'Pascal Engman is the master of the new generation... ...s irresistible reading.'

DAVID LAGERCRANTZ

'Completely impossible to put down.'

SARA BLÆDEL

'The absolute hottest Swedish crime novel of the autumn, I have read it twice. It's that good and *everyone* is talking about it!'

CAMILLA LÄCKBERG

'[T]his author just keeps getting better and The Widows is his best yet... Read the young thriller king Pascal Engman, he is indispensable!'

ANDERS KAPPRAKT, SWEDISH CRIME ACADEMY

'[I stayed up through the night to finish this book], then I lay down and thought about Dan Brown's The Da Vinci Code, this book that last did this to me, that overpowered me with the same never-wracking construction... Congratulations Pascal, you did it.'

ALEX SCHULMAN

THE WIDOWS

PASCAL ENGMAN

Translated by Neil Smith

Legend Press Ltd, 51 Gower Street, London, WC1E 6HJ
info@legendtimesgroup.co.uk | www.legendpress.co.uk

Contents © Pascal Engman 2024

Originally published in Swedish as *Änkorna* in 2020 by Bookmark förlag

Translated by Neil Smith

Print ISBN 9781915054432
Ebook ISBN 9781915054449
Set in Times.

Cover by David Grogan | www.headdesign.co.uk

Pascal Engman's debut novel *The Patriots* was published in 2017, and he has since become the best-selling Swedish crime novelist of his generation. He has been acclaimed by Camilla Läckberg, David Lagercrantz, The Swedish Crime Writers' Academy and others as a rising star of Swedish crime fiction. His novel *Femicide* was published by Legend Press in 2022.

Engman, who resides in his native Stockholm, was born to a Swedish mother and a Chilean father. Engman was a journalist at Swedish evening newspaper *Expressen*.

To Linnea. I love you.

*They are evil idealists and what they have done in
the yards behind their facades I cannot describe, cannot
change blood into ink.*

FROM THE POEM "CARILLON", FROM *THE WILD SQUARE*
BY TOMAS TRANSTRÖMER.

At least 400 ISIS terrorists have been trained to commit atrocities in Europe. They have been organised in different cells to carry out a wave of bloody attacks, according to what sources within the security services of Europe and Iraq have told the AP news agency.

One senior Iraqi security officer claims that the cell that carried out the Paris attacks has now spread to Germany, Britain, Italy, Denmark and Sweden.

ISIS is said to have dedicated training camps in Syria, Iraq, and possibly a number of former Soviet states, in which jihadists are given special training for attacks in Europe.

According to one source in the security services they are trained in combat technique, as well as surveillance and how to handle explosives. Previously, many attackers only received a few weeks' training.

"The strategy has changed now. Special units have been set up. Training lasts longer now," the source reports.

Panorama, the BBC's investigative news programme, claims that ISIS has a network consisting of a total of 1,500 recruits trained in terrorism, who could be planning new attacks in Europe, according to Swedish Radio.

Omni news service, 23 March 2016

2 years earlier

Vanessa knew from the start that it had been a mistake. A mistake to get involved, to install false hope by agreeing to become a mentor. All because she just couldn't stand the restlessness of not having a task, a purpose. At first, the idea had seemed good, noble even – to spend her suspension from the police, caused by a DUI, by volunteering at a shelter for unaccompanied refugee children, and focusing on teaching the girls self-defence. But she should have known as soon as she met Natasja that she wouldn't be able to just be a mentor to her without becoming emotionally invested in her life. Not when she heard Natasja's story and felt fully present in the moment for the first time in what felt like forever. When she spoke to Natasja, Vanessa didn't once think about Adeline, the baby girl she had lost to illness some years ago and who usually occupied her mind every waking moment.

Natasja had fled to Sweden from Syria on foot a few years earlier, after losing her entire family in a bomb attack. But despite all the tragedies she had already had to endure in her fourteen-year-old life, despite losing everything, Natasja still had a positive outlook on life. On one of the first occasions they met at the shelter, Natasja told Vanessa that she had to be happy, had to make the most of her life, had to enjoy it all. Because if she didn't, what was it all for? Then she might as well have died together with her family. But she didn't and that meant Natasja had to cherish her chance of being alive in every way.

Vanessa admired her attitude and strength and made the mistake of thinking that she could somehow help her, this teenage war refugee, despite the fact that she had proved previously that she was unable to take care of anyone, especially a child. She was destructive and unreliable and she should have stayed away from Natasja. But she didn't. Instead she reached out to Natasja to fill her own sense of emptiness, to give her company. And it had eventually resulted in the young girl going missing. One day she left the shelter with a friend and didn't return.

The employees at the shelter simply seemed to think she had left voluntarily, but Vanessa knew better. It didn't make sense, she had a Swedish residence permit and she loved living here. But the alternative, that someone had abducted her, also seemed unrealistic. Who would do it, and why?

It didn't matter that Vanessa simultaneously learned that she was allowed to return to her police again; she couldn't do it before she had found Natasja. She started her own investigation into her disappearance and it finally led her to the conclusion that Natasja had been kidnapped by the Swedish drug gang The Legion and brought to a clinic in Chile, along with several other unaccompanied refugee children, where criminals were waiting to steal their organs and sell them to their rich clients.

Vanessa had no choice but to head to Chile and try to save Natasja and with Nicolas's help she succeeded and brought Natasja to safety. Once back in Sweden, they decided that Natasja would move in with Vanessa and that she would become her legal guardian – a decision that made Vanessa very happy.

But the happiness was short-lived. Just a few months after the events in Chile, Natasja learnt that her father had survived the war and decided to return to him in Syria. It broke Vanessa's heart but there was nothing she could do, Natasja should be with her father, her real family. So here she was again, back where she started, all alone. With one child gone and the other on the opposite side of the world, desperately hoping every day that she would return to her in Sweden again.

Now

Vanessa bit her lip so hard she could taste blood. She closed her eyes and pressed all three buttons at the same time. She screwed her eyes shut so tightly that dancing patterns appeared on the inside of her eyelids. She leaned her head against one shoulder and hunched up in anticipation.

She didn't want to die. Not now. A few years ago she wouldn't have minded, but not today. Not now that she had Celine in her life, something to fight for. Something good. Something beautiful. Celine trusted her, she needed her.

Three.

She felt tears well up. Her lips were trembling, the sinews of her neck stood out as she straightened her back, forcing herself to stand tall. She wasn't going to die cowering. She wasn't going to give the terrorists that. No one would ever know how she spent her last moments, but she would know. She told herself that that actually meant something.

Two.

"Fucking murdering bastards," she whispered.

She drew air into her lungs and realised that it could be her last ever breath.

One.

Prologue

Every so often, twenty-two-year-old Molly Berg would be flown to palatial villas around the Mediterranean, told to wait, then sent home with an envelope stuffed with cash without her having to do anything except twiddle her thumbs. But at least she could usually play with her phone or read a book. This time a dour-looking guard had taken her phone off her the moment she stepped aboard the thirty-five-metre luxury yacht *Lucinda*. And she had managed to leave the book she was currently reading, Charles Bukowski's *Post Office*, at home in her apartment in Barcelona. The television could only get Spanish channels, and even though she had been living in Spain for the past few years, she could barely speak the language. But the payment was better than normal: fifteen thousand euros, per day.

Through the round porthole of the extravagant cabin Molly could see the coast of Majorca and Puerto Portals harbour. The shops and pavement cafés were full, the quay lined with luxury yachts. Tourists were wandering about, taking pictures of themselves in front of the boats. The largest vessels, like *Lucinda*, couldn't actually fit in the harbour, and were spread out in a fan just outside it.

Her stomach rumbled. Molly switched the television off and tossed the remote on the double bed. When she had been taken to the cabin she had been told to wait until someone came to fetch her.

She stood in front of the mirror.

"A girl's gotta eat."

She changed her voice, and said seriously:

"Stop talking to yourself."

She pinched the bridge of her nose with two fingers.

"Ok, sorry Molly," she said in a nasal voice.

She tied her dark hair up and pulled a black T-shirt on over her bikini top.

The corridor was empty. She made her way towards the aft, passing four closed doors before she reached some steps. A man in a white servant's uniform was on his way down, but stopped abruptly.

"The kitchen?" she asked with a smile. The man stared at her without answering. Molly put her hand on her stomach and moved it in a circle. "Food. I'm hungry."

The man gestured for her to follow him. He pulled a napkin from his back pocket and wiped his forehead before stopping in front of the wooden door and pointing to it.

Molly stepped into what looked like a small restaurant. In front of her a glass door led out onto the deck. There were five circular tables, all empty. The walls were adorned with black and white photographs of old ships. In front of one window there were silver dishes laden with fresh fruit, and an ice-bucket containing bottles of mineral water.

"I was kind of hoping for a hamburger, you mean bastard," she muttered as she looked disconsolately at the bowls of fruit. The blue sea outside the window looked very inviting.

She took a piece of mango, popped it in her mouth, then licked her fingers before she went behind the counter to look for bar-snacks. She opened a drawer and found some bottles of San Miguel. She pulled two out, drew a smiley in the condensation on one of the bottles, then put them down on the counter. She leaned over to have another look and found a bag of crisps and some cashew nuts.

"Thank fuck," she muttered.

Just as she was closing the drawer she heard the door leading out onto the deck open.

She snatched one of the bottles of beer and ducked down behind the counter so she wouldn't be seen. Two men were talking quietly. As the voices came closer she heard that they were speaking Arabic.

"Are the martyrs ready?"

"They're waiting for your signal. They're very eager, they've been waiting a long time…"

The voice was hoarse and Molly couldn't make out the rest. She sat there motionless and held her breath, regretting that she had hidden in the first place.

"And the target?"

One of the men opened a bottle. The bottle-top fell to the floor and he swore.

"In Stockholm, the capital."

"When?"

One of the dishes clattered, then the voices faded away as the men made their way back out on deck.

Molly slowly breathed out and cautiously got to her feet. She waited a few seconds before snatching up the crisps, nuts and bottles of beer. She went and stood by the wall, staring out at the deck. The men were nowhere in sight.

Molly raised the crisps to her mouth with shaking hands, then chewed mechanically. She no longer felt hungry. The two men had been talking about a terrorist attack in Stockholm.

She had met her fair share of bastards over the years, men with money and power who treated the women whose company they had paid for as commodities. Men who took pleasure in humiliating them and being rough. But she had never feared for her life. Not really. It was different this time, she could feel it in her whole body.

No one knew where she was. Her dad thought she worked in a clothing boutique in Barcelona. He didn't even have her address. And Marc, the man who arranged the jobs, wouldn't lift a finger if she disappeared.

But even if the men had found her, they couldn't possibly know that she spoke Arabic. She had a Swedish passport. She may not look typically Scandinavian, but she certainly didn't look Arabic.

She got up from the bed when she heard the sound of an engine out on the water. A small boat had just set off from the *Lucinda* and was heading towards Puerto Portals. On its stern stood a man in a blue cap. Was he one of the men she had heard talking?

The motorboat drew into the harbour, the man jumped nimbly ashore, and the boat turned back.

She would spend the next few days acting as a ditzy luxury escort. Under no circumstances must she let anyone realise that she understood Arabic.

Molly opened the second bottle of beer against the edge of the desk, took a deep swig, then wiped her mouth.

She let out a cough when there was a knock on the door.

"I'm coming," she called. She adjusted her hair, then opened the door. Outside stood a guard in a white shirt, with a shoulder-holster strapped across his chest.

"I need you to come with me," he said.

PART I

1

The road surface of Valhallavägen was partially submerged in water. Rain was tipping down onto forty-three-year-old Vanessa Frank's black BMW. A flash of lightning lit up the sky and she started to count. She got to five before a crack of thunder rolled across the sky, drowning out the newsreader's voice.

"Storm Gertrude is passing Stockholm on Friday night," a woman's voice was saying seriously. "The public are being advised to stay indoors and not venture out except in an emergency."

"No shit," Vanessa muttered, taking her eyes off the road for a moment to lower the volume.

A moment later she had to slam the brakes on as a cyclist crossed the road at high speed. She came within a hair's breadth of hitting his rear wheel.

Gertrude. Why didn't they give storms proper, fear-inspiring names like Odin or Thor? Something from Nordic mythology that would make people realise it was serious? Gertrude sounded like a dotty primary-school teacher with ragged fingernails and breath that smelled of coffee.

It had rained almost all of October, and it would soon be the middle of November. Vanessa was already thoroughly fed up of the darkness. She passed the Fältöversten shopping centre and wrenched the wheel to avoid a large puddle out of which the outline of an electric scooter stuck up. A few hundred metres later she was able to make out the flashing blue lights through the rain up ahead, close to Gärdet.

Vanessa turned into Oxenstiernsgatan and double-parked in front of the cordon that had been set up beside the Swedish Television building. She opened the car door, grabbed the umbrella from the back seat and opened it as she got out.

The strength of the wind made her stumble. A stern-looking

police officer in a raincoat with the hood pulled up took a quick look at her, then waved her through.

Vanessa turned right onto Taptogatan. Three floodlights had been set up, illuminating the pavement where a man was lying on his back beside an SUV.

Two forensics officers in white plastic outfits were erecting a temporary tent to stop the rain contaminating the scene. One of them caught sight of her and raised a hand to stop her coming any closer. Vanessa stopped ten metres from the body, and tried to find the right angle to hold the umbrella as she looked around. To her right the pavement led to a sloping patch of grass. At the end of the street she could make out the slides and swings in Gustav Adolf's Park.

The forensics officer gestured to Vanessa to follow her, and judging by the woman's height and way of moving, Vanessa realised it was Trude Hovland. She liked the Norwegian-Indian officer, and considered her more competent than most. She also had a dry sense of humour that Vanessa appreciated.

They went and stood in a doorway and Trude pulled her mask down under her chin.

"He's a fellow officer, Rikard Olsson. Shot twice in the back."

Trude wiped the rain from her forehead.

"Where did he work?" Vanessa asked.

Another flash of lightning lit up the dark sky.

"Team 2022."

"Gang-related crime, then."

The tent had now been erected over the body. Trude pulled her mask back up and left Vanessa alone in the doorway.

In recent years the threat to police officers and their families had grown in strength and intensity. Criminals no longer hesitated to open fire on individual officers' homes, or issue threats against their families. Officers working with organised crime were particularly vulnerable. Until Vanessa transferred to the National Homicide Unit from what used to be called the NOVA Group, she too had been the target of threats.

She took out her mobile to call her boss, Mikael Kask, to ask him to send more detectives. She dropped it back in her inside pocket when she remembered that she didn't yet have his number on the new phone she had bought from a talkative sales assistant in a shop on Kungsgatan earlier that day. Besides, her own number had changed, and her official phone was in the car. She had just decided to go and get it when the uniformed officer who had been guarding the cordon came trudging over, followed by a man in a black raincoat. When they caught sight of Vanessa they headed towards her.

The two men squeezed into the doorway. The man in the raincoat, who was in his thirties, held out his hand.

"Samer Bakir," he said in a strong southern Swedish accent, and Vanessa found herself thinking that it reminded her of the way Zlatan Ibrahimovic spoke.

"You're new?"

He pushed his drenched hood back and ran his fingers through his short black hair.

"From Malmö. I'm with Serious Crime, Central Division now." He gestured towards the illuminated tent. "What do we know?"

"A fellow officer. Rikard Olsson," Vanessa said, and the two men stared at her. The uniformed officer's radio crackled, but he showed no sign of answering it. Samer and Vanessa nodded towards it. He started, then turned away and asked the operator to repeat the message.

"Do we know if he was on duty?" Samer asked.

Vanessa shook her head.

"Can you call your boss and get more people here? I was first on the scene, and they don't yet know that the victim is a fellow officer."

"Haven't you done that yet?"

"New mobile, I haven't had a chance to transfer the numbers yet," Vanessa said, only half lying. The truth was that she didn't really know how to do it.

Samer felt the pockets of his jacket as the uniformed officer turned back towards them. He seemed shaken.

"They've found another body."

Samer's hands fell to his sides.

"Where?" Vanessa asked.

The police officer moistened his lips.

"A few hundred metres from here. On Gärdet," he said.

2

Axel Grystad was lying on his single bed with his arms folded behind his head, looking up at the cracks in the ceiling. The rain was pattering against the window, but seemed to be easing off a bit.

He was feeling miserable. The next day he would be saying goodbye to his nine-year-old son, Simon, and then it would be another week until he had him with him again. He lived for his weeks with Simon, the rest was just one long wait.

He heard footsteps in the hallway, then the door-handle was pushed down. His son opened the door, dressed in his blue pyjamas.

"I can't sleep."

Axel shifted back to make room for Simon on the edge of the bed.

"Why not?"

"I'm hungry."

They had eaten spaghetti bolognese for dinner only a few hours ago. Axel knew he ought to tell Simon to go back to bed so he wouldn't be tired when he got up to go to football practice the next day. But he felt nothing but joy.

He looked at Simon's face.

"Me too."

Axel peered at the window and concluded that the rain was indeed easing. He glanced at the alarm clock on the bedside table, its red digital numbers said it was half past nine in the evening.

"What do say about going down to the kiosk and getting a takeaway?"

Simon's face cracked into a smile, revealing that one of his front teeth was missing. He reminded Axel of an ice-hockey player being interviewed on television after a win.

"I'm going to try one of those wraps this time, like you normally have."

"You're going to love it. But we won't mention this to your mum. If she asks, the Grystad boys ate broccoli all week, and went to bed at the right time."

"Of course, Daddy."

Their hands met in a high five. Axel loved it when Simon called him "Daddy".

A few minutes later they were stepping out through the door onto Rådmansgatan in their raincoats. Simon leaned his head back and looked up.

"It's stopped raining," he concluded, dropping the football he took everywhere with him onto the pavement. He kicked the ball, then set off after it, his movements lithe and easy. Every time Axel saw him running like that he was filled with relief that his son hadn't inherited his own clumsiness and the under-developed motor skills that had made his own childhood such a nightmare. Simon was even good at football. Axel had never played any sports. Physical activity was forever linked to torment. He had never felt more vulnerable than he had during PE lessons. A lot of the most humiliating moments of his life had taken place in the changing rooms at school.

At first he had been worried when Simon said he wanted to start playing football. But since he started, Axel hadn't missed a single match or training session. He felt nothing but the purest joy when he watched his son chase after that ball. Simon shot, scored, was hugged by his teammates. Sometimes Axel felt like it was him flying across the pitch.

The ball came to a halt in a puddle and Simon stopped, lifted it up with his foot and kept it in the air with a series of kicks.

It's magic, Axel thought. This is my son, and he can do things like that.

"Watch!" Simon called, and started heading the ball.

A tingle ran through Axel when he thought about the foreign trip he had booked for the two of them. In a few weeks' time they would be flying off to watch Axel's favourite team, FC Barcelona. Axel had promised himself that he wasn't going to say anything before Simon's birthday.

The match was being played in one of the weeks when Axel wasn't supposed to have Simon, but when he asked Rebecca she had said that was absolutely fine. They were flexible and generous towards each other when it came to times and dates. Axel had often heard about divorced couples who did nothing but fight, but to him it had always seemed straightforward. If Rebecca and her husband Thorsten ever wanted to go away on a trip that spilled over by a few days, he had no problem with Simon spending those extra days with him. His son was the only thing that gave him any pleasure in life, he didn't really have any other friends.

He was happy enough with his job as an IT technician at Danske Bank. He was actually over-qualified for the job, and was aware that his duties were pretty basic. His workmates could have been kinder, though. He could feel the way they looked at him, the mocking smiles behind his back when he stammered and couldn't get his words out. But it could have been worse. Everything could have been worse.

Axel had Simon, Simon loved him, and that was all he needed.

He didn't know how he had managed to keep the Barcelona trip secret for so long. He decided that it was time to tell Simon while they were eating their takeaway. It would be the perfect end to the week.

Axel crouched down to tie his shoelace. A moment later he heard the sound of shrieking car-tyres. A thud moved out from his stomach, through his whole body. When he straightened up he saw a dark vehicle disappearing into the distance at high speed.

The traffic lights were green for pedestrians.

Simon lay on the crossing, not moving.

3

Vanessa walked out of the revolving door of the Swedish Television building, where she had spent the past hour examining the footage from the security cameras that faced Oxenstiernsgatan.

The rain had stopped. She tossed her umbrella in the boot of her BMW and looked around.

There was plenty of activity. The blue lights reflected off the facades of the modernist buildings and the grey concrete colossus of Swedish Television. She could see curious neighbours in windows and on balconies.

Every available patrol car in Stockholm had been called to the scene. Even the Rapid Response Unit was there, searching the area with weapons drawn, seeing as they couldn't rule out that they were dealing with a random act of violence. One reporter and a photographer were hanging about by the cordon, and more were surely on their way.

Vanessa looked over towards Gärdet. Two forensics vehicles had driven across the mud that made up the sports pitch at this point in the autumn, and were now parked by the stone formation that resembled a miniature Stonehenge. That was where the second victim had been found. She could see the forensics officers working, lit up by floodlights.

Samer Bakir came trudging over to the car. His white trainers were dark with damp and the bottom of his jeans spattered with mud.

"It's a woman in her twenties. I'd guess she's of Arabic heritage, same as me," he said.

"Shot as well?"

Samer reached down and tried to brush the worst of the mud off one shin.

"Stabbed." He gave up the attempt and straightened up. "In the chest and neck. How did you get on with the security cameras?"

"Not very well." A strong gust of wind whipped at Vanessa's hair and she shivered.

"What do we do now?" Samer asked.

Without answering, she opened the driver's door and got in the car. She started the engine and turned the heating up. Samer got in the passenger seat and rubbed his hands together to get his circulation going as he looked around the car.

There was a knock on the window and Trude Hovland's face came into view. She was holding up a sealed plastic bag containing a mobile phone. Vanessa gestured to her to get in.

"Rikard Olsson's phone," Trude said.

"Have you got the pin?" Samer asked,

"No."

Vanessa weighed the phone in her hand. She felt frustrated. Two murders in the same evening, in one of the calmest parts of Stockholm. She needed something to go on for the investigation to make any serious progress tomorrow. There was already a team in Rikard Olsson's apartment, which had turned out to be nearby, opposite the Garrison on Karlavägen, only a hundred metres or so from the scene of the murder.

"Where's the body?"

"About to be taken away," Trude said.

Vanessa opened the car door and walked quickly towards Taptogatan with Samer and Trude close behind her.

Two men were in the process of lifting Rikard Olsson into a van, and Vanessa asked them to wait. She folded the white blanket back to uncover the police officer's face. She pressed the button on the side of the iPhone, then held the screen in front of the dead man to activate the facial recognition software.

"Thanks," she said, before pulling the blanket back up.

While the body was loaded into the van Trude and Samer peered at the phone over her shoulder. The first thing that appeared was a photograph of a child in a swing. Vanessa sighed and pressed the green button with a white phone on it at the bottom left of the screen, to bring up a list of the most recent calls.

"Bloody hell," Samer exclaimed.

"Can you call and ask them to locate the recording?" Vanessa said.

The last number Rikard Olsson called when he was alive was the emergency number, 112. The call had been made at 19.04, and had lasted twenty-three seconds.

4

Axel Grystad was in the middle of the worst nightmare of his life. Several times he was so convinced he was dreaming that he had to pinch his arm.

He was pacing up and down a bare white corridor at the Karolinska University Hospital, clutching Simon's football tight. A short while ago the door to the emergency room where Simon was being operated on had swung open. Six people in green hospital outfits and masks over their mouths had been standing around Simon's small body. Axel knew they were doing their utmost to save his life.

He would never forget the scene.

Every time he closed his eyes he saw it again.

When he found Simon lying motionless on the tarmac, his first instinct had been to put him in the car and drive him to hospital himself. That would surely have been quicker than waiting for an ambulance? But a woman in her fifties had come running over. She was a nurse, and explained that moving Simon could damage his spine. He needed to be stabilised first.

"I've called for an ambulance, they're on their way," she had told him breathlessly.

The ambulance had arrived seven minutes later. Axel had sat on the kerb with his face buried in his hands while the paramedics spoke to the nurse. They quickly examined Simon's injuries, supported his back, then lifted him onto a stretcher. Axel had stood next to them, paralysed and silent and completely useless. He had felt ashamed of letting other people fight to save his son's life.

He was roused from his thoughts when a young nurse came up to him.

"You're Simon's dad?"

Axel nodded.

"They're still operating on him. Let me show you to the waiting room."

"W-will he be… b-b-be okay?"

The only people Axel didn't stammer in front of were Rebecca and Simon.

"We're doing everything we can," she said, gently putting one arm round him. "Come with me and we'll find you somewhere to sit."

She led him past the lifts into another, smaller corridor. As they were walking he felt tears welling up in his eyes. She sat him down gently on a sofa and sat down beside him.

"Simon's mum is on her way, I'll bring her here so you can be together."

The nurse stood up and the sound of her footsteps faded away.

A short while later Rebecca rushed in and threw her arms round Axel. He tried to explain what had happened, but she hushed him.

"They've already told me."

Axel couldn't think of anything to say. He didn't dare meet her gaze. Did she blame him? Did she think it was his fault? Obviously he should have been keeping a closer eye on Simon.

"They're still operating on him," he said, mostly to break the silence.

Rebecca's face was pale, her blonde hair pulled up into a ponytail. It struck him how like Simon she was – and how Rebecca and Simon were the most beautiful people on the planet.

"It's going to be okay."

"It all happened so fast. I just crouched down to tie…"

"I know you'd never do anything irresponsible when it comes to Simon."

"No, I wouldn't."

Rebecca took hold of Axel's hand and squeezed it. He leaned back, closed his eyes and tried to calm down.

Two police officers appeared in the corridor, and a nurse pointed them towards Axel. He put Simon's football down and went to meet them.

"I'll get some coffee in the meantime," Rebecca said, and disappeared.

The police officers introduced themselves with their full names, then asked Axel to sit back down and took his contact details. They asked him if he felt up to going through what happened again.

He explained that the car had been driving fast, and broke a red light. When he looked up Simon had been lying motionless on the tarmac. The driver hadn't stopped, just accelerated and disappeared in the direction of Roslagstull.

The police officer looked at him sympathetically.

"Did you see what sort of car it was?" he asked.

"I don't know anything about cars. It was black, that's all I saw."

"Registration number?" the other police officer asked.

Axel shook his head.

"S-s-sorry, it all happened too fast."

"I understand."

The police officers stood up, and one of them patted Axel awkwardly on the shoulder and said that they'd be in touch.

When he was sure they had gone, Axel took his phone out and went onto the Vehicle Registration Database. In the search box he typed the car's registration number: HNC 106.

5

Vanessa parked her car in the garage beneath Norra Real. Small drops of rain were still falling from the dark sky. Even though it was a Friday night, Vasastan was deserted, the only sign of life was a taxi passing by when she crossed Odengatan.

She stopped in Monica Zetterlund's park as she often did. She closed her eyes to listen to the music playing from the bench that had been placed there in honour of the jazz singer, and which played her music quietly all day and night. Vanessa needed sleep, the following day was going to be hectic, starting with a meeting at eight o'clock in Police Headquarters. The emergency call centre had promised to email the recording of Rikard Olsson's call as soon as they managed to identify it; they thought that would happen some time during the night. The dead woman still hadn't been identified, no mobile or ID card had been found on her. And so far they didn't know if there was any connection between the two murders.

As Vanessa was approaching her apartment she saw two denim-clad legs sticking out from the doorway of the building. She assumed a homeless person had taken shelter from the rain and fallen asleep. She crept the last few steps so as not to wake the sleeping figure, then saw its pink hair. It was Celine Wood, a thirteen-year-old girl she had got to know during the summer. During a mass shooting at Stockholm Stadium, Celine had been hit in the stomach and had come close to dying. For the past couple of months she had been moved between various foster families. Every now and then she ran away, came to see Vanessa and get a decent meal, then disappeared again.

Celine had grown thinner, and Vanessa couldn't help shivering at the sight of her jacket, which was far too thin for the cold November weather. She crouched down and gently touched her shoulder.

Celine opened her eyes.

"What have you done to your hair?" she yawned, reaching out one hand and running her fingers through Vanessa's recently bobbed hair.

"Look who's talking!"

Vanessa gave her a hug, tapped in the code and held the door open for Celine as she got to her feet and shuffled into the stairwell.

Up in the flat, they hung their coats up in the hall and Vanessa dug out a pair of white pyjamas that were far too big for Celine.

"How long were you waiting?" Vanessa asked.

"A couple of hours, maybe. I fell asleep pretty quickly, so it wasn't too bad."

"Have you been going to school?"

Celine didn't answer.

"You need to start going."

Vanessa inspected the freezer in a hunt to find something to eat while Celine sank down on the sofa. She seemed to have shaken off her tiredness.

"I've been thinking about that. Why does everyone make such a fuss about Greta when she skives off school, when I just get bollocked? That's pretty unfair."

Vanessa rolled her eyes as she put a Gorby's pie in the microwave. She set the timer for one minute.

"Greta has a plan. She's demonstrating for the climate, standing up against the system for a better world."

"I'm standing up against the system too. I'm a punk."

Celine got up from the sofa and walked over to the fireplace, took down a framed photograph and looked at it.

"She's really pretty."

The picture was of Natasha, the young Syrian refugee Vanessa had looked after two years ago. Now she was back in Syria with her father. Vanessa missed her so much it hurt. Every day she hoped that Natasha would get in touch to say she was coming back to Stockholm.

The microwave pinged and Vanessa took the pie out, put it on a plate and pushed it across the island unit. Celine put the photograph of Natasha back and sat down on one of the bar stools. One third of the pie disappeared in the first bite.

"I'm trying to be vegetarian, but I'll make an exception today. Don't want to seem ungrateful," she said.

"Another one?" Vanessa asked.

"If you insist," Celine said, with her mouth full. "Haven't eaten since yesterday. But then I struck lucky at Burger King. I had to wait half an hour before a rich bastard left half a Whopper. Damn, it was good. You can say a lot of things about you rich people, but you've got good taste."

Once Celine had eaten the second pie she lay back on the sofa. Vanessa went and sat down beside her.

"Aren't you going to eat anything?" Celine asked.

Vanessa shook her head.

"I'm not really hungry," she lied. There had only been two pies left, and Celine obviously needed the second one more than she did.

Celine closed her eyes and stretched out. The pyjama top rode up, baring her stomach. The scar left by the bullet that had almost cost her her life glinted white just above her navel.

"Sweetheart, you have to stop running away. And you need to go to school," Vanessa said.

Celine nodded and gave a weak smile.

"Can you stroke my hair? It feels so nice when someone else touches you."

Vanessa shifted closer to Celine and laid the girl's head on her lap, and ran her fingers through her pink hair. It was dirty, tangled and smelled bad.

Celine screwed her eyes shut and a tear trickled slowly down her cheek, leaving a white line on her dirty face. She wiped it away angrily. It wasn't long before she fell asleep. Vanessa reached for a cushion and gently tucked it under Celine's head before she stood up.

She took her mobile phone out. The sound file of Rikard Olsson's emergency call had arrived. She poured herself a glass of water, dug out her earbuds and sat down on one of the stools by the island unit before playing the clip.

"SOS 112, what's the nature of the emergency?" a female voice said.

The only response was heavy breathing and the sound of running footsteps. The wind was howling angrily in the background.

Vanessa pushed the buds deeper into her ears to hear better.

"Hello?"

Rikard Olsson still didn't say anything, all she could hear was his strained breathing and quick footsteps. His clothing rustled against the microphone. Was he being chased? All the evidence pointed towards that, not least the fact that he had been shot in the back.

"Hello?"

The operator's voice was sounding increasingly tense.

A couple of seconds passed.

"Who am I talking to?"

There was a sharp bang. Rikard Olsson cried out. A shrill, heart-rending scream. Then a thud. He must have fallen to the ground, and was now hyperventilating. Moaning. Then came the second shot.

"Hello?"

Rustling in the microphone. Then footsteps fading away. After ten more seconds, the only sound was the patter of the rain against the pavement.

6

It had been raining all night, and a thin layer of ice covered the puddles of water outside the hospital window. Axel Grystad was sitting opposite the woman he loved. But Rebecca's hand, which was resting on the table, was entwined with Thorsten's. Rebecca and Axel had been at the hospital since the previous evening. Thorsten had been home to the couple's apartment to fetch clothes and toiletries for Rebecca. He had slept there, but came back early on Saturday morning, and now they were eating breakfast together.

"God, I'm so sick of this hospital coffee," Thorsten said, gesturing towards the empty cup in front of him. He and Axel had each eaten a ham sandwich. Rebecca, who had been vegetarian for the past couple of years, had picked a turkey sandwich seeing as all the vegetarian options had run out. The slices of turkey that she had carefully removed lay lined up along the edge of her plate.

Thorsten stifled a belch and scratched his stubble.

"I'm just going to the toilet, does anyone want anything?" Rebecca said, pushing her chair back.

Thorsten and Axel both shook their heads.

Simon had been moved to the Intensive Care Unit. His condition was unchanged. The doctors still didn't know if he was going to survive. Every time Axel closed his eyes, he saw that thin little body surrounded by bleeping machines in his mind's eye.

Rebecca disappeared in the direction of the toilets. The atmosphere was often a little strained whenever Axel and Thorsten were left alone together. They had nothing in common, apart from the fact that they loved the same woman. But over the years that had seemed to become less important. Thorsten always treated Axel well when they met at birthday parties, or when they were picking Simon up or dropping him off. And Thorsten liked Simon, he treated him as his own son. And Simon loved Thorsten. Sure, for the first few years Axel had been worried that Simon might actually prefer his stepfather. Who wouldn't? Thorsten was funny, talkative and successful. He always seemed confident, no matter what the setting. The estate agency he had helped set up had a turnover worth hundreds of millions of kronor. He, Rebecca and Simon went on long, luxurious holidays in summer and winter alike, to places like Bali, Thailand, Dubai, the Maldives.

Thorsten was staring tersely at Axel. He helped himself to a bit of turkey from Rebecca's plate. A hospital clown with a white face and red hair was walking up a flight of stairs a short distance away.

"I don't know how many times I've told you not to let him play with that damn ball on the pavement," he said.

Axel was taken aback by the sudden burst of aggression. He pressed his lips tightly together and ran his fingers along the edge of the table. What could he say? Thorsten was right.

"This is your fault. You get that, right? It's your fault the boy's lying up there like a vegetable. If he dies, it will be your fault."

Every word, every syllable, cut into Axel.

He bowed his neck and nodded.

"I know. S-s-sorry."

Thorsten rolled his eyes.

"You've always been an idiot. But this… Do you have any idea of the suffering you've caused? Just look at her, she won't recover from this. Do you understand that? If he dies, then she's fucking finished. And then you'll have two lives on your conscience."

Thorsten snorted, then shook his head and pushed the plate away.

"But no doubt you'll get away with it. With your pathetic fucking stammer and your moronic behaviour."

Axel had never seen him like this, even if he had realised that Thorsten couldn't understand how Rebecca could have had a child with someone like him.

"If it wasn't for her, I'd have killed you by now." Thorsten gestured towards the toilets. "But she feels sorry for you."

The door to the bathroom opened and Rebecca headed back towards them. Half a metre from the table she stopped and looked at them.

"What are you talking about?"

Thorsten sighed and held his palms up.

"I was saying it like it is."

Rebecca leaned towards him.

"Meaning?"

"That it's Axel's fault we're here. Christ, Rebecca, someone had to say it. He gets away with everything. He's a grown man, so he ought to be able to hear it."

He no longer sounded so self-assured. Rebecca stared at him.

"Don't blame Axel. Do you hear? Not now. Not when our son is lying up there and might…"

She sat down and buried her head in her hands. Thorsten put his arm on her back, but she shook it off. He sighed.

"I'm going for a walk," he said tersely.

He snatched up his jacket, stuck his hands in his pockets and marched purposefully towards the exit.

Axel didn't know what to say. He hated seeing Rebecca sad, and was ashamed to been the cause of a row between her and Thorsten. He should have stood up for himself. At the same time, he was pleased that she had defended him. He couldn't help it, but he liked it. No one stood up for him like Rebecca did.

"Don't listen to him," she mumbled, still not looking up.

"He's right. I should never have let Simon take the ball with him, but he was just so happy when I let him. He was running, and… Nothing makes me happier than seeing him run."

Rebecca straightened up, tucking back a lock of hair that had fallen in front of her face.

"You mustn't talk like that. You mustn't talk about what he used to be like, or what he used to like doing. He's alive. Simon is alive, and one day he's going to play football again."

She shuddered and swallowed her tears, keeping them locked up inside her.

"You're a good father, Axel. Simon's always saying what a great dad you are. I knew you would be from the first moment I met you."

He hadn't told anyone about the registration number, not even Rebecca. He knew the address of the man whose name the car was registered in by heart now.

"I need to go home," he said. "Shower and change my clothes."

It was the first time he had ever lied to Rebecca, and he hated it. But he had no choice.

All he could think was that the person who had done this to Simon and Rebecca had to die.

7

The garden outside the window was grey and lifeless. The pool was hidden by a metal cover, and the view of the white stone wall that surrounded the plot and large house in Djursholm was obscured by two bare fruit trees. The upper floor had a view of the inlet beyond, but Nicolas Paredes's room was on the ground floor. It was approximately thirty square metres in size, and sparsely furnished.

A wardrobe and a bed. A desk and matching chair, and a noticeably empty bookcase.

With practiced movements, Nicolas put on his shoulder-holster and service weapon, a Glock 17, which he had a licence to use in Sweden. His formal title was security coordinator, which was the result of Swedish bureaucracy, but in practice it meant the same as when he had been responsible for the Karlström family's security in London: he was their bodyguard. Since the move to Sweden the security apparatus had been scaled back, and instead of four people now only Nicolas was guarding them. He had been surprised when his bosses told him that Johan Karlström wanted him to go with them.

But Johan was unpredictable. On several occasions Nicolas had had to contact his bosses to explain that Johan was making his job harder and exposing himself to unnecessary risks. Sometimes he had gone off in the car without warning, leaving Nicolas in restaurants or hotel lobbies. And on other occasions he had been almost openly hostile. As time went on, Nicolas had realised that there wasn't much he could do about that. Johan Karlström was the MD of Gambler, one of the largest online casinos in the world. And the gambling company was an important source of income for the AOS Risk Group. His British bosses always responded the same way: Keep him happy, just do your best.

Nicolas hoped that no one else would be up yet, but when he opened the door to the combined kitchen and living room he could hear the television. He was desperate to get away from the house. To escape Johan Karlström's condescending smile and the meanness he radiated. Nicolas's bosses had promised that they would organise an apartment for him sometime after Christmas, but for the time being he was forced to live with the family.

To his relief he saw that it was James, the Karlström family's ten-year-old son, who was curled up on the sofa on his own. He had a plate with a slice of toast and marmalade on his lap. Beside the television hung a large, black and white photograph of Erica Karlström in a bikini.

"How are you feeling?" Nicolas said, opening the fridge to get the eggs out. "Ready for the game?"

James nodded, but Nicolas could tell he was nervous. Even in London Johan, an ice-hockey fanatic, had insisted that his son play the game, and today James would be playing his first game with Djursholm Hockey.

Nicolas turned the coffee machine on, then cracked the eggs into a bowl and whisked them.

"Would you like some scrambled egg?"

"No thanks."

"Coffee?"

"No thanks."

"A shot of whisky?"

James turned round, shaking with laughter. Nicolas put the frying pan on the stove, breathed in the smell of fresh coffee from the machine, and went over to the sofa. He crouched down in front of the freckled boy.

"Seriously, mate. It's going to be fine. It's only a game, and you can only do your best. I'll keep my fingers crossed for you."

"Are you coming to watch?" James asked. His voice was high, fragile. Even though both his parents were Swedish, he had a British accent. He had been born and raised in England.

"I can't, I'm meeting my sister. It's her birthday."

It was two weeks to the day since the Karlström family left London for Stockholm. This would be Nicolas's first afternoon and evening off. The AOS Risk Group were organising a replacement from a Swedish security company.

"That's nice," James said, doing his best to hide his disappointment.

Nicolas went back to the stove just as Erica Karlström came downstairs in a white silk dressing-gown.

"Good morning," she said in a hoarse voice, kissing James on the head. The look in her eyes was vacant, distant. Nicolas realised she was under the influence. She had a habit of mixing sleeping pills and alcohol. He got two mugs out, filled them with coffee and handed one to Erica. She stared at it uncomprehendingly before slowly taking it.

"How are you getting to the game?" he asked.

"I'll drive. Unless that's a problem?"

Nicolas stirred the pan as Erica took a seat on one of the tall kitchen chairs. It was as if there was an invisible veil between her and the rest of the world. She put her elbows on the marble top in front of her and rested her chin on her hands. Her dressing-gown was only loosely tied and her breasts were visible. Nicolas turned away, suddenly awkward.

"Would you like some scrambled egg?" he asked with his back turned to her.

She didn't react, and was staring blankly in front of her. She seemed fully occupied trying to lift the mug of coffee to her lips. Nicolas cursed under his breath. He couldn't let her drive the boy. There had been a frost, they could have an accident. Drive off the road, kill a pedestrian. He pulled his mobile from the pocket of his jeans and pretended to study the screen as he ate a large forkful of scrambled egg.

"My sister isn't well, and I don't want to risk picking something up. Is it okay if I come with you to watch the game?"

James leapt out of the sofa and ran into the kitchen to hug Nicolas.

"Really?"

"Really."

Erica's expression didn't change at all, but Nicolas could sense her anger as she put the mug down hard on the marble worktop and left the kitchen.

"Do you want to get some practice in?" he asked.

James reached for the remote and switched the television off.

They fetched sticks and a ball from James's room and went out into the garden, where they set up two goals twenty metres apart. The boy took the ball and did few quick moves, until Nicolas darted out with his stick and snatched the ball away.

"Cheat, I wasn't ready!" James cried, and chased after him, but Nicolas had the advantage and managed to fire the ball into the goal.

Fifteen minutes later the score was 3-3, and they took a break. Nicolas leaned on his stick as he caught his breath while James leaned against one goal, his face bright red.

Nicolas caught a glimpse of Johan Karlström in the window. He was watching them expressionlessly as he raised a mug of coffee to his mouth. When their eyes met, Johan tapped his watch with two fingers. Nicolas put the stick down and went back into the house.

"We're going to get a new car," Johan said.

"When?"

"Now. We'll take the old one and head over there right now."

"I've promised to drive James and Erica to the game."

"What fucking game?"

"James has a game this afternoon."

Johan snorted.

"You'll be in time if you stop making a fuss."

A short while later Johan was sitting in the back seat, behind the passenger seat. Nicolas started the engine, opened the garage door with the remote control and drove out.

"You're priceless, Nicolas." Johan smiled at him condescendingly in the rear-view mirror. "Bodyguard and nanny, all in one."

Nicolas didn't answer. The garage door closed behind them.

"I daresay you'll start fucking my wife as well soon."

8

The gym on Kronobergsgatan was busy. The thud of heavy weights hitting the floor made the treadmill tremble. A man with a ponytail dressed in a wrestling tunic was groaning like a steroid-pumped porn-star as he raised a pair of dumbbells above his head and admired his own body in the mirror.

Freddie Mercury was singing "Flash!" in her headphones as Vanessa raised the volume and increased the speed of the treadmill. She lengthened her stride, felt the taste of iron in her mouth, and pushed herself for the last kilometre.

She didn't really enjoy training in the middle of the day, but she needed to clear her mind. She was thinking about the two murders that had landed on her desk the previous day, and about Samer Bakir, her new colleague. She didn't have anything against him, not really. There was nothing wrong with his self-confidence, with regard to either his job or women. He was attractive, with a disarming smile that Vanessa assumed usually worked on the women around him.

During the meeting about the two murders Samer had behaved well, suggesting sensible ideas and asking intelligent questions. The focus, naturally, had been on Rikard Olsson, considering the threats that came with his work with gang-related crime.

The woman's mobile had been lying in the mud a couple of metres from where she was found. Trude Hovland, the forensics officer, thought it might take a while to get it working, but Vanessa was expecting to get the list of calls before too long.

Oddly enough, she didn't feel terribly affected by the investigation, even though one of her colleagues had been found murdered.

Since the mass shooting at Stockholm Stadium that summer, when eleven women had been killed, it was as if nothing really touched her anymore. She was running on backup power. Almost six months had passed now, but the images she had seen hadn't faded. Maybe that was why she felt she couldn't really take on Celine, even though she knew she ought to.

The girl didn't have anyone. Her father was an alcoholic, her mother dead. She needed a friend, but she reminded Vanessa too much of all the things she wanted to forget. Maybe that was why she had cut herself off from Nicolas Paredes, who had been by her side when the two attackers had been killed. He had called several times after he moved to London, trying to stay in touch, but she couldn't bring herself to take his calls. He seemed to have given up now, it had been months since he last contacted her.

Her mobile buzzed when she had just one hundred and fifty metres left to run. Vanessa slowed the pace, then reached for her towel and wiped her face, neck and arms. She drank thirstily from the bottle of water, spilling some on her already drenched gym vest.

She opened the text, which was from Trude, telling her to check her email. She had sent the list of calls from the dead woman's mobile.

Vanessa scrolled down to the last number the woman had called.

"That's impossible," she muttered to herself. "Bloody hell, that's impossible."

She got off the treadmill, grabbed her water-bottle and towel and headed towards the changing-room. She didn't bother to shower, just put her winter coat over her sweaty gym clothes and rang Trude's number.

As the call went through she thought about the dead woman. She hadn't seen the body yet, she'd been told to concentrate on Rikard Olsson. The post-mortem was due to be conducted that day, and no other test results had come back yet. They knew nothing about her background or who she was. All they had been able to determine was that she had died from two well-directed stab-wounds, one to her chest and the other to her neck. Then she had been left to die in the mud on Gärdet.

But this changed everything.

"I need to see her," Vanessa said as soon as Trude answered. "Now."

"You'll have to go out to Solna. The post-mortem is about to start. Have you come up with something?"

Vanessa took a deep breath and tried to collect the thoughts that were swirling round her head.

"The last number she called before she died was mine. My old phone. The one I had before I got this one."

She ended the call and started running towards Police Headquarters to fetch the car. The endorphin rush she usually felt after a serious gym session had vanished, and had been replaced by a growing feeling of unease. Who was this woman? Was it someone she knew?

Her stomach clenched. She only knew one person who fitted the description.

9

Nicolas was sitting with Erica Karlström in a half-empty, creaking stand in an ice-rink in Tumba. The final period was approaching its conclusion. James, with number eight on his back, was the smallest on the team. The protective helmet was far too big for his slight frame, and the red jersey reached down to his knees. He had been allowed to play a couple of minutes, but had mostly sat on the bench with his head lowered. Nicolas felt for him. Erica had watched the game through a large pair of sunglasses, without showing any emotion. She hadn't even looked worried when James was tackled and forced into the boards, fell over and ended up lying on the ice. In fact she barely seemed to have noticed. He had seen her with James when she wasn't under the influence of medication, and then she was a loving, engaged parent.

"I'll get some more coffee, you can drink it in the car on the way home," he said.

She shrugged her shoulders.

When he returned with two paper cups and a chocolate biscuit to cheer James up, Erica had taken off her sunglasses.

She took the coffee without turning her head.

"I know you made up that stuff about your sister's birthday party being cancelled."

Nicolas pretended not to understand. He couldn't work out if it was an accusation or if she was grateful. Erica clenched her jaw, pulled out her sunglasses, fiddled with them, then put them back on.

The buzzer sounded. Djursholm Hockey had lost against Tumba, 6-2, and the players skated across the ice towards the changing-rooms.

In contrast to what Nicolas was expecting, James was in a good mood when he came towards them, dragging his hockey bag. The boy turned to Erica.

"Carl-Johan asked if I can sleep over at his," he said happily. "Can I?"

"Of course you can," Erica said with a relieved smile. "I'll courier your clothes and a toothbrush over if you send me the address later."

Nicolas, who had been keeping in the background, stepped forward.

"Well played, James. Have a good time, and see you tomorrow."

He hoisted the hockey kit onto his shoulder and followed Erica, who was already walking towards the car. He unlocked the new black Range Rover, tossed James's things in the back and got in behind the wheel. It was exactly the same as the old one, which had surprised Nicolas when Johan handed him the keys earlier that day. A short distance away Nicolas saw James and his teammate, deep in conversation, get into the back seat of an SUV. Out of habit, he memorised the registration number as he reversed the Range Rover.

It wasn't until they reached the E4 and were heading north that Erica cleared her throat. She lowered the volume of the radio.

"I haven't always been like this, you know," she said. "I can see that you despise me, and the judgemental way you look at me makes me sick."

Nicolas didn't respond.

"I was happy before I met Johan. God, I curse the fucking day he came up to me. I was twenty-four, what did I know? I'd been in a TV reality show a couple of years earlier, and my life was sliding out of control. I couldn't even get any gigs in bars. The last offer I got was to show my cunt on a webcam for fifty dollars. I was broke. I thought living with someone like Johan would give me some sort of security. Fucking hell…"

"Erica, I…"

She held her hand up towards Nicolas and he fell silent.

"Every day, every single fucking day, he reminds me how grateful I should be to him. For rescuing me from myself. From life as a white-trash single mother on benefit. I have everything, Nicolas, but in reality I have nothing. He can throw me out whenever he feels like it. Judge me as much as you fucking like, but I'm his property just as much as you are. The difference is that you can pack up and leave."

Nicolas felt sorry for her, but didn't know what to say to console her.

"Do you know why Johan wanted to get a new car?" he asked, to change the subject.

"I didn't even know he had," she replied, staring out at the gloomy blocks of flats before turning the volume back up again.

10

Vanessa parked the BMW in the empty car-park on Retzius väg in Solna. She squeezed between the bushes and cars and followed the signs to the mortuary. Her gym clothes were sticking to her body. She rang the door-bell of the large brick building and waited. Nothing happened. She tried again, and a moment late the lights went on. A man in his fifties, with glossy, slicked-back black hair opened the door. He had a pair of black glasses pushed up onto his forehead, and Vanessa could see a gold ring in his ear.

"Vanessa Frank?"

He held out his hand and Vanessa shook it quickly. He smelled of cigarette smoke. The man stepped aside and she walked into the large, stone-floored reception area.

"I'm Per Thysell. Your colleague said you wanted to see the unidentified woman who was found yesterday evening on Gärdet."

Vanessa nodded and held out her police ID. Per Thysell pulled his glasses down and peered at it before handing it back.

"Was there anything particular you were curious about? My assistant and I were about to get started."

"I just want to take a look at her."

Their footsteps echoed in the corridor. Per Thysell stopped in front of a thick, metal door and pressed a keycard to the reader. He tapped in a four-digit code with two fingers. There was a click and he opened the door. The cold that streamed out made Vanessa shiver. One wall was covered with stainless steel hatches. She took a deep breath. Her heart was beating hard. The pathologist walked over to one of the hatches, grabbed hold of the handle and pulled it open.

It would soon be over, soon she would be looking at the face of a complete stranger. And then she would go back home to

Vasastan. Shower. Wash her hair. Then stroll slowly to the local bar, McLarens, exchange small-talk with the owner, Kjell-Arne, drink a light, uncomplicated lager, trudge home and get a good night's sleep. Then carry on looking for the perpetrator without any personal feelings about the victim. There was bound to be a perfectly reasonable explanation for why the woman had phoned her. Unless she had just called the wrong number.

Per Thysell checked the ID-tag that was tied around a pale toe.

"Here she is," he said as he pulled the tray out then stepped back.

The harsh fluorescent light enhanced the beauty of the girl's face. Her thick black hair glistened. If it hadn't been for the two knife-wounds, it would have looked like she was sleeping, the way she had slept so many times in her room in Vanessa's apartment. She let her eyes move downward, past the dried blood on her stomach, past her genitals, down her thighs, all the way to her feet. The feet that had carried Natasha from Syria to Sweden, which had walked, tired and bleeding, all the way across Europe in search of a decent life. To Stockholm. To Vanessa.

Natasha ought to be in Syria with her father. Not here. Not lying naked on a stainless-steel tray in a mortuary in Solna.

Per Thysell was standing with his arms folded over his chest, silently watching her.

Vanessa tried to express what was going on inside her, but not a sound emerged from her lips. Her jaw had locked. She took a step closer to Natasha and reached out her hand, but pulled it back before she touched the girl's cheek. She couldn't bring herself to touch her, to feel the chill of her body.

A tear ran down Vanessa's cheek and dripped onto the tiled floor.

Per Thysell shuffled uncomfortably.

"Who is she?"

Vanessa replied in a thick voice:

"My everything."

She wiped the tears away and cleared her throat. Natasha had called her, had tried to get hold of her. Was it a last cry for help? Then someone had driven a knife into her. Questions were building up in Vanessa's head. Why was Natasha back in Sweden? And why hadn't she got in touch earlier?

Vanessa was struck by a terrible thought.

Could the murder be a way of someone taking revenge on her? There were plenty of people who wished her ill, who knew that by killing Natasha they could inflict a wound that would never stop bleeding.

"Send me the autopsy report as soon as you're finished," she said in a dull voice.

In her mind's eye she imagined Per Thysell cutting into Natasha's body. He and his assistant removing her organs, weighing them, taking notes. It made her want to throw up. She wanted to tell the pathologist to be careful, to treat Natasha gently, but she knew that wouldn't make any difference. Natasha was dead, and wouldn't feel anything.

Vanessa turned and left the cold-store. Per Thysell called after her.

She managed to start the car and drive a few hundred metres, and was passing the Karolinska University Hospital when the scream came.

She pulled over to the side of the road and put her hazard lights on. The cars behind her blew their horns angrily as Vanessa clutched the steering-wheel and screamed. After a while she slid over to the passenger seat, pushed the door open and threw up in the gutter.

PART II

1

It was Monday afternoon and Molly Berg was sitting on the roof terrace above her apartment on Banérgatan, engrossed in Charles Bukowski's *Factotum*. Her top half was wrapped in a thick padded jacket, and she was wearing grey fingerless gloves. The temperature was only just above freezing, but the cold didn't bother her.

She had grown up in Kiruna, almost one thousand, two hundred and fifty kilometres to the north. She was sixteen years old when she announced to her parents that there was nothing for her in the mining town. Not because of the climate or the permanent darkness during the polar winters, but because she felt so far away from everything. Isolated. Molly found a high school specialising in gymnastics in Stockholm, moved to a one-room flat in Solna, and hadn't been back to Kiruna since then.

From the age of twelve or thirteen she had realised that she had a particular effect on men. She knew she was beautiful, with her glossy dark hair, her big, brown eyes, high cheekbones, full lips and perfect skin. But there was something else as well. Something she couldn't put her finger on. All manner of men were drawn to her. Old, young, rich, poor. Businessmen and criminals. Artists and football players. They usually guessed that she was from Argentina or Brazil, maybe Colombia or Venezuela. In fact she was the result of a business arrangement between a Swedish mine-worker and a Thai waitress. He had been on the hunt for the kind of intimacy no Swedish woman wanted to give him, she wanted a decent life. Molly's father Robert had flown to Bangkok, surveyed the bars and strip-clubs, picked the girl he thought prettiest and took her home with him, with the promise of a new life.

Molly had been born a year later.

Now Siriwan had been dead a couple of years, and Robert lived on a farm outside Kiruna with his dog Joik.

Molly looked up irritably when a shadow was cast over the text. Her irritation quickly switched to delight when she saw who it was. She folded the corner of the page and tucked the book away in her Louis Vuitton bag.

"Back to yours or mine, darling?" Didrik de Graaf said in an affected voice that was considerably deeper than his usual voice. His short blond hair was combed forward into a short fringe.

"No one would ever believe you were hitting on me," Molly said as she sat up. "No matter how hard you pretend."

"Why not?" Didrik said, with feigned indignation. "I'm macho, aren't I? A real man's man?"

"First and foremost because you have a pink boa worthy of a long-dead opera diva wrapped round your neck. But mostly because your parents gave you the gayest name in the world. Didrik. I mean, was there ever any doubt that you were going to turn out to be a poof?"

Didrik pulled a chair over towards the ledge of the roof and sat down next to Molly. She put her feet up on the parapet as he lit a joint he had brought with him, closed his eyes and took a deep toke. He leaned his head back as he passed it to Molly. She drew the thick smoke into her lungs and held it there for a few moments before breathing out.

They looked at the lights of the city beneath them, the dark water.

"Do you miss Barcelona?" Didrik asked.

"Every day."

"Me too."

She could feel the marijuana start to work, making its way into her blood, calming her, shutting the noise out. Didrik's voice sounded muffled and distant. She took another small toke before handing the joint back to Didrik.

"You said you were going to stop…"

"Fucking for money?" she interrupted. "I can't do anything else. All I know how to do is be a whore, like my mum."

Didrik turned towards her with the joint dangling from the corner of his mouth.

"Don't say that."

"It's what I am. And what she was. A whore. She spread her legs for a better life. I do the same because it's the only thing I know how to do, and because I've been doing it since I was seventeen. Only I get paid more. That was Mum's problem, she made do with so little."

"Seriously, Molly. Find something else. Who the fuck needs money?"

"Not you, seeing as you're going to inherit something like two hundred million when your parents die. But the rest of us do." She smiled. Despite her sharp tone, she wasn't annoyed with him. She reached out her hand and stroked his cheek. It was nice that someone cared, for real. "Don't worry about me, I'm just talking crap. I'll find something else."

Didrik took a deep drag. His eyes were bloodshot.

"God, I miss Barcelona. I can't believe you persuaded me to come back home."

Molly stiffened. She hadn't even told Didrik about what she'd heard on the luxury yacht, *Lucinda*, back in the summer, the real reason why she had left Spain and moved back to Sweden. She had thought about contacting the police but hadn't dared. Since she got home she had been avoiding crowds and places she imagined the terrorists might target.

"What about Thomas? Have you heard anything from him?" Didrik asked with his eyes closed.

"We're meeting up this evening."

"Can I see the picture again?" He had persuaded Molly to take a discreet photograph of Thomas, the man she had met two weeks ago. She handed over her mobile. "God, he's handsome. I love Brits. Especially mysterious Brits who turn up in bars."

Molly laughed and the world spun. She wanted more marijuana, wanted to put more distance between herself and everything around her.

Didrik coughed, and smoke billowed out of his mouth.

"Have you told him what you do for a living?" he asked when he had recovered.

"No," she said, taking the joint once more. "But on the other hand, I don't know what he does either."

2

It was half past four and Mikael Kask was watching as Detective Inspector Vanessa Frank cleared her throat, reached for the glass of water on the desk and took a sip.

In the late 1980s and early 90s Mikael Kask had worked as a model in New York, before he trained to join the police. His career had progressed quickly. For the past couple of years he had been leading the National Homicide Unit, the unit which reported directly to the National Operations Department, and was tasked with supporting particularly complex investigations throughout Sweden.

He liked Vanessa, and considered her one of the best detectives he had worked with. But he, like most people, found it difficult to get close to her. Vanessa worked hard and tirelessly, but kept her distance from her colleagues. A lot of people thought she was difficult, but not Mikael. He was fascinated by her. She was charismatic in her own subtle way. And she was beautiful. When she got divorced from her film director husband, Svante Lindén, he had harboured hopes that something might develop between the two of them. Nothing serious, of course, but a brief romance. A few nights of fun. But Vanessa hadn't shown any interest in him, even if he was fairly sure she liked him. As a boss, anyway.

"So you had no idea that Natasha was in Sweden?" he asked carefully.

"Up until Saturday I thought she was with her dad in Syria."

"And you can't think of anyone who might have wanted to harm her?"

Vanessa shook her head slowly.

"Her whole family apart from her father was wiped out in the war in Syria. Despite that, there was no hate in her. I'm having trouble thinking that she could have made a single enemy, ever."

"Can you see any logical connection to Rikard Olsson?"

"No."

Mikael ran a hand through his perfectly styled hair.

"Why did she live with you?" he asked.

"I liked her, she liked me. She thought her whole family were dead. She'd crossed an entire continent to get here. The alternative was a residential care home. It was the right thing to do."

Mikael could see that she was working hard to keep her voice steady. It was unusual for him to see Vanessa fragile, and he didn't like it at all. He switched his Dictaphone off. Sighed. Focused on what he was about to say. This was the part of the conversation he'd been dreading. Vanessa would be furious, and would cause a scene. But the decision had already been taken, and he had been promised that he could call Samer Bakir in on a part-time basis.

"Considering what's happened, and the mental strain you've been under in recent days, it would be best if you took some time off."

Mikael did his best to adopt a stern expression.

"Okay," Vanessa said.

He was surprised, almost astonished.

"You're not going to ask how long for?"

"You're the boss, boss," she said in a monotone. "Was that everything?"

Without waiting for a reply, Vanessa stood up, went over the coat-rack by the door and pulled down her coat.

She left the room with Mikael's look of surprise burning into her back.

3

Outside the first snow of the winter was falling. Small, light flakes that melted as soon as they touched the ground, turning the tarmac a darker colour. Vanessa was driving her BMW towards Stadshagen. She had always respected Mikael Kask. He was competent. Fair. Always behaved correctly. At the same time, he was a notorious ladies' man. He was old-school masculine, a gentleman. Besides being obviously washing-detergent-advert handsome, tall, with a pronounced jaw and a large but fitting nose, and that carefully coiffed hair, he had a boyish self-assurance that she was reluctant to admit she found attractive. And not only her. There were always fresh rumours about his affairs with colleagues and lawyers. It was more the rule rather than the exception for him to have company in his bachelor pad on Kungsholmen. Even so, he always seemed to emerge unscathed when he ended these relationships. Vanessa had never heard anyone say a bad word about him, and assumed that he successfully managed to use his charm to avoid hurting anyone too badly. Recently she had come to understand that he had been seeing Trude Hovland. Even if they denied being infatuated with each other it was obvious, at least to Vanessa.

She passed the premises of the City Mission, where impoverished pensioners gathered to get a decent meal. The beautiful old buildings outside the car windows were replaced by taller modern edifices. In the yellow glare of the floodlights, a juniors match was being played at Stadshagen sports ground. The world was still turning, even though Natasha was dead. The buses were still serving their routes. Underground the metro trains were racing through their catacombs. Micro-dramas were happening everywhere. People were getting fired, falling in love, betraying their partners. Couriers in waterproof anoraks on bicycles with boxes full of pizzas, Thai takeaways and kebabs strapped to their backs, swished this way and that for slave wages.

"Everything's the same. I'm the only one who's changed," she said out loud.

The person who had killed Natasha was out there. Vanessa's head still felt heavy with the sleeping pills she had taken the past two nights, but somewhere in all the murkiness her thoughts were beginning to clear.

She felt a stabbing pain in her chest. Anguish? Grief? She breathed in deeply, then let the air out slowly through her lips to fend off her emotions.

She pulled into a parking space in front a grim nine-storey building and sat there with her hands on the wheel. People were emerging from the metro station, bags of groceries in their hands.

There were a number of hostels and a lot of sheltered housing in this part of Stadshagen, and property prices were lower here than in the rest of Kungsholmen because of all the drug addicts and alcoholics who hung around, hollow-eyed, in doorways and on street corners.

Vanessa thought about Nicolas. Maybe she should contact him, let him know that Natasha was dead. No, that would only complicate things. Steal valuable time from what really mattered. She was going to find whoever had killed Natasha, then she would deal with everything else.

Her phone rang, it was Celine.

"I can't talk now," she snapped. She felt a pang of guilt as she clicked to dismiss the call.

In her side-mirror she saw the person she was waiting for walking along with a sports bag on his shoulder. She didn't move. She waited until he had opened the door and disappeared inside. Shortly afterwards the lights went on in an apartment on the fourth floor.

4

Molly Berg watched Thomas as he chalked his billiard cue and circled the table, reading it. The word that described him best was stylish. He was calm, there was confidence in every movement, probably regardless of wherever he was or what situation he was in. She felt both safe and nervous in his company.

In his dark suit, white shirt and loosely knotted tie, he looked out of place among the rest of the clientele, which mostly consisted of noisy men in their twenties. The basement premises were full of rows of billiard tables, with a long bar counter along one side. Some of the men were perched on bar-stools, drinking beer until a table became free.

Molly thought a scruffy billiard hall was an odd place for a date. But on the other hand, she was glad Thomas hadn't suggested meeting in a hotel room where they could fuck and then go their separate ways. Not that she didn't want to have sex with him, but because she appreciated him showing that he didn't only want sex from her.

In fact they hadn't so much as kissed yet, even though this was the fourth time they'd met. He hadn't made any attempt to get physically closer to her on any of those occasions.

It was almost two weeks to the day since they had first met.

Molly had been eating dinner in her local pub on Banérgatan. Thomas had been sitting at one of the other tables. He too had been alone, with a copy of the *Financial Times* open in front of him. Every so often their eyes had met. He had been eating pasta, with a cloth napkin tucked into his collar to stop him spilling tomato sauce on his shirt. When it was time for coffee, he stood up, walked over to her table, and casually asked if she would like to have a drink with him. They had had a pleasant time together, scratching the surface of each other's stories and personalities, and amusing each other with observations about the other clientele. After a couple more drinks, Molly had been surprised when Thomas explained that he had to get back to his hotel and didn't suggest that she keep him company. He had waved for a waiter, paid for them both, them got to his feet.

"I'll be eating here again tomorrow, if you happen to be passing," he had said, before disappearing through the door.

To her surprise, the following day she had found herself sitting there expectantly waiting for Thomas to arrive. The atmosphere was more flirtatious than the previous evening. They had drunk more bottles of wine, and taken the occasional smoking break. That was when she had discreetly taken the picture she had shown Didrik a few hours ago.

They had sat there until the pub closed. Once again, the question she had been quite convinced was coming had not been asked. Instead Thomas had suggested that they meet the following week.

She had laughed and they had arranged to meet at a bar in Gamla stan, where the same thing happened. But even though they hadn't been physically intimate with each other, there was a charge between them was better than most things she had experienced.

"Check this out," Thomas said, winking at Molly, then leaned forward and hit the white ball. He got a perfect touch on the green ball, which rolled into the pocket.

"Nice," she said in English. "I'm going to get another beer, do you want one?"

"Yes, please. I'll pay." He put his hand in his back pocket, fished out a hundred-kronor note and eyed it uncertainly. "Is this enough?"

"I've got money."

Thomas waved the bank note.

"It's a point of principle. If you invite me out, you pay. Okay?"

She smiled, and took the hundred.

"No cheating," she said, gesturing towards the table.

Molly went over to the bar and ordered two large beers while Thomas went on playing. He always paid cash. That was a bit strange, but somehow fitted his persona.

He had told her he had landed in Stockholm that weekend. Molly had avoided asking him why he was back. In general, they told each other very little about themselves.

All she knew about Thomas was that he was staying at the Nobis Hotel on Norrmalstorg, and that he was here "to attend to some business", as he put it. He was polite and well-mannered. A perfect British gentleman, even if he looked like he was from the Middle East. His hair was short and black, with a neat side-parting. It was almost shaved at the sides. His skin was golden brown, his eyelashes long and dark. Was he going to take her to his hotel room after this? Molly hoped so.

She already knew he was good in bed. She could see it in certain men, from the way they carried themselves, spoke, looked at her. Thomas was one of those men, she was sure of it.

She returned to the billiard table with the beers. Two new players arrived at the next table. A man in his mid-forties with a sky-blue T-shirt from some heating company tucked into his pale jeans. He was with a small, pretty Thai woman, only a few years older than Molly.

She glanced immediately at Thomas, worried that he was going to make some comment, whisper something unpleasant. But he hardly seemed to have noticed them.

"Your turn," he said.

He handed her the cue, they were playing with the same one, and their hands touched. He left his where it was, their eyes met, then he smiled quickly and stepped back. A shiver of delight ran through her body. She wondered if he had noticed, and if he had touched her on purpose. It was frustrating, she was usually the one in control, not the other way round. Ever since she had realised the effect she had on men, she had learned to play on their desires. Their egos. Playing, challenging them, adopting different roles depending on what she wanted to get out of the encounter. But not with Thomas. No, he wasn't like other men. He didn't follow the rules. Sometimes she wondered if he was attracted to her at all. He seemed completely unaffected by her company, unconcerned by her appearance and attractiveness. That both disturbed and titillated her. He was something very unusual – a man she couldn't read.

She hit the white ball, but it missed. He laughed.

"You'll have to practice before next time."

She stifled the impulse to ask when that was going to be, then felt annoyed with herself for caring so much.

On the next table the woman was getting ready to play. The man was standing behind her, instructing her on what to do with one hand on her hip. She was smiling, but Molly could see it was a fake smile. She was tired of him, disgusted by the way he pawed at her.

Molly couldn't help wondering if her mum had felt like that when she was with her dad.

Thomas's mobile buzzed, and he took it out and looked at it thoughtfully.

"I'm sorry, I have to go," he said apologetically.

She felt disappointed. Nothing more was going to happen this time either. Thomas walked round the table towards her. She stiffened, suddenly very aware of how she looked and the way she was standing. But he just teased the billiard cue from her hand, turned and put it back in the rack on the wall.

He calmly drank a last gulp of his beer before they left the club. The wind had got up out in Odenplan, and it was snowing harder. Their breath coloured the air white.

"It's so cold," Thomas said, peering up at the sky.

"Not really," Molly said.

He smiled.

"Would you like me to get you a taxi?"

She shook her head and once again stifled the urge to ask him when they were going to see each other again. Instead she leaned forward and kissed him softly on his cheek.

"I've got a question, though," she said.

Thomas looked at her intently. For a moment she thought he looked disapproving, but that could have been her imagination.

"Oh?"

"What scent is that?"

"Versace. I don't know what it's called. A pale blue bottle. Transparent."

"I'm going to buy one like it."

"Who for?"

"My boyfriend, of course," Molly said. "See you!"

Thomas laughed.

As she waked home she decided that the evening hadn't been a failure, even though Thomas had cut it off early. She still couldn't put her finger on what it was, but there was something that made her weak at the knees in his presence. Maybe it was just as well to acknowledge it, she concluded. It happened so rarely. She hadn't felt this way in a very long time.

Admittedly, things had ended badly that time, and she had been forced to move to Barcelona. But she was still alive.

And this evening, she felt happy about that.

5

Samer Bakir's apartment consisted of a single room. From the ceiling hung a bare light-bulb that spread a harsh glare. The only furniture was a bed with no legs and a chair over by the window.

"Very feng shui," Vanessa said.

Samer closed the front door behind her.

"I haven't had time to get more than the bare necessities yet."

The air was damp, steam was coming from the bathroom. Samer's hair was wet and he was wearing a grey tracksuit. He went over to one of the cupboards in the tiny walk-through kitchen and took out two glasses, then opened the fridge to get a carton of orange juice. He looked questioningly at Vanessa, who nodded. She took her coat off and hung it on the back of the chair before sitting down. Samer handed her a glass and she took a sip.

"Thanks, that's good."

He remained standing, emptied his glass in two gulps, then refilled it.

"I heard that you knew her?"

"Natasha."

"Yes, Natasha."

Vanessa leaned forward and put the half-empty glass on the pale parquet floor.

"I've been taken off the case," she said. "But I want you to keep me updated on what's going on."

A short silence followed. Vanessa couldn't figure out what he was thinking.

"Yes, I heard. I'm standing in for you."

"Then you already know that she used to live with me, that I cared about her," Vanessa said quietly. The words were catching in her throat. All of a sudden she felt uncertain. Maybe she should just stand up and leave. Wait for the results of the investigation. After all, there was a reason why police officers weren't allowed to investigate crimes committed against people they were close to. Emotions got in the way of rational reasoning.

"Of course I can keep you informed. But you can't get involved in our work. You understand that?"

"Thanks."

Samer stepped over the gym bag that was lying on the floor and sat down on the bed. He pulled his legs up and leaned back against the wall.

"Why did she live with you?"

Vanessa fixed her gaze on her hands.

"I was suspended from duty after I was caught drink-driving." Samer raised his eyebrows and she went on. "While I was waiting for the inquiry I spent a couple of days a week volunteering, helping young refugee girls with their reading. Natasha was living in a care home. We found each other. A couple of months later she moved in with me."

Samer moistened his lips with his tongue.

"Natasha isn't a Syrian name, is it?"

"Her dad was a professor of Russian literature at Damascus University. Her younger brother was called Lev."

"Was?"

"The whole family apart from Natasha and her father died in an air-raid. She was smuggled out of the country and made her way to Sweden on foot."

Samer pulled one leg of his jogging bottoms up, revealing a hairy calf, which he proceeded to scratch with his fingernails.

"When did she return to Syria?"

"In December last year. When she left her father in the hospital before she came here, he had been close to dying, but he survived and managed to track her down. She went back to take care of him."

Samer looked at Vanessa sympathetically.

"You had no idea she was back in Sweden?"

She shook her head, then reached for the glass and drank the last of the juice.

"Have you found out how long she'd been back?" she asked.

Samer seemed to be considering his response, and took his time answering.

"All we know is that she was staying with Johannes and Ida

Lindskog in Bergshamra. They're on holiday in New York, and when Natasha didn't answer their calls they got worried and called us to report her missing. They're due to land at Arlanda early tomorrow morning. We'll know more then."

Vanessa got to her feet and took a few steps towards the door. When Samer began to stand up, she held her hand up towards him. He sank back onto the bed.

"I can find my own way out."

6

The house lay on a sloping plot surrounded by a white stone wall.

Axel had gone straight there from the hospital on Saturday, without any equipment. He had stood outside the fancy villa, trying to see in through the black gate, but to no avail.

It was now just after eleven o'clock on Monday evening, and this time he had brought his laptop with him. He wanted to know what sort of person could hit a child with his car, then drive away from the scene.

To check if anyone was coming he switched on the dash-cam in his car. He had installed it for his insurance company, in case he was ever involved in an accident.

Axel had failed his driving test seven times. Rebecca, who had been pregnant with Simon at the time, had stubbornly persisted in going for test-drives with him, even though he had wanted to give up.

"How else are you going to be able to pick our son up? Unless you're expecting me to drive him around all the time?" she had asked.

Eventually he had succeeded, even if he was still an insecure and probably unsuitable driver. Things that came naturally to other people took longer for him. He drove so slowly and carefully that Simon would often sigh out loud in the passenger seat. Axel smiled briefly at the memory and glanced towards the empty seat to his right.

The house seemed to be asleep, the windows beyond the tall wall were either dark or had their curtains closed.

Axel lay down in the back seat and took one last look out of the tinted windows. He pulled a blanket over his head so the light from the screen wouldn't illuminate the inside of the car, then set to work. Breaking into a wifi network was child's play. But the family that lived in the house had enhanced security, so it took him a few more minutes before he was in.

Every so often he checked the live feed from the dash-cam, to make sure no one was approaching the car.

It felt good to be doing something, not just sit helpless while Simon fought for his life. He started by mapping the web traffic to get a better idea of the family. Even if the car, a Range Rover, was registered in the man's name, it was hard to know who had been behind the wheel on Valhallavägen last Friday.

Even though only three people were registered as residents of the villa, a fourth person seemed to live there. That surprised him, because it was unlikely that such a wealthy family would have a lodger for financial reasons. Could the fourth person, who – according to what Axel could tell from the web traffic – was called Nicolas Paredes, be some sort of butler? A chauffeur?

It would probably have been enough to copy the hard-disks he had gained entry to onto his own laptop, but he was starting to get hooked on finding out more and lost track of time.

He checked the dash-cam again. A man with a labrador on a leash was cautiously approaching the car. Axel closed the laptop and lay motionless under the blanket. The man seemed to be circling the car, trying to see in through the windows. Axel waited a few minutes before opening the laptop again and copying the contents of the hard drives.

He could look through the data he had gathered while he was at the hospital. He checked there was no one nearby, then crawled into the front seat and drove away.

7

The sun had just risen when the SAS plane from New York landed on time at 08.20. There were five taxi-drivers holding up signs in the arrivals hall at Arlanda. Weary, suntanned travellers trudged out from the baggage reclaim area pulling their luggage. Some of them were wearing colourful flip-flops and sun-hats, and stared unhappily at the wet sleet outside the panoramic windows.

Vanessa went over to the information desk and held her police ID up to the man behind the desk, who looked at it with a distinct lack of interest.

"I need to get a message put out," she said, then took a sip of the coffee she had bought from 7-Eleven. She felt rested even though she hadn't slept more than a few hours. The previous evening she had promised herself that she wasn't going to take any more sleeping pills. She needed to stay sharp, despite the pain of Natasha's death.

She leaned her back against the counter and took a large gulp of coffee as an announcement over the speakers asked Johannes and Ida Lindskog to go to the information desk in the arrivals hall. There was no way she was going to sit at home waiting for her colleagues to find something. She needed to be proactive. Neither Mikael Kask or Samer Bakir were going to stop her being part of the hunt for Natasha's killer. Besides, she knew that the focus of the early part of the investigation would be on Rikard Olsson. A murdered police officer was always prioritised, no matter what the public message might be. Given that he had been working with gang-related violence, there was a clear level of threat that was hard to ignore.

A couple in their twenties emerged from the crowd, moving

quickly in Vanessa's direction. She held up her police ID once again as she noted that Johannes and Ida Lindskog were considerably younger than she had expected.

"My name is Vanessa Frank, I'm a police officer," she said.

"We thought you were going to be waiting for us at home?" Johannes Lindskog said.

"Change of plan." Vanessa gestured for them to follow her. "I'll drive you home and we can talk in the car to save time."

Ida got in the passenger seat while Johannes put their cabin cases in the boot and got in the back seat. Vanessa pressed record, then put her mobile next to the handbrake as she started the car.

"How long had Natasha been staying with you?"

"Natasha?" Ida exclaimed in surprise. "You mean Zahra?"

Vanessa, who had been keeping her eyes on the car in front, turned her head and met Ida's gaze. She quickly recovered from her own surprise.

"Yes, I mean Zahra."

"Since May," Ida replied. "That's right, isn't it?"

Johannes murmured in agreement from the back seat. So Natasha had been in Sweden for at least six months without getting in touch. And she had been using a false name. To make it harder for Vanessa to find her?

"What did she do during the day?"

"She had a number of casual jobs. Back in the summer she worked in a café, and in the past few weeks she was working at an Asian restaurant in the shopping centre in Solna."

"I'll need to ask you the names of those places later." Vanessa pulled out onto the dual carriageway and passed under a bridge. The air traffic control tower got smaller and smaller in the rear-view mirror. "Did she spend much time with other people?"

"A girlfriend came to visit her a couple of times."

Johannes leaned forward.

"Her name was Sabina, wasn't it?" he added.

"Do you have any contact details for her?" Vanessa asked as she turned off towards Stockholm.

"I'm afraid not. They only used to say a quick hello to us before going into Zahra's room."

"Age?"

"She was probably the same age as Zahra. Maybe a year or two older."

They drove past fast-food restaurants, warehouses, petrol stations and industrial estates on their way towards the city.

"When was the last time Sabina came to the flat?"

"Two or three weeks ago. I don't know more precisely than that," Ida said.

The traffic got heavier the further south they got. When they reached Kista Vanessa slowed down and they joined a long line of flickering brake-lights moving slowly forward ahead of them.

She took a sip of her coffee, which was now cold.

"Had Zahra seemed at all worried recently?"

Johannes leaned forward again.

"No, not at all. She seemed just as cheerful as always. She was the first person who replied to our advert, and we made up our minds at once. This is all so tragic."

"It's horrible," Ida added.

For some reason Vanessa was feeling irritable. She liked the young couple, but it annoyed her that they were talking about Natasha as if they knew her better than she did. The situation felt surreal. Natasha was dead. Murdered. And she had stayed away from Vanessa. Something was wrong. Badly wrong.

"Did she pay her rent on time? Was she a good lodger?"

"Exemplary. She went to work, then came straight home. She kept to herself, but she was always pleasant. Sometimes the three of us would watch television together in the evening, but we didn't really socialise much more than that."

The traffic eased slightly on the smaller roads leading to Bergshamra. The apartment blocks rose up around them with their small squares and parks, followed by an ICA supermarket.

"I remember there was one thing that was a bit strange," Ida said, nodding towards the small square in front of the supermarket. "I'm sure it isn't important, but still. It was here, by the shop, last Tuesday. I was buying some sweets for the flight."

"What happened?"

"Well, Zahra was standing outside talking to a man. You need to turn off here, by the way," Ida said, pointing.

Vanessa slowed down and turned off.

"Why did you react to that?"

"Because, like we said, we never saw Zahra talk to anyone

apart from Sabina. And it looked like they were deep in discussion. When Zahra saw me the man quickly disappeared. We walked back to the flat together, and I asked her who he was."

"What did she say?"

"That she didn't know him, he had just been asking for directions. But that's not what it felt like. They were talking a bit too long for that."

"What did he look like?"

"I only saw him from the side. He was wearing a grey jacket and a cap."

"Was he an ethnic Swede?"

"I don't think so. He had a black beard."

"How tall would you say he was?"

"At least a head taller than Zahra."

Natasha, Vanessa thought. Her name was Natasha. No matter what you think and how well you think you knew her, her name was Natasha.

"And what time was this, roughly?"

"It was still light out, so sometime between 1.00pm and 3.00pm?"

Vanessa turned the engine off when they reached the couple's address. She pressed *stop* and saved the recording before asking for Ida's phone number. As she made a note of it she saw movement from the door of the building. It opened and Samer and another man stepped out onto the pavement.

Vanessa helped Johannes to get the cases out of the boot before jumping back in the driver's seat. Samer leaned over and tapped on the passenger window, gesturing to her to open it. She ignored him, started the car and drove back towards the ICA supermarket.

8

Molly Blom was lying on a sunbed by the edge of the pool in Sturebadet, wrapped in a white towelling dressing-gown. The muscles in her back and thighs were aching after her session in the gym, and she felt pleasantly relaxed. The other clients' voices formed a comforting background noise.

The clientele of the venerable bathhouse at this time on a Tuesday morning were mostly housewives from the upper-class parts of Stockholm who had dropped their children at preschool and were meeting friends to drink celery juice and have a massage. They probably assumed Molly was one of them, not least because she was also sipping a glass of green celery juice. I've probably had sex with the husband of at least one of them in the past five years, she thought to herself.

She closed her eyes and dozed off.

It had all started after she moved to Stockholm to go to high school. Molly had frequented the nightclubs around Stureplan, and because she wasn't old enough she had bought an ID card from an older girl. It was like stepping into a different world. An exclusive world to which only the chosen few had access. The roles were clearly defined. The men paid. The young women were trophies to be played with, replaceable accessories.

One day Molly got a message on Instagram from a man who said his name was Marc. He asked if she wanted to fly down to Dubai for a party. She could take two girlfriends with her, and the men would pay for hotels and drink. She and her two friends would also get three thousand dollars each. A week of paid partying. Molly agreed eagerly, and found two friends to go with her. The men, who were American, were pleasant and well-behaved. The fact that they were married wasn't something that bothered Molly. They bought designer clothes, bags, jewellery for her and the others, invited them to fancy dinners, took them to exclusive beaches, and in the evenings they went dancing in nightclubs. Obviously they ended up in bed together, but that was mainly because that was what happened when you spent time together drinking. At least that's what Molly convinced herself.

When she got home Marc contacted her again to ask if she'd be interested in carrying on. The men had been happy.

More trips followed: Los Angeles, Miami, Rio de Janeiro, Ibiza, London, Paris, London again, Athens.

Molly was more and more in demand, the payments grew, the presents became more numerous and more expensive. She said nothing to her parents back in Kiruna. She ended up having to buy a trunk for the money, which she kept under her bed in her one-room apartment in Solna. It would be tricky for her to go into a bank and explain why a high-school student had more than half a million kronor in used banknotes, in three different currencies.

The months passed. Marc and Molly's collaboration intensified. He offered to help her to launder the money. She didn't pay any attention to the details, but a couple of weeks later she had an account with a foreign bank, where the money from the trips built up. She was also starting to get bookings in Stockholm. She could get up to forty thousand kronor from Swedish businessmen for a night in one of the fancy hotels. Foreign sports stars, musicians, performers and businessmen all wanted to meet up with her in Sweden. Molly gave up high school.

But then everything changed.

Jamal, a guy only a couple of years older than her, moved into the same apartment block in Solna. He worked the same strange hours as Molly, and lived on the floor below her. One summer evening they started talking on their balconies, and Molly went down to Jamal's flat and sat on the wobbly chair on his balcony. They talked until the sun went up. While their neighbours went off to their boring jobs, leaving their snot-smeared kids at preschool, Jamal and Molly went on smoking, drinking whisky from the bottle, talking about their dreams and ordering takeaway pizza for breakfast. They had cracked the code for how to live without letting yourself get beaten by society, even though they had both been born without anything. That was what they thought, that was what they said. Molly stopped working with Marc and moved in with Jamal. She went to meet his family in Rinkeby, and got on well. For the first time in her life she was part of a loving community where people accepted her for who she was.

Of course Molly understood how Jamal earned his living, and where those bundles of cash came from. But instead of feeling scared, she thought it was exciting when he tucked his Glock into the waistband of his trousers before going out. He asked her not to ask any questions, and she accepted that. They dreamed of moving abroad. Jamal was going to arrange it, fight for the pair of them, get the money they needed. They would have kids and live a secluded life. They would raise a whole gaggle of children and look after stray dogs on a large farm somewhere in the Pacific.

Everyone was scared of Jamal, because they saw a tattooed gangster who wasn't afraid of anything. Everyone except Molly. He treated her kindly, with respect. Listened to her advice. Paid attention to her. Praised her. Encouraged her.

Molly was roused from her doze by someone tweaking her big toe. She opened her eyes and saw Didrik grinning at her. She made room for him to sit down on the sunbed. In the pool, wealthy pensioners were slowly swimming up and down.

"You're the only person in Sweden who still wears Speedos," she said.

He bounced up, grabbed the waist of his minuscule red trunks, pulling it out and let it snap back noisily.

"Why hide something God put a lot of effort into creating?"

He raised one arm, clenched his fist and kissed his bicep.

Molly laughed.

"Is that why he forgot to give you a working brain?"

Didrik pulled a face.

"Let's swim."

Molly threw off her dressing-gown, revealing a black bikini, and they jumped, shrieking and splashing, into the heated, clear blue water. The pensioners shot them disapproving looks as they clambered out, laughing, and lay down side by side on the sunbed.

"Aren't you working today?" Molly said as she tried to catch her breath.

"I'm not well."

"Again?"

"You sound like my beloved father. But you have to understand that you and I belong to Gen Z. We don't have any future prospects. The world is going to hell anyway. If the climate crisis doesn't turn the planet into a burning inferno, we'll only die of some virus or in a terrorist attack."

Molly flinched instinctively when Didrik mentioned terrorism.

But he went on babbling and didn't notice her change of mood. The torrent of words continued.

"...I mean, we might as well take so many drugs it kills us. What do you say?"

He rolled over onto his stomach and looked at her expectantly. Molly pulled herself together and ran her index finger from his forehead down to the tip of his nose.

"If you say so," she said. "I'm hungry. Shall we order a stupidly expensive salad and get told to shut up by oil-smeared posh women with gold jewellery that rattles?"

"Sounds good."

Still in their dressing-gowns, they went upstairs to the café, ordered two salads and sat down at a table with a view of the pool.

When they were finished, they leaned back and drank green tea. Molly's mobile buzzed. It was Thomas, wanting to meet up. In her apartment, at half past three.

Molly smiled and held her phone up to Didrik so he could read the message.

"What happened to playing hard to get? Are you really going to jump the minute he calls?" he asked.

"I can't help it. There's something special about him, something I haven't felt since..."

Molly fell silent and swallowed.

"Jamal?" Didrik concluded. "And you know how that ended."

This time he saw the effect of his words on Molly. He reached across the table and took hold of her hand.

"Sorry. I didn't mean that."

"I know. Don't worry."

She gathered her things together and went down to the changing-room, where she showered, dressed and applied her makeup extra carefully. She had a few hours to kill before Thomas showed up, and decided to take a walk through the city.

She stopped abruptly in the middle of Stureplan. A man bumped into her shoulder and muttered something. But Molly didn't hear him. She took her iPhone out of her bag and looked closely at Thomas's text.

See you at yours, it said.

At hers?

No one apart from Didrik knew where Molly lived. She was certain she had never given Thomas her address. How could he know where she lived?

9

Vanessa leaned her head back and studied the grey blanket of cloud that covered the Stockholm sky. Last year the city didn't get more than nine hours of sunlight throughout the whole of November. So far this month the sun hadn't appeared for a single minute, but at least it had stopped raining.

There was a security camera mounted to the right of the entrance to the ICA supermarket. Vanessa ignored the female beggar's mechanical greeting and went into the shop. A teenage boy with a red face and spiky hair was yawning behind the only till that was open.

"I'm from the police, and I need access to the recordings from the camera by the door."

"You'll have to talk to Gurra. The boss, I mean. He's in the office."

Vanessa followed the cashier's directions and found herself facing a thick metal door with a glass window. She cupped her hand, pressed her face to the glass and peered into what looked like a stockroom. She banged on the door before going in.

A large, red-haired man in a white polo shirt with the ICA logo on the chest emerged from the rows of boxes. He looked surprised.

"Gurra?"

The man nodded.

"Vanessa Frank, I'm from the police." She held up her ID.

"Okay. So how can I help you?"

"The security camera facing the entrance to the store. Can I take a look at the recordings from last week?"

"I've got a lot to do…"

"Me too. Best to get this out of the way quickly," Vanessa said, cutting him off.

Gurra held out his long arms, then turned and walked back into the stockroom. He showed her into a small, windowless office that smelled of sweat and stale fast food. The only furnishings were a desk, two chairs, and a bookcase stuffed with files. There was a computer on the desk, with an evening paper spread out in front of it, next to a steaming cup of coffee and a half-eaten cinnamon bun on a paper napkin.

Gurra moved the mouse and the screen came to life. He clicked on an icon the shape of a camera and eight square, black and white pictures appeared. Vanessa leaned over Gurra's shoulder. One of the cameras showed an image from outside, while the other seven showed images of the store's interior.

"What day are you after?"

"Last Tuesday, from midday."

He opened a new window, changed the date and tapped in the time. Vanessa pulled the other chair over and Gurra made space for her.

"What are we looking for?" he asked.

"A teenage woman. Black hair. She should be talking to a man, possibly bearded, wearing a cap," Vanessa said, without taking her eyes off the screen.

"Exciting," he said with a yawn. "Want me to fast-forward?"

"Go ahead."

The people in the square started moving faster, like they were in an old newsreel. Pushchairs criss-crossed the screen. A class of preschool pupils in overalls marched past. A Securitas van drove up and stopped. The driver got out, walked into the store and came out again with a box in his hands, then the van disappeared.

Gurra lost interest and reached for the cinnamon bun, and took a bite. Sugar and crumbs scattered across the desk and he absentmindedly swept them onto the floor with one hand.

He picked up the cup of coffee and raised it to his lips.

"Stop," Vanessa said.

Gurra froze and looked at her in surprise, his cheeks bulging with a mouthful of the bun.

"The film, Gurra. Not your coffee."

He swallowed and put the cup down.

"Sorry."

The clock on the screen said 13.37. Gurra rewound a few seconds. He stuck one finger in his mouth to loosen a piece of bun.

Vanessa felt a pain in her chest when Natasha appeared on the screen.

She was facing the camera, wearing a thick, dark jacket. Vanessa guessed it was black or dark blue. Suddenly she turned her head. A man was approaching from the right, and stopped with his back to the camera.

Vanessa studied Natasha's face. There was no doubt that the girl seemed afraid. The man appeared to be talking to her. Natasha nodded, held her arms out, shook her head. Backed away. The man nodded. On the back of his neck, just below his hairline, there was a mark. A scar, or a tattoo, perhaps? Vanessa leaned even closer to the screen and looked at the man. It looked more like a large birthmark.

The conversation went on for twenty-three seconds, then the man put his hands in his pockets and disappeared from the picture. Ida Lindskog appeared, exchanged a few words with Natasha, then went inside the supermarket while the girl stayed where she was, looking towards where the man had disappeared.

"Where did he go?" Vanessa asked.

"Towards the metro, maybe. Or the car-park."

Ida Lindskog came out again carrying a plastic bag. She waved to Natasha, who gave a strained smile and went over to join her. They walked off in the same direction as the man.

"I want you to send me the recordings from all the cameras, even the ones inside the shop. Everything that was recorded between eleven o'clock and six o'clock."

"Sure."

Vanessa grabbed a post-it note and pen from the desk and wrote down her personal email address.

"Are we done?"

Vanessa stuck the post-it note to the computer screen.

"We are." She patted Gurra on the shoulder and stood up.

There had been no mistaking the fear on Natasha's face. She was going to find the man in the recording. She would hunt him to the ends of the earth if that was what it was going to take.

10

Nicolas was out walking among the oversized houses of company directors and tech-millionaires in Djursholm. The sun was just visible as a brighter patch behind the clouds covering the sky. The trees around Samsöviken were leafless and anorexic.

He met very few pedestrians, and most of those were upper-class mothers with pushchairs or dog-walkers. Some of the other people out running were followed by bodyguards who observed him warily. In his black leather jacket, balaclava, dark jeans and heavy boots, he didn't look like a typical Djursholm resident.

Sweden and Stockholm had changed. The wealthiest had begun to install panic rooms, company directors and industrialists were accompanied by bodyguards who protected them and their families from kidnapping and extortion. Pretty much every day there were newspaper reports of fresh explosions and shootings in the suburbs. Gangs of youths drifted around the city centre, stealing mobiles and coats from other youngsters. A couple of years ago, just after Nicolas had been forced to leave the Special Operations Group, the elite division of the Swedish Armed Forces, he had personally helped to encourage the growth in panic rooms and bodyguards. Together with a childhood friend, he had abducted two directors and extorted money from their families. Vanessa Frank had put a stop to their activities. She had let Nicolas go unpunished in exchange for him accompanying her to the far south of Chile to rescue Natasha.

Since then, an unusual friendship had developed between him and Vanessa. A friendship that had occasionally bordered on… well, something else. Last summer, before he accepted the job in London, he had come close several times to asking her exactly what was going on between them. But something held him back. Held Vanessa back. It was as if neither of them wanted to expose themselves, risk stepping over the invisible boundary out of fear of ruining their relationship. After Nicolas moved to London he had tried to stay in touch, but Vanessa had stopped answering his calls and texts. He didn't understand why. He didn't mean her any harm. Quite the reverse. There was no one he wished more happiness than Vanessa Frank – no matter what happened between them. She was difficult, hard to figure out, but in all his thirty-one years Nicolas had never met anyone he felt a stronger connection with.

He stopped by a jetty and looked out across the water of Samsöviken. On the far side of the water lay Lidingö. He took out his mobile and called Vanessa's number. A soulless female voice told him that the number was no longer in use.

When Nicolas got back to the house and was passing the large living room, Erica was sitting at the dining table in lacy underwear with a bottle of red wine in front of her. The lighting was low, turned down. There was a crackle from the open fireplace where flames were licking the logs.

"Would you like a glass?" she asked.

"I'm good, thanks."

"You don't want to keep me company for a while?"

Erica got to her feet, picked up the bottle of wine and walked slowly towards him. Her high heels and the fact that she was drunk made her walk unsteady. Nicolas looked away, fixing his gaze on the fire.

"Don't you think I look nice?" she whispered. "Look at me."

Erica grabbed his hand and placed it on her hip. She leaned forward, her breath smelled of wine and mint. Nicolas removed his hand.

"Stop it," he said, looking her in the eye.

She backed away, raised the bottle to her lips and took a swig. She wiped her chin and laughed.

"If Johan told you to fuck me, you'd do it. Is that what you want? For him to ask you to do it?"

Nicolas felt sorry for Erica. He didn't want to take advantage of the situation she was in.

"I want to do my job. I don't even think this is what you want. You're just... unhappy. And drunk."

She snorted.

"Don't tell me what I want. And I've seen the way you look at me. I know you want it too."

Erica took a step forward and hit him in the chest with her right hand. Nicolas didn't flinch.

"Am I so disgusting? Do you despise me so much that you don't even want to fuck me?"

She hit him again.

Nicolas turned and began to walk towards his room.

Erica let out a sob. But she was right. From the very start he had noticed the way she looked at him. And he had been worried, by what it meant, and about his own reaction. He was attracted to her. But he couldn't do anything, couldn't ruin everything. He'd get the sack, would have to start from scratch once again.

Nicolas stopped and walked back. Put his arms round Erica. Felt her tears run down his neck.

"Hush, now," he whispered. "It's going to be okay."

He held her tight, pressing her slim body to his. Erica misinterpreted the gesture and tried to kiss him, and Nicolas let go of her and backed away.

As he walked to his room, he heard the sound of the wine bottle smashing against the wall.

11

Axel found an empty space in the windy car-park and managed to get his Volkswagen Passat inside the white lines after a few attempts. His body was trembling as he opened the door and the wind grabbed at his clothes.

He followed the arrows towards Skärholmen Shopping Centre. The pocket of his jeans was bulging with the bundle of notes he had withdrawn a short while ago.

The doctors had made their pronouncement. All Axel and Rebecca could hope for now was a miracle. And if that miracle didn't happen in the next few days, Simon was going to die in his bed in the Astrid Lindgren Children's Hospital.

Axel hadn't been able to stay there, just sit there watching life drain away from his son. The hospital was full of sick, dying children, whose distraught parents, their faces red from crying, wandered the long, sterile corridors like ghosts.

Rebecca had looked surprised when he said he had to go off on an errand. He had never felt such anger as the rage now coursing through his body.

He took the escalator down into the sleepy shopping centre, passed a Clas Ohlson store and a couple of noisy young mobile-phone salesmen from Telenor, and made his way towards the food court.

The name of the restaurant where he was meeting the man was Alhambra. Thorsten's insults from the weekend were echoing round his head. The problem was that he was right. It *was* Axel's fault Simon had been so badly hurt, that his lungs only worked with the help of machines. But there was one person who was more responsible than Axel. The person who had been driving Johan Karlström's car. He still wasn't entirely sure if Johan himself had been driving, but everything pointed towards that.

If Simon didn't survive, Axel's last act in life would be to take revenge. There was no other option. And he wanted to be prepared for the worst.

The weapon he was going to buy would end two lives, his son's murderer's, and Axel's own. He would never be able to live with the guilt if Simon died.

The man he had arranged to meet via a site on the Darknet would be wearing a red cap. It was easier to identify him than Axel expected, only two of the tables belonging to the Alhambra were occupied. One was being used by a noisy young family, the other by the man wearing a red cap. Axel was feeling uncertain, nervous. The man met his gaze, Axel raised his hand in greeting and walked over to him. He wiped his mouth with a napkin, pushed his plate away and stood up.

"Hi, I'm the p-p-person you're meeting," Axel said.

The man ignored Axel's outstretched hand. scratched his scalp, then pulled off the red cap and put it in his pocket.

"Follow me." He started walking towards the exit and Axel followed him. They crossed a square where greengrocers were shouting out their prices as clouds of white steam exploded from their mouths. He almost had to run to keep up. They entered a housing area. The tarmac was covered with pools of water. A rusty bicycle with no wheels lay abandoned in a bare shrub. The man stopped at a white metal door, looked around cautiously, then gestured to Axel to hurry up.

"Down here." The man opened the door, which led to a flight of steps.

Axel felt hesitant. He could easily be robbed, the man knew he had fifteen thousand kronor on him. Maybe there were more men waiting down there.

Axel was pathologically afraid of violence. How many times in his childhood had he lain curled up on the ground, desperately trying to protect his head from getting kicked? Listening to the laughter, the mocking cries as his schoolmates egged each other on.

"Make him piss himself! Make him piss himself!"

"Hey, wake up. I haven't got all day."

Axel made his way down into the darkness and almost tripped on the bottom step, but managed to keep his balance. Suddenly the light went on. The walls were lined with storage units, and a clutch of copper-coloured water-pipes ran along beneath the ceiling. The air smelled of damp and mould. The man walked past him, took out a silver-coloured key and pushed it into the sturdy padlock hanging on the nearest storage unit. He stepped inside, pulled on a pair of thin gloves, then grunted as he moved several boxes.

He opened one of them and felt around inside it.

"Come in."

On top of one of the boxes lay a black pistol. Beside it was a small box of brass-coloured bullets.

"Cash first."

Axel reached into his pocket and put the bundle of notes in the man's outstretched hand. He wondered what he was expected to do now. Should he check the gun? Ask for a bag? The man stamped his foot on the uneven cement floor as he counted the money.

Axel leaned forward and tucked the Glock in one jacket-pocket and the bullets in the other.

"Th-thanks," he mumbled, then turned and started to walk back to the stairs.

12

The clock on the wall said it was ten past three in the afternoon.
The moment Molly stepped into her large, carefully furnished hall
she could tell something was wrong. The light was on. Footprints
on the pale wooden floor led into the three-room apartment.

"Hello?" she called.

"I'm in here," Thomas replied.

She stifled the urge to turn and rush out of the apartment. Instead
she took off her Adidas trainers and put them on the shoe-rack.
For a moment she wondered if he had prepared some kind of role-
play. With her heart pounding in her chest, she followed the damp
footprints that led into the living room. He was sitting on the large,
pale armchair beneath the chandelier. She studied him hard, trying
to read the situation. Had she misjudged him? Was he a madman?

"How did you get in?" she asked.

"Sit down," he said curtly. "We need to talk."

His voice was measured, but left no room for discussion. Molly
put down the bag containing the change of clothes she had taken to
Sturebadet and sat down on the sofa. The atmosphere between them
had changed, and she felt uneasy.

"I need your help," he said.

He was looking at her intently.

"With what?"

"Next week you've arranged to meet a man, one of your regulars.
The managing director of Gambler, Johan Karlström."

Molly felt a growing sense of anxiety spread through her body,
she opened her mouth to protest but Thomas indicated that she
shouldn't interrupt.

"We need to be honest with each other, Molly. I know how you
make your living, and I'm not going to judge."

She stared at him. His face was expressionless.

"Who are you?" she asked.

"That's not what we're going to talk about."

"Why would I help you?"

Thomas gestured towards the round coffee-table between them. Molly hadn't noticed that there was a brown envelope lying on the mirrored glass surface.

"Open it," Thomas said.

"No."

She shook her head, and demonstratively put her hands in her lap. She moistened her lips. Her heart was beating harder and harder in her chest.

"Do as I say."

Molly grabbed the envelope and weighted it in her hand.

It was lighter than she had expected. It felt like it contained nothing but a few sheets of paper. She opened it. Photographs, at least twenty of them. Taken from a distance, through windows. Pictures taken from close-up, probably with a hidden camera. Molly on all fours in the cabin on the *Lucinda*. You could see her face clearly, but not the man's. Molly with his cock in her mouth. Molly dancing naked with a vacant expression in her face, high on ecstasy on the deck of the *Lucinda*. Molly in a red dress at a dinner in London. Molly snorting a line of cocaine from a tray at a party with a famous politician. Molly and Didrik on her terrace in Barcelona. She looked through them faster and faster, the trembling of her hands getting worse with each photograph. They must have been following her for months.

"There's video footage as well," Thomas said.

She blushed and put the pictures down.

"Who are you? Who the hell are you?" she said dully.

"MI6."

"MI6?"

Molly spat the question. She was angry. Her apartment on Banérgatan was her refuge. It was the only place on the planet where she felt safe. Thomas had invaded her sanctuary. And was threatening her. There was no other way to interpret the situation.

"The British security service. At the moment we're conducting a joint operation with the Swedish security service. And now we need your help."

Molly let this information sink in. She was trying to think

clearly, even though she felt sick. Did this have anything to do with what had happened on board the *Lucinda*? Or was he lying? Could he in fact be working for the men she had had sex with on the boat? Thoughts were swirling round her head, with less and less clarity.

"What do you want from me?"

"We want you to do us a favour. That's all."

"And if I refuse?"

"You won't."

"If I refuse?" she repeated tersely, even though she could already predict the response. She wanted him to say it out loud.

"Then I'll send these pictures to your father, who thinks you work in a clothing boutique. Your clients are powerful, in some cases world-famous. I daresay both the British tabloids and the evening papers in Sweden would be interested in them. You'd be on every front page, in every news bulletin. You'd be the most famous whore in the world."

That's not all, Molly thought. I'd be hunted down. A lot of the men I've met would want to see me silenced. Killed. They'd assume I was the one trying to get publicity.

A year or so ago a Russian woman described in the papers as a fashion model had been found dead beneath a skyscraper in Bangkok. Molly knew who the woman was, she had met her at parties in various villas in the Mediterranean. Spaced out. Talkative. Untrustworthy. There had been no doubt that she was in the same line of business as Molly. The woman's death, combined with what she had heard on board the *Lucinda*, had prompted Molly to look for a way out. But now, thanks to Thomas, Molly would have to make herself a target again.

13

Vanessa was sitting at a window table in McLarens on Surbrunnsgatan. Two of the regulars, dressed in leather waistcoats, were standing unsteadily by the bar, throwing darts that were hitting pretty much everything except the dartboard. From the television behind the bar, a newsreader was talking monotonously about the wretched state of the world. Vanessa poked aimlessly with her fork at her vegan pasta with tomato sauce as she held her mobile up in front of her. She was watching the short clip of Natasha and the unidentified man outside the ICA supermarket which had arrived that afternoon. It was impossible to make out what Natasha was saying. She had forwarded the recording to Trude, who had sent it for analysis. A lip-reading expert was going to be taking a look at it the next day, in the hope of learning something about the conversation.

Even so, she had a feeling that Mikael Kask and the others on the team weren't taking Natasha's death seriously. They appeared to regard her as a random victim, someone who just happened to get in the way.

But Vanessa needed to know why Natasha had been murdered, no matter what the motive was. She needed to reach a conclusion in order to be able to move on. And something told her that what she had seen in the security-camera footage meant something. While Mikael Kask and the others were focusing on Rikard Olsson, she might as well head in a different direction.

The only person she had let into her life in recent years had been Natasha. And Nicolas, if he counted. But now Natasha was dead and Nicolas had moved to London. Right now, it was probably just as well that he had left Sweden. There was a connection between them after what had happened in recent years, but she was scared of letting him get too close to her. Sure, she was attracted to him, painfully so. And there was no one she trusted more. But he was over ten years younger than her. There'd come a time when he wanted children. And she wouldn't be able to give him that, she was too old. More than anything, she didn't want to run the risk of being vulnerable again. That was why she had stopped responding when he had tried to contact her. It was better for her to stay away.

There was Celine too, of course. Wherever she was at the moment. Vanessa felt guilty about blowing her out the last time she got in touch. But she couldn't handle the responsibility. She picked up her mobile to call and ask how she was.

Someone roared her name. She looked up and saw Gusten, another of the regulars, over by the bar. Beside him was the guitar case he took everywhere with him. He jumped down from his bar stool and came over to her.

"How are things, Constable?" he asked.

"So-so."

"Have you heard this one?" Gusten cleared his throat. "Life is like a sewage pipe, long and full of shit."

"Nice. But I don't really like poetry, Gusten."

He shuddered and turned back towards the bar. A dart flew past his back, but he didn't seem to notice.

Vanessa felt comfortable in the poorly-lit bar. The atmosphere was friendly, the food perfectly okay, and the other customers mostly kept to themselves. McLarens' owner, a Norwegian called Kjell-Arne, appeared to have temporarily given up his attempts to make the bar hip.

The door opened, letting in a gust of cold air. Vanessa turned her head when the new arrival stopped at her table.

It was Samer Bakir.

"You didn't pick up when I called. Trude said I might find you here." He pulled out the chair opposite Vanessa and sat down. She raised her eyebrows, but said nothing. "Nice place."

"What do you want?" Vanessa asked wearily. She was expecting a lecture for having spoken to the Lindskogs and going to the ICA supermarket even though she had been taken off the case.

The two dart-players appeared to pick up on her irritation with the unexpected company even though they were drunk. They put their darts down and ambled over to the table, and stood there with their legs far apart, their hands resting on their belts as they fixed their eyes on Samer.

"Is this clown bothering you, Sheriff?"

"It's okay," Vanessa said.

One of the men put a large hand gently on her shoulder.

"Just say the word and we'll throw him out."

"I'll let you know if that becomes necessary."

As they returned to the dartboard Samer shrugged his jacket off and hung it on the back of his chair. Vanessa took a sip of beer and looked at him calmly.

"What do you want?" she asked again as she put her glass down.

He leaned forward across the table.

"Bringing in a lip-reader to find out what Natasha was saying isn't going to help."

"Why not?"

"Because she's speaking Arabic."

Vanessa stared at him. Samer leaned back, finding it hard to hide his satisfaction at the look on her face.

"So what's Natasha saying to him?"

Samer sighed.

"Give me your mobile."

Vanessa pushed it over to him and Samer moved his chair so they were sitting next to each other. He pressed to play the clip. Natasha's mouth moved.

"'I promise I won't betray you'."

Three or four seconds passed while Natasha listened to what the man was saying.

"'Please, let me live. I'll never betray you'," Samer said when her lips began to move again.

He stopped the clip and handed the mobile back to Vanessa, then moved his chair back to its original position on the other side of the table and sank down onto it.

He scratched his stubble.

"Stop working against me, Vanessa. I want to catch whoever killed them as much as you do. But you can't run your own investigation. That isn't going to work."

PART III

1

Vanessa was sitting on the bench in Monika Zetterlund Park, immersed in a printout of the post mortem that the pathologist, Per Thysell, had sent her. It was half past eight in the evening and the temperature was just below freezing. She was wrapped in a thick black winter coat that she had bought at an outlet store a couple of years ago. It wasn't the most elegant item in her wardrobe, but it kept her warm. She had spent the day trying to get hold of the manager of the care home Natasha had been living in when she first got to know her. Eventually she had succeeded. The manager, whose name was Lars Gustafsson, remembered Natasha well. And Sabina, the friend mentioned by the Lindskogs, and whose surname, according to Lars Gustafsson, was Haddad. Vanessa had got hold of the girl's last known address and was planning to pay her a visit the following day.

She read on in the autopsy report. She had to stop several times and check the text back. There were things in Per Thysell's report that seemed completely fantastical.

"Vanessa?"

Samer was slipping cautiously down the short icy slope to the bench, where he stopped. To fight the cold he was wearing a pair of thick woollen mittens and had a black woolly hat pulled down over his forehead.

"What's that sound?" he asked.

"Monica Zetterlund."

"Can we take a walk? It's too cold to sit here."

The walked, side by side, down Roslagsgatan towards Odenplan, where they turned right towards the City Library.

"Have you found any connection between Natasha and Rikard Olsson?" Vanessa asked.

"No, nothing."

"It can't be a coincidence that they were killed at almost the same time."

Vanessa tried to read Samer's face, but failed.

"What do you think of the autopsy report?" he asked, gesturing towards the folder in Vanessa's hand.

"What can I say?"

They passed a busy tapas restaurant, customers holding glasses of red wine behind the window, salsa music spilling out onto the street. Vanessa didn't reply until they had walked past.

"Natasha was seventeen, not over twenty as they claim."

Samer looked at her quizzically.

"And it says she'd given birth," Vanessa went on irritably. "I knew her. She hadn't had any children."

"She has scar tissue in her uterus," Samer said tentatively. "You read that for yourself."

He looked serious, and concerned. Vanessa stopped abruptly in front of a large advertisement featuring a radio presenter with a big, phosphorescent smile.

She raised her finger towards Samer.

"Natasha didn't lie. Not to me. You get that? I don't care what you and that damn pathologist think. Here, take the damn thing."

She pushed the folder against his chest. Samer took it.

She had been thinking of asking him to go with her to Rågsved the following day to talk to Sabina Haddad, but he could forget that now. He had shown he couldn't be trusted. Samer and the others didn't care about Natasha, they were only interested in Rikard Olsson, even though the security camera footage from the ICA supermarket clearly showed that she was being threatened.

Vanessa started walking, and Samer hurried to catch up with her.

"If you can't accept the findings of the post mortem, there's no point me wasting my time keeping you informed. I'm doing this for your sake, because I know you cared about her. Because I know what it's like to lose someone far too young."

Samer put his hand on Vanessa's shoulder to slow her down. She suppressed the urge to brush it off.

"I used to live in Rosengård," he said. "Every other person who was found dead in Malmö was someone I either grew up with or used to play football with. That's why I ended up moving here. So I didn't have to keep investigating who killed them. In most cases, their murderers were also friends of mine. No matter what I did, no matter how damn good I was at my job, I couldn't win. Do you think I like living in an empty apartment in a city where I don't know anyone? No, I don't. But I have to, because the alternative is to carry on finding my old friends shot, and having my life threatened whenever I bring in the childhood friend who fired the gun."

A blue bus drove past along Odengatan.

Steam was coming from their mouths, and their faces were close together now.

"I don't care how many gang-members you grew up with. Natasha wasn't lying," Vanessa said.

Samer turned his back on her and walked towards Sveavägen. Vanessa saw him stop for a red light, before he carried on up the hill towards Odenplan.

2

Thirty-two-year-old Hamza Mansour liked the thick darkness and desolation that took over the forest in winter. He was free to roam around there undiscovered, avoid other people and all the silly problems that followed in the wake of human life.

But now he was out of the forest, the tree-line behind him. He glanced at the black Casio watch on his wrist. 20.57. In front of him lay tarmacked roads, concrete buildings, cement viaducts.

Welcome to Skärholmen, a sign said.

He passed a bus shelter, the ground around it littered with broken glass, sparkling in the glow of the streetlamps.

Hamza pulled his scarf tighter around his face. Someone had tipped a rubbish bin over, the contents lay strewn on the ground. Two bus-drivers were talking quietly as they smoked. Behind them, up on the hill, the concrete tower-blocks rose up. When Hamza was little, he used to think they looked like spaceships ready to launch if you tilted your hear back and squinted.

He stopped in the square. Groups of idle youngsters were scattered around the benches talking. He glanced towards the basement housing the mosque, but there were no lights on. A small man walked past, hunched over. Hamza caught a glimpse of his lined face as the old man hurried past. Wasn't that Stig, Hamza's old teacher? Used to be really active in the local community. The only person who ever really cared.

Hamza stifled the urge to call Stig's name. Instead he stood in front of a café and watched him disappear into a side-street.

Two of the youngsters had got up and were following him. Something in the way they were moving alerted Hamza about their intentions. When he was in his teens he had mugged well over thirty people, getting hold of mobile phones, cash, designer jackets. But it was mostly the kick, the fleeting feeling of being powerful, in control, that he had been after.

That morning he had read that mugging by youngsters in Stockholm had increased by three hundred percent in four years. And pretty much all of the offenders had been carrying a knife or a pistol. The two little brats who had gone after Stig were probably armed too.

Hamza had pretended to carry a knife when he mugged people. But his appearance, size and unpredictability had been enough. A couple of slaps and then grabbing them by the throat usually got him what he wanted.

He weighed up his options. He really shouldn't intervene, that would be stupid when he was supposed to be staying below the radar. But he couldn't just let them attack Stig, could he? They might kill him. Stig had always stood up for Hamza, had defended him, the only person who believed in him when everyone else doubted him.

Now it was Hamza's turn to protect Stig, even if the old man would never know. There were some things you just had to do as a human being. Making sure that the old man with the big heart didn't get mugged by a couple of little hooligans was one of them.

Hamza set off after the youths at a half-run.

He caught up with them in the car-park below the apartment block where Stig lived. They were staying ten metres or so behind the old man, who hadn't realised the danger. Hamza assumed they were planning on following him into the stairwell, then jumping him once he had unlocked the door to his flat, so they could tie him up and empty the flat of valuables.

He crouched down behind the row of cars and waited until Stig had stepped inside the stairwell before making his move. One of the guys had just reached out his hand to catch the door. Hamza tackled him with full force, and the young man was so shocked that he lost his footing. He flailed with his arms to defend himself, but he stood no chance. Hamza's body was ready to fight, every sinew ready to cause damage. He banged the young man's head against the ground, hard enough to give him concussion.

The second youth came on the attack with his knife and Hamza threw himself at him. He clenched his fists and parried his blows, then saw a chance and slammed his right fist into the guy's nose.

The mugger's head jerked back and he staggered before falling and lying still. Hamza sat astride him, locking his arms with his knees, and punched him twice in the face. Then he stopped, reached for the knife the guy had dropped and raised it above his chest.

3

From the highest point on Vanadislunden Vanessa had an impressive view in two directions. In one direction were the rooftops with the centre of the city in the distance, and in the other the buildings on Frejgatan and Tulegatan that surrounded the park. She stopped on the slope and looked in through the illuminated windows at the small scenes of people's lives. The apartments were like televisions stacked on top of each other, showing different films.

Her argument with Samer a short while ago was nagging at her. Her chest was heaving with each breath.

Vanessa forced herself to keep climbing the hill, towards the old water-tower that resembled a medieval castle. In the exercise area for dogs, a few animals of various sizes were racing around, watched by their owners. There weren't many people on the paths that criss-crossed the park. On one bench sat a woman with blazing eyes, muttering to herself. She was rocking from side to side with her arms clasped round her, maybe she was coming down from a high.

Vanessa kept going. She pulled off her hat and stuffed it in her coat-pocket.

She was waiting for a call from a colleague in Malmö; she had texted her shortly after Samer walked off. Hanna Jackson worked with Vanessa in what used to be the NOVA Group, but had fallen in love with an artist from Malmö she met on the internet, and had been working for Malmö Police for the past couple of years.

Vanessa's phone vibrated and she answered at once. After the usual pleasantries she got straight to the point, and asked Hanna to promise to keep the contents of the conversation confidential. Even if they had never really seen each other socially, Vanessa trusted her. She asked what Hanna knew about Samer, what sort of impression she had got of him from working together.

"Nice guy. Very ambitious. He was smart, and popular," Hanna said. "But there were things in his background that complicated matters."

"How do you mean?"

"Well, he grew up in Rosengård, which was obviously an advantage in many ways. He knew who we needed to talk to, knew the people there, and they trusted him. But it also made other things harder. For him. For all of us. A lot of the people we were investigating were old friends of his, guys he had grown up with, and knew, or at least used to know. There was a fair bit of talk about that internally. And because he's a migrant, there was all the usual gossip behind his back – he was only there to fill a quota, that he was treated more leniently because he had a non-European background."

"Anything particular that stood out?"

"It wasn't really anything to with us, with his work, but a couple of months ago there was talk about him being investigated by the Special Investigations Unit. That was probably one of the reasons why he left Malmö."

Vanessa stopped. The Special Investigations Unit only looked into crimes that police employees were suspected of committing.

"What do you mean?"

"I don't know how much of it was true, but his best friend was a renowned jihadist who had returned to Malmö. What the hell was his name? Hassan something. I can look it up later. Either way, rumour had it that they had met up after he came back, and were seen talking."

"How did it end?"

"Samer got suspended for a couple of weeks, the whole thing was obviously very inappropriate, but evidently they accepted his explanation. I don't know what he told them, but it seems like no crime had been committed. Nothing that could be proved, anyway, seeing as he kept his job. But that wasn't enough for a lot of our colleagues. As a result, people in the department stopped talking to him. The situation became untenable. A couple of months later he announced that he'd got a job in Stockholm."

They ended the call and Vanessa lowered her phone and looked out over Sveavägen. According to Samer, he had left Malmö of his own volition, to stop being personally involved in the crimes he was investigating. But what Hanna had said told a very different story. Samer had more or less been forced out. Vanessa didn't know what to believe.

4

Hamza stopped the knife when it was just centimetres from the unconscious young man's chest. He tossed it aside, and heard it clatter across the tarmac. It was like he had been in a trance. His body started to shake when he realised how close he had come to ending the guy's life. Now he could see how young they were, no more than fourteen, maybe fifteen years old.

He got to his feet and went over to check on the other mugger. Blood was seeping from the back of his head. Hamza took his gloves off and checked his pulse.

The guy was alive.

They were both alive.

He breathed out. He had stopped them from attacking Stig, but he didn't want them to get hurt. Not seriously, anyway. He hoped that Stig would sleep soundly in his bed tonight, unaware of how close he had come to being mugged. None of the neighbours appeared to have noticed the disturbance.

His clothes were sticking to his body. The adrenalin hit was slowly fading. Hamza picked up a handful of wet snow and held it against his face to cool down. To reset his brain. He moved the cold hand to the back of his neck and let a few drops run down his spine. He leaned over and put the young mugger in the recovery position, then went over to the other one and did the same thing.

But he couldn't just leave the boys there, they could freeze to death if no one found them. He forced his way through the bushes that surrounded the apartment block, making his way to one of the windows. He peered into the darkened flat, then banged on the window. He crouched down so as not to be seen. The light went on and a woman peered out into the darkness. Hamza stayed perfectly still. The woman disappeared, then the door to the building opened a minute or so later.

She came outside, and there was a man with her. They went over and looked at the two unconscious muggers, shaking them and talking, trying to get a response from them. The man took out his mobile phone and put it to his ear.

There was no need for Hamza to stay any longer. He burst out of the bushes and ran. The woman cried out in shock and the man called out after him. He carried on across the car-park at top speed, heading for the edge of the forest.

5

The instruments on the dashboard were telling her that the roads were icy, but Vanessa was staying a fair bit above the speed limit. It was after rush-hour and there weren't many cars about.

Her best chance of getting hold of Sabina Haddad was in the evening. While she was waiting for the right time she had visited the gym for the first time since she found out Natasha was dead. She had tried to run the grief away, but that had failed. She had spent the rest of the afternoon trying to get hold of Celine in order to apologise to her, but that hadn't worked either. The girl wasn't taking her calls, and Vanessa was starting to get worried. She hoped that Celine had a warm bed somewhere, so she wasn't having to sleep outside in this weather.

When she was passing the Forest Cemetery Vanessa turned the satnav on and tapped in the address – Vedevågslingan 5 – she had been given by Lars Gustafsson, the manager of the care home where both Sabina Haddad and Natasha had lived. It wasn't long before she pulled up some way onto a footpath in front of a greyish white ten-storey block. She switched the engine off, walked over to the entrance and tried the door. Locked. You needed either a keycard or the code to get in. She went back to the car and kept an eye on the road behind her in the rear-view mirror. There weren't many people about, so she would easily be able to spot any who turned off the main road towards number 5.

Vanessa called Celine's number again and the call went through, but there was no answer. The voicemail clicked in. Celine had recorded some sort of gibberish before she started to speak Swedish.

"If you didn't understand what I said, that's because I said in Mandarin that you should leave a message after the tone."

Vanessa sighed.

"Celine, it's me again. I sorry I cut you off the other day. I... Natasha has been found dead, so I'm not really myself. I hope you can forgive me. Can't you just give me a call to let me know that you're okay?"

She ended the call.

Her stomach was rumbling, the way it had often done when Vanessa was a teenager and had tried to starve away what little fat she had on her body. There had been so few things she could control back then, and how much she ate was one of them. She used to make herself sick, go on diets, exercise like a maniac.

She stretched, and looked at her reflection in the rear-view mirror. Who was that old face trying to fool? She was still the same insecure upper-class rebel with an eating disorder. Maybe she should just start the car, reverse out onto the street and drive back to her flat in Vasastan. Let Samer and her other colleagues investigate Natasha's death. She was too emotionally involved. Too deeply, horribly emotionally involved. And something like that was unlikely to end well.

But she wanted to meet Sabina, talk to someone who had known Natasha and could remind her of what she was like. Not just refer to her as a murder victim or summarise her in some dry autopsy report.

Vanessa caught a glimpse of movement and quickly got out of the car. A man walked past, balancing carefully on the icy tarmac with bags of shopping in his hands. She tucked in behind him, and saw him put his bags down and pull out a black keycard.

"I'm visiting a friend," she mumbled.

He nodded amiably and they got in the lift together. He pressed the button for the seventh floor and the lift started to move.

"Which floor?"

"Nine," Vanessa said.

He tapped the button for her.

There were five flats on the ninth floor. There was no Haddad on any of the doors. Vanessa went down one floor and found the right door, furthest away from the lift. She rang the doorbell and waited. Nothing happened. She opened the letterbox and looked in. The flat was dark, but in the yellow light that seeped in from the stairwell, Vanessa could see a free local newspaper and two envelopes on a brown doormat.

She unbuttoned her jacket and sat down, leaning back against the door to wait.

Arguments, voices from television sets, music, children crying. Sounds from the flats spread through the concrete. The automatic lighting went out, leaving the stairwell in darkness.

It went on again a couple of times while she was waiting. Each time she got to her feet.

After an hour she heard the lift machinery start up again. The lift rose up through the building. Vanessa pushed away from the door and got to her feet. The lift door opened and out stepped a young, dark-haired woman. She was carrying a Lidl bag in one hand as she felt around in her jacket pocket with the other, presumably looking for her keys.

"Sabina?" Vanessa asked.

The woman stopped abruptly and looked up in fright. They stared at each other for a moment before she dropped the bag of shopping and threw herself down the stairs. Vanessa called out to her to stop, then rushed after her.

6

Nicolas meted out a series of kicks and blows to the punch-bag. The bag was swinging back and forth and his body was reacting to its movements on autopilot. Even if the exercise was primarily physical, the goal was not to have to think.

He breathed out, with his back towards the rowing machine as he drank some water with his towel round his neck. The door to the basement gym opened and Erica Karlström walked in. She stopped when she spotted Nicolas. For a moment it look like she was thinking of turning round, but she nodded coolly and put her towel and water bottle down. She went over to the stereo and connected her mobile to it.

"You don't mind me putting some music on, do you?"

She didn't give Nicolas any chance to reply before a heavy bassline began to thud from the walls. He smiled. Erica took up position on the exercise bike. He watched her discreetly in the mirrored wall. She was wearing a tight white gym top and a small pair of grey shorts. Her blonde hair was pulled into a tight bun.

Nicolas stood up and began to attack the punchbag furiously. He noticed Erica glancing at him, but pretended he hadn't seen. Although it distracted his focus from the punchbag, he realised he liked it.

Even during the first weeks in London there had been a tension between them. Glances. Smiles. But Nicolas had quickly become aware of her problem with alcohol, that distant look in her eyes and her sluggish movements. The smell of mint and vodka in the afternoon when he drove her to James's school.

But it was as if there was a tacit agreement among those around her not to notice any of that. And socially Erica was more effective than most people, at least when she was in the mood. She had responsibility for afternoon activities and collections at James's private school. And she had been a charming, entertaining hostess at the large social gatherings held in the Karlström family's home in Kensington.

The decision to move back to Sweden had been a sudden one.

It had all started when Johan Karlström, in his capacity as Gambler's managing director, had been called in for an interview by the British Financial Offences Authority. Nicolas had waited outside. Johan hadn't said much afterwards. But the following morning he had asked, via the security company, if Nicolas would like to move back to Sweden with the family for a year.

The level of security was going to be stepped down, with Nicolas on his own in the role of security coordinator with the occasional assistance of Swedish colleagues. He had hesitated at first. He had only just started to feel at home in London, he liked his apartment and the part of town it was in. For the first time in several years he wasn't having to live incognito. So why had he decided to accept the offer?

Partly because of the money on offer, of course. His salary was one hundred and twenty thousand kronor per month, before tax. He had never even dreamed of earning that much money. And even if the work was often boring, it was pretty comfortable.

But then there was Erica, and his concern for her. He could see that she was slowly falling apart. And Nicolas was fond of James. He liked the quiet, kind boy who looked at the world with cautious, intelligent eyes.

He didn't want to leave them alone with Johan Karlström, whom Nicolas in his more generous moments found cold and unkind, and at his worst thoroughly despised. But mostly it was the chance of once again being close to his sister Maria that appealed to him. That, and Vanessa.

Even if nothing had come of trying to meet up with her, Vanessa was often in his thoughts. There was unfinished business between that he couldn't let go of. He felt hurt that she was keeping him at arm's length. It wasn't the fact that she was ignoring him, he just thought she could at least have given some sort of explanation. Not just disappear and change her phone number.

He aimed one final kick at the punch-bag, and finished off with a series of punches.

Erica jumped down off the exercise bike just as Nicolas was

taking another breather, but because she immediately got on the rowing machine, he sat with his back against wall this time, catching his breath.

Erica grabbed the handles, kicked off with her legs and straightened her back. Her skin was glowing with sweat, her face red from exertion.

"What are you going to do about the threats Johan has received?" she suddenly said.

Nicolas stared at her uncomprehendingly.

"What do you mean?"

"Well, isn't that the sort of thing we ought to talk about, you and me? That is why you work here, isn't it?"

He pushed off against the wall and stood up, then walked round the punch-bag.

"He hasn't said anything about any threats to me."

7

Sabina was unexpectedly fast. Vanessa could hear her pattering footsteps, but got a glimpse of her back two floors below and realised that she was gaining on her. One more floor and she was right behind Sabina. Vanessa launched herself at her and managed to grab her foot. Sabina fell to the floor screaming. She held her arms up defensively as Vanessa jumped on her.

"Don't hurt me."

"I'm not going to hurt you," Vanessa gasped. "I'm from the police. I just want to talk to you."

"The police?"

Sabina lowered her hands and stopped struggling, and Vanessa nodded. She held out her hand to help the girl to her feet.

"What do you want from me?" Sabina said, still defensive. Vanessa was holding her close in case she got it into her head to start running again.

"It's about Natasha. Can we go up to yours and talk? Let's take the lift this time, okay?" Vanessa pressed the button.

The flat consisted of two rooms. Vanessa thought it felt impersonal, there were no photographs or ornaments, but it was tidy and smelled clean. Sabina showed Vanessa into the kitchen where she put her bag of shopping on the worktop and switched the kettle on. She took two mugs out of a cupboard, put a teabag in each of them, then sat down at the kitchen table opposite Vanessa.

"Nice view," Vanessa said.

In the distance, above the lights of the city, the illuminated Globe Arena rose up towards the sky.

"You're Vanessa."

"How do you know that?"

"Because Natasha's talked about you. She lived with you, before she went back to Syria."

The words overwhelmed Vanessa.

"Natasha's dead," she said in a single exhaled breath. She could see no reason to withhold the truth. "She was found stabbed to death on Gärdet last week."

Sabina put her hand over her mouth. Her gaze darted about before she closed her eyes.

"I need answers to some questions."

The kettle clicked then fell silent, but Sabina showed no sign of getting up. She seemed to have taken the news hard. Vanessa poured water in the two mugs, then put one on front of Sabina.

"When did you last see Natasha?"

"About three weeks ago, at hers."

"Did she seem worried about anything?"

Sabina took a sip of the tea, pulled a face at how hot it was and pushed the mug away.

"Worried?"

"Frightened."

"No, she was the same as normal."

Vanessa stared at Sabina to see if she was holding anything back, but the young woman calmly met her gaze. But her reaction in the stairwell said it all. She was clearly frightened of someone or something. Possibly of the same man who had threatened Natasha.

"Why did you run?"

"There's always a lot of things going on around here."

"I think you're lying."

Vanessa reached into her jacket and pulled out her iPhone, tapped in her code and found the security-camera footage from the supermarket. She pressed to play it, then put the phone on the table. Sabina leaned closer and watched the clip without showing any emotion.

"Who's that man?"

"How should I know? You can't even see his face."

"But you can see the fear in Natasha's," Vanessa said. "You were her friend. She must have told you."

Vanessa waited a few moments before repeating what Natasha had said to the man.

"I don't know who he is," Sabina said curtly.

"Did Natasha have a boyfriend?"

"No, not as far as I know."

Vanessa pulled up a picture of Rikard Olsson and held her

mobile in front of Sabina. A connection, there must be some sort of connection, she thought.

"Do you recognise this man?"

"No."

"Are you sure?"

"Yes. Who is he?"

"He was a police officer, and he was found dead a hundred metres or so away from Natasha. I think the same person murdered them both."

"I've never seen him before."

Vanessa put her phone back in her jacket pocket, toyed with her mug and decided to change tack. She couldn't go on putting more and more pressure in Sabina, but she was clearly hiding something out of fear for her own safety.

"When did you come to Sweden?" she asked.

"13 August 2015."

"One month before Natasha?"

Sabina shrugged her shoulders.

"I don't know exactly when she arrived."

"How did you get to know each other?"

"We met in Tyresö, at the care home. We became friends there, then lost touch for a while."

"What do you do for a living?"

"I'm a cleaner." Sabina stretched out her yellow T-shirt with her fingers so Vanessa could read the words on her chest. *HomeClean Ltd.* "I'm not a criminal, I don't know who killed Natasha or that policeman. Natasha was my friend, my best friend. If I knew who wanted to hurt her, then obviously I'd tell you."

Vanessa found herself thinking of the autopsy report. She didn't want to ask, but she had to.

"This will sound odd, but do you know if Natasha had any children?"

Sabina looked blankly at Vanessa.

"Children?" She leaned forward. "No, Natasha didn't have any children."

"And she was seventeen?" Vanessa asked, then lowered her voice. "She didn't lie about her age so she could stay in Sweden?"

Sabina hesitated and raised the mug to her lips. She took a sip.

"I need to know," Vanessa said.

The young woman shrugged. At the same time Vanessa heard the buzzing sound of a text message arriving from the living room. She glanced at Sabina's mobile which was on the table, and concluded that it wasn't that one. Sabina didn't seem to react.

"Maybe. She would hardly have been the first. But I think she'd have told me. And you."

Vanessa leaned back and nodded in relief. Natasha wasn't a liar, she wasn't making it up. Not for Vanessa. Per Thysell could go to hell. There was something wrong with the report.

She leaned forward again, resting her elbows on the edge of the table.

"When did Natasha come back from Syria?" she asked.

Sabina thought.

"In March, I think."

"Why did she come back?"

"She said she couldn't see any future in Syria. Sure, the war may be pretty much over, but the violence and killing are still going on. Bombs. Shootings. It isn't a good place for a young woman."

"The couple she lived with thought her name was Zahra?"

Sabina pulled a surprised grimace.

"That sounds strange."

Vanessa swallowed. Steeled herself to keep her voice steady.

"Why didn't she contact me when she came back?"

"I don't know," Sabina said quietly. "I honestly don't know."

Vanessa took a deep breath and let the air out slowly through her nose.

"Did she think I was angry with her for leaving Sweden? For leaving... me?"

She didn't want to ask, but she had to. The question had been nagging at the back of her mind since Natasha had been found dead. Vanessa was terrified of the answer. Could she have hurt Natasha without realising it, said something that made her think she didn't want her staying with her?

"She never said a single bad word about you. She loved you. She said you saved her life."

Vanessa could feel her eyes start to prick, and raised the tea to her mouth and took a sip.

8

Erica Karlström smiled mischievously at Nicolas before kicking off with her feet and starting to row again.

"Johan hasn't said anything to me about receiving any threats," Nicolas repeated as he went over to the rowing machine and stopped her.

Erica made an attempt to pull free, but he had a firm grip of her shoulder. In the end she gave up and turned towards him.

"Do you care?"

"It's my job to…"

"Your job."

Erica snorted and knocked his hand away.

"You need to tell me what this is about. You and James could be in danger."

She ignored him, and went on rowing with her eyes fixed firmly on the mirror in front of her. Nicolas firmly wrested the handles from her and let them spool back to their place at the foot of the machine.

"I'm serious," Nicolas said.

He turned her head so that their noses were almost touching.

"Show me that you care, then."

Erica got up, standing so close to him that he could feel the heat of her body. She barely reached his chin, but was glaring at him intently. She moved even closer and Nicolas took a step back.

"Show me that you care about me, Nicolas."

She pushed him in the chest and he backed away another step. Erica followed. Nicolas was wrestling with himself. He wanted her. Erica wanted him. But if he let this happen, there was no way back. He swallowed. She pushed him again. He backed away another step, and felt the wall behind him. Erica moved even closer.

"Show me that you care about me."

She pressed herself against him. Nicolas put his hands on Erica's waist and spun them both round, so that she ended up standing against the wall. Holding her tightly, he lowered his head and kissed her.

9

Vanessa was lying naked on the sofa in her combined kitchen and living room, looking up at the plaster detailing in the ceiling. It was almost time for dinner, but she didn't have the inclination or energy to cook. She decided to head down to McLarens instead. After all, it was Friday.

Her hair was still damp from her long session at the gym and the shower that followed, and now she was waiting for the residual sweating to die down. The window onto Roslagsgatan was open, and a stream of winter air was pouring into the apartment.

She had been feeling calmer since her conversation with Sabina Haddad the previous day. In spite of everything, Natasha had been the person she always said she was. Even so, she couldn't help wondering why Sabina had tried to run when she found Vanessa waiting outside her door. She definitely seemed worried about something. Vanessa doubted she was telling the truth when she claimed not to know who the man Natasha was talking to outside the ICA supermarket was.

She hadn't yet decided if she was going to tell Samer what she had found out. What Hanna Jackson had told her was nagging at her. At the same time, she remembered the way her own colleagues had talked about her behind her back. Not least her male colleagues. She had been accused of being difficult, pushy, and awkward. And when she got promoted, several of the younger, more testosterone-fuelled officers had declared that she "needed a good fuck", "should be put in her place", and "needed cock". Her upper-class background hadn't helped matters. At the time she had persuaded herself that it didn't affect her, but now, in hindsight, she wasn't so sure. She didn't want to subject Samer to the same thing, and had no intention of telling tales to senior officers. So she decided to keep what she knew to herself for the time being. To trust him. She could hardly suspect him simply because they didn't share the same opinion of how the investigation should be conducted. And how would she have reacted if one of the murder victims hadn't been Natasha? In all likelihood, she too would have focused on Rikard Olsson.

Vanessa jumped when the doorbell rang. She reached for the dressing-gown draped over the back of the sofa, pulled it on and tied the belt. She peered out into the stairwell through the peep-hole.

"Thank God," she muttered, and unlocked the door.

She hugged Celine, who kept her arms by her sides as she let herself be embraced. Her cheeks were ice-cold.

"Where have you been? I've been worried."

"You have?" Celine wondered in surprise.

"Yes. Of course I have."

Vanessa pulled her gently into the hall and closed the door.

"I'm sorry Natasha's dead. I didn't want to bother you."

"You never bother me, remember that. Otherwise I'll get it tattooed on your forehead."

They smiled at each other, then Vanessa gave Celine another hug, holding the girl's head tightly to her chest.

"Sorry," Celine whispered. "No one's ever been worried about me, so I didn't realise there was any rush to get in touch after you called. Then my phone ran out of charge."

"No, I'm sorry, Celine," Vanessa said. "I'm the one who behaved badly. I should never have said what I did when you phoned. I mean, we're friends. Are you hungry?"

Celine pulled a face.

"Mostly cold."

Vanessa rubbed the girl's upper arms to get her circulation going. A bag that Celine had been holding, without Vanessa noticing, fell to the floor. It contained a package wrapped in red gift paper.

"It's Dad's birthday, so I bought him a shirt," Celine said.

What little Vanessa knew about Celine's dad was that he was a serious alcoholic, used to beat the girl black and blue, and had been evicted from his flat in Bredäng towards the end of the summer. He had lost custody of Celine, and that's why she was being shuttled between various official bodies, care homes and foster-parents.

"Have you arranged to meet up?"

Vanessa was having trouble concealing her surprise. Celine looked away, embarrassed.

"He doesn't know I've bought him a present," she mumbled. "I can't get hold of him, but I know where he's living. It's quite a long way. I don't want him to be alone on his birthday. I was wondering… if you…"

Vanessa wasn't sure it was a good idea for Celine to see her father. Even so, she could understand why she wanted to.

"Would you like me to come with you?" Celine nodded, her eyes firmly fixed on the floor. "Of course I'll come."

Vanessa had made Celine wear a pair of woollen tights, a hat and a thermal vest that was far too big for her and stuck out beneath the sleeves of her jacket. As they were walking out onto the street she noticed a man who seemed familiar.

"Vanessa Frank?"

She told Celine to wait, and walked over to the man.

"My name is Max Lewenhaupt, I'm a reporter at *Kvällspressen*."

At once, Vanessa realised why she knew him. He was the evening paper's new star reporter. His by-line picture seemed to get bigger with each passing day.

"I know it was you who killed one of the attackers after the attack on Stockholm Stadium last summer. You're a hero. A real hero. I've tried calling you loads of times."

Vanessa studied him. So this was the person who had called her several times a day for about a month or so. Who had made her change her phone and number. If he hadn't done that, Vanessa could have answered when Natasha called, and she might still be alive today.

"I want to ask if you'd be interested in doing an interview. A serious portrait of a hero. The whole of Sweden is going to love you," he said with an ingratiating smile.

In spite of Vanessa's attempt to stay calm, Max Lewenhaupt must have seen the suppressed anger in her face. He took a step back, until his back was against the façade of the grey 1920s building. He glanced at the fists that she had unconsciously clenched, but which were still hanging by her sides.

"Listen now, Lewenhaupt. I will never talk to you, or any of your colleagues. We have freedom of the press in this country, you can write whatever the hell you want, but you can do it without my help."

"But…"

Vanessa's eyes darkened. She raised her hand to grab hold of his jacket, but stopped when she heard Celine's voice.

"Vanessa, let's go. There'll only be trouble otherwise."

She turned her head in confusion, then gave a strained smile followed by a quick nod. She turned back to Max.

"Don't ever call me again," she said, raising a warning finger right in front of the reporter's nose, before she felt Celine's hand on her arm. They had got no more than ten paces away when Max called after them.

"What about the Syrian woman and the murdered police officer, then? What do you know about them? Is it true that they were having a relationship and it was a crime of passion?"

Vanessa spun round, but Celine tightened her grip on her arm to hold her back.

"Calm down. You'll end up in prison," she hissed.

Even though the girl was holding her back, the distance between Vanessa and Max Lewenhaupt was shrinking by the second.

"No. Just no," Celine said. "Who's going to catch Natasha's killer if you're not allowed to be a police officer anymore because you threw a punch at this arsehole?"

Vanessa stopped. She started threateningly at Max Lewenhaupt before turning on her heel and heading towards the garage again. Celine turned to the reporter and formed her hand to make it look like she was masturbating.

"Stay away from Vanessa, you *fucking wanker*," she called out in English, so loudly that it echoed across Roslagsgatan.

Vanessa couldn't help smiling. She put her arm round the girl's shoulders and they walked off to the garage together, side by side.

10

The woman got up from the table in the dining room of the Bank Hotel and walked slowly towards Johan Karlström.

"Hello, darling," she said, with a seductive smile.

Nicolas had seen her before, together with Johan in London. But back then he had no idea that she was Swedish, and had assumed she was a high-class South American prostitute.

Johan gestured for Nicolas to stay in the bar while he led the woman back to the table. Nicolas sat on a bar-stool and asked the bartender for a coffee. None of the other guests had taken any notice of Johan. There was nothing to indicate that he had been recognised or was expected. It was going to be another boring evening in a hotel. A waiter carried cocktails over to Johan and the young woman, who were already deep in conversation.

Nicolas felt his phone vibrate in his pocket.

He glanced around the room, then discreetly took out his mobile and checked the message. It was a naked picture from Erica. He recognised the background, the photograph had been taken in the ground-floor bathroom.

Can't wait till next time, the message said.

With his cheeks burning, Nicolas quickly slipped the iPhone back in his pocket, and checked that Johan and the young woman were still sitting at the table. Perhaps it was because he didn't like his client, but he didn't feel any guilt at what had happened. He detested the cold, even cruel way Johan treated the people around him. The strange thing was that Nicolas would still have been prepared to give his life for him. He wouldn't hesitate to throw himself in front of a bullet meant for Johan. Out of duty as well as instinct.

But even if he wasn't feeling guilty, the situation was far from ideal. He either had to bring his affair with Erica to a swift conclusion, or hand in his notice.

After they had had sex with each other up against the wall of the gym, she had led him up to Johan's office and tapped in the password to his computer. Evidently she made a habit of checking Johan's emails. Nicolas had wondered if that was her way of exerting some measure of control over him. Of showing herself, and now Nicolas too, that she wasn't Johan's toy. That she knew what was going on in his life.

Erica had opened his email folder and shown him the threatening messages sent from an anonymous Hotmail account. They were written in English. In the past week Johan had received three emails from the same sender. He hadn't replied to any of them.

The bartender tapped Nicolas on the shoulder and pushed a white cup over to him.

"Thanks."

The threats appeared to concern Gambler's online casino. Maybe they were from a dissatisfied customer. Johan appeared to have guaranteed this individual some sort of preferential treatment in the system at some point, but Nicolas didn't understand exactly what this meant. Despite that, he was debating whether or not he should report these threats to his bosses. His job description from AOS Risk Group didn't include breaking into the client's emails, and certainly not sleeping with his wife.

But why hadn't Johan mentioned anything about the threats to Nicolas and the security company he paid so handsomely every month to protect him? Either he wasn't taking them seriously, or he had something to hide.

11

Rysseviken lay in an area of forest in Haninge, and was a dumping ground for individuals the authorities wanted to hide away from the rest of society. Residents weren't expected to live free of alcohol or drugs, as long as their drinking and drug-taking happened within the area. The hovels were full of addicts, the destitute, convicts out on probation and other outcasts.

Vanessa stopped the car on the patch of rough tarmac that served as a car-park and switched off the engine. Darkness settled around them at once. Celine was clutching the birthday present tightly in her arms.

"Are you okay?" Vanessa asked.

Celine nodded, then moistened her lips.

"Just a bit nervous. I haven't seen him for a very long time."

"I can come in with you if you like?"

"You don't have to."

"I know, but I will, unless you'd rather see him on your own."

"I'd rather not. He hasn't always been that nice to me."

"Nor was my dad. The funny thing about dads is that we still like them, and are ridiculously desperate for them to love us. Or at least accept us. Don't you think?"

Without waiting for a response, Vanessa pushed the door open. Someone was yelling over by the edge of the forest. Some distance away, a group of hunched figures were standing round a fire burning in an old oil-drum.

"Do you know where he lives?" Vanessa asked.

"Not really."

"Wait here and I'll ask."

Vanessa walked round the wreck of a car, its wheels replaced by plastic crates that were holding it up, and went over to the group by the fire.

"Good evening. I'm looking for an Englishman, his surname's Wood."

No one said anything. Their mouths were all clamped shut, and they were all staring into the fire. Vanessa took a step closer and held out her hands to warm them.

"I recognise you," one man wearing a bobble hat said. He coughed, cleared his throat and spat into the flames. Both his front teeth were missing. "You're a cop."

The group looked at Vanessa with renewed intensity. She vaguely recognised the man from an old case.

"I am. And you're a fence and a thief, if I remember rightly. But I'm not here to swap CVs, I'm here with a girl who wants to give her dad a birthday present."

A murmur rose from the group. A woman with greasy, carrot-coloured hair and whose face kept twitching, pointed at Celine who was craning her neck to see what was going on.

"Is that the girl?"

"Yes."

The woman shakily lifted a filthy finger to her mouth, bit her fingernail and spat the fragment into the fire.

"If it's Kenny you're looking, he lives over there," she croaked, pointing towards a ramshackle barrack.

"Thanks," Vanessa said.

Even though the window was open, the small room reeked of poverty: alcohol, sweat and smoke. A dirty jacket hanging from the curtain-pole above the window was swinging in the breeze. The wallpaper, which had once been white, shone nicotine-yellow in the glare of the naked bulb hanging from the ceiling. The floor was littered with dirty clothes, empty cans, bottles and fast-food wrappers.

Kenny Wood was lying on the bed staring blankly in front of him with heavy eyelids. He was badly drunk, his jaw hanging limply down towards his chest.

"Who's there?" he grunted in English.

Vanessa felt the air go out of Celine when she saw the state her father was in.

His nose was blue-grey and swollen, his cheeks were red with shallow, thin blood-vessels. He looked like he didn't have long left.

"It's me, Dad," she said quietly, and took a cautious step inside the room. Vanessa regretted driving her here. This was a mistake. What good would it do Celine to see her dad like this? Vanessa suppressed the urge to walk in, pull the man off his bed and drag him to one of the basins in the corridor to sober up.

"I've brought a present. Today's your birthday."

Kenny Wood let out an empty, echoing laugh. Celine held the present out to him. He made no effort to take it. The girl's arms hung in the air for a while before she reluctantly lowered them.

"Take your crap and get out of here," Kenny said in Swedish. "I don't want to see you."

"Dad... please..."

Vanessa took a step closer and put her arm round Celine's shoulders, pressing the girl's head to her.

"Come on, darling, let's go," she said quietly.

"No," Celine protested. "It's his birthday. He'll be happy if we just wait a bit. Won't you, Dad?" Her voice was catching in her throat. "I have to look after him. He can't stay here."

"Why don't the two of us go home? It isn't that he doesn't want to see you, he just doesn't want you to see him like this."

Kenny struggled to sit up on the bed.

"Get the fuck out of here!" he roared, spraying saliva. He waved frantically towards the door with both hands. "Now! Get the fuck out, you little cunts!"

Celine stood frozen to the spot, staring at her father as tears ran down her cheeks. Vanessa gently turned her round and guided her out of the room and along the corridor.

"This isn't how I thought it would be," Celine whispered.

When they drove into the garage beneath Norra Real a little less than an hour later, snow was falling in heavy flakes and an icy wind was blowing. The 7-Eleven sign was glowing invitingly, and there was a sign in the window saying that the first saffron Lucia buns of the season were on sale.

"Would you like one?" Vanessa said, pointing.

"I love Lucia buns."

"Me too," Vanessa said, opening the door. "But you know what I like even more?"

Celine shook her head.

117

"The dough. When I was younger I used to go into shops and ask if I could buy uncooked buns. Shall we try?"

Celine's eyes were red from crying, her cheeks still streaked with tears. The young man behind the counter looked surprised when Vanessa explained that she didn't want cooked buns, but rather the uncooked dough.

"I don't know if I'm allowed to do that. Besides, they're stone-cold because they've been in the fridge."

"I'll pay the same price."

He shrugged, got out a paper napkin and put two lumps of yellow dough on it. They sat down at one of the tables in the window and looked out at Odengatan. Celine took a bite of the soft dough and closed her eyes in delight.

"What a life hack," she said.

"Life hack?"

"Don't you know what a life hack is?" Celine asked in astonishment with her mouth full of dough. "It's a trick that makes like a bit easier."

Celine took another bite, leaned back in her chair and smiled. Vanessa couldn't believe that she had behaved so dismissively towards the girl. She was only a child. And Social Services and the other authorities weren't doing a thing. Vanessa could no longer close her eyes to that, she couldn't let the girl's life be ruined. It wasn't about trying to replace Natasha, it wasn't actually about Vanessa's feelings at all. This was about helping a child who needed help.

She had made her decision. Celine would move in with her. It would be an upheaval, it would cause problems and arguments, but that couldn't be helped.

"In that case, I know another life hack," she said.

"What?"

"You. You're a living, breathing life hack. Get a couple more lumps of dough and we'll take them with us," she said, handing Celine her bank card. Vanessa stood up and went to wait by the door. She had a voice message from a missed call from her boss, Mikael Kask. He sounded focused and matter-of-fact. Vanessa suspected that Samer had told him about her excursion to Arlanda and visit to the ICA supermarket.

"The pathologist has been in touch. I haven't had time to read the whole autopsy report, but he's drawn attention to the fact that

Natasha once broke her leg. Thysell says there's something strange about the pins in the bone. If you're still interested, give me a call tomorrow."

The message ended. A woman's voice asked if she wanted to hear it again.

Vanessa clicked to end the message. A broken leg? Natasha had told her she had broken her leg as a child in Damascus. But what bearing could that have on a murder investigation so many years later?

Celine held a paper bag up triumphantly to Vanessa, who opened the door, took her bank card back, and let the girl walk out first.

They walked home through a heavy shower of snow.

"I'll only stay tonight," Celine said. "I know you want to be left in peace. I'll be okay on my own tomorrow."

"Nonsense. You can stay as long as you want."

"What about the authorities?" Celine said tentatively.

"Never mind them. They're 'fucking wankers'," Vanessa said, in English.

12

Nicolas heard the lift bell, got up from the sofa and rushed over to help Johan Karlström stay on his feet. Behind him stood the young woman, now wearing a white fur coat, also looking very unsteady on her feet. She didn't seem to be in such a bad state as his boss, but she was clearly high too. Johan's pupils were dilated. There were traces of white powder, which Nicolas assumed was cocaine, beneath his nose. He reached up and discreetly wiped Johan's face, pulled one arm around his own shoulders and helped him to stand. Three hours had passed since Johan and the woman had gone up to a suite, with Nicolas told to sit and wait in reception.

"How are you getting home?" he asked the woman as he escorted Johan towards the exit.

"I'll walk."

"We'll give you a lift," Nicolas panted.

Two of the hotel's guests were pointing and laughing at them. Johan grinned and waved at them. The automatic doors slid open, and the bitter winter air hit their faces. Nicolas dragged Johan across the cobblestones in the narrow alleyway to the Range Rover. Just as Nicolas lifted him into the back seat, a blood vessel in his nose broke and blood started to pour onto his white shirt. Taken by surprise, Johan held one bloody hand up in front of him.

"I'm bleeding, Nicolas. I'm bleeding. Save me!" he yelled dramatically, then burst out laughing.

Nicolas laid him down and closed the door as the woman got into the passenger seat. He checked the side-mirrors, then pulled out. A pair of headlights came on behind them.

"Where do you live?"

She hesitated.

"Banérgatan. Head along Strandvägen, that's the quickest way."

Nicolas pulled up at a red light. There was a lone blond man in the car behind. The same car had been behind them since the hotel. Nicolas craned his neck to try to see the model and registration number, but the car was too close.

On the pedestrian crossing a man stopped abruptly, leaned forward and threw up. Nicolas glanced at the young woman. She was beautiful in a way that was almost physically affecting. She turned her face towards him, and in the glow of the dashboard lights he saw that her throat was red and swollen. She quickly pulled up the collar of her fur coat.

"Are you okay?" Nicolas asked.

She nodded tersely.

"Sure?"

"Yes, for fuck's sake."

Her mobile phone rang.

She dug about in the handbag on her lap and pulled out an iPhone. Nicolas heard a man's voice. The lights changed to green and Nicolas put his foot down, and the distance between them and the other car increased.

"I'm on my way," she said in English, and hung up.

Nicolas slowed down, letting two taxis overtake, and turned off. The car that had been behind them earlier was still there, following them. At Narvavägen Nicolas turned left, along the avenue, then into Banérgatan.

"Let me out here."

He stopped and the woman jumped out.

Nicolas reversed the car, then followed Narvavägen to the Karlaplan roundabout, where he turned off onto Karlavägen.

The car that had been behind them was gone. When they had reached Östermalm School, Johan began to move anxiously.

"Stop the car."

Nicolas pulled into a narrow, cobbled side-street. The turn-of-the-century buildings stretched up proudly towards the sky. He checked their surroundings. Empty. Quiet. He opened the door and pulled Johan up into a sitting position, before doing his best to support him as he got out of the car. He fell to his knees at once, tried to get his balance, but his body was lurching back and forth.

"I just need some air," he said.

Nicolas leaned against the black body of the vehicle and looked at his watch.

It was half past eleven.

"You're alright, you know, Nicolas. You know that, right? That's why we wanted you to come to Sweden with us." Nicolas looked at his boss in astonishment as he put one hand on the kerb to stop himself falling forward. He was clutching his chest with the other hand. "I'm grateful to you for doing this for me. I'm not always the easiest fucking person to deal with."

13

That morning the doctors had told Rebecca and Axel that it was only a matter of time before they would have to turn Simon's life-support off. He was going to die.

Axel had made a decision. He was going to force Johan Karlström to tell him who had been driving the car. Kill him, if things were as he suspected, and if necessary also the man who, he had realised after watching the family, was their bodyguard.

The thought of making the driver suffer was the only thing stopping him from falling apart. Axel had never fantasised about harming another person before, let alone killing someone. Even during the worst of the bullying when he was at school, he had never tried to fight back, but now he was consumed with the thought of vengeance. It was different when it concerned Simon. He was Axel's responsibility, it was his job to protect him in life. And whoever had been driving that car had stolen that from Axel. He had never felt anything that came close to the fury that filled him now. In a way, he was glad that he felt like that, that he wasn't so very different to other people after all.

He couldn't bear seeing Simon suffer anymore. He had said goodbye to his son, gone home to get the pistol, then had gone to the villa in Djursholm. He had watched as Johan Karlström and the bodyguard drove away, and decided to follow them. They had driven into the city, to a luxury hotel close to Berzelii Park.

Axel had parked outside, before going into the lobby and spotting the bodyguard at the bar.

He had gone back outside and moved his car so he could see the Range Rover, and that was when he realised that the registration number had changed. Unless it was a new car? Either way, it was a sign that Johan was aware of what had happened, and was now trying to cover his tracks. The rage inside him had only grown.

Johan was an evil man. He had realised that from what he had found in his computer. When the bodyguard emerged with the obviously inebriated Johan and a young woman, he had followed their car. They stopped outside a building in Banérgatan and let the woman out.

The SUV had performed a U-turn and for a moment Axel and the bodyguard's eyes had met through their windscreens.

Had he been rumbled? Everything pointed to that, so now Johan would be prepared. Perhaps it would make sense to wait until the following day? Axel looked out at the street as he considered his options.

The woman was still standing outside the building. It looked cold out there. The wind was tugging at her hair, blowing it about. She wrapped her arms round herself. Why didn't she go inside if this was where she lived?

There was something about her that piqued his curiosity, making him forget his fury for a moment. Was it sympathy he felt? Had Johan Karlström harmed her as well? He was torn between following the Range Rover and staying where he was.

Axel turned the engine off as a man came walking along from Strandvägen.

He went over to the woman, who handed him something. It was impossible for Axel to see what it was from that distance. They exchanged a few word before the man carried on walking, towards Stureplan.

Axel pressed *record* on the dash-cam, then threw himself down when he realised the man would be walking past his car.

14

The black puck left long, straight tracks in the snow. Nicolas and James were standing in the garden, each clutching a hockey stick and making long passes to each other. Johan and Erica Karlström were still asleep.

Nicolas was thinking of going to see his sister Maria. He wanted to get away from the house and clear his thoughts. Not least after the chaotic behaviour the previous evening. Nothing disgusted him more than Johan buying sex. And he was also going to have to talk to Erica. Explain to her that what had happened on Thursday evening couldn't be repeated.

Johan lobbed the puck to Nicolas, who dribbled it past an imaginary opponent and sent it back with a backhand pass.

"Nice," James said.

An upstairs window opened and Johan Karlström stuck his head out. His hair was sticking up, and his face was ashen and grey. But there was no doubting the fact that he was angry.

"Get up here at once!" he yelled, pointing at Nicolas.

The window slammed shut. Nicolas and James looked at each other in surprise, before Nicolas shrugged his shoulders and put his stick down.

"I'll be back soon," he said.

Even as he tried to make light of it to James, he was deeply worried. If Erica had said anything about the two of them, or if Johan had found the picture she had sent Nicolas, it was all over. He would be fired. He stopped and drank a glass of water at the island unit in the kitchen before he went upstairs and knocked on the door of Johan's office.

"Come in," Johan called.

He was sitting at the large mahogany desk by the window, but flew up when Nicolas walked in.

"That bitch stole my mobile phone yesterday. I've looked everywhere, but it's not here. You'll have to go round to hers and get it. Right now."

Nicolas breathed out. So it wasn't about Erica. But at the same time he couldn't help feeling alarmed. A stolen mobile could be used for blackmail. No one knew what videos, photographs, audio-files and emails might be on it.

"Calm down," Nicolas said. "I've got a couple of questions."

Johan stopped and stood there with his arms folded, leaning against the desk.

"What?"

"Has anyone contacted you about it, asking for money?"

"No."

"You're not the target of any attempted blackmail?"

Nicolas looked intently at Johan, who shook his head quickly.

"No. Now get going."

"I need to call AOS and check how they want me to deal with this. I can't just break in and accuse her of stealing your mobile."

Johan stared at Nicolas.

"Do whatever the hell you want, but this is precisely the sort of situation I pay you to deal with. Get me my phone back, or you can start looking for a new job."

Nicolas parked the car in the snow-covered avenue in the middle of Narvavägen. He pulled up the hood of his top, his hair was still wet from the quick shower he had taken when he got changed before driving into the city. There were families and couples walking towards the Djurgården Bridge, and two men went past on cross-country skis.

When he had explained the situation to AOS, they had told him to do as Johan said. Go and see the woman and politely demand the return of the mobile phone. If she wasn't home, he was to get back to them for further instructions. Nicolas waited as a snow-plough rumbled past. He crossed the road and walked quickly towards Banérgatan. He stopped outside number 4, waiting for one of the neighbours to go in or out. He stayed close to the door so he couldn't be seen through the windows, and cursed the fact that he hadn't worn warmer clothes.

Twenty minutes later he was let in by someone delivering advertising leaflets. Nicolas stepped into the ornately decorated stairwell and studied the list of residents' names on the wall. Just as Johan had said, the woman's surname appeared to be Berg.

She lived on the fifth floor, one from the top.

He took the lift, passing the guy delivering leaflets on the way, and got out. He pulled the grille closed behind him and shut the door. He rang the doorbell and waited. Nothing happened. He rang again, then put his ear to the door to see if he could hear any noise inside the apartment, but it was totally quiet. Nicolas sighed, took out his mobile, put his ear-buds in and dialled AOS.

He gave his name and explained the situation.

"Is the door locked?"

Nicolas gently tried the door handle, and the door moved. It was unlocked. He hung up, glanced around quickly to make sure he was alone, then stepped inside and closed the door behind him.

He found himself in a spacious hallway. There was a built-in set of shelves, laden with designer handbags and shoes, all in a jumble. An assortment of jackets hung from the coat-rack. Nicolas took another step and wondering if he should take his boots off, but decided to keep them on. He quickly wiped the soles on the doormat.

The floorboards creaked alarmingly. He crossed the hall and entered a large, light living room with a chandelier hanging from the ceiling. The room was expensively furnished. Lots of panelling and ornate plasterwork. The whole apartment felt extravagant. He headed towards a closed sliding door that he assumed led to the bedroom. He knocked quietly – the woman might be asleep in there.

And she might call the police if she got scared.

Besides, it was far from certain that she had taken the phone. It could just as easily have been left in the hotel room, even if Johan claimed he had already phoned the hotel.

Nicolas slid the door open and walked in.

Just as he saw that the bed was empty, he heard the floor creak and detected movement behind him. He spun round, and at the last moment managed to parry the masked man's attack.

15

Hamza was pulling a trolley behind him. It contained a carton of eggs, a couple of Findus ready-meals and a jar of Nescafé. He had his cap pulled down over his forehead, and was wearing a blue padded jacket he had bought second-hand.

The City Wholesale store in Kungens kurva was full of noisy families with kids and couples shopping for the weekend. Hamza remembered how he and his two younger siblings used to tear about in there, while their mum Shadia tried in vain to keep them under control as she worked her way through her shopping-list. These days his parents lived in Akalla, on the other side of the city.

The winter darkness had really been getting him down. But suddenly the clouds had parted and the sun had broken through. Hamza had thrown on his outdoor clothes and gone for a walk through the snow-covered forests before spotting the City Wholesale sign and making his way there. He hadn't been able to resist the temptation, despite the risk of running into someone from the past. But his appearance had changed in recent years, and his thick black beard made him practically unrecognisable.

He headed towards the row of tills and got in the queue. He felt in his pocket for his crumpled banknotes. There was only one person ahead of him in the queue, an older man. Hamza couldn't see his face because he was wearing a brown padded hat with ear-muffs. But he recognised the voice straight away. Stig. Hamza considered moving to a different till, but made do with pulling his cap even lower and keeping his eyes on the floor.

The young cashier started to scan his items. Stig was standing at the end of the conveyor belt, putting his own purchases in a plastic bag.

"That comes to 249 kronor," she said.

Hamza held out three hundred-kronor notes, then took the change. Stig was still standing there, even though he had finished packing.

"Hamza? Is that you?"

Stig was squinting at him, and Hamza pretended to be surprised. Stig stepped forward and gave him an enthusiastic hug. Hamza let himself be embraced by the thin, fragile man. Stig patted him on the back, then took a step back and looked up at him.

"I haven't seen you since you were a little lad."

The old teacher's reaction was touching. How many boys must he have known in his lifetime?

"Where have you been?"

"I've been living in Malmö. Got a job down there. So that's where I've been," Hamza lied, in accordance with the replies he had practiced.

Stig's eyes had got caught by Hamza's hands and bruised knuckles. He opened his mouth as if to say something, then seemed to change his mind.

"And now you're home again?" he asked.

Hamza put the last of his things in his bag.

"Yes, now I'm home."

"It's good to have you back."

They ended up standing outside in the car-park. Stig held out his hand, and Hamza shook it.

"You're welcome to call in for a coffee one day. I still live in the same place."

Stig turned and padded off through the snow, the heavy bag bouncing against his leg. He got no further than a few metres before he looked back over his shoulder.

"You're welcome to come now, if you haven't got anything else to do?" he said hopefully. "But I'm sure you're busy."

"Coffee would be great," Hamza said. "Give me the bag, I'll carry it."

Hamza vaguely remembered the dark, three-room flat. Stig always used to invite the most troublesome boys home, where he tried to talk to them, support them, lent them adventure books to read. Now it smelled of loneliness and old man. Stig went into the kitchen to make coffee, and put two dry Danish pastries on a plate.

"I'll be right with you."

Hamza looked around the narrow kitchen. On the windowsill was a photograph of a young woman. He recognised her. Stig's daughter. He stood up and went over to take a closer look. She must be ten-fifteen years older than him, and had short, jet-black hair. Her eyes were serious and dark. He recalled that she had done her training at the preschool he attended, hadn't he sat on her lap at some point? Later on he used to say hello to her if they ever passed each other in the shopping centre.

"Petra."

Hamza put the photograph back. Stig was standing in the doorway with a book in his hand. He put it on the table, then came and stood next to Hamza, and ran his fingers over the frame.

"Didn't she used to work at the Squirrel Preschool when I was there?"

Stig lit up.

"She did her work-experience there."

"Everyone used to fight about who got to sit on her lap. How is she?"

Hamza regretted the question the moment he asked it.

"Not so good. She's back inside at the moment, she's had a pretty tough life, my Petra. Boyfriends who haven't always been very nice, drugs."

"Inside?"

Stig nodded.

"In a mental hospital. Even if they aren't called that anymore."

"Do you go and see her?"

"It's been a year or so since I last went. I can't handle the journey, the hospital's quite a way outside Jönköping. The surroundings are beautiful, but it's too far. And I've lost my driving licence, because I suffer from epilepsy. And… well, she hardly recognises me. That's the fault of the medication. Do you have children, Hamza?"

He nodded.

"Two. A boy and a girl."

"Our children are the best, most valuable things we have in this world."

Hamza felt his throat constrict with loss. Mazhar and Amina were dead. Murdered. Blown to pieces. His hands started to shake and he clenched his fists to stop them shaking.

Stig put the frame back, picked up the well-thumbed book

and handed it over. Hamza saw that it was the *Adventures of Huckleberry Finn*.

"You used to love this one. Open it and you'll see."

Hamza opened the book.

"The last page."

He turned to the final page and recognised his own childish handwriting. He held the book up to the light and squinted, trying to read what it said.

I want to go to Mississippi too. If I behave, am good and don't fight, and if I become a pro in the NHL, I promise to take my friend Stig with me.

Skärholmen, 17 August, 1999.

Beneath that were Stig and Hamza's signatures.

Hamza laughed.

"But you haven't kept your promise not to fight," Stig said, with sudden seriousness in his voice.

He tapped Hamza's swollen knuckles with his forefinger. The sudden touch made him start.

Coming home with Stig had been an unnecessary risk, but his desire for human contact had been too great. Since he came home he had been living in isolation in his flat. It was months since he last had a meaningful conversation.

"It isn't what you think," Hamza said, forcing himself to look his old teacher in the eye. "I do mixed martial arts. The gloves are thin. If you manage to land a decent punch, this is what happens."

Hamza lifted his hand and spread his fingers.

"If you say so."

It was impossible to tell if Stig believed him. Hamza closed the book, then ran his palm over the front cover before handing it back to him.

"Keep it," Stig said.

16

Nicolas understood instinctively where the blow was going to land, and managed to deflect it with his left arm, but he underestimated the strength of the attack. He only just managed to evade a kick that shattered a standard lamp. The attacker was driving Nicolas back, further into the bedroom, and he had his hands full just trying to defend himself. The kicks, punches, combinations – this was no ordinary martial arts enthusiast. Everything suggested military training.

He realised he was in a tricky situation.

Eventually Nicolas saw an opening, blocked one kick with his lower left arm, and went on the counterattack with a series of punches and kicks that should have knocked out any opponent. Now it was Nicolas's turn to push the masked man back, but he felt far from certain that he was going to get out of the apartment alive.

The man's strength, reaction times and close-combat abilities surpassed those of most people he had ever come across.

They stopped to catch their breath, staring at each other before they started fighting again. Nicolas parried, kicked, punched, but could feel his strength inevitably begin to fade. At the same time, the force of the other man's attack was also diminishing.

Eventually Nicolas got a chance to put an end to it. The man took aim at his face with his left hand, but Nicolas saw the blow coming. He moved out of the way, felt the punch graze his cheek, and grabbed the man's arm, bending it backwards hard, dislocating the man's shoulder. He let out a roar and came on the attack again with his arm hanging uselessly by his side. But now that the man's left arm was out of action, Nicolas could concentrate on his left side, and floored him with a well-aimed right kick.

Nicolas was on top of him in an instant, using his bodyweight to pin him to the floor, and holding his left arm across the man's throat until he lost consciousness. He rolled over onto his side and caught his breath for a few seconds, before putting the man in the recovery position and tearing off his black balaclava.

He had dark features, and appeared to be in his thirties. Black hair, brown eyes. There was no doubt that he had some sort of military background. What was he doing in the home of a top-class Swedish prostitute?

Nicolas searched the man's pockets, looking for anything that might identify him, but found nothing but a few banknotes and a white key-card that presumably came from his hotel room. In the man's inside pocket he found a rolled-up, sealed envelope.

The man was showing signs of regaining consciousness. Nicolas reached for the cable from the smashed lamp, then unceremoniously dragged the man to the radiator below the window and tied his right wrist to it.

His body was aching and throbbing, and his arms covered with bruises. Nicolas turned one of the armchairs round so he could keep an eye on the man, and sank down onto it.

The man opened his eyes and looked around groggily. He was breathing heavily, feeling his ribs with his tied right hand.

"Who are you?" Nicolas asked in Swedish. No reaction. He asked again, this time in English.

The man shot him a hostile glare, then moved and grimaced in pain.

Nicolas looked around the apartment from his seated position. The man had already been there when he came in. The balaclava indicated that he didn't want to be identified. Had he been planning to steal something? Had he harmed the young woman?

"Where is the girl?"

The man clenched his jaw and stared past Nicolas into space. He realised the man wasn't going to talk.

Nicolas looked more closely at the envelope he had taken from the man's pocket. He got laboriously to his feet, then went out into the hall, looking for the kitchen. He took a kitchen knife down from a magnetic strip on the wall, then returned to the living room. The man looked indifferently at the knife in Nicolas's hand.

The envelope contained photographs.

He leafed through the first few and saw that they all featured the high-class prostitute in various intimate situations.

Blackmail. But why? Did the man belong to some foreign criminal gang, or could he be working with the woman to blackmail wealthy businessmen?

Nicolas quickly looked through the rest of the photographs, and noted that Johan didn't seem to feature in any of them. He didn't understand at all, and it was obvious that the man wasn't planning to give him any answers.

He could hardly call the police, seeing as he had entered the apartment without permission, and it would be hard to explain what he was doing there. Instead he put the knife down within reach of the man, put the photographs back in the envelope, then took it with him when he left the apartment.

17

Molly Berg was driving at one hundred and twenty kilometres an hour. Fresh snow was swirling round the tyres. The further north she drove, the deeper the snow was, and the more beautiful and wild the natural landscape. Fewer people, fewer cars. Less of everything, except snow. She felt free. Almost happy. She had done as Thomas had asked: she had stolen the mobile and given it to him. She had already been driving for six hours in the hire-car she had picked up from Avis early that morning.

First Aid Kit's "Emmylou" was playing through the speakers. Molly felt the song talking to her: "I was born to endure this kind of weather". To her surprise, she found herself looking forward to getting there, to seeing her father. Perhaps that was because of the insecurity and fear she had felt in the past few days, the past few months? No one could reach her in her father's cottage, ten kilometres outside Kiruna, no one could threaten or hurt her.

The closer she got, the more she felt that this was where she belonged. At heart, she was a Norrlander. How could she ever have left all this?

The petrol gauge was telling her that she would have to fill up soon, and through the swirling snow she could see the red sign of a Circle K filling station. Molly pulled off the road. An articulate lorry was parked by the side of the road next to the petrol station, and she assumed that the driver was taking a break. She jumped out of the car, opened the petrol tank and stuck her card in the machine. She breathed in the smell of petrol, which she had always loved, still humming "Emmylou". Every so often a car or truck would rush past on the road. When the tank was full, she screwed the lid back on and walked towards the door of the shop. The guy behind the counter had trouble tearing his eyes off her, but that didn't bother her. On the contrary, she found his staring amusing.

She tucked a bag of cheese puffs under her arm and got a Diet Coke from the chiller. She lingered by the newspaper and magazine stand, looking at the colourful, glossy covers. She recognised the player on the cover of one of the football magazines. She had slept with him a year ago in a hotel room in Chelsea. She moved along the shelf, and found herself staring into the ice-blue eyes of Sweden's young justice minister, Magnus Moheden, on the cover of *Kvällspressen*. The Social Democrat politician, spoken of as a potential future prime minister, was another client of hers, even if she hadn't seen him for a while.

The headline beneath the photograph said: *Now the imams are being deported.*

What sort of life had she been leading in recent years? Here – far away from Stockholm and Barcelona, the parties on Dubai and luxurious suites in London, at a petrol station somewhere just south of Umeå – it all felt very unreal. She would never have been to explain that to the cashier. How could she ever make anyone understand? But she had been given a second chance. Two second chances, in fact.

The first was when she managed to escape alive from the luxury yacht last summer. The second was yesterday. She was convinced that Johan Karlström would do all he could to ruin her life if he found out she had stolen his mobile. But Thomas had promised that the pictures of Molly had been destroyed, and that they wouldn't need her anymore. She hoped he could be trusted. In a business where discretion was everything, Molly's future was still wrecked. In a way, that actually felt like a relief. It left her without many options. She had amassed a fortune of around twenty million kronor, if you included the apartment. That was more than her dad had earned in his whole life, probably more than her mother's entire family had earned in a hundred years. The money was laundered and clean. Now she just had to figure out what she was going to spend the rest of her life doing.

Molly put her purchases on the counter and deliberately smiled her most seductive smile at the blushing teenager.

"That comes to seventy-three kronor, please," he said, his throat flushing bright red.

Molly swiped her card, shook her head when he asked if she wanted the receipt, and wished him a good day.

18

Celine and Vanessa were sitting on the sofa, while an enthusiastic chef and smiling presenter prepared vegetarian tapas together on television. Vanessa had just got out of the shower, and was wearing her white dressing-gown, while Celine was wearing a pair of Vanessa's gym leggings and a white T-shirt emblazoned with the text *Living Legend of Instagram*.

Later that day they were planning to go into the city to buy clothes and toiletries for Celine. But Mikael Kask was coming round first. Vanessa had reluctantly called him back after the message he left on her voicemail the previous day. Even though he was bound to yell at her for getting involved in the investigation, she needed to know what he meant when he said there was something strange about Natasha's broken leg. If he was going to fire her, so be it. She didn't need the money that working in the police gave her, and she was still going to catch Natasha's killer.

Vanessa stood up to go and get dressed, pulling on a pair of black jeans and a black polo-shirt. When the doorbell rang she was drying her hair in the bathroom.

"Be polite," she said to Celine as she walked past the sofa to answer the door.

Celine stood to attention and gave a salute. Vanessa laughed before letting Mikael Kask in. Celine lowered the volume of the television, then held out her hand.

"Celine Wood," she said seriously, and curtsied.

"Mikael. Erm... Kask."

"Can I offer you some saffron dough?" She held out the 7-Eleven bag from the previous evening.

Mikael eyes darted between the girl and Vanessa in confusion.

"No, thanks. I'm fine."

Vanessa showed him in and asked Celine to stay in her room.

"Well-behaved girl," Mikael said when Celine had closed the door. "Who is she?"

"Celine Wood, as she said."

"The girl who got shot at the Stadium?" he asked in a low voice.

Vanessa nodded. She made a note to tell Celine that polite didn't mean behaving like a butler, even if she had found the performance amusing.

"She's had a difficult time since then, so now she's staying here for a while. I told her to be polite before you arrived, she's normally much less... stiff."

"Well, you've certainly got the space," Mikael said, looking round at the huge apartment.

"Can I get you anything?" Vanessa asked. "There's coffee, tea, apple juice. All sorts, really."

"In that case, coffee."

They sat down at the island unit in the kitchen. Mikael, who was still wearing his coat, took it off at last, revealing a tight white T-shirt and an impressive pair of biceps. Vanessa poured two cups of coffee from the machine and pushed one over to Mikael, who took a sip and nodded appreciatively.

"Samer's told me about the Lindskogs and what you did. It's great that you got hold of the recording from the supermarket so quickly, but you can't undermine your colleagues like that. That really isn't good. You understand that?"

"Yes."

Mikael looked her sternly in the eye.

"As you know, we've been focusing on Rikard Olsson. We believe that the reason why Natasha was murdered has something to do with his work, rather than anything to do with her."

"And I don't agree."

Silence descended on the kitchen. Vanessa was looking at him defiantly. She knew Mikael Kask well enough to know that he was building up to something. He pushed his cup away and drummed his index finger on the edge of the counter.

"Did Natasha ever tell you that she broke her leg when she was around four or five years old?" He sounded serious.

"Yes?"

"And she told you the same thing she told the Migration Office

– that she was born and raised in Syria? And that she had never set foot in Europe before she arrived in the autumn of 2015?"

Vanessa nodded. Her good mood from earlier had vanished. There was something in Mikael's eyes that made her steel herself. Whatever he was about to say, it was bad news. She reminded herself to stay calm, she needed him on her side if she was going to carry on being told what was happening in the investigation.

"Just spit it out."

"The flexible pins inserted into Natasha's leg are manufactured in France. That treatment couldn't possibly have been offered in Syria in the early 2000s. It was only available in France, possibly Belgium. According to Thysell, there's no way a Syrian hospital could have had access to those pins and the skills to use them."

Vanessa opened her mouth to protest, but Mikael held his palm up towards her.

"And the MRI of her knee showed, just like the x-rays of her wisdom teeth, that she was at least twenty years old."

Vanessa stared at Mikael. She was searching for an explanation, but without success.

So Natasha was older than she had said. It wasn't unusual for refugees to lie about their age, which in itself wasn't that remarkable. Vanessa had trouble imagining why they wouldn't lie, out of desperation, if it would help their chances of being allowed to stay. Even so, she felt obliged to defend Natasha.

"If she lied about her age, it was because she wanted to stay in Sweden. And like she said, her father was a professor of literature at Damascus University. It isn't impossible that he had contacts in France, and that she was operated on there if the fracture was serious?"

Mikael sighed and scratched his stubble.

"What?" Vanessa said irritably.

"We've been in touch with Damascus University. No one knows anything about a professor of Russian literature with Natasha's surname. I'm sorry to have to say it, Vanessa, but Natasha wasn't the person she claimed to be. You need to accept that as soon as possible if you're going to be of any use in this investigation."

Mikael stood up pulled his coat on, then walked round the island unit and put one hand on her shoulder.

"I'm sorry," he said.

"What do you think happened when they were murdered?"

Mikael held his arms out.

"Rikard Olsson was being chased, you heard the emergency call he made. The man Natasha seemed to be afraid of is interesting, of course, but we're sure Rikard Olsson was the primary target. He had been involved in an operation against the Sätra network. Some of their members were seen in Östermalm that evening. We're looking for the perpetrator in those circles."

"Why are you and Samer spending so much time trying to make Natasha look like a liar? What's the point?"

Mikael picked up his cup, poured away what he hadn't drunk and put it down on the draining board.

"To get you to wake up so you can return to work and the investigation. All the evidence suggests that she was just in the wrong place at the wrong time."

"What about the man outside the supermarket? What was it that she promised not to betray?"

"We're looking into that." Mikael raised his voice. "But damn it, as of now you need to realise that the death of a colleague…"

Vanessa stood up so abruptly that her stool fell over.

"What, Mikael? What were you about to say? That his death is more important than Natasha's?"

Mikael slowly shook his head.

"You know that isn't what I meant."

He bent down and picked up the toppled stool.

"Obviously everybody is just as important. But for God's sake, Vanessa, Rikard Olsson was a police officer. Investigating gangs. Hitting their drug-dealing, stopping them in the streets, messing with them. You know there are guys in these gangs who like to impress their mates by proving just how fucked up they are. And how do you do that? By shooting a police officer. We need to catch them, to show that we're not going to let this go unnoticed."

PART IV

1

The temperature had risen on Sunday, and by lunchtime on Monday the streets and squares of Kungsholmen were a mess of slush and grit. Vanessa was still mulling over her meeting with Michael on Saturday. She felt confused. And she couldn't deny that his reasoning made sense.

The bright yellow newspaper billboard outside the tobacconist's on St Eriksgatan made her stop in her tracks. She found herself staring at black-and-white passport photographs of Natasha and Rikard Olsson. Above the pictures the newspaper blared: *Mystery baffles police – who killed the young refugee and gangland cop?*

Vanessa opened the door and an electronic bell rang out. She snatched up a copy of the *Kvällspressen* and paid. Tucking the newspaper under her arm, she set off towards Fleminggatan.

She had arranged to meet Sabina Haddad in a salad bar in less than four minutes. The young woman had told her that she was supposed to be cleaning an apartment on Kronobergsgatan, and that she really didn't have time to meet, but Vanessa had promised it wouldn't take long. When she arrived, Sabina was already sitting at a table close to the queue snaking its way towards the counter. Vanessa asked what she wanted.

"Greek salad, please," Sabina said. "Takeaway."

In spite of the number of people, the queue moved quickly. Vanessa ordered two Greek salads to take away, pressed her bankcard to the machine and was given a turquoise ticket. She poured two glasses of water and went and sat down.

"I need to go in a minute," Sabina said apologetically. "I have to get to my next flat, and it's on Södermalm."

"What do you know about Natasha's childhood in Syria?"

"Not much. We never spoke about the war."

"I mean before the war," Vanessa said. "Did she ever say anything about her family?"

"Only that her dad was a professor at the university. And she talked about her younger brother, Lev. He used to keep fish in an aquarium, and was killed in a bombing raid."

Sabina fell silent, and a voice called out from the counter:

"Number 17."

Vanessa quickly checked her ticket, then turned her attention to Sabina again.

"I have reason to believe that Natasha didn't grow up in Syria, but in France, or possibly Belgium. Was there anything she ever told you that might support that?"

Sabina stared at Vanessa in astonishment.

"Definitely not," she exclaimed, sounding almost insulted. "Whoever's saying that is lying. Natasha was born and raised in Damascus."

"You never heard her... I don't know, speak French?"

Sabina laughed. She shook her head.

"No."

The situation was absurd. Natasha was the person who Vanessa had been closest to after her divorce from Svante. She was one of the most warm-hearted, considerate people Vanessa had ever met. And now here she was, sitting in a salad bar on Kungsholmen, asking Natasha's friend to try to figure out what was true and what was false in what Natasha had said.

"Are you sure?" Vanessa said softly.

"Yes." Sabina leaned forward and put her hand on top of Vanessa's. "Completely sure. She couldn't speak a word of French. Nor can I. What's making you ask these things?"

"Details that don't make sense."

Sabina slowly withdrew her hand and left it lying on the table.

"How are you coping?" Vanessa asked. "Natasha was your friend too."

"Obviously it's hard. It might sound harsh, but when you've lived through a war, you learn how to deal with death. It's like everything else. It becomes second nature."

"Don't you have any family either?"

Sabina gave her a sad smile and shook her head.

Vanessa knew she was pushing too hard with no real justification. Sabina hadn't committed any crime, the only thing she was guilty of was knowing Natasha. She adopted a gentler tone, and tried to think of something conciliatory to say.

"Do you want to go back one day, like Natasha did?"

Sabina sighed.

"There's nothing to go back to. Only graves and ruins. My life is here now."

The woman at the counter called their number. They both stood up at the same time. Vanessa took the bag containing the salads and handed it to Sabina.

"Take both of them, I'm not feeling hungry. I really am sorry. Get in touch if there's anything I can do."

"Thanks."

When Sabina had left, Vanessa sat down again opened the *Kvällspressen*. Just as she had suspected, the article mentioned on the billboard was written by Max Lewenhaupt. He began by giving an account of the discovery of the two bodies eleven days ago, describing in detail the degree of violence they had been subjected to. Then he moved on to talk about Rikard Olsson's and Natasha's lives. He had got hold of the Lindskogs, the couple Natasha had been living with, so a lot of it was based on what they had said. The section about Rikard Olsson was longer and more detailed, which Vanessa took to mean that Max Lewenhaupt and his editor thought their readers were more interested in a policeman who was working on organised crime than in a young refugee girl.

The article ended with two former police officers speculating about the motive. One of them claimed it could be revenge from some gang Rikard Olsson had infiltrated. The other suggested that this was probably a crime of passion, and encouraged the detectives to find the connection between the two victims.

Vanessa screwed the newspaper up and tossed it in the bin on her way out.

2

It was half past three in the afternoon and the sun was already setting. The last rays were clinging to the high-rise apartment blocks in Skärholmen when Hamza got to the square. In recent days it had felt like he needed to get things sorted out urgently. Say goodbye. He suspected that they would soon be getting in touch, and he wanted to be ready. Maybe it was his encounter with Stig that had prompted these thoughts. Hamza couldn't let go off the photograph of Petra. Every time he closed his eyes, her serious, almost accusing face appeared in his mind's eye. Then Stig's face, contorted with grief when he talked about her. The old man had a car, a rusty old Opel Astra. Hamza could drive him to visit her, couldn't he? See to it that he met his daughter? It was worth the risk.

Hamza went up the steps from the square. The sun had vanished and darkness made him walk faster, feel freer. The satellite dishes on the concrete walls shone like hovering, one-dimensional planets. He looked out across the yard where he had grown up, where he had played football, had fights, chased other children and been chased by them. He remembered it as being much bigger, much more beautiful. Now he saw just how run-down and tragic it really was.

Instinctively he looked up at the fifth floor. There were lights on in the living-room window. The television was flickering, but his family had moved. His father, Abbas, was now sitting in a flat on the other side of the city, watching the news from Iraq. He was probably hitting the loose arm of his chair with his fist, muttering about the stupid, ignorant children he had been cursed with. Hamza felt himself growing angry even at the thought of that. But his father hadn't always been like that. Hamza remembered those first years in Sweden. Back then, whenever their relatives called from Iraq, his father told them what a wonderful country he had ended up in.

He lied, telling them that he had a permanent job, a big salary, that he could speak Swedish. He had called his new homeland "the cold paradise at the end of the world". The truth was that he was always hanging around the Job Centre, sometimes drove an unregistered taxi, refused to go to integration classes. He thought they were a waste of time. Abbas had never managed to get a permanent job. He had become more and more apathetic. Eventually he stopped going to the Job Centre at all, just sat in the café with the other unemployed men, smoking Prince cigarettes, drinking black coffee, and becoming more hollow-eyed and thin-haired.

Life was slipping from his hands. All this while his children, Hamza, Nadira and Ahmed did all they could to fit it, all they could to integrate into their new homeland. Their father, who had encouraged them to study, to fight and achieve, mocked their efforts.

"Don't you see that the Swedes despise you?" he used to say. "They need cheap labour. People to clean their streets and work in their fast-food restaurants. That's why we're here. Don't pretend otherwise. Just look at me. Those bastards have stolen my best years from me."

In the end, his words had begun to affect Hamza. His grades had got worse, he got into more fights, the hatred and feeling of exclusion grew.

He wondered how Ahmed and Nadira were doing. He hoped they were happy, that their father hadn't broken them too. But he knew he mustn't think about them too much, because that made him weak.

He sighed, took one last look at the apartment window, then turned to walk back to the square.

It was only four hundred metres to Stig's door. Hamza was going to call and tell the old man that he could drive him to visit his daughter, if he wanted. But it would have to happen soon.

As soon as they contacted him, Stig and everything else would be of secondary importance.

3

Nicolas saw her in the distance, outside the Bollywood Indian restaurant on Roslagsgatan. He looked at her thoughtfully until she had almost gone into the building. He rushed across the street as fast as he could, his body was sore after his encounter with the man in Molly's flat.

"Vanessa."

She stopped, quickly pulling her hand back from the keypad by the door, and turned round. Her new bob suited her. It framed her face, which only looked more beautiful each time he saw it. She looked at him with her usual friendly seriousness, without saying anything. Nicolas felt like he was intruding.

"I read about Natasha," he said quickly. "I realise that you don't want to see me, but I need to know what happened."

"Aren't you in London?"

"I live here now."

"In Stockholm?"

The look on Vanessa's face was still expressionless. Nicolas found it impossible to figure out what she thought about the fact that he was back. He suggested that they drive somewhere more secluded for a talk. Vanessa followed him to the Range Rover, which he had parked in Tulegatan.

"Nice car," she said, running her hand over the wood on the dashboard. "I hope there isn't a kidnapped banker in the back?"

Nicolas smiled.

It felt surreal to be so close to Vanessa again. But she seemed different. Tense. Wary. They crossed the avenue, turned off next to the Sophia Hospital and carried on driving along the narrow roads behind Stockholm Stadium. Nicolas switched the engine off, unfastened his seatbelt and leaned back.

"I didn't know Natasha was back in Sweden," he said after a while.

"Me neither." Vanessa seemed to be struggling for words. "She came back some time in March and was living with a couple on Bergshamra."

"She didn't contact you?" he asked, unable to conceal his surprise.

"There's a lot that's unclear about her background. It looks like she was hiding a whole lot of things. There's evidence to suggest that she actually grew up in France. Or Belgium. That she was older than she said. Not only that, but a couple of days before she was found dead, she was threatened by a man. We have video footage from where it happened, and she looked terrified. Then, just minutes before she died, she called me. But I'd changed my number."

The words were pouring out of her now, Nicolas was struggling to keep up.

"Do you have any idea of what happened?" he asked.

Vanessa took a deep breath and calmed down.

"No."

She took her seatbelt off and rubbed her face with her hands. She looked away and stared towards the stadium. Nicolas waited for her to go on, but Vanessa seemed to have finished. He didn't want to push her. Losing Natasha was the worst thing that could have happened to her. Not least because he knew what she had been through earlier in her life.

"Do you ever think about it?" she asked softly, pointing towards the brown brick walls of the stadium.

"Sometimes," he said curtly. "Do you?"

"Fairly often. More and more, in fact. Or rather, I did until Natasha was found dead."

A man ran past them, wearing a hi-viz tunic over his running gear. Vanessa watched him until he disappeared from sight. She turned to Nicolas. Suddenly she reached out her hand and stroked his cheek, then moved up, across his forehead, and tugged gently at his cropped hair.

He considered asking why she had stopped calling him, and never answered when he called, but he didn't know if he felt up to hearing the answer.

"What are you doing back here?" she asked.

"I'm working as the security coordinator for a Swedish family.

They've just moved home from London and asked me to come with them."

He changed position, and felt a sudden stabbing pain in his chest. Vanessa looked at him quizzically.

"What is it?"

"Nothing."

"Are you hurt? Let me see."

She switched the light on, undid his jacket and lifted his T-shirt. She stared at the bruising on his ribs, touching them gently with her fingertips.

"It's nothing," he said, pulling his T-shirt down again.

"What happened?"

He gave her a brief account of his encounter with the unknown man in Molly's apartment, and the pictures he had found.

When he stopped talking, Vanessa asked what he had been doing there, and soon he had told her all about Johan and his work for the Karlström family. He left out the bit about having sex with Erica. Not because he had done anything wrong, but because he wasn't sure what Vanessa would think about it. Would she be disappointed in him? And if there was one person he didn't want to disappoint, it was Vanessa.

"What sort of photographs?" she asked.

Nicolas opened the door, went round to the back of the vehicle and returned with the envelope, which he had hidden in the first-aid box. He handed it to Vanessa, who leafed through the pictures.

"Bloody hell, I don't think I've ever seen a more beautiful woman," she muttered. "Blackmail, do you think?"

She handed the pictures back.

"But who by?" Nicolas said. "Either she has pictures like that taken so she can blackmail her own clients, or someone else forced her to do it by threatening to expose her."

Vanessa shrugged her shoulders.

"What do you know about her?"

"Nothing beyond the fact that her name is Molly Berg, and that she's some sort of exclusive, international escort."

"Would you like me to find out more?"

"Could you?"

"I'm a police officer. And it sounds like your unpleasant boss or whatever you call him is in a difficult position."

"Thanks."

They looked at each other warmly. In spite of the gloomy subjects they had spent the past half hour talking about, there was no one whose company Nicolas enjoyed as much as Vanessa's.

"Are you seeing anyone?" she asked, as if in passing.

He couldn't lie to her. She looked at him with amusement, aware that he was wrestling with his conscience.

"I slept with Erica Karlström last week," Nicolas eventually said. "I don't know why, it just happened."

Vanessa pursed her lips and nodded slowly. It was impossible to determine what she was thinking.

"Is she beautiful?"

"She looks like you."

Vanessa laughed. She reached for her seatbelt and put it back on.

"Are you driving me home, then?"

4

Vanessa was the only customer in McLaren's. Kjell-Arne was getting the place ready for the evening, setting lit candles out on the tables. She still felt annoyed about her encounter with Nicolas the previous day. Bloody Nicolas! The last thing she needed right now was him waltzing back into her life, complicating everything. Even so, she had volunteered to help him. The simple reason why she had done so was the loyalty she felt towards him. The complicated but still obvious one, which she didn't really want to think about, was that she wanted to see him again. Vanessa googled Erica Karlström and found a number of old glamour pics.

She studied them intently before forcing herself to focus on the two documents from the Migration Office that she had in front of her.

"It's going to be a good night," Kjell-Arne said as he passed her table. She moved her coffee-cup so he could put one of the candles down.

"Sure," she replied without looking up from the documents.

Younger versions of Natasha and Sabina looked up at her from the files. They contained the girls' histories during their first few months in Sweden, as well as the investigations conducted in response to their applications for residence permits.

Sabina's file said that she had been registered as an asylum seeker in the middle of September 2015, on the 23rd, to be precise, even though Vanessa clearly remembered her saying that she had arrived in Sweden at the end of August that year.

So she had been lying. The date of her registration was the same as Natasha's.

The two of them had then moved through the system and the country together. They lived in the same refugee hostels and homes.

Why hadn't Sabina told her the truth? A lie was a lie, and now Vanessa would have to find out why.

The door opened and three men ambled in and went over to the bar.

Vanessa sat there thinking for a while before she looked up the details of HomeClean Ltd online. She found a number for the owner and managing director, Goran Zelinsky, and pressed *call*. As the phone rang she saw Kjell-Arne looking at her disapprovingly as he filled a glass with beer from the tap. She got through to voicemail, and left a short message asking Goran to call her. She hung up as Kjell-Arne wiped his hands on his apron and came over to her table.

"What is it?" Vanessa asked. "I'm working."

"That's what worries me. We have a new policy. No work calls, no mobiles in here. I want this to be a place where people can leave their work at home. Where you live for the moment. Come with me, I'll show you."

He led her over to the bar. There was a bucket with a handwritten note taped to the side: *Here we leave our work at home – fine for non-compliance: 10 kronor.*

"You can't be serious," Vanessa said. "Most people here have been unemployed since the millennium."

"They're between jobs."

Vanessa sighed.

"I need to make calls for work. Besides, you know perfectly well that Leif and I are the only regulars with jobs."

Kjell-Arne squirmed.

"Leif got fired last week."

"That's shit. Say hi to him from me."

"Will do. But I'm serious. Ten kronor per call. The money's going to charity."

"Which one?"

"Alcoholics Anonymous."

"You're kidding?"

Vanessa went back to her table, found a 100-kronor note in her coat pocket, strode back to the bar and dropped it in the bucket.

"That means I've got nine calls credit, right?"

"Yes."

Her phone, still in her hand, vibrated. Vanessa held it up demonstratively and Kjell-Arne threw his arms out.

"Eight left."

He went back behind the bar as Vanessa clicked to take the call. It was Goran Zelinsky, the managing director of HomeClean.

"Thanks for calling back. My name's Vanessa Frank, I'm a detective. I was wondering if you had time to meet up so I can ask you a few questions?"

"What's this about?"

"One of your employees."

Goran Zelinsky didn't say anything.

"You're not in any trouble. I promise. I just need to talk to you about Sabina Haddad."

Vanessa pulled her chair out and sat down.

"Can we do this over the phone?" Zelinsky asked.

"Preferably not."

Goran Zelinsky sighed loudly, making the phone crackle.

"I live on Liljeholmstorget. Can we get this done this evening?"

"I'll call you when I get there."

5

Axel Grystad knew he only had a few minutes left to live. He had written two documents which he had left at on the kitchen table at home. One letter explaining his actions, and a will leaving everything he owned to Rebecca. He didn't know if the will would be legally valid, it hadn't been witnessed by anyone, but he hoped it would be acceptable. He wanted Rebecca to know how grateful he was, and how much he loved her.

That weekend he had been wracked with anxiety about his decision. He had set out several times, but kept turning back before he even got to Djursholm. Instead he went back to the hospital to sit by Simon's side. But on Tuesday morning something snapped. It was Simon's birthday, and when he opened the newspaper he saw an advert for the match in Barcelona that they should have gone to see.

Axel pulled up outside the Karlström family's house. This time he didn't care if he was seen.

He knew that the woman, Erica, and the son, James, were at hockey practice.

He was going to ring the doorbell, shoot Johan Karlström, and the bodyguard if he had to, then call the police, turn the gun on himself and end his own life before Simon breathed his last breath. The phone-call was important, because he didn't want Erica and James to have to find the bodies. He was sure Johan was the one who had been driving, not least because he had got a new car so soon after the accident. Besides, he didn't think a woman was capable of leaving a child to die.

Axel reached over to the car stereo to play Lars Winnerbäck's "Du hade tid", *You had time*.

He took the pistol out of his rucksack, weighing it in his shaking hand. He thought about the list he had found a week ago on Johan's computer, where he ranked the prostitutes he had slept with according to the number of points he had given them. And the money he had hidden in various accounts around the world. Money-laundering. Mostly Axel thought of how this repulsive man had run Simon over and left him to die. Johan Karlström was a cruel man. A gangster, a bully. His wickedness had spilled over onto Axel, infecting him.

He saw Rebecca's face in front of him. He leaned his head back, thinking about that single night they had shared together, ten years ago.

Axel had been living in a sub-let one-room apartment on Tomtebogatan while he was working as a programmer for a gambling company. Late one evening he had met Rebecca when he was walking past the metro station at St Eriksplan.

She had been drunk, and dropped her mobile phone. Axel had lent her his, and she had called a friend who hadn't taken her call.

They had chatted for a while as Rebecca smoked Camel Lights. She had asked questions, and Axel had given taciturn, evasive replies. People didn't usually ask Axel questions, and if they did, they only did it to make fun of him. But not Rebecca. She had been happy, curious. In the end she had asked what his name was.

"Axel Grystad," he replied, holding his hand out.

She laughed. Not cruelly or mockingly. More in fascination.

"Rebecca Maria Thorén," she said, then praised him for having such good manners.

He got embarrassed, which amused her even more.

"Listen, Axel Grystad, I don't suppose I could crash at yours? You've probably got a spare sofa, right?"

"I don't know, I was thinking of getting something to eat." He pointed towards the all-night kiosk.

"My treat if you let me sleep on your sofa. I'll be gone before you wake up in the morning, unless you want to have breakfast, obviously. I make pretty mean pancakes. Deal?"

She ordered falafel. Axel did the same. As they walked down Rörstrandsgatan, Rebecca talked, telling him that she was studying law but really wanted to be a vet. The words just kept bubbling out of her. There was so much to do, so much to experience.

"Have you ever been in love?" she asked as he tapped in the code for the door.

"I don't think so."

"Have you ever had a girlfriend, then?"

He remembered that he considered lying, inventing a girlfriend to make himself seem normal. He didn't usually care, but with Rebecca he was suddenly very conscious of the impression he was making. But it felt like she would see through any lie immediately. And he realised that it really didn't make any difference to her if he had ever had a girlfriend or not.

"I've never had a girlfriend. It's just never quite happened."

"I've had loads of boyfriends." Rebecca laughed. "Not that it's made me particularly happy. Do you know what gets to me?"

They stopped outside the front door while he dug about in his pocket for the keys, which were on a chain so he wouldn't lose them.

"No?"

"Girls who hold back so that guys don't think they sluts, who say that the guy has to earn it." She stuck two fingers in her mouth and pretended to throw up. "That turns sexuality into some sort of fucking prize. As if we don't get horny too. Do you get what I mean?"

"I think so."

They entered the flat and Rebecca went straight over to the stereo.

"Have you got any good albums?" she asked.

"No, but I can download something."

"Good. Do you like Lasse?"

"Lasse?"

"Lars Winnerbäck. Download something by him and I'll sort the food out. I've already bought all his albums, so he can hardly object. And you're a potential new buyer, after all."

Axel found a site where he download Lars Winnerbäck's album, "Söndermarken", *Broken Lands*. Rather tentatively he put the first track on, "Faller", *Falling*. Leaving the music playing, he opened the balcony door to get some fresh air.

"Shall we eat outside? It's a nice night, and it isn't really that cold," Rebecca said.

They sat out on the balcony with their coats on. Rebecca talked with her mouth full, gesticulating with the hand holding the falafel roll for emphasis. Up until then Axel had always looked upon encounters with new people as rather frightening. With Rebecca it was different.

When it was time to go to bed, he made up a bed for himself on the sofa so she could have his bed. She protested, but Axel insisted.

It was the best evening of his life. And suddenly he realised that he hadn't stammered once.

"Axel, are you awake?" Rebecca whispered. "Wouldn't you rather sleep here? It's much cosier sleeping together."

Axel lost his virginity at the age of twenty-three, to the sound of Lars Winnerbäck's "Timglas", *Hourglass*, playing in the background.

The next morning Rebecca went home and Axel assumed he would never see her again. But three months later his doorbell rang. Rather surprised, he opened it. Rebecca asked him to sit down because she had something important to say.

"I'm pregnant."

"Congratulations," Axel said.

"It's your child, and I'm keeping it. You don't need to take any responsibility for it, but I thought it was right to let you know."

He remembered thinking it was like winning the lottery twice. He had never imagined becoming a father. Still less that the woman he would have a child with would be as beautiful, intelligent and funny as Rebecca.

"I'd be happy to take my share of the responsibility. I'm just happy."

She eyed him suspiciously.

"You are?"

"Yes."

A small frown appeared between her eyebrows.

"Axel, are you in love with me?" she asked.

"Yes, I am. And I'll never stop. But I know you're not in love with me, so you don't have to worry."

Rebecca shot him a look full of sympathy.

"I like you, Axel. You're a very unusual person. You're so incredibly kind. But as you say, I'm not in love with you."

"That doesn't matter. I'm just proud to be having a child with you."

When Simon was three years old, Rebecca had married Thorsten Lindgren. Axel had sat with Simon on his lap at the wedding, watching the woman he loved, the woman who was the mother of his son, swear eternal loyalty to another man. It had been painful, but he had been happy for her sake.

Axel took a deep breath. He looked out through the windscreen, at the house where the man was he was going to kill lived. Rebecca had given meaning to his life by giving birth to Simon. And now Johan Karlström had taken that away from him.

His grip on the Glock tightened. Just as he was about to open the car door, his phone rang. He looked at the screen in surprise, and saw that it was Rebecca.

6

Goran Zelinsky was almost two metres tall, and was dressed in a dark padded jacket and a hat with earmuffs that framed his friendly, gentle face. They met in the middle of Liljeholmstorget and Vanessa suggested that they go inside the shopping mall to stop them freezing. They walked silently through the sliding door, past Wayne's Coffee, and Vanessa pointed to an empty bench next to a large potted plant in one of the walkways.

"Like I said, I'd like to ask you a few questions about Sabina Haddad," she said when they had sat down.

"Fire away," Goran said as he took off his leather gloves.

"How long has she worked for you?"

"Since January."

He tucked the gloves in the pockets of his padded coat.

"And she does a good job?"

He took his hat off and Vanessa was surprised to see that he was bald.

"She's excellent, actually. She's conscientious, punctual. She's never called in sick. She does extra shifts at weekends and in the evening if necessary. Speaks good Swedish. We have quite a high turnover of employees. The women move on, especially the good ones, but I really hope that Sabina will stay. That's why I was worried when you called. Is she under suspicion for anything? Has any of our clients contacted you?"

There was something very sympathetic, almost gentle, about Goran.

"No, not at all."

He looked at her quizzically.

"She's not earning extra doing… other work?"

"What do you mean?" Vanessa wondered.

He hesitated.

"We had a girl who earned extra money as… well, you know. She was offering some of our male clients extra services, if you get what I mean. Sabina has taken on some of her jobs. That's why I was worried."

"I'm sure there's nothing untoward about her approach to her job."

Goran seemed to relax slightly. He toyed idly with his hat.

"I don't really know what you're after, but Sabina is very popular. Monsieur Karlsson, whose cleaning and laundry we take care of, has never been happy before. He used to want to change his cleaner every other week until he met Sabina. Then he finally stopped phoning every Friday to ask if he could have someone different."

"Do you know if there was any particular reason?"

"Why do people like each other? God knows. He's a pensioner. A lonely older man."

Vanessa was about to ask how Sabina had applied to work for HomeClean Ltd, but stopped herself. She leaned forward and tilted her head . She rewound the conversation in her head. France. Belgium. French. Natasha. The flexible pins in Natasha's leg.

"Why 'Monsieur'?" she asked slowly.

He looked at her uncomprehendingly.

"How do you mean?"

"Why do you call him Monsieur Karlsson?"

"Oh, I see." Goran smiled. "That's what the girls who clean his flat call him. He's a bit of a Francophile. You know, berets, cigarillos, paintings of Napoleon on the wall."

Vanessa stared at him.

"Does Sabina speak French?"

"I don't know. That wouldn't be a crime, would it?" He burst out laughing.

7

"See you soon" Rebecca said, and hung up.

Axel could hardly comprehend what she had said. It was incredible. A miracle. Simon wasn't going to die. He was going to live. Axel dropped his phone and buried his face in his hands, then shouted out loud with delirious joy. Then he wept quietly for a while before trying his tears. He cast one last look at the house before putting the key in the ignition again. He was just about to start the engine and drive away when he caught a glimpse of movement outside the car.

When he turned his head he found himself looking straight into the barrel of a pistol. The next second the driver's door was yanked open, a powerful hand seized hold of his arm and dragged him out of the car with almost superhuman force. Axel was paralysed with fear as Nicolas Paredes pressed the pistol against the back of his head.

"Where's the gun?"

Axel couldn't speak. His chest was pressed against the car as Nicolas Paredes patted him down.

"Why are you watching my client?"

Axel stammered something incoherent. He was terrified, in shock.

"Who are you working for?"

Axel was struggling to get the words out, but all he managed to utter were guttural, unintelligible noises.

"W-w-working for?"

"You followed us from the hotel last week. Now you're here."

His nervousness and fear were making the whole thing worse. It couldn't end like this, with the bodyguard shooting him. Not now. Not when Simon was going to live.

"He ran over my son," Axel finally managed to say. "He almost killed Simon."

Nicolas looked at him questioningly.

"What did you say?"

"My son, Simon, he got run over." Nicolas was blinking uncomprehendingly. "By Johan Karlström," Axel added.

Nicolas opened his mouth to say something, but nothing came out.

"I don't know anything about your son. Or Johan running him over. What makes you think that?"

"It was the Range Rover," Axel said tersely.

Nicolas glanced quickly behind him.

"Can we sit in your car?" he asked, lowering his pistol.

Axel nodded. Nicolas kept the pistol in his hand as he walked round the car and opened the passenger door. He sat down, keeping the gun on his lap with his hand over it. Axel couldn't help noticing the obvious difference in his way of handling it. For Nicolas Paredes the pistol was almost like an extension of his body, he didn't seem to need to think about it being in his hand. Axel realised it would be ridiculous, an act of suicide, to reach for the Glock under his seat.

Nicolas looked at him calmly and asked him to tell him the whole story, right from the start. He seemed genuinely surprised. Axel stammered his way through the sequence of events, from the moment he and Simon went out to get some food. His eyes welled up as he told his story.

"I really am very sorry about what happened. But I don't understand why you've got it into your head that it was Johan?" Nicolas said when Axel finally fell silent.

"I s-s-saw the registration number. The car was registered in his name, and now he's replaced it with a new one, the same model. Why else would he have done that?"

"I use that car too. So does his wife. When was your son hit?"

"Friday, 8 November."

Nicolas leaned his head back and closed his eyes. He rubbed his eyes, and suddenly looked very tired. Axel interpreted the resigned look on his face as confirmation that Johan had been the driver.

"Why haven't you gone to the police?" Nicolas asked after a while.

"If he was even found guilty, he might have got a few months in prison, while my life would have been ruined. I can't go on living without my son. Up until just a couple of minutes ago I thought he was going to die. That was why I…"

Nicolas nodded.

"The gun under your seat. Can you slowly reach down and put it between the steering-wheel and the windscreen?"

Axel looked at Nicolas in surprise, and Nicolas smiled back at him.

"H-how did you know?"

"You keep looking between your seat and my gun. You don't have to be a genius to figure out what you're thinking."

Axel reached under his seat, got hold of the pistol and put it where Nicolas had told him. He glanced at the bodyguard, who was sitting motionless as he stared out into the darkness.

His shocked reaction when Axel had told him about Simon had been genuine. There was no doubt about that.

"How is your son now?" Nicolas asked after a while.

"I've just been told that he's regained consciousness. He's going to survive."

"I'm very happy for you." Nicolas looked Axel in the eye.

In spite of his physical strength, and the rough way he had dragged him out of the car, Axel thought there was something gentle and sensitive about the man.

"I need to ask you for something." Axel looked curiously at Nicolas, but remained silent. "I want you to give me your ID-card."

"What for?"

"Because I say so," Nicolas said, with sudden sharpness in his voice.

Axel reached for his wallet at once, opened it, pulled out his ID and handed it over. Nicolas held it up in front of him for several seconds before handing it back.

"Okay, Karl Axel Grystad, I think you should go to the police and report what happened. Don't come round here anymore." He opened the car door and disappeared through the gate towards the large house.

8

Hamza spread the tatty mattress out on the floor, got the blanket and laid it on top of him. There was a cold draft from the window, which didn't fit properly. But he was used to it, and the draft didn't really bother him. Heat was worse. After his years in Syria and Iraq, he knew what heat and thirst could do to a person.

He smiled when he thought about how happy Stig had been when he offered to drive him to see his daughter next weekend. The old man had wrapped his arms round his neck, pressing his thin body against his and whispering: "Thank you, thank you, thank you."

Hamza pulled out the laptop he had hidden behind the radiator in case anyone broke into the flat. He switched it on without much hope. He had done the same thing every day for four months. He logged into the gmail account. His jaw dropped with surprise when he saw that there was a new file in the drafts folder. Someone had made an electronic dead-drop – writing an email that never gets sent, and which therefore can't be traced. With his hand shaking, he moved the cursor to the folder. Clicked to open it.

A time and a place.

Nothing more.

He had been waiting so long, he had started to wonder if they would ever contact him. He had wondered if he was the only one left, or if they had forgotten him. His doubts had nagged away at him, making him consider fleeing while there was still time. If the security service had caught the others, then he ought to be next on the list. But they were evidently still out there. Free. Still capable. And now they wanted to get hold of him. That could only mean one thing: it was getting closer.

The hour of vengeance was getting closer.

He closed the laptop and put it down in the floor. He knew he wasn't going to get any sleep for several hours.

Not after that.

"Thank you, God," he muttered, closing his eyes.

His life would have meaning again.

Finally, he was going to die a martyr.

PART V

1

Hamza was stamping his feet to keep warm. Groups of students walked past him on their way to the metro station at Stockholm University. It was Thursday afternoon and the area of grass that separated the various institutes had turned into green-brown sludge. He scanned his surroundings again, trying to identify the person he had arranged to meet.

"Peace be with you, brother."

Hamza spun round, and found himself looking into a pair of dark eyes. He returned the greeting, grasped the outstretched hand, and estimated that the man was in his fifties. His head was bald, birdlike, and sat on top of a tall, thin body.

The man gestured towards Frescati Hall, and they walked side by side along the tarmac path. He pulled out a packet of cigarettes and held it up towards Hamza with a questioning expression. Hamza shook his head. The man stopped, took his glove off and lit a cigarette with a 7-Eleven lighter.

"My name is Farid," he said, white smoke billowing from his mouth.

Unique, Hamza thought. A suitable name for the man who had finally called him to take revenge and die.

There were fewer students around them now, and the few who remained were heading in the same direction as them. To his left Hamza could see the Museum of Natural History, and from beyond the impressive building came the noise of traffic. In front of them was a large meadow. There was a hill at the end of the meadow, then blocks of 1960s buildings. They turned onto a different tarmac path.

"I had started to think you were never going to get in touch," Hamza said.

Farid glanced at him with a smile.

"We've had a few problems," he said. "But we're ready now."

"Tear them to pieces with gunfire and bombs, or stab them with a knife."

The words Hamza was quoting were those of the dead ISIS-leader, Abu Bakr al-Baghdadi.

"The problem is that the kuffars have got used to things, the terror effect has diminished," Farid said, exhaling smoke. "But it is precisely as Abu Bakr said, that one attack in the West is worth a thousand times more than one in the Middle East. But the small attacks that our brothers and sisters have carried out no longer have the political impact we hope for. We need to think bigger if we are to defeat the Crusaders."

Hamza shared his analysis.

They passed through a tunnel and carried on up the road on the other side.

"What will my role be?"

"One thing at a time. I appreciate that you are keen, but you must have patience."

"I have felt very alone."

"I understand that too. But you are no longer alone."

A large sign said *Campus Lappis*. They climbed several flights of steps, and came to a small square with a pizzeria called The Professor, a small ICA supermarket and a sushi restaurant. After yet another flight of steps they turned right. On the ground floor of the blocks of residences Hamza could see laundry-rooms and shared kitchens where students were cooking food together. The majority of them were exchange students rather than ethnic Swedes. They reached a large courtyard surrounded by six-storey apartment blocks. Hamza read the street sign: *Professorsslingan*. At its centre was a small, tarmac football pitch and a climbing frame. A large pride flag was hanging from one balcony, and there was a strong smell of cannabis coming from one open window.

"Here," Farid said, pointing towards a door numbered 37. He pulled out a keycard and held it against the reader. They took the lift up to the fifth floor, got out, and Farid unlocked the flat. He let Hamza go in first before closing the door behind them. It was a four-room apartment, with three bedrooms, a spacious kitchen and a balcony that looked out on the football pitch. Farid immediately opened the balcony door, sat down on the sofa in the living room, and lit a cigarette.

"This is where you'll all live. At first we were thinking of getting an apartment near Järva, but you're closer to the target here. And you'll blend in with all the exchange students."

That was good thinking. Besides, the risk of random police checks was lower here than in the crime-ridden suburbs.

"How many of us will there be?" Hamza asked.

Farid held up his hand and folded in his thumb and forefinger.

"Three."

"When?"

"I mentioned that we have had problems. So we have been forced to think again, adjust certain details, but within a few weeks, God willing, we will have struck."

"What sort of problems?"

Farid's face darkened.

"Partly economic. But we have also encountered traitors. Weak apologies for Muslims whose faith isn't as strong as yours and mine. For that reason I am obliged to be secretive, even with you, brother. Until it is time, no one must know too much, not even you."

Hamza thought that sounded wise. He would have to be patient, even if his body was itching now that he had finally been contacted. He wondered where Farid had been, and if he, like Hamza, had fought for the Caliphate.

"When do you want me to move in?"

"Immediately," Farid said and got to his feet, before handing over the keycard and keys to the apartment to Hamza. Then he put his hand in the pocket of his jeans, pulled out a folded sheet of paper in which there was a small, brass-coloured key. It looked like it fitted a padlock.

"From now on our communication will mostly take place via this address. Go there this evening. Then you can move your things in here."

Hamza studied the sheet of paper and saw that there was writing on it. He memorised the address before he asked for Farid's lighter and set fire to the note.

"I'll leave the flat first, you can follow in fifteen minutes. It's unnecessary for us to be seen together again."

Farid tucked his lighter in his jeans pocket and walked out to the hall. He opened the door.

"I'm sorry about what happened to you and your family," he said in Arabic.

"We have all had to make sacrifices," Hamza said.

"They're going to pay for it."

"If God wills it."

Farid held out his hand. Hamza grasped it and they looked each other in the eye before Farid carefully closed the door.

2

Molly was lying curled up on the sofa in the living room, dressed in dark blue leggings. The fire was crackling cosily, and her father's Norwegian elkhound Joik was snoring on the floor in front of her. The sound of axe-chopping out in the yard stopped abruptly and Molly looked up from John Steinbeck's *The Grapes of Wrath* when the outside door opened a short while later. Her father, Robert, stamped the snow from his shoes on the hall mat, muttered something, then put the logs down.

"Are we going, then?" Molly asked, putting her book down.

It was just before seven in the evening, and the sun had gone down a few minutes after one o'clock. The temperature was ten degrees below freezing.

They crossed the dark, snow-covered yard towards the four-wheel-drive Chevrolet pickup.

"Can I drive?" Molly asked.

"Sure."

"Really? What if I drive us off the road?"

Her father smiled.

"If it makes you happy, that feels like a small price to pay."

"Even if we crash?"

"Even if we crash."

She put her foot on the step below the door, got into the driver's seat and leaned forward to familiarise herself with the various buttons and controls. She adjusted the back of the seat, then started the engine. She watched as the farmstead disappeared from view in the rear-view mirror. The ICA supermarket in Kiruna was ten kilometres away.

"Doesn't it get lonely?"

"A bit. But I'm used to it now. It was worse in the first few years after your mum died."

"Were you disappointed that I didn't move back home then?"

"No, Molly. You must never think that. Some people like living this way, others don't. You chose to leave and find your own path. You weren't happy, and then it makes sense to move somewhere else."

"I should have come to the funeral."

"Everyone's free to make their own decisions, sweetheart."

"Do you miss her?"

Her father nodded, then gazed out into the darkness.

"Every day."

"I used to think she was a bit difficult."

"The difficult ones are the best ones."

Silence descended, as it often did between them. It had always been like that. But the silence wasn't oppressive. During the previous few days they hadn't mentioned Molly's mother Siriwan except in passing, and Molly had yet broached the really serious questions, the ones she wanted answers to. The questions that had first arisen when she was growing up, and which she had carried with her in recent years.

The bare trees stood out as silhouettes by the side of the road. They hadn't yet seen another car.

"Can I ask something?" Molly said, gripping the steering-wheel tighter. "Did you never notice the way people used to look at the pair of you? How they whispered? All that pointing and laughing?"

"I'd have to have been deaf and blind not to. But it didn't really bother me. My life was lonely. None of the women here would have me. And when I saw your mum, I fell in love."

Behind them a car was approaching, its headlamps lighting up the inside of the car and her father's face.

"But she didn't love you," Molly exclaimed. She bit her tongue. She'd blurted out the words without thinking, and was now worried she'd upset her father. "Sorry, I didn't mean that."

"Your mum chose between selling sex to different men every night, living on a mattress on the floor and still never earning enough to feed herself because she had to send money home to your grandparents. Or coming to Sweden with me. A secure life. No more going hungry. No more men. That was the choice she had. And I was faced with the choice between living alone, or inviting her into my home."

"She was a whore."

Molly felt tears welling up in her eyes, and wiped her cheek against her shoulder.

"I don't want you to call her that. She was your mum. And I loved her."

There was no anger in his voice, just resignation and disappointment.

The car behind them was still there, it showed no sign of wanting to overtake them.

"How could you love her? She was mean. Her whole existence centred around making me beautiful so I could marry a rich man. Her only plan in life was to capitalise on my appearance. She hated it when you took me out into the forest or onto the lake to go fishing. She said it was dangerous, but it was really only because she didn't want my skin to be spoiled. Bloody hell, Dad. That's messed up."

"I didn't share her views on that, you know that."

"Did you know that she was unfaithful to you?"

"Yes."

"And you still loved her?"

"More than anything. After you."

Molly shook her head forlornly.

The Luossavaara and Kiirunanvaara mountains rose up like dark shadows on either side of Kiruna. The city was located north of the Arctic Circle, and every single one of its twenty thousand or so inhabitants was connected in some way to the mine that produced seventy-five thousand tons of iron ore every day.

The mine was the nerve-centre of the city, its beating heart, its reason for being. Like most people, Robert worked there too, and had done since he was a teenager.

The sky above them was lit up by the lights of the city. It was surrounded on all sides by wilderness. Mountains. Forests. Snow.

"See how beautiful this is?" he said. "Like an oasis of civilisation in the middle of the wilderness."

Molly got a trolley and was struck by how satisfying the everyday act of filling it with things was. Almost meditative. During her years in Barcelona and the past few months in Stockholm, she could count the number of times she had cooked a meal from scratch on the fingers of one hand. She either ate out, or had a takeaway delivered. She was struck by a happy memory of her time with Jamal. They got into the habit of doing a big shop for the whole week every Sunday in Sundbyberg. Mostly junk food. Ready-meals and rich sauces. Things they could cook quickly in a frying pan. But those shared excursions made them feel grownup, like a family.

Molly stared at her full trolley and realised why she had avoided spending any time in supermarkets.

It had been after one of her shopping trips with Jamal, when they were putting the groceries in the boot out in the car-park, that the car containing the two masked men had appeared. Molly had been standing with her back to them when she heard the two shots. She spun round and felt the bullet whistle past her head, then threw herself down behind the car. Jamal's motionless body lay on the tarmac. She had been convinced that the shooter was going to get out and kill her too, but the car had disappeared, tyres squealing. People came running towards her. Molly had got up and stumbled away in confusion. She went home to her apartment and, almost in a trance, put her cash, valuables and makeup in a cabin bag. She went to the Central Station and bought a ticket to Copenhagen. She kept heading south by train until she reached Barcelona.

She was roused from her memories when her father put a large bag of dog food in the trolley, then turned and disappeared into another aisle again.

Molly saw a man over by the vegetable counter waving discreetly at her. It took her a few seconds to realise that it was Thomas. She felt herself start to panic. What was he doing here? He had promised to leave her alone. She looked around quickly, making sure that her father was out of sight, then went over to him. His arm was bandaged, his face swollen. She stopped next to him, grabbed a bag and slowly filled it with apples.

"I need to talk to you. Tomorrow. Come to the Scandic Ferrum hotel tomorrow afternoon."

Molly shook her head desperately.

"Forget it," she whispered. "I did what you asked. You promised I wouldn't…"

"You have to," he hissed, still without looking at her.

"Why should I?"

"Because your country needs you. And if that isn't enough,

then for the same reason as last time. Because otherwise I'll show your father what you've been getting up to in the past few years," he said, nodding towards her father, who was slowly heading towards them.

Thomas walked away discreetly. Molly tied a knot in the bag and met her dad at the trolley.

"Who was that?" he asked.

"Just a tourist, one of those hikers," Molly replied nonchalantly.

"Did he fall down a mountain or something?"

Her dad smiled as Thomas limped off towards the tills.

"Something like that."

Molly made space for the apples in the full trolley.

"Apples? I thought you hated them?"

"Things change, Dad."

3

After leaving the flat in Lappkärrsberget and going to Torsplan and signing in at the 24-hour gym, Fitness World, under a false name, Hamza had wandered around the dark, wet streets of the city centre. As agreed, he had bought a gym bag so as not to attract attention at the gym, and had filled it with newspaper. He had noticed a change in himself. He saw the people in the shops and cafés and on the streets as enemies. Targets. The coming attack would wipe out their complacent, self-assured attitude. He would show them what it was like not to feel safe anywhere on the planet.

Not far from the places in the Mediterranean where Swedes went on holiday, thousands of Muslim women and children were being kept imprisoned in large camps, in terrible conditions. Guarded by Kurdish monsters. Without access to clean water. People whose only dream had been to live under sharia law in a country of their own. The Caliphate had by no means been perfect, far from it. But just as with every new nation, a few sacrifices were required. He didn't support everything their leaders had done, but he knew they were wise men who wanted the best for all Muslims.

He decided to have a quick meal at Kebab House on Vasagatan. Outside the window the crowds began to thin and the amount of traffic diminished.

Hamza thought about Stig, and how he would have to get in touch to postpone their arranged excursion to Jönköping. Was Stig an enemy too? Not exactly. It was important to remember that they too had been created by God. There were many Swedes he didn't wish any harm to. But they were part of a system, of the Western imperialism that had oppressed Muslims for centuries. It had started with the Crusades, when Europeans travelled down to the Middle East to bathe in the blood of Muslims, and continued with the conquests of the colonial powers to grab the oil and natural resources, right up to today's aerial and drone bombardments and attempts to wipe out Muslims in what Western leaders called "the War on Terror".

At the table next to his sat two teenage girls with rouged cheeks and heavily made-up eyes, each eating a kebab. In Raqqa they would have been whipped if they had left the house tarted up like that. Perhaps the punishment was too harsh, but the law was there to be followed. Sharia existed for the sake of humanity. How else was a society supposed to stick together? And who possessed greater knowledge than the learned men who were appointed to make sure that the Word of God was followed? If Westerners wanted to let their daughters dress like prostitutes and behave like whores, that was their business. Hamza didn't care. But they had gone to the Middle East to wipe out the newly-established Islamic State, and to stop Muslims who wanted to live according to the Koran, so they would get a taste of the same medicine. It was war. And in war soldiers weren't the only ones to die. Hamza, of all people, knew that. He wiped his mouth, looked at the time and decided to walk back to Torsplan.

The staff in the gym had gone home by the time Hamza pressed his finger against the reader to the left of the door. He entered an airlock, repeated the procedure and tapped in a four-digit code. He headed towards the changing-room, and fleeting smile crossed his lips when he saw that the padlock that had been described to him was hanging from locker number 11. The first letter of the alphabet, twice: AA. "*Allahu Akbar*, God is most great," he whispered, then quickly checked that he was alone before inserting the key and turning it.

A black gym bag, almost identical to the one he was carrying on his shoulder, lay inside.

He glanced behind him once more, opened the zip and put his hand inside. His fingertips touched metal and he realised it was a pistol. Hamza closed the bag without any further examination of the contents, then put the bag he had brought with him inside the locker before closing and locking it. Now all he had to do was fetch his few possessions and move them to the flat in Lappkärrsberget, then he was ready.

4

Vanessa was sitting right at the back of Thelin's café on Odengatan. After making sure that Celine got off to school okay, she had decided to brave the morning darkness to get some time to think through her next move.

It was Friday, and the tables around her were empty. Apart from a couple of high-school kids by the window and two white-haired pensioners sitting opposite each other, she was alone. Hans Karlsson, the man Sabina Haddad cleaned for, had confirmed over the phone that she spoke fluent French. The talkative pensioner had said he thought her accent was Belgian, so Vanessa had decided to contact Mikael Kask. There were too many lies in Sabina's backstory for her to ignore them. And Natasha's story didn't make sense either, she had to admit that. She had to get Mikael to realise that they risked missing other lines of inquiry if they continued to focus exclusively on Rikard Olsson.

Mikael answered on the second ring.

"Good morning, Vanessa," he panted.

She raised her eyebrows.

"I hope you're out running."

"Correct."

"Well, that's better than the alternative. I need to talk to you."

"Come and see in my office later today."

"Perfect," she said, and ended the call.

She gathered together Natasha and Sabina's Migration Office documents and put them in the correct folders, then pulled out a third folder about Molly Blom.

The luxury escort Nicolas had asked her to look into had no criminal record. She was mentioned briefly in an old report from the Criminal Intelligence Service regarding an abandoned surveillance operation. She was suspected of being involved with a known gang-member who was later executed outside an ICA supermarket in Sundbyberg. But that was all.

Nicolas was due to show up anytime. Vanessa thought about their meeting on Monday, and her reaction when he told her he had slept with Erica Karlström. Jealousy was probably too strong a word, but it had bothered her. Naturally, Nicolas was free to do whatever he wanted, seeing as she was the one who had kept her distance and put an end to whatever they had had. Even so, it annoyed her. Was there really any reason to throw that business with Erika Karlström in her face? Even if Vanessa was the one who asked, did he really have to tell her everything?

"What are you thinking about?"

She had been so immersed in her own thoughts that she hadn't noticed he was suddenly standing in front of her.

"Just some idiot I met the other week." She had never seen Nicolas looking so elegant before, he was dressed in a dark suit, leather gloves and black overcoat. "Are you going to a graduation ball?"

Nicolas looked down at his clothes and smiled.

"I've just dropped Johan off at the office, he likes me to be dressed smartly. Have you got what I asked for?"

She pushed the file across the table. Nicolas took his gloves off and looked quickly through the contents.

"Can I take this?"

Vanessa nodded. Nicolas drummed his fingers on the back of the chair. She thought about asking if he'd like to sit down, he was obviously waiting, but instead she began to gather her things together.

"I have to go," she said, stuffing the other two folders in her handbag.

"I can give you a lift."

"You don't even know where I'm going."

"I've got a few hours to myself before I have to pick Johan up, so unless you're going to Germany or something, I can drop you off."

"The coffee here is good, you can sit here and pass the time."

Nicolas seemed disappointed, even if he did his best to hide it.

"I'll do that, then."

Vanessa got up from the table. Did he have to be so nice, even though she was so dismissive, almost rude?

"See you," she said.

A few hours later Vanessa opened the door to Mikael Kask's office just as her mobile rang. She told Samer where she was and suggested that he join them. She sat down, and noticed a glass containing a greenish liquid on her boss's desk.

"What's that?" she asked.

"Celery juice. Try it," he said encouragingly. Vanessa hesitantly raised the glass to her lips, took a sip and pulled a face. "It's really healthy. Everyone's drinking it these days."

"Are you one of those it-girls?" Vanessa teased.

Mikael smiled and reached for the glass, raised it in a toast to Vanessa, and drank the contents down in one.

There was a knock on the door. Samer came in, raising one hand in greeting. He sat down on the second visitor's chair.

Vanessa put the two folders on the desk. Mikael glanced quickly through them.

"Sabina Haddad was Natasha's friend."

The two men stared blankly at her.

"You haven't questioned her?"

Mikael looked at Samer, who shook his head.

"The couple Natasha lived with mentioned her," Samer said.

"Sabina Haddad told me that she arrived in Sweden on 13 August 2015." She looked from one man to the other. "That isn't right. She arrived the same day as Natasha. And they stuck together in Sweden, right up until Natasha moved in with me."

"What do you think that might mean?" Samer asked.

"I don't know. But that isn't the only thing Sabina has lied about."

The atmosphere in the room was gradually changing. Both Samer and Mikael were looking at Vanessa intently.

"She speaks fluent French. A fact she kept quiet about. Maybe it doesn't mean anything, but I thought I should let you both know."

Neither of them said anything. Mikael looked down at his desk.

"So she's lying?" Samer sighed. "A refugee girl who tells lies. Is that what you've got? Let me tell you something – refugees lie. You of all people ought to know that. Not because they're bad, but so they can stay in Sweden."

He leaned back and looked up at the ceiling.

"We've talked about this, Vanessa," Mikael said wearily, patting the folder about Natasha. "I want to catch the person who murdered them. But we do that by focusing on Rikard Olsson. All the evidence suggests that Natasha was in the wrong place at the wrong time.

Rikard Olsson was a police officer. He lived under constant threat. He had enemies, people who are very prone to resorting to violence."

Samer cleared his throat to interrupt, but Mikael held his hand up towards him.

"This girl, Natasha," Mikael went on, more gently. "She lied to you. Bloody hell, Vanessa. You need to let go of her. I don't know what you think you can get out of Sabina Haddad. But the fact that she lied to you about her knowledge of French isn't enough to change anything."

"I'm not saying you should arrest her and charge her with the murders of Natasha and Rikard Olsson. I'm saying she's lying about things she has no reason to lie about. She's pretending to know Natasha less well than she actually did. There could be something in their background, something Natasha knew about her. Boy trouble, maybe, or an argument about money. Can you check out her alibi, or at least talk to her?"

Mikael Kask leaned back and folded his arms.

"It sounds harsh, but Natasha was collateral damage."

Vanessa kept her eyes fixed on him for a few moments, then snatched the files and stood up. She heard Mikael calling her name behind her.

5

The city of Kiruna was moving. Because the seam of iron ore ran beneath the centre of the city, the decision had been taken to move the city three kilometres to the east, or else the built-up area risked collapsing into the mine. The thousands of Kiruna inhabitants who were affected included both the living and the dead. The remains of the dead were being moved to a new cemetery. The living had been bought out and given new homes by the mining company, LKAB.

Houses that were considered of cultural and historical value were lifted onto specially constructed vehicles from the Netherlands and rolled away. Molly wandered around the city centre that would soon no longer exist. No matter what she felt about it, Kiruna was undeniably her city. Some things in life were transitory, but the streets of your childhood shouldn't be, she thought. Not that she harboured any particularly fond memories of Kiruna from when she was growing up, but it was as if she saw it all in a new light now. The cinema. The cafés. It wasn't Barcelona, it wasn't London, but these streets were hers.

And now everything was going to be flattened.

She wandered down to the well-stocked bookshop on Meschplan. The shelves were overflowing with local authors, international bestsellers and modern classics. She picked two of the latter, Ernest Hemingway's *A Farewell to Arms* and Isabel Allende's *The House of the Spirits*. As she said thank you and took the brown paper bag, she noticed with amusement that her Norrland accent had made a temporary comeback.

The Scandic Ferrum hotel lay practically next door to the civic centre, Folkets hus. Molly could feel her body getting nervous as she reluctantly crossed the square towards the entrance to the hotel. She hoped Thomas just wanted answers to ask a few questions, even if she realised that was wishful thinking. He had evidently gone to considerable trouble to find her. The lobby was full of men and women in colourful traditional Sami costumes.

Thomas was sitting in an armchair close to the reception desk, and got up with an effort when he caught sight of Molly.

"Let's go up to my room."

Molly followed him to the lifts. They went up to the fifth floor in silence, then got out and walked along a long corridor. The fitted carpet muffled the sound of their steps. Thomas stopped outside room 525, pulled out a white keycard and held it to the reader, which turned green. He held the door open and let Molly go in first.

Outside the window the mountains and fells were lit up beautifully by the setting sun.

"This view is just incredible," Thomas said.

"A shame it's only light for an hour or so each day, then," Molly said. "What do you want with me? What are you doing here?"

She put the bag containing her books down on the bed. Thomas picked it up, checked the contents, then put it back down.

"I need to ask you to put your mobile in the bathroom," he said. Molly rolled her eyes, opened the bathroom door, put her phone on the washbasin, then went and stood in front of him.

"I need to pat you down."

"Are you serious?"

He nodded and Molly held her arms out.

"Watch out, or you'll trigger the bomb I'm carrying round my stomach."

Thomas grimaced as he bent down to feel between her legs. I hope it hurts badly, Molly thought. She could see the irony of the situation. Her hopes back when she first met him, that the two of them would end up alone together in a hotel room, had come true at last. But this wasn't the Grand Hotel in Stockholm, it was the Scandic Ferrum in Kiruna, and the way he was touching her body was anything but romantic.

When Thomas was finished he rubbed his ribs and gestured to Molly to sit down on the armchair by the window. He sank down onto the bed. He looked at her seriously for a few seconds, then crossed his legs and began to talk.

"I need your help," he said.

"I've already helped you, and you promised to get rid of the pictures. But you lied. Why should I let you trick me again?"

"Molly, I don't want to blackmail you. But you're not giving me any choice. We need your help. You're Swedish, and your country needs you."

"Really? So tell me. What's this all about?"

"Obviously I can't go into detail. But the alternative is that I pay a visit to your father and tell him who his daughter really is."

The loneliness Molly felt was suffocating.

"Why don't you contact someone else? How come I'm the only person who can help you?"

Thomas seemed to be struggling to hold back his irritation.

"Because the person we want you to meet is a client of yours. Someone who trusts you."

"Who?"

"You'll find that out in due course. I want you to come back to Stockholm with me this evening."

"That's impossible," Molly exclaimed. "How do you think I could explain that to my dad?"

"Tell him whatever you like," he snapped. "It's hardly the first time you've lied to him."

He calmed down, but that wasn't enough for Molly. It was becoming increasingly obvious that behind the charm and the polished exterior there was something deeply troubling. Something unpleasant that she wanted to steer well clear of. But in spite of her aversion to Thomas she did feel a duty to Sweden, to do as he said. She had done her research. From articles in foreign newspapers she had realised that it wasn't unusual for different countries' security services to blackmail young women to get information. Besides, she didn't exactly have a choice.

"Go home and say your goodbyes. The plane leaves at 18.30, we'll meet at the gate," he said, handing her a SAS plane ticket with her name on it.

6

Vanessa put the folders on the roof of her BMW and leaned back against the car door. She felt confused. Neither Mikael nor Samer shared her belief that Sabina Haddad ought to be investigated more closely. Quite the reverse, in fact. To make matters worse, they had made her start to doubt herself. Was she losing her grip?

Samer walked past with his gym bag. He looked at her warily.

"Are you okay?"

He put the bag down on the ground and walked up to her. A police car drove past. Vanessa watched the rear lights rather vacantly until they disappeared round a corner.

"You know what the worst thing is?" she said slowly. "It's that it was the pair of you who made me realise that there was something that didn't make sense about Natasha's background in the first place. You knocked her off her pedestal. That broken leg. And the fact that her dad didn't appear to exist. That she was older than she had told me."

"So what do you think, Vanessa?"

"I think she knew something that cost her her life."

Samer raised his eyebrows.

"What?"

"Something about Sabina Haddad. Or about the man outside the ICA supermarket in Bergshamra."

"Such as what?"

Vanessa bit her tongue. She wasn't going to say anything about her suspicions. Not yet. Samer would think she was mad.

"I don't know. But maybe she found something out and confronted Sabina."

"How do you mean?" Samer asked with a trace of a smile.

"There's been a long, terrible war in Syria. War creates secrets, loyalties, hatreds. And that doesn't vanish simply because someone comes to Sweden."

Samer looked at her for a few moments before nodding.

"You could be right, but I'm not saying that you are. I'm not as convinced as the others that Rikard Olsson was the target. I agree that it's problematic that Sabina Haddad seems to have lied about apparently unnecessary things. Knowing French is one thing, but also that she had known Natasha longer than she said, that they arrived on the same day."

A drop of water hit Vanessa's cheek. A mixture of snow and rain began to fall, and Samer hoisted his bag onto his shoulder.

"Where are you going?" she asked.

"I was thinking of going to the gym."

"I can drive you to save you getting wet. Jump in."

Samer told her the address. Vanessa reversed out, turned the car and set off towards Scheelegatan. The sleet was getting heavier. On the pavements people were seeking shelter in doorways and shops. She leaned forward to see better, and increased the speed of the windscreen wipers.

Behind the window of the gym people were running on treadmills. Vanessa stopped the car and put the handbrake on, but left the engine running.

"See you," Samer said, pulling his hood up over his cap.

"Yup," Vanessa said.

She watched as Samer ran, hunched over, through the slush towards the entrance. She started blankly at the umbrellas hurrying past. She wasn't going to let go of Sabina Haddad, not yet, at least.

Instead of turning right onto St Eriksgatan, she turned left towards the Essinge motorway. She switched the Bluetooth on and connected her phone to the car's speakers as she headed south. Celine answered almost immediately.

"What are you doing?" Vanessa asked.

"Reading your horoscope."

She couldn't help smiling. There was something sweet about the fact that Celine read her horoscope as well every day, even though she had no interest at all in star signs.

"What does tomorrow look like for this poor old Leo then?"

"In summary – you're not going to meet the love of your life. But you might have luck if you're a gambler."

"I'll try to stay away from men and buy a scratchcard. I can live with that. Was school okay?"

"Fine."

"Good. I'll be home around seven, we can go and get something to eat and then settle down on the sofa to watch a film, if you like?"

"Sure."

Half an hour later Vanessa was driving through Rågsved. When she reached Sabina Haddad's street she had to park a short distance away because a removals truck was parked on the path where she had left the car last time. A couple of removal men were busy carrying a plastic-wrapped sofa in through the door. Vanessa reached into the back seat for her umbrella. Just as she was about to get out of the car, she caught sight of Sabina. The young woman was dressed in a thick padded coat, and was heading out of the building towards the car. Vanessa was about to let her know she was there, but ducked down instead to stop her seeing her. She waited a little while before slowly sitting up again.

Sabina had passed the car and was heading towards the metro station. Vanessa opened the door and put her umbrella up. She opened the boot and dug out the bag containing a change of clothes that she always kept there, rummaged through the items until she found a black hat, then pulled that on her head before closing the boot and setting off after Sabina.

7

Hamza was standing in Stig's hallway, completely drenched, with rain trickling down his face.

"Come in," Stig said cheerily, gesturing with his hand.

Hamza shook his head. He stayed on the hall mat to save him wetting the floor with his squelching shoes.

"It's going to be so wonderful to see Petra again. I can't thank you enough for your offer."

Hamza squirmed, and couldn't bring himself to look Stig in the eye. Only now did the old man realise that something was wrong.

"Is everything okay?"

"I'm not going to be able to drive you tomorrow."

Stig looked at him uncomprehendingly, as if he was expecting him to start laughing and say he was joking. As the seconds ticked past it seemed to dawn on him that Hamza was serious. His disappointment showed in every pore of the old man's face.

"Has something happened?"

Stig leaned against the wall.

"My aunt had died. I have to go to the funeral," Hamza lied.

It was impossible to tell if Stig believed him. His gaze was glazed and unclear.

"Sorry."

Stig nodded quickly. He took a step towards Hamza, then stopped, evidently at something of a loss.

"Of course you must go to the funeral," he said. "I'm sorry for your loss. I didn't mean to make you feel bad. I was just looking forward to seeing her again."

"Maybe we can go another time," Hamza said.

Stig smiled without any enthusiasm.

"Don't worry, Hamza. I have no right to expect anything. I understand that you're busy."

Hamza wanted to get out of the flat as quickly as possible. Away. Forget Stig and focus on what was important. His mission. That was why he had to erase Stig from his life. Since Farid had contacted him, the circumstances had changed. Not least for Stig's sake, he had to step back from helping him. Their friendship could ruin his life. Hamza couldn't take any risks. The police and journalists would look under every stone once everything was over. But it was as if the old man's sadness had left him incapable of action.

Hamza felt behind him for the door-handle, found it and opened the door.

"See you," he said.

Stig raised his hand in a wave.

The underground train rushed past Slussen towards Gamla stan. The lights of the city reflected off the dark water now that the rain had suddenly stopped. Vanessa was at the other end of the carriage from Sabina. She was doing her utmost not to look at the young woman in case she was spotted, but from the glimpses she had got she couldn't escape noticing that Sabina seemed nervous.

She kept looking round. It was as if she was a completely different person to the calm, relaxed woman Vanessa had met earlier. Was she scared of something?

Sabina had lied about the date she arrived in Sweden, about her close friendship with Natasha, and the fact that for some unexplained reason she spoke French. What was Vanessa not seeing?

The train pulled into Gamla stan station. A gang of youngsters were standing smoking on the platform. One of them spat in the direction of the train as it started to move, and the woman just across from Vanessa looked alarmed.

Vanessa got ready to get off, assuming that Sabina was going to get off at the Central Station, but she didn't move as the carriage filled with passengers. When they were between the Central Station and Hötorget Sabina took out her mobile and held it to her ear.

She said a few words, nodded, then hung up.

When the train pulled into the station at Odenplan she stood up, pushed her way through the crowded carriage and got off. Vanessa waited until the doors were just about to close before getting out. She caught sight of Sabina's back in the sea of people heading towards the escalators.

Vanessa decided it was better to be safe than sorry. Following someone on your own was practically impossible, the police always worked in teams of at least two people for that very reason. She pulled out her phone and called Samir's number. She quickly explained the situation, where she was, and said she needed his help. To Vanessa's relief, he didn't ask any questions, just said he was on his way.

Sabina took the exit to the left, and made her way up the steps. Vanessa stopped and looked down, pretending to look for something in her handbag when she realised that Sabina had stopped at the top of the stairs. Had she been seen?

When she dared to look up again, Sabina was gone. Vanessa hurried to the top of the steps and looked around, and was convinced that she had lost her until she spotted her again outside Burger King a short distance away on Odengatan. Skirting round a large puddle, she set off after her. Because there were fewer people in the streets, she was able to keep her distance and reduce the risk of being seen. Sabina headed down the hill, past the Hard Rock Café, and stopped at the crossing on Sveavägen. Vanessa waited by the Central Library. Sabina took out her mobile again. The call lasted no more than a few seconds, then she put it back in her pocket.

The lights turned green. Sabina crossed Sveavägen, then turned right immediately to go to the bus stop in the middle of Odengatan. Vanessa followed her slowly. If Sabina was going to catch a bus, obviously it was going to be much harder to follow her without being seen. Vanessa checked her mobile. Samer was going to call her when he got close to Odenplan.

She heard footsteps behind her. She was about to turn round when she caught a glimpse of movement out of the corner of her eye.

The next moment everything went black.

8

Nicolas knocked on the door of Johan Karlström's office. He waited until Johan called "Come in", then pushed the door open. Johan was tapping at the keyboard of his MacBook on the large mahogany desk. He took no notice of Nicolas, who stopped on the dark fitted carpet.

There was something odd about the whole situation. Ever since Nicolas had failed to bring back his mobile phone, Johan had been very quiet. He hoped that was because of what had happened with Molly Berg, and not for any other reason. Nicolas had reported it to AOS Risk Group, and had been told that he had acted correctly. As a result, the matter was considered closed.

"You wanted to see me?" Nicolas eventually said, and Johan raised one hand towards him to stop him. He lowered it again and continued to attack the keyboard with rapid, firm movements.

"There," he finally said, closing the screen.

He looked at Nicolas expressionlessly until the silence was interrupted by his mobile phone ringing. Johan pressed *answer*, then held his phone out to Nicolas.

"There," he said happily. "For you."

Nicolas took the phone, glanced quickly at the screen and noted the call was from a British number.

A male voice asked in English if he was talking to Nicolas Paredes.

"Yes."

Johan was watching Nicolas with a thin smile.

"Your employment with Johan Karlström is terminated with immediate effect."

Nicolas looked at Johan, who was leaning back in his chair with his hands folded across his stomach.

"Understood. I'll head back to London tomorrow."

"No need. AOS Risk Group is no longer in need of your services."

"What did you say?"

The man patiently repeated what he had said. Nicolas realised what had happened. Through Gambler, Johan Karlström was a significant client of the security company, generating income worth tens of millions of pounds each year. Johan must have given them an ultimatum that Nicolas should not merely be transferred, but dismissed from the company altogether. Nicolas clicked to end the call and put the phone down on the desk.

Johan Karlström was looking at him with amusement.

"You should have asked my permission before you fucked my wife. Who knows, I might even have let you?"

Had Erica told him? No, because then she would probably have warned him. Or said something, at least. There was no point speculating about who had said what. The fact remained: Nicolas had made a mistake, and now he had to deal with the consequences. It had only been a matter of time before the whole thing came to light.

Nicolas turned to go back to his room and pack his belongings. Halfway to the door he stopped and turned back.

"You should be careful with Molly Berg," he said. "There are things in her past that worry me."

He didn't say that for Johan's sake, but for Erica and James's. He was risking their safety, their lives. Johan demonstratively opened the screen of his computer again.

They turned into the airport precinct and her cabin bag slid across the back of the pickup.

Molly couldn't help noticing how disappointed her dad was, even though he was doing his best to hide it. Right from the start she had said she would be staying for at least another week.

"You're sure it's nothing I've said or done?" he asked quietly. "I know I can be a bit gruff and thoughtless at times. But I don't mean any harm."

His voice was low, so subdued that she could hardly hear him over the noise of the engine.

"I have to get back for work."

"But I thought you'd taken the time off?"

He found an empty parking space and pulled into it.

"One of the girls in the shop is ill, so I have to cover for her. I'm sorry."

She put her hand on her father's as it rested on the gear-stick.

"I've enjoyed being here. I've even learned to like Kiruna. It just took me a few years to recognise its charms."

Her father turned towards her and raised his eyebrows in surprise.

"Good grief. So... you'll be back?"

"Yes, Dad. As soon as I can get more time off. Maybe for Christmas?"

She patted the back of his hand and tucked a strand of hair behind her ear.

"You're welcome whenever you want to come. And if you want to move back up here to get away from the big city, there'll always be a room for you with me and Joik."

"I should get going," Molly said quietly.

Her father squeezed the steering-wheel with his large fists.

"It's been wonderful having you here. I'm so glad you came."

They got out of the car. He lifted the case down from the back of the pickup, put it down on the snow-covered ground and pulled the handle out. Molly hugged her dad, and he wrapped his arms round her and held her tight.

Molly turned and pulled her case through the snow. Halfway towards the entrance she turned round. Her dad raised his hand to wave. He looked so lonely, she thought as she waved back. It felt like she was seeing him for the last time. She wanted to hold onto that moment, prolong it, but she forced herself to carry on into the terminal building.

Forty-five minutes later she had passed the security checks and was sitting in seat 14A. Both seats on either side of her were empty. She could see the back of Thomas's head a couple of rows in front of her. She hated him. The cabin crew closed the doors, then ran through the last routines before take-off as the half-empty plane taxied towards the runway.

Molly toyed with the safety leaflet, unable to bring herself to take out either of her newly-bought books. Anxiety was rolling through her stomach in waves, but that had nothing to do with their impending take-off and flight. It went deeper, was bigger than that. What did Thomas want her to do? And who was the person she was going to meet? The pilot accelerated, the plane hurtled down the runway and her body was pressed back in her seat. The wheels lost contact with the ground.

Outside the window the trees, cars, airport buildings and terminal grew smaller and smaller. The plane shuddered. She turned her head to see the thousands of lights of Kiruna in a sea of darkness.

"Like an oasis of civilisation in the wilderness," she muttered.

Vanessa was lying in the recovery position on the pavement, surrounded by a group of people. She screwed up her eyes, put her hand to the back of her head, and grimaced when it stung.

Samer crouched down in front of her and patted her on the cheek. He wasn't wearing a jacket, and Vanessa realised he had laid it over her so she wouldn't freeze. Her clothes were drenched.

"Are you okay?" he asked. Vanessa tried to sit up, but sank back to the ground. Her headache felt much worse, flaring through her nervous system. "There's an ambulance on its way."

The people who had gathered around Vanessa began to drift away.

She remembered Sabina standing at the bus-stop. After that everything went black. Someone had hit her from behind.

"How long have I been lying here?"

"Three, four minutes, I think."

"Not longer?"

How could Samer have found her so quickly? Unless she was remembering wrongly, he had said he was going to call her when he got to Odenplan. Perhaps he had. She hadn't checked her phone. Vanessa patted her pockets and felt that it was still there.

"A crowd had gathered round you, people wanting to help. I rushed over and saw it was you."

Samer held her under her arms and lifted her carefully so she was sitting up on the pavement.

The sound of an ambulance siren was getting louder from the direction of Norrtull.

"How do you feel?"

"Like one of those scary warning pictures on cigarette packets in other countries."

Her head was spinning. She put her hand down on the pavement to brace herself so she didn't lose her balance.

"You didn't see what happened?" Samer asked.

"No. I caught sight of something out of the corner of my eye, then everything went black. What do the witnesses say?"

"I haven't actually spoken to anyone, I was concentrating on you. Shall I call for backup?"

"No, don't bother."

The ambulance did a U-turn at the junction of Odengatan and Sveavägen and pulled up. The street corner was lit up by the flashing blue lights. The few people who were lingering made room for the paramedics who hurried over and crouched down next to Vanessa. Samer looked on as they examined the back of her head. Vanessa wondered what she ought to be doing. The most urgent thing was to find out who Sabina had phoned. That was probably the person who had knocked her unconscious. She thought about asking Samer to look into it, but something was stopping her.

"This needs stitches," one of the green-clad women said.

The paramedics each took one of her arms and helped her to her feet, then led her carefully towards the ambulance. They opened the back door and helped her sit down on the trolley. One of them gave her a white compress and told her to hold it against the back of her head. Vanessa held her mobile phone up with her other hand and looked at the screen. Samer hadn't texted her to say he was at Odenplan. He hadn't called either. She sent a quick text to Celine and explained that she was going to be a few hours late, but that there was no need for her to worry.

"I can get a taxi to the local clinic in Sabbatsberg," she told the paramedics. "I'm fine."

9

Through the pane of glass Axel saw Rebecca's wavy hair as she leaned over their son's bed in the dimly lit room. He soaked up the scene, imprinting it on his brain. He loved them so much. Unconditionally. He must have moved, because suddenly Rebecca looked up. Her eyes were red from crying. He pushed the door open and entered the room, and she put a finger to her lips and pointed at Simon, who was asleep. She stood up, gestured to Axel to follow her, and they walked out into the corridor together. Axel closed the door carefully and turned towards her.

"What's happened?" he asked tentatively. He reached out his hand to touch her, but thought better of it and pulled it back. A nurse walked past pushing a rattling trolley. It was Saturday afternoon and there was an atmosphere of calm in the hospital department.

"Is it Simon?" Axel asked, feeling anxiety spread through his body. "Has he got worse again?"

Rebecca quickly shook her head.

"No, don't worry. Simon is fine."

Axel breathed out.

"So – what is it?"

He looked at her quizzically, waiting for an explanation, but instead she slipped her arm under his and led him along the corridor by his elbow, towards the lifts. "Can we go and talk downstairs? I'm so tired of sitting here."

They went down to the cafeteria. Axel suggested that Rebecca sit down at a free table, then hurried off to get coffee for himself and tea for her. While he was waiting in the queue he looked around the room. Simon had been moved out of Intensive Care, and his new department seemed to share a building with the maternity ward. The tables were full of new parents holding tiny bundles, waiting to be discharged and allowed to go home.

Axel thought back to his encounter with Nicolas Paredes earlier that week. He was so grateful that Nicolas had stopped him from doing anything stupid. How had he even contemplated the idea of killing another human being and abandoning Simon and Rebecca? Nicolas had advised him to report what had happened to the police. Part of him just wanted to forget Johan Karlström and move on. Devote all his time to Simon and make his life as good as possible. But part of him was telling him that he couldn't let Johan get away with it. Was there some other way of punishing him? Of preventing the same thing from happening again? Next time it could be another child, one that might not survive.

He paid for the drinks and returned to the table, and put the cup of tea down in front of Rebecca.

She mumbled her thanks and ran the palm of her hand over her face. Axel waited, anxious not to pressure her into talking.

"Do you remember that we sat in this cafeteria before Simon was born?" Rebecca asked. "After you fainted in the delivery room?"

"I just lay down to have a rest, that's all," Axel said with a smile. "It was taking such a long time."

Rebecca looked at him sceptically, then laughed. He was filled with warmth.

"Okay, let's say that's what happened."

Then she sighed, wrapping a lock of hair around one finger and looking at the new young parents a couple of tables from them.

"Do you think they understand?" she said in a low voice. "What they've got ahead of them, I mean. All the worry. That life is never going to be the same."

"I've never felt like that, not the worry, anyway. Not before the accident, at least. My life wasn't the same, but that was only ever a good thing."

"You're very positive all of a sudden."

"But it's true. Even if Simon hadn't woken up, I… I wouldn't have had any regrets, if you understand what I mean?"

"I do."

A short silence followed. Rebecca raised her cup with both hands and took a sip. She leaned back.

"Thorsten wants a divorce."

The words didn't really sink in, Axel couldn't quite absorb them. He must have misunderstood her. No one in their right mind would be capable of leaving Rebecca. No, it must be a misunderstanding.

"I went home earlier to pick up some clothes. Seeing as I haven't been keeping an eye on the bills and so on while I've been here, I opened the drawer where we usually keep unpaid bills. And found a load of divorce papers. He got them on Wednesday, 6 November. That was when he signed them, anyway."

"Two days before Simon…" Axel left the sentence unfinished.

"Yes. He must have delayed saying anything when all this happened," she said quietly.

Axel wanted to comfort her, say that everything would be alright, but he couldn't find the words. He felt miserable on her behalf. Sure, he loved Rebecca, he was in love with her and would never stop being in love with her, but he didn't want to see her sad.

"Is there anything I can do?"

She sniffed and shook her head. Axel thought she looked more beautiful than ever.

There was something special, something intimate in the way she had dared to share her vulnerability with him. Like a confidence.

10

A police helicopter was buzzing in the air. Hamza heard a whistle, and a moment later Farid's form emerged from the shadows behind the water tower. They walked towards each other. Behind them the worn, drab concrete of the post-war housing project rose up. Below them, on the E18 motorway, the headlamps of the cars formed a snaking chain of light. No one who didn't live there ever came here. The rest of Sweden just hurried past. As Hamza had been walking from the metro station in Hjulsta he had heard shots being fired. Hjulsta shopping centre and the small square had been full of police and the other emergency services.

Farid shook his hand and thanked him for coming at such short notice. Hamza had been told that something urgent had happened and that they needed to meet via a message left at the gym.

"We have a problem," Farid said. His face looked worried, the circles under his eyes were dark and deep. "Our attack needs to happen earlier than we originally planned. That isn't ideal, but it's manageable."

"What's happened?"

"One of our people is close to being found out."

Hamza watched the police helicopter as it disappeared towards the south. His encounter with Stig was still fresh in his memory. That, combined with all the police officers and the helicopter, was having an affect on him. He was starting to have doubts. The situation felt unreal. What could he do against a state, against an entire country?

The good, the faithful were so few in number.

The unfaithful, the wicked, there were so many of them.

God was testing him, making him waver.

"Do we really stand a chance against all this?" he heard himself ask.

"Hamza?" Farid took a step forward, put his hands on his shoulders and fixed his eyes on him. "Are you having doubts?"

Only then did Hamza notice that Farid was carrying a rucksack. An old Haglöfs rucksack, the sort Hamza once had for school.

197

"Sometimes it feels like we're the only ones left. The only ones alive."

Farid let go of him. He fished a cigarette from his jacket pocket and turned away to shield his lighter from the wind.

"Nothing could be more wrong. There are thousands of us spread across Europe. Dormant cells. We must show our Muslim brothers and sister the true face of the kuffars. Make them wake up. Men like you and I sacrifice ourselves so that Muslims the world over can live a decent life. So that they don't have to see their families bombed, see our way of life insulted."

Hamza rubbed his face. Farid took a deep drag on the cigarette, then exhaled. The smoke dispersed in the cold air.

He turned round, then told Hamza to stand next to him. With the glowing cigarette between his index and middle fingers, he pointed out across the Järva plain.

"Rinkeby. Tensta. Akalla. Hjulsta. From each of these places young men set off to populate the Caliphate, giving up everything to create a safe haven for Muslims. A place where we can live as God wants us to live. A land where we are no longer oppressed. Most of them are dead. They died for God. But not you. Not yet. Why?"

Hamza shrugged his shoulders.

"You are one of the chosen ones. That's why we brought you home. That's why you managed to escape the captivity of the Kurdish monsters. So that you can help us take our revenge. You will be a *shaheed* – no one deserves that more than you."

"Haven't we lost? Aren't we alone?" Hamza whispered.

"No," Farid exclaimed forcefully. His voice was angry. He raised his cigarette to his lips with trembling fingers and took another drag. His face relaxed slightly. "I understand that it looks that way, but God is testing us. How could we, the people fighting for his honour, for his word, be defeated?"

Farid took out his mobile phone, opened the image library and turned the screen towards Hamza. Images of dead, dark-haired children. Women crying. The victims of war. Any of the dead children in the pictures could be Amina or Mazhar. Or the children of people he had lived side by side with in Raqqa. Neighbours, friends, acquaintances. Brothers he had fought alongside, who had sacrificed themselves in the struggle.

"Look at them, Hamza. This is what Western peace means. Western justice. This is what they want to do to all Muslims. Or at least those who don't want to live the way they do. Those who refuse to praise homosexuals, those who refuse to allow women to paint themselves like whores, those who refuse to let our faith and our prophets be insulted."

Hamza turned his face away. Farid switched the screen off and put his phone away.

"You are an acclaimed warrior, one of the greatest. Women and children all over the Caliphate told stories about you, about your heroic deeds. Do you know where those same stories are told now? In the camps. Where they are waiting for us to liberate them. In camps like Ein Eissa and al-Hol. Where they are humiliated every day, where they are close to breaking, and where the only thing that keeps them alive is their hope in men like you. Are you going to tell them that we have lost, that we are abandoning them? Surrendering them to the Westerners without a fight? Are you going to betray them?"

Hamza shook his head.

"No."

Farid was right. What was the alternative? For him to go to the Job Centre and look for a job? He had nowhere to go. No friends, nowhere he belonged.

Farid lit another cigarette and shrugged off the rucksack. From one of the outside pockets he pulled a newspaper cutting containing a man's picture.

"I want you to start plotting this man's life this evening."

Hamza read the man's name. He was surprised, this wasn't what he had been expecting. He had imagined a football stadium, possibly a department store. He opened his mouth to ask Farid what their goal was, but he shook his head.

"The less you know at this stage, the better. This man, 'Khenziir', is going to die, that's all you need to know."

"*The pig*. An appropriate code name."

Farid nodded. He sucked hard on his cigarette.

"When am I going to meet the others?"

"In two days' time, on Monday. One of them, anyway. You need to give them this."

Farid held the rucksack out to Hamza, who took it and weighed it in his hand.

"What's inside?"

"Take a look, and you'll realise why I can't keep it at mine."

Farid dropped the cigarette and crushed it beneath his shoe. Hamza quickly opened the zip of the rucksack. When he saw that it was an explosive vest, his heart began to beat faster, more eagerly in his chest.

Axel was lying on the carpet in Simon's room with his hands clasped behind his head. He couldn't help smiling. He was surrounded by toys, football posters, clothes – things he never thought Simon would have any use for again. Now he saw them in a completely different light.

He had been lying like that since he got home from the hospital. He looked at the time and saw that it was already half past five in the evening. He had had a lot to think about. Not least what Rebecca had told him, that she and Thorsten were getting divorced. But above all, he needed to think of how he could be there for Simon when he was discharged from hospital. The doctors had told them that there was a strong chance that he wouldn't be able to walk again.

There was an unopened roll of black bin-bags on the floor by the door. Axel had bought them some time in the terrible days when he thought his son was going to die. To put everything in, all the things he could no longer bear to look at, to get rid of them. Now he was pleased he hadn't done that. Simon was going to live. Axel wondered if he should get rid of anything to do with football, so that his son wouldn't constantly be reminded of his dreams. Unless that was the wrong way to go about things. Maybe he and Simon could go and watch another FC Barcelona match in a few months' time?

Either way, Axel was going to devote all his time to making his son happy.

His thoughts were interrupted by the doorbell ringing. For a moment he hoped that it was Rebecca. Perhaps she was upset, wanted to talk. He half ran through the flat, then pressed his forehead to the door and looked through the spy-hole. But it wasn't Rebecca, it was Nicolas. The man who worked for Johan Karlström.

Axel watched as Nicolas rang the bell again. He must have heard that Axel was inside the flat. What did he want? Nicolas didn't look threatening, he didn't seem angry. And he had actually let him go after he told him about Simon.

Hesitantly, Axel reached for the door handle, waited a couple of seconds, then turned it and opened the door.

"Thanks," Nicolas said.

"What are you doing here?"

"I need to talk to you."

"What about?" Axel asked, wondering if he might have made a mistake after all. Could Johan Karlström have sent Nicolas here to threaten him?

"Is it okay if I come in? I really do just want to talk to you. Nothing else."

Axel stepped aside. When Nicolas leaned forward Axel jerked back.

"It's wet out," Nicolas said calmly as he unlaced his shoes. "I don't want to make a mess. That's all."

Axel showed him into the living room. The door to Simon's room was still open and Nicolas peered in.

"Your son likes football?"

"It's his favourite thing in the world."

"How's he doing?"

"He's awake and talking."

Axel couldn't help smiling, and Nicolas looked genuinely relieved.

"That's good to hear."

Axel gestured towards the sofa and Nicolas sat down. Axel settled down on the armchair. He couldn't help thinking how strange it was that the man sitting on his sofa seemed so gentle and friendly: even though he was evidently capable of violence, he didn't seem like an aggressive oppressor.

"Perhaps I should start by saying that I no longer work for Johan Karlström," Nicolas said, resting one hand on the arm of the sofa. "But I'm worried about his family. I think he's mixed up in something that might jeopardise their safety."

When Axel didn't reply, he ran his fingertips thoughtfully over the rough fabric.

"His family are innocent. And I think you might have seen something, seeing as you've been watching him for the past few weeks. Maybe you know who's blackmailing him, and why? I would never reveal where the information came from. I promise."

Axel's eyes darted about the room. He licked his lips.

"You do know something. Don't you?"

Axel considered his options. He had decided to find out all he could about Johan Karlström. See if he could find something he could use against him, and he had found out quite a lot. But Nicolas was right – his family were innocent.

"You promise to keep me out of it?"

"Yes."

Axel nodded slowly.

"Johan is laundering money through Gambler. Huge amounts."

"How?"

"Gambler owns online gambling sites around the world. They're one of very few companies that permit gambling with bitcoins. You know, the cryptocurrency. It's impossible to trace, which is why it's used for money laundering."

Nicolas held his hands out.

"How?"

"Poker. A number of players fill their accounts with bitcoins and lose systematically to one chosen player. The chosen player withdraws their winnings in dollars, say, and they get recorded as gambling profits. Ta-dah. The money is now clean."

"But…"

"Why are they blackmailing him now?"

Nicolas nodded quickly.

"All poker sites have warning systems, precisely to avoid this. But those warning systems can be shut down manually. For the past three years Johan has been instructing his technicians on Malta to do that for certain selected players. But six months ago he emailed them and told them to stop doing it."

"Why did he do that?"

"I don't know," Axel said.

"But that was when the threats started?"

"Yes."

Nicolas looked at him in surprise.

"How do you know all this?"

"I know everything about Johan Karlström." Axel smiled.

"Who are the players whose privileges have been withdrawn?"

"That I don't know."

He found himself thinking of the evening when he had followed Johan and Nicolas from the Bank Hotel, and saw the beautiful young woman.

"I think I might know who one of the players is," he said in a low voice. Nicolas looked at him intently as Axel got up from the armchair.

"You'll have to come with me to my car."

12

Hovet ice-hockey rink was packed, and the crowd was venting its
anger at the referee. On the ice a match between Djurgården and
Brynäs, the team from Gävle, was into the third period, and the score
was 2-2. The smell of the ice was mixed with beer and hotdogs.
Djurgården had just incurred a penalty and in the row below Hamza
a man in a Djurgården sweater stood up and pointed to the rink.

"You fucking bastard ref!" he cried.

Hovet would have been the perfect target for an attack, Hamza
thought. Not least during an ice hockey game, or one of the concerts
the arena often hosted. There were television cameras everywhere,
the game was being broadcast live throughout Sweden. The attack
would be caught on camera and circulated by news media around
the world. Wake the cells that had been dormant in Europe, instil a
bit of courage in supporters who had been waiting in silence.

The security check at the entrance had been sloppy, the stewards
had barely looked in the bag Hamza had taken with him out of
curiosity to see what the security procedures were like. Now that
he knew, he almost hadn't needed to go the flat in Lappkärrsberget
to drop the rucksack off. An older man in a neon-yellow vest had
asked him if he had any alcohol with him. Hamza had shaken his
head, the man had opened the bag, looked down into it for a couple
of seconds, poked his gym clothes, then lazily waved him through.

Hamza looked down at the rink again. He was fascinated by the
way the players skated, the ease with which they moved across the
ice. Even as a boy he had loved hockey. More than football, which
was what all the other boys in Skärholmen played.

He had nagged his dad to let him join a hockey club, but his father
had refused for several years. The equipment was too expensive.

"Only Swedes play ice hockey. And the Swedes hate you, so

why should I pay good money for you to make a fool of yourself?" he had said.

But eventually his father had given in. He took Hamza to the Salvation Army, bought a pair of rusty skates and some worn leg and shoulder pads that had to be at least ten years old. After school Hamza had taken the bus by himself to the outdoor rink in Huddinge, almost quivering with excitement. But in the changing-room the other boys in the team, all of them Swedes, had laughed at his kit. And what had looked so easy turned out to be practically impossible.

Hamza had dragged himself across the freshly prepared ice. He fell. He got up. He fell again. The coaches had shaken their heads. At the end of the training session he had stood there, leaning against the boards with tears pricking his eyes.

He had realised that his father was right. Even so, he couldn't bring himself to tell the truth when he got home. Over the next few months, every Tuesday and Thursday Hamza had packed his ice hockey kit and walked about in the forests around Skärholmen. He stayed away from the flat so his father would think he was still playing. Partly out of fear that he would be beaten for wasting the family's money, and partly because he didn't want to prove his father right.

Hamza started when the crowd exploded. On the ice the blue-clad Djurgården players were celebrating winning 3-2. Above them, on the giant screen, the camera zoomed in on Khenziir – the man who was going to die – as he raised his fist in triumph. Hamza turned round and glanced up towards the box where he was standing and applauding, surrounded by suited bodyguards. Khenziir did a high-five with another VIP guest. Apologising as he went, Hamza made his way towards the exit of the arena.

Something inside him had woken up. He felt guilty about Stig. Why couldn't he do the old man this one last favour? Farid and the others could hardly object. Stig had been the only person who had ever really been there for him.

If he wanted to see his daughter one last time and it was in Hamza's gift to make that happen – then wasn't it Hamza's duty, as a Muslim and a fellow human being, to help him? Stig was no imperialist, he wasn't one of the infidels who oppressed and humiliated Muslims. On the contrary, the old man tried to do everything right. For everyone. No matter where they came from. If more people had been like Stig, Sweden would have been an easier place to live.

Hamza took out his mobile phone. He could still remember Stig's home number. Sometimes he used to call when he had been walking around the forest alone for too long and it was too cold. Stig had always opened his door to him back then, promising not to tell anyone that he wasn't playing hockey.

The day after tomorrow, on Monday, he would drive Stig to see Petra. If they set off from Stockholm early, they could be back before dinner, when he was supposed to hand over the suicide vest.

Farid would never know. It wouldn't entail any risk to the attack. And Hamza would be able to die with peace in his heart, secure in the knowledge that he had paid his debts.

13

Nicolas and Axel were back in the living room after fetching the dashboard camera together. Axel sat down on his armchair, put his laptop on his knees and inserted the memory card from the camera. The screensaver was a picture of a woman with a small child in her arms.

"Is that Simon and his mum?" Nicolas asked.

Axel nodded.

"Rebecca."

His tone of voice told Nicolas that Axel was reluctant to talk about her. He had earlier pondered the fact that there didn't appear to be any sign that anyone other than Axel and Simon lived in the flat.

Axel was unusual, but sympathetic. Nicolas felt for the lost, stammering man whose wiring was evidently a little unreliable. As a result, he was surprised to see Axel's fingers flying over the keyboard, he had never seen anyone work so adroitly on a computer. It was like watching a concert pianist.

Within a matter of seconds a new window opened on the screen. It showed a street at night.

"So this is from the evening when you followed us from the Bank Hotel?" Nicolas asked.

"You'd just dropped the woman off in Banérgatan."

Nicolas leaned closer to the screen.

"There – look." Axel froze the image and Nicolas saw Molly. She was talking to a man.

"Wait a moment, the man comes closer." Axel pressed play. The picture started to move again.

The man walked right past the car.

Axel slowed the speed of the replay, and now Nicolas had a clear view of Molly and the man she was talking to. Nicolas recognised him instantly.

PART VI

1

It was half past seven on Monday morning when Vanessa and Mikael Kask met in his pedantically tidy office in police headquarters on Kungsholmen. There was just over a week to go until December took over, the sun hadn't yet risen, and the scene outside the window was dark and unappealing.

Vanessa had brought her takeaway coffee, while a red-eyed but evidently alert Mikael drank his celery juice before fetching a cup of coffee from the machine in the kitchen.

There had been no sign of Sabina Haddad yet, he told her. Her flat had been watched all weekend following the assault on Vanessa. An alert and a description had been issued to all patrol cars. Her phone, or at least the number they could connect to her, was switched off.

The stitches in the back of her head itched. Vanessa still felt groggy, even if the worst of the headache had abated.

"What about the list of calls? Do we know who she called?"

Mikael shook his head.

"Her mobile number hasn't been active since 15.00 on Friday. No incoming or outgoing calls."

"Which means she has two mobiles. I saw her call someone." Vanessa said nothing for a few moments before going on. "When I went to see her, we drank tea in the kitchen, and I heard a mobile phone buzz. It wasn't the one on the kitchen table, and it wasn't mine."

Mikael drummed his fingers on the desk.

"I want you to be part of the investigation again," he said. "What you've managed to find out with your own private inquiries could prove useful, if nothing else."

"So you're not angry with me?"

"Let's move on from that. Your suspicions about Sabina appear to have been correct."

Vanessa was surprised. She had always regarded Mikael as something of a stickler for the rules. Neat and orderly. Maybe seeing Trude had changed him.

"So what do we do about Sabina?" she asked.

"We get into her flat today, take DNA samples and send what we find to France and Belgium for analysis. As you know, the information held by the Migration Office isn't always reliable, especially not if she entered Sweden using a fake passport."

"Good," Vanessa said. "Where's Samer?"

"He called yesterday to say he wasn't feeling well. I told him to stay at home today."

Vanessa thought about Samer as she drank the last of her coffee. She couldn't shift the feeling that there was something odd about him. How could he have appeared so quickly when she was assaulted? Sure, what he had said could be the truth, that he had seen the people gathered around her and hurried over. But in that case, why hadn't he already let her know that he had arrived at Odenplan, as they had agreed?

She wondered if she ought to tell Mikael about her conversation with Hanna Jackson and Samer's suspected connections to extremists in Malmö. She prolonged the decision by pressing the takeaway mug into the overflowing wastepaper bin under the desk. She decided to keep the information to herself for the time being, but at the same time to investigate further without saying anything. The situation was too serious to do nothing.

"Where are you going?" Mikael Kask asked as Vanessa got to her feet.

"I need to talk to Trude," she said, and left the room.

Vanessa walked towards Stockholm Court House where she had arranged to meet Trude. They exchanged a quick hug, and Vanessa suggested that they take a short walk in Kronoberg Park.

It was getting lighter as they walked around among the tired-looking Stockholmers on their way to work. Vanessa had been feeling uneasy since Mikael told her that Samer had called in sick.

"I need access to the geographic locations of Serious Crime's cars."

"You just have to go into the Storm system and look, surely?"

"Yes, of course," Vanessa said hesitantly. "But I'm probably going to need someone sitting at a computer to keep me updated and give me directions."

Trude stopped and turned towards Vanessa. A class of preschool children in bright yellow vests was walking past them in a crocodile. Trude waited until they had gone past.

"What's this about?"

"Samer. He's off sick today, but he's got a car because he was on call. His time is divided between Serious Crime and us at National Homicide. If that car starts to move, I want to be able to see where it's going."

Trude raised her eyebrows.

"I've been told something that troubles me, I just want to check it out for my own peace of mind," Vanessa said.

"Is this really any of your business?"

"I know it sounds odd. But if I'm wrong, I'm going to look like an idiot, and it also casts suspicion on him in a way that really isn't fair. And I probably *am* wrong."

Vanessa handed over a note of her log-in details for Storm, and the code for the police radio in Samer's car.

Trude glanced quickly at the note, nodded and put it in her pocket. Vanessa realised there was one more thing she needed to sort out. Samer knew what her car looked like. She took out the keys to the BMW that was parked in the garage and dangled them in front of Trude.

"Can we swap cars?"

2

They had passed Jönköping, and according the GPS on Hamza's mobile, they were approaching the clinic where Stig's daughter Petra lived.

Hamza had taken care to stick to the speed limit so as not to get stopped by the police. He had left the rucksack Farid had given him in Stig's flat seeing as he wasn't going to have time to fetch it from Lappkärrsberget in time to hand it over at IKEA at Kungens kurva that evening.

Stig was wearing a white shirt and worn brown jacket, and his hair was neatly combed and slicked down with water. He was in a good mood, and every ten minutes he thanked Hamza for taking the time to go with him.

"It means so much to me, Hamza, I don't think you can begin to imagine." Stig was holding tightly on to the wrapped gift he had brought to give to his daughter.

"What are you giving her?" Hamza asked.

"Oh, it's nothing special. Just a framed photograph of the family, so she can remember the way things used to be," Stig said proudly.

Hamza had no photographs of his children. The war had swallowed up everything. During the first months after Mazhar and Amina died he had been worried that the memory of their faces would slowly fade away, until in the end he wouldn't be able to conjure them up. But now he knew he wasn't going to live long enough to be able to forget.

They turned off the main road. Hamza braked and checked the GPS, and concluded that they were going the right way.

Not long after that a large, red-brick building rose up in front of them. They passed the gates and drove until they reached a tarmac car park. Hamza clenched his jaw and cast a discreet glance at the digital clock on the dashboard: 11.25. He would be back in good time. And hopefully he would feel better then, free from the guilty conscience that had been nagging at him.

They got out of the car and crossed the car park towards the entrance.

Stig was impatient, walking a couple of paces ahead of Hamza with the parcel in his arms. The glass door led to a reception desk, from behind which a woman with short hair looked up.

Stig introduced himself and Hamza sat down on a sofa.

He glanced up at the ceiling but couldn't see any surveillance cameras. Not that it really mattered if his visit was registered. Once the police and Security Service had found out that he was alive, he would be dead for real.

While the receptionist tapped at her computer to register Stig on their system, he turned round with a broad smile and gave Hamza the thumbs up.

3

Vanessa had spent the first hours following her meeting with Mikael Kask studying the state of the investigation. There was a lot of material, but just as she had already concluded, the detectives had focused almost exclusively on Rikard Olsson. Even if that was partly understandable given the nature of the threats against him, it was still a dereliction of duty to ignore other possibilities.

She had just grabbed her jacket and was heading down in the lift to go and have lunch at Ciao Ciao on Hantverkargatan when Trude called. Vanessa had been so immersed in her reading that she had almost forgotten their conversation in Kronoberg Park.

"Samer's on the move."

Vanessa patted the pockets of her jacket to check that she had taken the keys to Trude's Alfa Romeo with her.

"Where am I going?"

"He's heading south on the E4. He's just reached Alby, pretty much."

"I'll call back once I'm on the road. Let me know if he changes direction."

An hour and a half later Vanessa had turned off the motorway and was driving into Nyköping. Her stomach was rumbling, she hadn't had time to eat anything since breakfast.

She parked Trude's Alfa Romeo on Hospitalsgatan, close to St Nicolai Church, and wondered if she would ever be able to trust anyone again after Natasha's lies. Or if she was doomed to spend the rest of her life suspecting that people weren't what they told her they were. She didn't want that to be the case, but she didn't know what she could do to avoid it.

Shrugging off her thoughts, she got out and set off towards the almost deserted Storgatan. A group of alcoholics were sitting on a bench, passing a bottle between them. A lone woman hurried past.

Vanessa passed a tapas restaurant and reached a beige building belonging to the Philadelphia Pentecostal Church. On the ground floor was a restaurant called The Larder. To her right, in the car park, was the car in which Samer had driven there.

From her position on the street corner, Vanessa tried to catch a glimpse of him.

Her phone started to ring. She retreated a few steps so she couldn't be seen from the restaurant, then held her iPhone to her ear.

"What is it?" she snapped irritably.

"Monday blues?" Mikael Kask chuckled. "And you seemed so pleased to be back at work this morning."

Vanessa moved so she had a view of the restaurant again.

"Something like that. Was it anything urgent?"

"Fairly. But where are you?"

Vanessa didn't want to go into detail, but at the same time she was reluctant to lie.

"Near The Larder."

"Somewhere new for lunch? Haven't heard of that one."

"Mikael, what's this about?"

A bus pulled up at a stop nearby, blocking her view. When it pulled away she caught sight of Samer inside the restaurant. He was sitting facing the window. For a moment Vanessa thought he had seen her, but he went on talking to the person opposite him.

"Vanessa, are you still there?"

She clicked to end the call.

At Samer's table, with her back to the street, sat a dark-haired woman.

Vanessa couldn't see her face, but judging by her profile and hairstyle, she thought she knew who the woman was.

Sabina Haddad.

4

Molly opened the front door and stepped out onto Banérgatan. Grey cloud had parked itself on top of Stockholm, and there was an icy cold wind blowing. The temperature had risen, and the weather forecast on TV4 had said they would probably be getting snow sometime later that day. She turned off Strandvägen and crossed the bridge to Djurgården.

In recent days she had felt like she was being watched the moment she stepped out of her apartment, but assumed that she was just being paranoid. She pulled up the zip of her black Fjällräven jacket, right up to her chin, then pulled the hood up. Thomas still hadn't got in touch, the last thing he had said was that she should stay at home and wait for him to contact her. He guessed that would be towards the end of the week. She turned right at Nordiska Museet, walked past the Josefina restaurant and carried on along the shore. Most of the people she passed on the path were housewives dressed in exercise gear. Molly thought about calling her dad, just to see how he was and show that she was thinking about him, but decided not to contact him until all this was over.

She heard footsteps behind her and had to turn right round to look seeing as the hood was blocking her vision. A lone man jogged past her at speed. She breathed out. She needed to talk to someone, to do something. She took out her phone, put her ear-pods in, dialled Didrik's number. The phone rang, but he didn't answer. She thought gloomily that there was no one else she could call. She was alone. She had spent the past few years running – from cities, people, situations, as soon as she was expected to make any sort of emotional effort. But she couldn't run from her own loneliness.

She heard footsteps behind her back again.

"Molly."

She spun round. It took her a few seconds to recognise him. Johan Karlström's bodyguard, the one who had waited in the Bank Hotel and then drove her home. He was wearing a black parka jacket with the hood pulled up.

He took a step closer.

"I don't know if you remember me, but my name is Nicolas, and I used to work for Johan Karlström."

"Used to?"

He nodded quickly.

"I'm no longer employed there. But I need to talk to you."

Molly glanced behind him, but couldn't see anyone else there. He must have realised what she was thinking, because he smiled.

"You're not being followed. I've been watching since you left home."

"What do you want to talk about."

"The mobile phone you stole from Johan. I want to know why you did it."

Molly turned and began to walk away. He caught up with her and kept pace with her. They passed two women walking in the opposite direction.

"Is someone blackmailing you?" he said once they had passed. "Is that why you're scared?"

"Leave me alone."

"I only want to help you, I promise."

She pursed her lips and sped up.

"I went to your apartment to look for the phone the day after you met Johan. There was a man there. I don't know what you're caught up in, but I'm genuinely worried about you, and about Johan's family. He has a son and a wife. They could end up getting hurt. You too."

Molly stopped abruptly.

"What were you doing in my flat?"

He put his hand in his pocket and pulled out a sheet of A4 paper that he held up in front of Molly. The printout showed her and Thomas outside her building, the same night she handed over the phone. A jolt of fear ran through her body.

She struggled to stay calm.

"Who is he?" Nicolas asked. "Who's he working for? Is he threatening you?"

Molly looked directly into his eyes.

"If you don't leave me alone, I'm going to scream for help," she said quietly, then walked off.

"Wait." He caught up with her as he felt in his jacket pocket. He pulled out a pen and an old till receipt, quickly wrote something down and handed it to Molly. "My number, in case you ever need to contact me."

5

Vanessa crouched down behind a car so she wouldn't be seen. She thought about going to get the Alfa Romeo; she could keep her distance in the car without losing them, seeing as Trude could direct her. That was probably the correct strategy. Find Sabina's hiding place, wait and see what was really going on and who she met. Vanessa stood up, looked over towards the restaurant, and felt her heart start to race when she couldn't see Samer and Sabina. She looked over at the door and saw that they were on their way out.

But there was something that didn't make sense.

She moved closer. Samer and the woman were moving towards his car, deep in conversation. She was the same age, had the same colour hair and was the same height as Sabina – but was it really her? Vanessa was growing increasingly uncertain. She moved parallel to them on the other side of the street. When the woman turned towards Samer and put her arms round him, Vanessa got a glimpse of her face.

It wasn't Sabina. But who was Samer being so affectionate towards? Vanessa turned round and began to walk quickly back towards St Nicolai Church where she had parked.

From the car she called Trude and asked for Samer's position, and was told that his car was driving slowly east through Nyköping and was now next to Gripsholm Park. Vanessa set off after them, but without hurrying. She felt relieved, even if she still thought Samer's excursion was a bit odd. After all, he had lied about being ill, and had used a police vehicle for personal business. And had driven all the way to Nyköping. And he had never said anything about there being a woman in his life. Not that he was under any obligation to tell Vanessa everything, but there was still something shady about his behaviour. She considered setting off back to Stockholm and raising the subject with him later, but decided to find out where they had gone anyway.

Her mobile buzzed.

Jupitervägen 39, the screen said. Vanessa tapped the address into the GPS on her iPhone and put her foot down.

The street was lined with yellow, low-rise apartment buildings with balconies. The gardens were edged with muddy lawns and bare hedges. She caught sight of Samer's car. She checked in her mirrors that there was nothing behind her and backed into a free parking space four cars behind his.

Twenty minutes later Samer emerged from one of the buildings.

Before he unlocked the car he turned and waved up at one of the glassed-in balconies. She caught a glimpse of the woman from The Larder on the third floor.

Vanessa started the engine, drove up and parked so that Samer couldn't get out. He looked at her in surprise. Vanessa wound down her window, and a few seconds later Samer did the same.

"What are you doing here?" he asked nervously.

"I wasn't feeling great this morning, and I've heard that the Södermanland air can work wonders if you're not feeling well."

Samer blushed.

A car pulled up behind Vanessa and the driver started gesticulating angrily.

"Stay here, I'll be back," she said, and pulled into a free parking space further along the street. She got out and walked back, then got in the passenger seat. The car smelled strongly of aftershave.

"I am actually ill," he said.

Only now did Vanessa realise that he had made an effort to look smart. He was wearing a neat shirt under his jacket, he was clean-shaven, with just a dark triangle of stubble below his bottom lip. His black hair was neatly combed.

"So I see. Were you sneezing so hard that your moustache slipped down onto your chin?"

"What do you mean?"

Vanessa pointed to her own chin. Samer laughed. They sat in silence for a short while.

"Who is she?" Vanessa eventually asked.

"Who?"

"The woman on the balcony, Romeo."

Samer put his hands on the steering-wheel and sighed.

"Her name is Noor."

"Why all the subterfuge?"

"Because her brother's trying to find her."

Suddenly Vanessa got an idea of why he was being so secretive. She thought back to her conversation with Hanna Jackson. She had checked out the name of the jihadist afterwards.

"Is her brother's name Hassan Jaber?" she asked.

Samer stared at her.

"How did you know that?"

Vanessa shot him a thin smile. He sat up.

"Okay. I'm a Shia Muslim, she's Sunni. Hassan has come back from ISIS. He used to be my best friend, until he started to see me as the enemy. Sunni extremists hate Shia Muslims, and when he came back and found out that his sister had fallen in love with me, she had to get out of Malmö."

He glanced up at the empty balcony.

"I tried to talk to him. Reason with him. But it didn't work. He's blinded by hate. He said he'd cut her throat. His family may have disowned him, but it was still safer for Noor to move up here. She'll never be safe in Malmö while Hassan is alive."

6

Hamza had followed Stig up to his flat to fetch the rucksack he was going to hand over at Kungens kurva.

During the drive back to Stockholm from the clinic where Petra was being cared for, Stig had been unusually quiet and introverted. The old man had insisted on paying for the petrol, but Hamza had refused. Now he was standing in the hall with his shoes on.

"Sorry I was so quiet on the way home."

"Was it difficult seeing her?"

Stig nodded.

"I'm pleased I was able to see her, but at the same time it was hard. She wasn't really herself."

Hamza put his hand on the old man's shoulder.

"I couldn't help thinking that it was probably the last time I was going to see her in this life."

"Don't say that. She could still get better. Wounds heal. Both the ones we carry inside us, and the ones on our bodies. The ones inside us just take longer."

Stig smiled at Hamza.

"That's a kind thought. And hopefully you're right. I'll do everything I can to stay alive for the day when Petra is Petra again."

Hamza glanced at the rucksack on the hall floor, then at his watch. He had an hour left before he was due to hand it over. He had plenty of time, and could easily walk there.

"Is it okay if I use your toilet?"

Stig gestured towards the bathroom door and stepped back. Hamza closed the door, pulled down his zip and relaxed. He had done his best for Stig. The debt was repaid. Now he didn't need to have a guilty conscience.

He flushed the toilet.

He looked at his face in the mirror. The attack was getting nearer. He was going to shave that night. Pray. Wash properly. It would feel strange not to have a beard, but it was necessary if he didn't want to arouse any suspicion.

Now he could focus all his attention on what was going to happen, on vengeance, on waking up all the Muslims of Sweden, of the world.

He could hear Stig walking up and down in the hall.

"I can't let you pay for the petrol, Hamza. You've already done so much. I'm going to put…"

Hamza jerked, leapt for the door and pushed it open. But it was too late. Stig was standing hunched over the open rucksack.

"What's…?"

He fell silent. The old man's gaze swung between Hamza and the suicide-vest he was holding in his hands.

7

Vanessa was driving slowly over Västerbron towards Kungsholmen.

It was rush hour, and the traffic on the bridge was moving at a snail's pace. A car was parked by the side of the road, it looked like the driver had skidded, and was now standing looking at his crumpled bonnet while he waited for a tow-truck. Vanessa felt relieved after her conversation with Samer. She considered his explanation plausible, and it matched what she had been told by Hanna Jackson in Malmö. She considered the matter closed. Her mobile began to ring, a call from a number not in her contacts.

"This is Kenny, Celine's dad," a hoarse voice said.

Vanessa immediately suspected the worst. If anything ever happened to Celine, the authorities would contact Kenny rather than her. Her grip on the steering-wheel tightened.

"Is Celine okay?"

"Yeah, don't worry. I wondered if you had time to meet?"

Vanessa breathed out. Anxiety was replaced by curiosity.

"When?"

"As soon as possible."

"Do you want me to bring Celine?"

"No, you're the one I want to talk to."

Vanessa fell silent, wondering what on earth he could want, but decided that he was at least sounding reasonable.

"I'll be there."

It was clear that Kenny Wood had done his best to smarten up both himself and his threadbare room in Rysseviken in advance of Vanessa's visit. All the clutter and rubbish, all the empty bottles and clothes had been pushed into one corner. He had showered, and was wearing a passably clean college sweatshirt with just a few old food stains across the chest and stomach. The window was wide open to air out the stench of dirt and alcohol.

"Thanks for coming," he said.

He pointed to a rickety chair. While Vanessa sat down he closed the window and sat down on the bed. She felt conflicted. The human wreckage in front of her had harmed Celine more than anyone. He had beaten her black and blue. Left her to fend for herself for long periods. But he was Celine's father. No matter what he had done, it was obvious that she still loved him.

"I want to start by apologising for my behaviour when you here last time."

Vanessa looked at him expressionlessly.

"You should be apologising to your daughter, not me."

Kenny pulled a face that was hard to interpret.

"I haven't always been like this." He gestured around him, and had to pull his thoughts together before he went on. "Somewhere along the way my life went off the rails completely, and the only consolation I could find was in the bottle. Everything else was less important, including Celine."

"It isn't too late yet."

Kenny smiled sadly.

"You're a police officer, aren't you? You've seen plenty of people like me, and you know that isn't true. I've only got a matter of months left to live, maybe less than that. I've got hepatitis C and cirrhosis of the liver. People who live the way I do usually kill themselves in the end. The first thing I'm going to do after you leave here is drink. Every day, up to Saturday. And then it will be Sunday and the off-licences will be closed and I'll lie in here, trying to sleep so Monday comes quicker and I can get on the bus to buy more of my medicine."

Vanessa knew he was right. There was no point pretending otherwise. Kenny Wood was beyond salvation. She looked at his hands, they were shaking from abstinence. He had beads of sweat on his brow. He drove the nail of his index finger into his thumb.

"Why did you want to talk to me?"

"Celine. I want to make sure you'll take care of her."

His hands were shaking more violently now, and he clasped them together in an attempt to stop them.

Kenny was obviously past the point where any advice could help him.

"Pour yourself something to drink," she said.

He sighed with relief, got up with an effort and opened a bag beneath the window. He pulled out a green can of Åbro beer, opened it greedily, tipped his head back and drank.

"Thanks," he said. He pulled out another can and took it back to the bed with him. He wiped his forehead on his sleeve.

"I'm already looking after her, she's living with me," Vanessa said. "I think she's pretty happy."

He leaned forward and licked his lips.

"I want you to look after her properly."

Vanessa raised her eyebrows. Kenny took a deep swig of beer, then started coughing.

"I was at Social Services today. To get the right papers." He stood up again, went over to the bag on the floor and fished out a plastic folder. "I want to do this before it's too late."

On his way back to the bed he handed the folder over.

Application for adoption, she read at the top. She pulled out the documents and leafed through them. Kenny had filled them in in jagged, childish writing. He had signed them. All that was needed was her signature and the process would be underway.

Vanessa was touched. She looked down at the filthy floor.

"Obviously I need to check with Celine to see what she thinks," she mumbled.

"She worships you. Even in the state I was in last time, that much was obvious."

Kenny smiled weakly, leaned back and raised the can to his lips. Vanessa sat there for a while, feeling overwhelmed, until eventually she got to her feet. Kenny did the same.

"Look after my little girl," he said seriously.

He held out a large hand. Vanessa grasped it and looked him in the eye.

"I promise I will," she said quietly, clenching her jaw and nodding slowly. She knew this would be the last time she saw him alive.

"I know you will," he said.

8

Hamza and Stig stared at each other. The cramped hall felt claustrophobic. Stig's hands were shaking as they held the white suicide vest. Hamza thought the old man looked like a frightened animal. He knew what he had to do, but his body didn't want to obey him. His brain was desperately trying to find another way out, but there wasn't one. He couldn't let Stig live.

Hamza took three slow steps towards Stig, who put the vest down and tried to say something. As Hamza came closer Stig raised the palms of his hands towards him, the five-hundred-kronor note sailed through the air down to the floor. His lips were trembling, but he hardly tried to defend himself when Hamza's hands closed around his throat. With a quick movement Hamza lay Stig down on his back, holding him down with the weight of his body as he continued to squeeze.

Stig gurgled, pleaded. His eyes were full of terror.

"Why did you open the rucksack?" Hamza whispered. "Why?"

He turned away and stared at the wall, and felt tears spring to his eyes, run down his cheeks and onto Stig's bright red face. The old man's legs were flailing helplessly as the colour of his face turned darker, almost blue. Stig began to lose consciousness, his movements were growing weaker, the guttural noises quieter.

"I'm sorry," Hamza said. "Forgive me."

Afterwards he sat with his back against the wall, looking at the lifeless body.

He reached for the five-hundred-kronor note, held it up, then tucked it into the back pocket of his jeans.

Somewhere on the other side of the wall someone flushed a toilet, and he heard fragments of conversation. What was he going to do with the body? Roll it up in something before it started to smell? Should he contact Farid and tell him what had happened, ask for advice? No. They might interpret it to mean that he couldn't be trusted, or be so angry that they excluded him. And Stig's only living relative was Petra. Hamza had read about a man who hadn't been found in his flat on Södermalm for three years. He hoped Stig wouldn't have to lie there for that long.

Moving the body would be a risk, too great a risk, especially when there were only days left before Khenziir was to die.

There was nothing to connect Hamza with Stig. And even if there had been, it didn't actually make any difference. He would already be in heaven with the other martyrs, surrounded by his brothers, when the police began to investigate the murder.

"Why did you have to be so stubborn, why couldn't you just let me pay for the petrol? You needed the damn money more than me," Hamza sobbed, feeling his voice fail.

Sure, there had been prisoners of war whose throats he had cut, sobbing infidels he had felt sorry for and would rather not have had to kill. But he had done it out of duty and respect for his superiors. And war was war. But that was nothing compared to how he felt now that he had killed Stig. It was as if he had killed part of himself, part of his childhood. The old man deserved a better fate after all he had done for boys like Hamza. Not ending his days being strangled like an animal in this meaningless way.

Hamza went into the kitchen and found some plastic bags that he used to seal the ventilation in the bedroom. Then he picked Stig up and carried him in there. His body was light, it was like carrying a child.

He lay Stig on the bed, and closed his staring eyes before leaving the room. He searched through the drawers in the kitchen, found a roll of duct-tape and sealed the cracks round the bedroom door so that the smell wouldn't seep out and prompt the neighbours to call the police.

He found Stig's keys hanging in a cupboard in the hall, picked up the suicide vest, put it back in the rucksack, then left the flat and locked the front door.

9

Mark Lewenhaupt looked out across the newsroom of the *Kvällspressen*. The large clock on the wall said it was quarter past five. He had been out to Stureplan, where he had had a meal, then caught a taxi back at the paper's expense. He could treat himself like that these days. The days when he had to spend every working hour hunched over his computer were in the past.

That autumn he had been given a permanent position, he earned forty-five thousand kronor a month and shared a desk with the most important contributors, close to the main newsdesk. In recent months he had been the runaway leader of the paper's internal competition to see who could get the most front pages. One out of every three lead stories had been written by him. In the weekly letter sent out to everyone who worked for the paper, he had been picked out for particular praise by the editor-in-chief, Tuva Algotsson.

Even his father, who had been utterly opposed to him becoming a journalist, had during the course of one dinner suddenly praised a scoop Max had been responsible for. His time was now, and he was making the most of it.

Max scrolled through his inbox, which had filled up during the hours he had been gone. It contained the usual mix of emails from crazies, people complaining about miscarriages of justice, conspiracy theorists, invitations to premieres, and ordinary readers who actually wanted to discuss articles.

He stopped at one message with the heading: *She belonged to ISIS*. The sender had included a mobile phone number. If it had been from one of the men calling themselves friends of the fatherland, and whose full-time occupation appeared to be writing emails to reporters, there would never have been a phone number. It was probably from a drunk, or a conspiracy theorist who, in their excitement at seeing yet another dark-haired person in the paper, had forgotten to delete their phone number from the signature of their email – but it wouldn't do any harm to call.

Max put his headset on and put his feet up on the desk as he tapped the number.

A woman answered. She had a strong accent, and asked if she could get her friend Yussuf to help with translation.

Four minutes later Max realised he was sitting on the biggest scoop of his career.

He hung up, then immediately called a taxi, grabbed his coat and hurried out of the newsroom. After telling the taxi-driver to take him to an address in the Stockholm suburb of Tensta, Max realised that if he played his cards right, this could be two separate scoops, as long as he managed to handle Vanessa Frank the right way.

10

Vanessa got out of the shower, reached for a towel and dried herself in front of the steamed-up mirror. From the other side of the door she heard the television being turned on, and realised that Celine had come home. She smiled. She was happier with Celine in her life. She had more to look forward to than just shuttling back and forth between crime scenes and her flat. Eating alone in front of the television or in the company of the regulars at McLarens. But could she cope? Did she dare invest so much of herself in someone else? Leave herself exposed. Vulnerable. Again. In one way, she had already made her choice.

She wiped the mirror with the towel. Stepped back. Studied her naked body intently. The scar on her forehead when she had intentionally driven into a truck on Sveavägen to get away from a gangster and eventually find Natasha, who had been taken to Chile by a criminal gang.

Vanessa turned so she was standing in profile, and ran one finger over the scar at the top of her left arm. That one was for Celine. She had consciously let Tom Lindbeck stab her there in order to buy time to draw the pistol tucked into her waist and fire the nine-millimetre bullet that put an end to his orgy of killing. In her mind's eye she could still see the abrupt switch from triumph to surprise as she put the gun under his chin, pulled the trigger and blew his sick brain all over the roof of the galley of the boat last summer.

That was how fragile life was. One microsecond, one bullet. That was how slender the difference between being alive and being dead was. It could have been Vanessa lying six feet under while Tom Lindbeck lived on, locked away in one of the country's overflowing prisons.

Those were two of the three scars that had defined her life. The third was inside her, like a tear in her soul. Adeline's death in Cuba in the late nineties.

Only three people knew that Vanessa had given birth to a daughter when she was twenty-three. With Natasha's death, that number was now down to two. Nicolas, and the girl's father, Camilo, who she hadn't seen or heard from since she fled Cuba in such a hurry.

She had been the daughter of a wealthy company director from Östermalm who fell in love with a Cuban soldier, left everything behind and, to her father's horror, moved to a Communist dictatorship in the West Indies.

Vanessa wondered if she had been happy in those months on Cuba, those months with Adeline in the small, shabby flat in Havana. Truth be told, she couldn't really remember more than small fragments of that time. Sometimes hazy images of people she had met, places she had been popped into her mind. Beaches. Bars. Nightclubs. She could smell the sun and petrol fumes. Sometimes she wondered if it was just a fantasy her brain had concocted.

Death had come to Adeline in the insignificant form of a bacterium that the Cuban health service could do nothing to treat. Vanessa groaned as the hospital room in which her daughter had drawn her last breath appeared in her mind's eye. The fluttering curtains in front of the open window, the sound of Havana's streets outside, the lifeless little body.

She reached for another towel, wrapped it round her head like a turban and shook the memories off. She rubbed herself with skin cream, then opened the bathroom door.

Celine was sitting cross-legged on the sofa, dressed from head to toe in orange, with matching fingernails. Vanessa stopped abruptly and stared at her in surprise.

"Should I ask?"

"Ask what?" Celine said.

"Why you're going around dressed like the Sun King."

Celine looked down at her trousers and top.

"Oh, this. It's no big thing. I'm just having a phase of dressing entirely in orange. Let's just call it my orange phase."

"Why?"

Celine shrugged nonchalantly.

"Why not?"

"Okay," Vanessa said. She carried on towards her bedroom, but stopped between Celine and the television.

"Is it something political?"

"No."

Celine leaned to one side to see the television.

"And you're feeling okay?"

"Yes, why wouldn't I be?" Celine asked in surprise.

"You know I'm here for you if there's ever anything? You know we can talk?"

"I've certainly noticed that you can," Celine sniggered.

Vanessa went into her bedroom. She closed the door and got out a pair of jeans and a white T-shirt. She removed the towel from her head and switched the hairdryer on. She needed to talk to Celine about becoming her legal guardian, as soon as possible. There was no point putting it off.

Over the roar of the hairdryer she heard the doorbell ring. When Vanessa peered out into the living room there was no one there, and realised that Celine had already gone to answer the door. She hid the papers Kenny had given her in her wardrobe.

"Who is it?" she called.

"It's that trained monkey again," Celine replied.

Vanessa looked out into the hall and saw that it was Max Lewenhaupt.

Celine shut the door on him. The reporter opened the letterbox.

"I need to talk to you," he said. "It's important."

Celine crouched down and looked through the slot.

"Someone ought to call the circus he's escaped from," she muttered.

Vanessa asked her to go back into the living room.

"I can handle this."

"Sure?" Celine asked seriously.

"Sure," Vanessa said, then opened the door and stepped out into the stairwell.

11

Hamza was waiting with the rucksack by the exit from IKEA at Kungens kurva. His body felt heavy and tired. A young couple were loading large pot plants into the back of a car. A family walked past, the children perched on top of the oblong boxes on a trolley. Hamza looked around. Who was he supposed to be meeting? Maybe it was someone he would recognise from the war. A brother-in-arms, someone else from the suburbs he had fought alongside?

That was what he hoped.

Stig's staring, accusing eyes kept appearing in his mind's eye. He looked down at the hands that had taken his life. Shuddered. He shook off the image of his hands squeezing the old man's throat.

Stig shouldn't have had to die.

But perhaps that was what God wanted. Perhaps God had wanted Hamza to be tested, to prove himself worthy of the task that lay ahead of him?

A young woman was watching him warily. She was standing a short distance away, by the trolleys. Their eyes met and Hamza looked away. But she started to walk towards him with firm steps.

She said the predetermined phrase. But he didn't react, just started at her in surprise, unable to answer.

"If the sun doesn't rise tomorrow, it is God's will," she repeated.

"And if the moon falls, it is God's will," Hamza replied, still shaken.

She smiled at his surprise, then led him away towards an empty part of the car park.

Hamza had heard of them – the widows who had been sent to Europe.

Some of the Caliphate's women whose men had fallen remarried other fighters. Others who were particularly capable and faithful had been selected, sent to training camps and then seeded into the stream of refugees heading north. Once they were in Europe, their task was to integrate into society. To keep a low profile. Get a job. Not rouse any suspicions. Live a dormant life until they were called. The woman in front of him was evidently one of them. He looked at her dark eyes, her black hair tied up in a ponytail, the beautiful features of her face.

"You can call me Sabina," she said.

12

It was just before ten o'clock in the evening when Vanessa parked her BMW outside the Punjabi Masala in Tensta. Cold rain was falling. She crossed the street, stepped over the railing around a car park and found herself standing in front of a six-storey building.

Vanessa tapped in the code for the door and took the lift up.

If felt as if she had reached journey's end. Her conversation with Max Lewenhaupt had been the last piece of the puzzle, and if it checked out, she could no longer deny what she had begun to suspect a couple of days ago. She had agreed to go along with his suggestion without hesitation. An anonymous interview in which she talked about her involvement in the events at Stockholm Stadium in exchange for him giving her the source who had emailed him. If she agreed, Max would first check that the woman, whose name was Malika, was happy to talk to Vanessa.

She had agreed straight away.

The front door opened and she was hit by a cacophony of voices and music. A man with a salt-and-pepper beard and a friendly smile showed Vanessa into the flat. He pressed the palm of his hand to his chest and gave a short bow.

"Yussuf."

She copied his gestures.

"Vanessa."

Behind him in the hall stood a small, hunched woman in her thirties, wearing a headscarf.

"Malika?"

The man confirmed that this was Malika.

The flat was full of people, a mix of adults and children, and when Vanessa had been shown into the living room, Yussuf explained that nine people lived in the three-room apartment. The others spread out in the bedrooms and kitchen so that Malika could speak to her undisturbed.

Yussuf stayed to interpret.

"Only little Swedish," Malika said, holding up her thumb and forefinger one centimetre apart.

Vanessa sat down on a creaking leather sofa, sipped the sweet tea she had been offered, then turned to Yussuf.

"Ask her to tell me what she knows about the woman in the newspaper."

Yussuf switched to Arabic. Vanessa understood the word Raqqa, and listened intently even though she didn't understand.

"Malika was captured by ISIS, and was taken as a slave to a house in Raqqa. Raqqa is a city in Syria…"

"I know where Raqqa is," Vanessa said, trying to conceal her impatience.

"She says the dead woman in the paper was the wife of a foreign ISIS fighter who lived in the house next door. She saw her several times. She was a member of Hisbah."

Vanessa closed her eyes. The world was quaking. She wanted to wake up from this nightmare. But she knew she wasn't dreaming. The curious faces that were peering in at them. The sweet tea. Malika's quiet confidence.

"Hisbah?" she whispered.

"The women's morality police," Yussuf said.

Vanessa opened her eyes and looked at them.

"Newspaper wrong. Not Syrian. European," Malika said.

"From which country?"

Malika shrugged.

"Belgium? France?"

Vanessa turned to Yussuf.

"Ask her if she's sure." Yussuf seemed to want to protest. "Please, just do it."

Before he had time to repeat the question, Malika spoke.

"Yes. Sure," she said, tapping her chest twice as if to underline her words.

Silence fell.

"What happened to her husband? The ISIS fighter?"

Malika looked uncomprehendingly at Vanessa before turning to Yussuf. He quietly translated Vanessa's question. When he had finished, a fleeting smile crossed Malika's lips. She drew her hand across her throat in a gesture that left no room for misinterpretation.

"He died in the fighting," Yussuf said after Malika had given a more detailed account of what happened. "After the funeral the woman, who was one of two wives, was never seen again."

"When was this?"

Yussuf turned to Malika again.

The woman reflected.

"Early 2015."

Vanessa sipped her tea while the rain outside grew more intense. The downpour was drumming against the window and the balcony railing.

"Why did she wait so long before saying that she recognised her in the newspaper?"

Malika held her hand up to Yussuf, who fell silent.

"Scared. Very scared," Malika said, looking seriously at Vanessa.

"But not anymore?"

"Yes." Malika tried to speak a couple of times, but failed and turned to Yussuf again. She was speaking quietly, more quietly than before. Vanessa waited for Yussuf to interpret.

"Daesh mustn't win. Not again. Not here as well."

The rain had eased slightly by the time Vanessa got back to her car. She was clinging tightly to the steering-wheel, but couldn't bring herself to drive away. The fact that Natasha, if that was even her real name, had belonged to one of the largest, most repugnant terrorist groups in human history was incomprehensible. Even so, what Malika had said was logical. Vanessa had no cause to doubt what she had said. She had no reason to lie or make anything up.

Vanessa pulled out her phone and called Samer.

"I need to talk to you," he said when he answered.

"Is everything okay?"

Vanessa didn't say anything for a few moments. The rain hammered on the car roof. Poured down the windscreen.

"Natasha was a member of ISIS."

"What do you mean?"

Vanessa gave him a summary of what Malika had told her, and Samer listened without interrupting. When Vanessa was finished there was silence at the other end.

"Could it have been a refugee, one of ISIS's victims, who recognised Natasha and killed her?"

"I don't think so. You saw for yourself what she said on that recording outside the supermarket. 'I promise I won't betray you.' I'm starting to think that the man who threatened her was a member of ISIS. We aren't exactly short of returnees in Sweden. According to the Security Service, there are at least one hundred and fifty people who went and fought for their bloody Caliphate back in the country."

"You're right. The question is, what do we do now?"

Vanessa checked her wing-mirror and waited for a car to pass before pulling out.

"We need to contact the Security Service," she said tersely. "They know who the returnees are. I'm guessing the man outside ICA was one of them and is in their register."

13

Hamza and Sabina had left IKEA and were walking past the tarmacked car parks outside the hypermarkets where people were bringing out television sets, bags of groceries and clothes. They carried on, into the forest that surrounded the nearby lake, Gömmaren.

It was pouring with rain. The moon was shining through the ragged branches. Hamza realised that even if he and Sabina had been neighbours in Raqqa, he wouldn't have recognised her. All the women in the Caliphate's capital city were forced to wear the niqab when they were outside. Now her long, dark hair was shining damply in the moonlight.

He was feeling emotional, thinking that she was an angel. God's very own angel of death.

They stopped by the shore of the lake.

"This is good," Hamza said, looking round.

Through the rain they could hear the distant sound of traffic, like buzzing insects over on the E4. Sabina took her gloves off and quickly began to take her jacket off. Hamza turned away so as not to embarrass her. He opened the rucksack, took out the suicide vest and studied it.

"I'm ready," Sabina said. He turned round, keeping his eyes fixed above hers, but he couldn't avoid seeing skin and the outline of her body. She took the vest and carefully pulled it over her head. She shivered. Hamza tightened it, and showed her the button she should use to detonate the explosives. She quickly put on her thick jacket again, pulled the zip up and jumped on the spot a few times to warm up again. Hamza got ready to go back, but she touched him on the shoulder and suggested that they stay for a while.

"I haven't spoken to anyone for several days," she said. "I've been hiding in a basement. That's why I have to wear this, in case they find me."

Only now did Hamza hear that Arabic wasn't her first language. He realised that she too had grown up in Europe.

"Where are you from?"

"Belgium."

They looked at other curiously. They could easily have passed each other on the streets of Stockholm without knowing that they shared the same struggle.

"You're one of the widows of Raqqa?" Sabina nodded. Hamza couldn't help noticing that she looked proud.

"My husband was murdered by the Kurdish swine. We only had one year together."

"May God have mercy on his soul."

Sabina bowed her head.

"And you?"

"I lived in Raqqa with my wife and two children. They died in an air-raid, the whole house was flattened. I never remarried. Instead I devoted all my time to defending the city against the infidels. In 2017 I got wounded and was captured, but I managed to escape a couple of months later. When I got back, the siege was into its last days. I managed to get back in, and found one of my commanders, who gave me a fake passport and ordered me to travel to Europe."

"Then we both have people whose deaths we want to avenge," Sabina said in a low voice.

"What was your husband's name?"

"Mohamed. He was from Gothenburg. He hated Sweden, hated the people here. He told me how the Swedes treated him, how they took his honour from him, forced him to live a life of sin, a life of drugs and stealing. That's why I was pleased when I was sent here to kill kuffars."

It was as if she had transformed in front of Hamza's eyes and had become a different person. Her voice was vibrating with anger, full of rage and derision. He understood, and allowed himself to be swept along. It was a wonderful feeling, finally being able to speak to someone who understood what he had been through, someone who had been there, in Raqqa, in the Caliphate. He would have liked to stay for hours, talking about his children, his wife, the memories he had kept hidden inside himself for so long. They walked slowly towards Skärholmen, where they were to part.

Sabina would continue to stay hidden for a few more days, so as not to risk the others in the group being caught. If she was found, she would kill herself by detonating the explosives.

Hamza was going to take the metro to the flat in Lappkärrsberget. In six days' time, they were going to strike.

Less than a week from now, on 1 December, Khenziir was going to die.

14

Vanessa took her mobile out and looked at the website of *Kvällspressen*. The interview she had given Max Lewenhaupt had just been published. It had gone quickly, it was only a couple of days since he had told her about Malika in the stairwell outside her flat. Her identity was concealed, just as he had promised.

She stretched out on the sofa with the back of her head resting on the arm, and looked up at the ceiling. She was hungry, she hadn't had time to eat lunch or dinner. Where was Celine? Just as she was about to get up and investigate the freezer in the hunt for something edible, her phone buzzed. It was Mikael Kask.

"I'm on my way home from a meeting with Security Service and I think we need to talk," he said in a tense voice. That was unusually to the point for Mikael; normally the introductory pleasantries went on a bit too long for Vanessa's liking.

"Now?"

"Unless you've got something better to do?"

"How about we meet in McLarens on Surbrunnsgatan?"

It had started to snow. Vanessa had just ordered a cheeseburger and sat down at her usual window table when Mikael walked in. He stopped at the bar to order before coming over and sitting down opposite her. It was unusual to see him looking so dejected.

"Thanks for agreeing to meet, I needed someone to talk about this with."

He put down a glass of what appeared to be low-alcohol beer.

"What's happened? You seemed to so positive this morning," Vanessa said, sucking up a large gulp of Coke through the paper straw. She pulled a face, pulled the straw out and put it on the table. She raised the glass to her mouth.

Mikael glanced behind him at the almost empty bar, then leaned closer towards her.

"We've heard from the Belgian police. Both Sabina and Natasha are from Brussels. Sabina was reported missing by her family, and was assumed to have made her way to Syria to join ISIS as early as 2013."

"Then we have to do everything we can to find her," Vanessa said.

"Not we," Mikael said. "The Security Service have taken over. We're shut out."

"Why?"

"They're suggesting that Natasha's murder could indicate that a terrorist cell in Sweden has been activated. And that an attack could be imminent."

"That doesn't seem to be an unreasonable supposition," Vanessa said. She lowered her voice. "The Christmas shopping crowds?"

"Maybe. I didn't find out much more than that before I was asked to leave the meeting."

Their conversation was interrupted when the kitchen door next to the bar opened and Kjell-Arne came over with Vanessa's hamburger.

She popped a French fry in her mouth, then offered them to Mikael.

He quickly shook his head.

Vanessa took a bite of her burger then put it back on the plate.

"You're usually pragmatic, Mikael, you don't tend to get territorial like a lot of other male bosses. It's the job of the Security Service to prevent terrorist attacks, so isn't it simply logical that they take over?"

"I thought you'd be more upset," he said in surprise.

Vanessa realised that he was right; she too was surprised. But the fact was that their investigation was treading water. And if the situation was as serious as the Security Service claimed, it would be ridiculous to argue about it.

The main thing was that the terrorists' plans, assuming that they actually had any plans, were stopped.

"I want to catch whoever killed Natasha. I want to find out the truth about what happened, why she didn't phone me. But we're stuck, that's just a fact. We haven't got anything. And more than three weeks have passed. Maybe it's just as well to move on and let a fresh team investigate it?"

Mikael rubbed his eyes.

"Maybe you're right," he said, then covered his mouth before yawning. "When did you get to be so bloody wise?"

"After the attack on Stockholm Stadium last summer, I think."

He raised his head and looked at her seriously.

"Do you think about that a lot?"

"Sometimes," she said. "But less and less."

"Good."

He had trouble hiding the fact that he wanted to say more, but couldn't find the words.

Vanessa considered telling him about the interview, but changed her mind. Not because she had done anything wrong, but because it didn't actually make any difference. It was her recollections of what had happened in Stockholm Stadium, her memories, her wounds, and who she chose to share those with was nobody else's business.

"Go home and get some sleep now, Mikael. I'm just going to finish this, then I'm going home too."

15

In the *Kvällspressen* newsroom, Max Lewenhaupt was leaning so close to the screen of his computer that the desk was pressing into his chest. His article, headlined *She killed the incel terrorist – now police hero talks about those dramatic final moments*, had been posted online an hour ago, and was already the most read article on the site. According to the logic of the new media, articles were posted on the site in the evening even if they were going to on the front page the following day. Max was delighted with the text, as were editor-in-chief Tuva Algotsson and head of news, Bengt "the Bun" Svensson, even if they had muttered about having to anonymise Vanessa Frank's identity.

"Shame to have to hide such a fucking gorgeous woman," Bengt had said as he tucked a portion of chewing tobacco the size of a cowpat under his top lip and ambled back to his desk. But a promise was a promise. Max had given his word.

One of his colleagues, Victoria Selander, stopped on the other side of his computer.

"What a story," she said admiringly. "Most read this week, I reckon."

"This month," Max said without looking up. "At least. Maybe this year."

That was something else he had noticed since his byline picture had got bigger in recent months, that more colleagues came over and wanted to talk to him. Give him praise. Invite him to dinner and drinks. He was in two minds about that. On the one hand, he appreciated their new-found admiration for him, but on the other their fixation on his status bothered him. It was very middle-class, as his mother would have said. Plenty of the people who suddenly wanted to socialise with him wouldn't have noticed him at all if he hadn't been one of the newspaper's brightest stars. Not to mention the old schoolmates who had suddenly started to get in touch on Facebook. And the other day he had received his first invitation to a film première. Max wasn't thinking of going. Not that he had anything against people who went to film premières, but he wanted to be incorruptible, he didn't want anyone ever to be able to think that he owed a debt of gratitude, or was otherwise reluctant to write the truth. He was a journalist, not a celebrity.

"How long are you staying this evening?" Victoria asked.

"Another hour or so."

"Then what?"

"Then I'm having dinner with my older brother, he's home from London," Max muttered.

Victoria gave up, turned and went off to her desk over by the newsdesk. He realised she thought he was being unfriendly, but the thought of seeing his successful big brother who worked for a financial company in London irritated Max. Besides, Samuel was their father's favourite, and had, like him, been appalled when Max had informed the family that he was thinking of becoming a journalist. Samuel hadn't been in touch since Max graduated, but last week he had contacted him and asked if he wanted to meet up over dinner. He was evidently considered successful enough now to be seen in public with. But what annoyed Max most was that he had allowed himself to feel flattered, that he actually cared about the approval of Samuel and the rest of his family.

He stood up, put his coat on and packed his laptop in his bag. The newsroom was half empty, only the nightshift remained. He might just as well grab a beer on his own in some bar to build up his courage before he met his brother.

Max set off towards the central desk, where Bengt, as always, had his feet up on his desk. But he stopped when a short person with pink hair appeared from the corridor. There was something vaguely familiar about the girl, even if he couldn't quite place her. She was wandering around between the desks, looking around, going up to the remaining reporters and looking at their faces. Max watched her with amusement. In the end she stopped next to Victoria, who pointed in Max's direction. The girl caught sight of him, and at that moment he realised who she was. She was the peculiar girl who lived with Vanessa Frank. The one who had called him a wanker.

She came rushing over to Max, who stood there waiting with his arms folded. When she was a metre away from him she stuck her hand in her bag, pulled out what looked like a Danish pastry, and threw it at him. Max ducked. The pastry missed his head by a few centimetres and hit one of the television screens.

"You leave Vanessa alone, do you hear?" she yelled.

Max tried to calm her down, but she was beside herself with rage.

"Don't you realise what you've done? You've forced her to talk about something she doesn't want to talk about. You're disgusting. If you write another word about her, I'll make sure you regret it. You don't hurt Vanessa. You just don't do that."

Reporters and editors had got up from their desks and were moving closer out of curiosity.

"Calm down," Max said. "Can we talk about this in peace and quiet?"

"Forget it. Fucking... blabbermouth!"

She spun round and pointed at the reporters who had gathered round them.

"You should all be ashamed of yourselves. You've hurt the kindest person I know, the only person who's ever given a damn about me, who's stood up for me. My only real friend."

She had tears in her eyes.

She pulled up her T-shirt, revealing a vicious-looking scar.

"This is where he shot me," she said, pointing. Max started at the large, vivid pink line. "Vanessa saved my life. She killed him because of what he'd done to me and the others. Not you. You earn money by forcing her to talk, even though she doesn't want to."

A heavily-built Securitas guard was approaching. He strode up to the girl and grabbed her hard by the shoulder.

"Let go of me, you fucking Neanderthal," she yelled as he picked her up and started to drag her away.

Max and others stood there, frozen to the spot.

"Take it easy," Max called. He caught up with the guard. The girl was kicking her legs, struggling to get free. "Let her go."

The security guard stopped. His face was red with anger.

"No chance. She tricked her way in here. I'm going to call the police, they can take care of her."

"Let her go now," Max roared.

"But..."

"No fucking buts. Let go of the girl now."

He put her down on the floor.

Max waited until he had turned and lumbered away. He put one hand on the girl's shoulder and gently led her away to one of the meeting rooms. He opened the door, pulled out a chair and patted the back of it with his hand. She hesitated, then sat down.

"Do you want a Coke or something?"

"I'm not allowed Coke on weekdays," she replied sullenly.

16

The hospital room was lit up by a weak lamp on the table next to Simon's bed. His eyes were closed, but Axel knew that he wasn't asleep. There was something about his breathing that gave it away. Axel's couldn't say exactly what it was, but he knew instinctively, after the hundreds of hours he had spent by his son's side when he was trying to sleep.

He knew that Simon needed sleep, that it did him good. But he just wanted to hear his voice for a little while, after all the hours they'd lost.

In the end he couldn't help himself.

"Are you pretending to be asleep?" he whispered.

His son smiled and opened one eye. Axel laughed.

"I knew it."

He got up from the armchair and carefully approached the edge of the bed so that Simon didn't have to turn his head too much to see him. He reached out his hand and ran it gently through his son's blond locks. His face was thin, his cheekbones clearly visible through the pale skin.

"Do you know what I want, Dad?" Simon asked.

Axel shook his head.

"A wrap from the kiosk. We never got there."

"I'll go and get you as many wraps as you want after you've been discharged tomorrow," Axel said. "Then we'll eat them round at your Mum's. You're going to be living there for a few weeks. But I'll come and see you every day."

They had agreed that Rebecca and Thorsten's flat was more suitable while Simon was still convalescing.

"Where is she at the moment?" Simon asked, glancing towards the empty armchair where Rebecca had sat practically nonstop for the past few weeks.

Axel didn't want to say too much. It wasn't his business to tell him about the divorce, and about how sad Rebecca was. Earlier that evening she had texted him to say that she needed a break from the hospital, to sleep in her own bed. Axel had happily volunteered to sit with Simon overnight.

"We need to be extra nice to Mum for a while," he said.

"Is she sad?"

"It's, well… it's grownup stuff. It's going to be fine, but we need to do what we can to help her."

"But we always do that?"

Axel nodded.

"We do."

Simon felt for his hand. He took it and squeezed it gently. They didn't speak for a while.

"Dad? Are you in love with Mummy?" Simon asked quietly.

Axel was surprised. He opened his mouth to reply, but closed it again when he saw the sympathetic look on Simon's face. His expression was so considerate, so anxious, that it made Axel feel uneasy. It wasn't his job to be worried about his dad.

"I-I-I like her very much. But she loves Thorsten, doesn't she?"

Simon nodded thoughtfully.

"Does that make you sad?"

Axel shook his head quickly.

"It's probably best if you get some sleep now," he whispered, then stood up and leaned over carefully to kiss his son's forehead. "Goodnight, my boy."

A short silence followed.

"When am I going to be able to play football again?"

"I don't know," Axel whispered, and felt something break inside him. "I don't know."

"Goodnight, Daddy."

Quarter of an hour later, Simon was snoring softly.

Axel sighed and looked at his peaceful face for a while before turning out the light. He thought back over the past few weeks, which without doubt had been the most tumultuous he had ever experienced. Neither he nor Rebecca had yet been able to bring themselves to tell Simon that his doctors had said he would probably never be able to walk again.

How could they? That would mean killing their son's dreams. But he knew they were getting close to the point where they couldn't drag it out any longer. He was planning to spare Rebecca and tell Simon himself. She had been through enough already. And Axel would do everything in his power to hold both her and Simon up, carrying them through the difficult time that lay ahead of them. They needed him. He was so pleased that Nicolas had stopped him from attacking Johan Karlström. Axel's death would only have made things even harder for Rebecca, at a time when she needed him most. And Simon would forever have been the son of a murderer. Axel wasn't like that, he believed in justice, not physical violence.

He leaned forward and took his laptop out of its case. He connected it to the mobile broadband he always had with him. In recent days he had been thinking more about Johan, who had carried on living his life as if nothing had happened.

The maximum penalty for driving away from a traffic accident was six months' imprisonment, and the maximum penalty for money-laundering was six years. It was a simple choice. Axel wasn't going to let Johan Karlström get away. He was going to track down his transactions, find evidence of money-laundering, and give the prosecutor an easy path to a guilty verdict.

Six years in prison was nothing compared to a lifetime in a wheelchair, but at least it was something.

17

The *Dagens Nyheter* skyscraper lit up the dark winter sky. The taxi drove away and Vanessa leaned her head back and studied the white letters one last time before going through the revolving doors into the building that housed the editorial offices of both *Dagens Nyheter* and *Kvällspressen*. She announced her arrival to the Securitas guard, who muttered unhappily before he picked up a phone and dialled a number.

"They'll come and get you shortly."

Vanessa waited on one of the sofas by the windows looking out onto Gjörwellsgatan. A snowplough was mounding up the snow in the pulsating orange glow from the rotating light on the roof of the cab.

A young woman emerged from a glass door. Vanessa got to her feet and shook hands with her. They went up in the lift in silence, and came to a revolving door. The woman took out a passcard, tapped a code and indicated that Vanessa should go through first. They reached a large, well-lit open-plan office full of cluttered desks, screens, half-empty coffee cups. Most of the desks were empty, only the large desk in the middle of the enormous room was surrounded by people working in front of computer screens. The woman gestured towards a room with glass walls. Celine was sitting in there, staring sullenly in front of her with her arms folded while Max Lewenhaupt was standing by a whiteboard. Vanessa opened the door.

Celine looked down at the table, shame-faced, as Max turned to face Vanessa.

"She showed up here, angry about the interview," he said.

Vanessa looked over at Celine, who glanced back anxiously.

"Sorry," she said. "But I got so angry. I knew you didn't want to do it, that he had forced you. I know I got it wrong."

Vanessa felt herself flush at the sight of the girl. Obviously it was wrong of her to turn up here and cause trouble, but she had done it to protect Vanessa. And she was grateful for that, even if she wasn't about to show it. Not yet, anyway.

"How did you get in?"

"I said I was the editor-in-chief's daughter," Celine muttered.

Vanessa stifled a laugh, took a couple of steps towards the table and pulled out a chair next to her.

"How are you feeling?"

"I'm a bit hungry."

Max smiled.

"Maybe you should have eaten that Danish pastry instead of throwing it as me."

Vanessa raised her eyebrows.

"Danish pastry?"

"They didn't have any cream cakes in the shop."

Vanessa put her arm round Celine and pulled her closer.

"You did the wrong thing. But I still think it was lovely that you wanted to protect me."

Celine wrapped her arms round Vanessa, who waited a moment before standing up.

"Have you apologised to Max ?"

She shook her head.

"Go ahead, please."

Celine walked over to Max, held her hand out and looked him in the eye.

"Sorry I threw a Danish pastry at you. And for calling you a blabbermouth. And for all the others things I said that I can't really remember."

Max shook the outstretched hand.

"It's fine. And Celine, I think it's good to stand up for your friends. But you have to do it the right way. You're welcome to phone or email next time you have an opinion about something we publish."

Vanessa and Celine walked in silence beneath Lilla Västerbron to get a taxi at Fridhemsplan. Rålambshov Park spread out below them. A woman walked past towards the water of Riddarfjärden with a large dog on a lead.

"Are you very cross with me?" Celine asked.

"No. But it was a silly thing to do. You could have got into serious trouble."

"Sorry."

"It's fine."

"I just got so angry when I read that article. Not that there was anything wrong with it, but because I knew you didn't want to do it. Have you read it?"

Vanessa nodded.

"He and I had an agreement. I didn't like it, but I did my bit, and he did his. You can't just do whatever you feel like simply because you're angry."

"I know."

"Did you go to school today?"

Celine nodded eagerly.

"Yes. I go every day. I promised you that I would."

Vanessa smiled, put her arm round the girl and pulled her closer to her.

"Good. That's important for your future."

Celine sighed.

"But the future's so far away."

PART VII

1

It was half past six on Friday morning when Mikael Kask left Barry's Bootcamp with his gym bag over his shoulder. In one hand he was holding a smoothie, and with the other he was scrolling through Tinder as he crossed Smålandsgatan. He had eleven new matches.

He was a late bloomer, his mum had always said that. After his time modelling in New York, and a brief period as a television announcer, he had applied to Police Academy at the age of thirty. He had soon been identified as senior officer material and treated accordingly. Three years ago he had been appointed head of the National Homicide Unit. But in spite of the valuable work he did there, he still didn't feel like a grown-up. Or rather he wasn't leading the sort of life he had imagined that grown-ups led when he was younger. The most obvious difference was that he didn't have children, and was nowhere near being married. Instead, ever since his years in New York, he had gone from woman to woman. The longest any of his relationships had lasted was two months. And he had never even considered having children. Why would he? Up until a year ago he had been happy with his carefree bachelor life. He owned a three-room apartment at a good address on Kungsholmen, and had recently bought a summerhouse on the island of Ingarö. He could go to a fashionable gym with influencers, television stars and actors at any hour of the day or night. He knew them all. Maybe it was childish, but he liked the freedom, being able to come and go as he liked, and being able to immerse himself in his work if he needed to.

And then there were the women. They seemed to be drawn to him, it had always been that way. He actually preferred women as friends too, he found the laddish banter that often developed between men rather difficult to deal with. Even if he didn't have any objection to having a few beers with old friends from his childhood on Södermalm, he never felt the same emotional attachment as he did with women.

His Tinder account was set for women between the ages of twenty-five and forty-five. Maybe that was a bit creepy, but he didn't look like he was fifty-one. He had thought about raising the lower age-limit to thirty. But if twenty-five-year-olds wanted to sleep with him, why should he turn them down? It was their choice. And he always behaved decently. He didn't want any broken hearts or tears. He hated letting people down.

Mikael tossed the empty smoothie container in a bin as he crossed Norrmalmstorg. He carried on towards Stureplan, and stopped outside the Scandic Anglais to wait for the bus. The front of the Sture Gallery was lit up by an enormous illuminated billboard of a recently divorced influencer who was advertising Armani perfume. Angelica? Was that her name? She had been at Barry's last week, and had talked to him and asked his name. A few years ago he would probably already have seduced her and would now be cooling the relationship off.

But now there was Trude Hovland. There was something about her that had changed him. Maybe it was because for the first time he had met a woman who was even less keen than him on playing happy families. Trude came and went as she liked, and their relationship – if it could even be called that – was conducted entirely on her terms. Even though almost a year had passed since the first time they slept together, he was nowhere close to getting fed up, either of the sex or of seeing her. Mikael thought about phoning to see what she was doing, but decided against it. It was an unspoken rule that she was the one who contacted him when she wanted to meet up. It was also understood that they weren't exclusively seeing each other. Two weeks ago he had seen her kissing a guy in a bar. He hadn't raised it with her, and wasn't even sure if it had upset him. Anyway, the rules were clear. Trude hadn't done anything wrong. Even so, he still wished she would show him a little more affection, or at least say that she liked him.

His mobile buzzed. It was Katarina Fredriksson, head of Serious Crime at the Southern District of Stockholm Police.

"We've got something I think might interest you. A dead man found in Skärholmen today. His name is Stig Boström."

"I don't follow?"

Katarina chuckled.

"Okay. Stig Boström was found strangled in his flat on Tuesday, and we found traces of DNA. We ran a family search and found that the DNA is a close match to a man named Ahmed Mansour. This Ahmed has convictions for robbery, assault and firearms offences, but he's got an alibi, because he's currently in Kumla Prison. The father also has an alibi, and there are no other male relatives in Sweden. But Ahmed does have an older brother, Hamza Mansour, who went off to Syria. He's been reported dead. The family received a call about a year ago from someone claiming to represent the government in Raqqa. But now we've found DNA that probably belongs to him in this flat. Weren't you looking for people with connections to ISIS?"

The bus pulled up and Mikael got on, nodded to the driver and held his card against the reader.

"We were working on that, but now the Security Service have taken over," he said with his hand cupped over his mouth to stop the other passengers hearing.

"That's a shame. We're snowed under and were thinking of asking if you could help us. We haven't really got time to investigate this seeing as we've got two armed gangs in the southern suburbs who are currently shooting merry hell out of each other."

Mikael stopped in the aisle of the bus, thinking hard. He had a lot of respect for the Security Service, but they weren't homicide detectives. It wouldn't do any harm to take a quick look at the case. Vanessa was available, and Samer was still working part-time for the National Homicide Unit seeing as another post had become vacant.

"I can ask Vanessa to take a look at it."

"Frank?"

"Yes."

The bus stopped on Kungsgatan. The doors opened and a woman with a pram got ready to get on. Mikael tucked his phone between his ear and his shoulder and helped her lift the pram on board.

"Good. I'll send you what we've got."

2

Molly Berg was sitting on her sofa drinking tea. She was wearing a dark-blue silk dressing gown she had been given as a present during a trip to Dubai. Her hair was pulled up into a knot on top of her head. Just as Thomas had told her, she had stayed at home, except for her walks on Djurgården and trips to the supermarket. She had politely turned down Didrik's suggestion that they meet up. She had passed the time reading and watching box sets on Netflix.

Molly had decided to follow Thomas's instructions to the letter. And trust that if she helped him with this, then he would leave her alone. But she hated him more than she had ever hated anyone. And she was frightened. Frightened that he was going to ruin her life, and wreck the relationship she had built up with her dad. He had already broken into her apartment twice, and had gone all the way up to Kiruna when he couldn't get hold of her in Stockholm. It was obvious that he wasn't going to give up if he didn't get what he wanted.

That was why she hadn't said a word to that guy, Nicolas, even though every part of her had been desperate to talk. To beg for help. Looking back, she was happy with her decision.

As soon as this was finished, she would sell the apartment and get out, breaking off all contact with Marc. She was blown. Those photographs were out there, they were never going to go away. Molly would have to spend the rest of her life running away from them. She would start by going north. Maybe she'd end up in Kiruna after all? She could get a normal job, be near her dad. She could carry on building the relationship with him that had started to develop when she was up there recently. She wouldn't have to worry about money, the sale of the apartment alone would keep her going for at least ten years if she was even reasonably careful.

She jumped when the doorbell rang. It was only a few minutes past eight in the morning. It must be Thomas. Perhaps it was going to happen at last. Even if she was feeling nervous, she was desperate to get this over and once with, so she could start living again.

She pulled the belt of her dressing-gown tighter, because she wasn't wearing anything underneath it, checked that nothing showed in the hall mirror, then walked towards the door.

3

The sun was rising over Skärholmen when Vanessa and Samer walked into Stig Boström's deserted flat.

Samer was carrying a folder of photographs taken by the forensics team when the body had been found, as well as a brief report on the state of the investigation. Beyond conducting a forensic search of the crime scene and a bit of knocking on doors among the neighbours, the Southern District hadn't had the resources to delve any deeper into the murder.

The flat felt gloomy, there were faded photographs from a bygone age on the walls, and there was a signed poster from an Ulf Lundell concert in the 1980s on the wall. Vanessa couldn't help thinking that it felt like Stig Boström had constructed a museum to the past, rather than living to create new memories. As if he had been waiting for death, and had had his wait dramatically curtailed.

The bedroom door was open. They stopped in the doorway and Samer held up the forensic team's photographs so Vanessa could see them.

Stig Boström's body had been lying on the bed.

In the pictures, his jaw was hanging open towards his chest, and his eyes were closed. If it weren't for the grey colour of his face and the swollen stomach making his T-shirt bulge, the picture could have been just an old man having a rest.

Vanessa looked away from the photograph and went and stood at the foot of the bed. She looked up, towards the ventilation grille, which had been covered with plastic bags.

"Whoever killed him put a lot of effort into stopping anyone from finding the body," she said.

"They wouldn't have done that unless…"

Samer's phone rang and he fell silent. He turned away and

walked out into the living room. Vanessa saw him hold the phone up to his ear as he picked up a pack of pills from the coffee table and look at it.

She heard fragments of the conversation, but soon lost interest.

According to the post mortem, Stig Boström had barely been dead twenty-four hours before he was found. The bed, which had now been stripped, had been neatly made. If he had been strangled in the bedroom, there should have been more mess. Stig Boström would have kicked his legs, rolled back and forth, fighting for his life. But the covers beneath him had been smooth and neat, according to the photographs.

No, he wasn't murdered in the bedroom, Vanessa thought. And the flat was too neat for it to have been a burglary. Samer cleared his throat in the doorway.

"That was the clinic where the daughter, Petra Boström, is a patient. We can visit her today."

"Good, let's set off straight away, then we can see Hamza Mansour's family after that, if there's still time. You were about to say something about how Stig Boström came to be found?"

Samer nodded.

"Yes. He wouldn't have been found if one of the neighbours didn't usually leave her kids here some evenings when she went shopping. She knocked on the door on Monday evening, but there was no answer. She thought he'd forgotten, and came back on Tuesday morning. When he didn't answer she called 112. Two of our colleagues got into the flat and found him on the bed."

"The front door was locked?" Vanessa asked.

"Yes."

She turned to look at the empty bed again.

"The perpetrator strangles him, moves the body into the bedroom. Blocks the ventilation and cracks round the door so that the smell of the body doesn't alert the neighbours."

"Why do you think the body had been moved?" Samer asked.

Vanessa pointed to one of the photographs in his hand.

"The bed was neatly made. Not a crease out of place."

4

"We'll be there the whole time, even if you won't be able to see us," Thomas said, leaning closer to Molly. "There's nothing to worry about."

"Will you be there too?"

His brown eyes drilled into hers.

"Yes, I'll be there too."

He was wearing the same suit he had been wearing the first time they met. She was struck by how long ago that felt, like another lifetime.

"On Sunday, then?"

The Thomas she was talking to now was more like he had been back then. Calm, gentle. Nothing like the agitated, unpleasant man of their last encounter. His face had almost healed completely now.

"7.00pm. The room is already booked."

"And this is the last time?"

He leaned back, adjusted his tie and smiled his crooked smile. She couldn't help thinking he was handsome, even if the attraction she had one felt towards him had evaporated completely. It was funny to think that less than a month ago she had been mildly infatuated with him, hoping that they might get together.

"After that you'll never see me again. I'm sorry I wasn't able to keep that promise last time, but this time it will definitely happen."

He reached into his inside pocket and pulled out an envelope.

"I bought something for you," he said, handing it over. Molly opened it and took out a sheet of A4. It was confirmation of a plane ticket in her name for a flight to Kiruna on Monday.

"The morning flight. Seeing as I forced you to leave so quickly, I thought this was the least I could do as thanks for all your help. What you're doing is brave, very brave. And important."

She was feeling calmer. She was going to be able to see her dad again, and Didrik. As soon as this was over, she was going to call him.

Because if there was the slightest risk that she might get hurt, Thomas wouldn't have bought her a plane ticket, would he?

5

Hamza's head ached and he was feeling faintly nauseous. He had dreamed about Stig last night. Again. He woke up in a cold sweat, and had trouble getting back to sleep. He had walked around the empty rooms of the flat, then gone out for a short walk in the forest, but nothing had helped.

He jerked when the doorbell rang. He got up quickly, snatching up the pistol from the table and moved swiftly into the hall. He took aim at the door, ready to fire while he peered out into the stairwell through the peephole. Farid. Hamza was immediately worried. He tucked the pistol in the back of his waistband, gently disconnected the explosive device that was attached to the door, and opened it.

Farid stepped inside and closed the door.

"Has something happened?" Hamza asked anxiously.

Farid wiped his shoes on the doormat, removed the cap that he had been wearing low over his forehead, and cast a quick, disinterested glance at the explosive device.

"We're going to pick up the weapons you're going to be using on Sunday."

"Now?"

Farid nodded.

"I told you the other day. What's going on with you? Get some clothes on."

A short while later they pulled out onto Albanoleden. Farid lit a cigarette and held it in the hand resting on the steering-wheel. They drove down into the tunnel and headed south. On the radio a newsreader announced that two people had been found shot in a car in Fittja.

"We're going to Hallunda, aren't we?" Hamza asked.

"We are," Farid said.

"Then we'll have to be careful, that's not far from that shooting. Isn't it better to wait until everywhere isn't crawling with police? There might be roadblocks."

Farid grunted something inaudible in response, then sucked hard on his cigarette.

Hamza looked at his face in the rear-view mirror. He ran one hand down his freshly-shaven cheek. It felt odd, and he missed his beard. He considered telling Farid about Stig, but decided to stay quiet. Maybe it would be best to move the body? But where could he hide him? No one would miss Stig. No one would report him missing. By the time the housing company began sending reminders about the rent it would be too late. Then Khenziir would be dead, and probably Hamza as well. He saw Stig's body lying on the bed in his room in his mind's eye. It had probably already begun to swell up and smell. He wondered if it was covered with fat flies like the bodies in the cities and by the roadsides during the war.

Stig had deserved a better death, but then so had plenty of others. The police would probably never been able to link his murder to Hamza. He had been keeping an eye on all the newspapers' websites, and hadn't been able to find anything about a man found dead in Skärholmen.

The murder would remain unsolved.

And what did it really matter? The history of the world was full of people who hadn't deserved to die. Hamza had several deaths on his conscience. Young soldiers from the Shia militias who had begged and pleaded for their lives while their deaths were filmed on mobile phones. Kurdish Peshmerga women he had allowed his men to rape for hours before they were killed. Yazidi boys whose throats he had cut without hesitation, their warm blood washing over his hands. Was it because of the war that had been raging all around him at the time that their deaths hadn't bothered him as much?

But the war was still going on, in spite of everything. In two days' time he was going to kill a man who really did deserve it. He hoped that would please God.

"It will be you and Sabina who go to the hotel tomorrow," Farid said.

He wound his window down and tossed out the cigarette butt.

"The widow?"

"Exactly. Don't let yourself be taken in by her beautiful face." Farid smiled. "She is very faithful, and very effective. In Raqqa

266

she was a member of Hisbah. A friend of mine told me a story about her."

Hamza looked at him curiously.

"She and her husband had two Yazidi slaves. A mother and daughter. The girl was five years old or so, and didn't know her place. Kept running about. Ran away. Didn't do what Sabina said. So do you know what she did?"

Hamza shook his head slowly. Farid took his time. He fished out his cigarette packet, quickly lit one, then put his lighter down. He blew out a cloud of smoke and chuckled.

"She chained the kid up in the garden in 50° heat, in the full sun. Let her slowly cook to death while her mother cried in despair."

6

Samer and Vanessa had been shown into a room by a stressed secretary. There was a conference table in the middle of the room, and a whiteboard at one end with points from the most recent staff meeting written on it in green.

Samer had been told over the phone that they would stand more chance of getting through to Petra Boström if they saw her in person. But it wasn't certain that they would be able to speak to her, because any evaluation of whether she could cope with a meeting would be made closer to the time. Going door-to-door in Stig Boström's building hadn't come up with anything, and Vanessa was hoping that they might get answers to at least a few questions. The latest phone call to the clinic had seemed to indicate that a meeting could actually go ahead.

They had just sat down at the conference table when the door opened and a tall man walked in. He looked pretty much as Vanessa expected a consultant psychiatrist would look. His head was shaved, the stubble of his beard reddish-brown, and his steel-rimmed glasses concealed a pair of curious, alert eyes.

"Nils Gysander," he said with a Småland accent, holding out his hand before sitting down opposite them.

"Is Petra Boström on her way?" Vanessa asked.

Nils Gysander made an apologetic gesture.

"After we told her of her father's death we had to administer a strong sedative. She was better this morning, but suffered a relapse about half an hour ago. We had to increase the dose. She's beyond reach at the moment, I'm afraid."

Vanessa looked at him with disappointment.

"How long has she been a patient here?"

"For almost three years."

"What for?"

"As I'm sure you know, details of our patients are bound by an oath of confidentiality."

Nils Gysander titled his head slightly and pursed his lips to a thin smile. Vanessa felt her frustration growing.

"How was her relationship with Stig Boström?" Samer quickly interjected. He had evidently noticed Vanessa's reaction.

"Without saying too much, it was good, as far I could tell. They were very close, or at least they were until she ended up here."

"Did he visit her often?"

"No," Nils Gysander said. "As I understand it, he had trouble getting here."

"In what sense?"

"I don't know the details, which was why I was rather surprised when he called a few days ago and wanted to see her. That was the first time in about a year."

Samer and Vanessa both leaned forward on the table.

"When was he here?"

"On Monday."

"How did Petra seem afterwards?" Vanessa asked. "Was she... upset?"

Samer went on quickly, before Nils Gysander had time to answer.

"Naturally we respect Petra's integrity, we're just trying to built up an understanding of the last few hours of her father's life."

He smiled ingratiatingly.

"Petra was happy, very happy," Nils Gysander said. "The visit seemed to have done her good, and we always encourage relatives to visit as much as they can. As I said before, I don't really have anything to say about their relationship, it seemed loving, normal. That's really all I can say."

Twenty minutes later Vanessa reversed the BMW out from the car park. It was snowing. The seats were cold, the windows steamed up. She turned up the temperature on the heater.

Samer cocked his head and peered up at the building they had just left.

"So he came down here to see his daughter for the first time in a year, then he was murdered. Probably that same evening," he said thoughtfully.

"Almost as if he knew he was going to die," Vanessa muttered as she drove out through the gate. "Do you think we'll have time to talk to the Mansour family today? In this weather I'm going to have to take it fairly gently on the way home."

"There's something bothering me," Samer said slowly, without any indication that he had heard what Vanessa had said.

"What is it?"

She hunched over the steering-wheel to see better.

"Stig Boström had epilepsy. I'm guessing that was why he couldn't drive all the way down here. He'd probably already lost his driving licence. After you've had an attack, you're not allowed to drive for a certain number of months."

Vanessa eased off the accelerator pedal.

"How do you know he suffered from epilepsy?"

"The medication on his coffee table, Lamictal. Noor takes the same thing. So how did he get down here?"

Vanessa pulled over by the side of the road, glanced in the rear-view mirror, then did a U-turn.

7

Hamza and Farid were on the E4, close to Älvsjö, on their way back to the flat in Lappkärrsberget. There wasn't much traffic, and Farid stuck a couple of kilometres per hour below the speed limit, and stayed in the right-hand lane. The weapons were in the boot, and Hamza was feeling calm.

Everything had gone smoothly. They had parked the car outside a rundown housing complex in Hallunda, Farid had tapped in the door-code, and they had gone down into the basement storage area. There he had pulled out a small key, opened one of the storage compartments and pointed to a bag. Using the torch on his mobile phone, they had quickly checked the contents, then took it with them, put it in the boot and drove away.

"So, on Sunday?" Hamza said, mostly to break the silence.

Farid turned his head, met Hamza's gaze, and nodded.

"You'll get the details tomorrow. But we know where he's going to be."

"How can we know that?"

"We know. You're going to be close. Very close."

Farid looked up at the rear-view mirror and his face tensed. Hamza looked in the side mirror and instantly saw what he had reacted to. There was a police car behind them, so close that Hamza could see the policemen's faces. He opened the glove compartment and pulled out his pistol, checked it was loaded and slipped it into the pocket in the door so he could reach it quickly. He glanced at Farid, who was clutching the steering-wheel tight.

"Take it easy," Hamza said. "They're not going to stop us, they have no reason to."

Just as he said that, the blue lights went on. The car pulled up alongside them and the police officer in the passenger seat gestured to them to pull over at the side of the road. Hamza realised he had no choice other than to shoot. There was too much at stake. The entire attack risked being ruined if they were caught with two automatic weapons. The police would investigate them, which would lead to the potential exposure of the whole cell. Everything would have been in vain. They would be arrested, charged and found guilty, and nothing would change for the defenceless women and children in the camps in Syria.

"If they ask to look in the boot, I'll have to shoot them," Hamza said.

Farid, whose whole body was shaking, nodded quickly. Hamza looked at him anxiously, his body language was anything but relaxed and self-assured.

Their speed was decreasing. The speedometer showed seventy kilometres an hour.

"Have you got your driving licence?"

Farid nodded again. Beads of sweat were breaking out on his forehead, and he wiped them off with one hand.

Fifty kilometres an hour.

"You need to calm down. Just answer their questions, and if it goes wrong I'll shoot. Then all you have to do is get us out of here. You can do it."

Hamza could feel his derision for Farid growing by the second. He was weak, he hadn't had to cope with more than a couple of hours in the Caliphate. It was obvious that he had never done any real fighting.

They pulled over. The police car stopped next to a road-sign about twenty metres behind them. Hamza took a deep breath and found himself thinking about the two men who had been found shot in a car in Fittja.

"Where's my mobile?" he muttered.

"What?" Farid hissed.

"Nothing," Hamza whispered as he found his phone in the cup-holder between them.

8

Vanessa and Samer huddled beneath the same umbrella as they made their way back through the snow to the reception area at the clinic.

Samer hurried over to the desk, where a woman with short hair and glasses looked up.

"Were you working here on Monday?" Samer asked, holding up his police ID.

"Yes?" the woman said hesitantly.

Vanessa looked around the room, trying in vain to spot a security camera. There was a sofa and a set of chairs, and a table with a Selecta coffee machine. On the coffee table was a stack of newspapers and a couple of magazines.

"So you were here when Stig Boström arrived to visit his daughter?"

She nodded and rubbed her chin with a long, red fingernail.

"Do you know if there anyone with him?"

"Yes. There was another man here with him."

Vanessa and Samer exchanged a quick glance.

"Can you describe him?"

"He was of, erm, foreign heritage, I think we say now?" she said, her gaze flitting about anxiously. "He had black hair. Dark eyes. He sat there and read a couple of magazines while Stig went in to visit the resident."

Vanessa took out her mobile and showed an old photograph of Hamza Mansour they had been sent from Serious Crime, Southern District earlier that day.

"Was it him?"

She nodded.

"You're sure?" Vanessa asked.

"Not entirely, maybe. But I think it was him."

After asking if any of the areas visited by Hamza Mansour was covered by security cameras and being told that they weren't, they left the building once again and walked back across the car park as the snow swirled around them. They got in the car without saying a word.

"What are you thinking?" Samer eventually asked.

"I think that Hamza Mansour killed Stig."

"But he's dead. He's supposed to be dead."

"There was a war, and in many ways that war is still going on. It's impossible to keep track of who actually died, or is being held in captivity, or has made their way back here. Someone called his parents and said he was dead, and they in turn called the police and reported that. We've got no way of going down to the war zone and demanding to see a death certificate and post mortem report, because those just don't exist."

Samer nodded, his eyes fixed on the wall in front of the car.

"Yes, of course you're right. But why did he kill Stig? And where is he now?"

9

Keeping his back straight, and with his phone on his lap, Hamza dialled 112. His heart was pounding in his chest and he clenched his fists and tried to breathe slowly. The call went through.

"What are you doing?" Farid hissed.

Hamza ignored him.

Behind the car one of the police officers indicated that the driver should get out. Farid undid his belt and opened the door.

"Hurry up and get out. Close the door," Hamza said quietly.

"112. What's the nature of the emergency?"

Hamza pressed to put the phone on speaker. He made sure he was looking straight ahead in case either of the officers decided to take a look inside the car. He moved his lips as little as possible.

"There's been a shooting in Sätra. Automatic gunfire. Four men have been shot. They're bleeding, dying, please, get here quickly."

Farid and the police officer were standing facing each other outside. The policeman's hand was resting on his service weapon, and he was gesturing towards the car. Farid was gesticulating unhappily, shaking his head.

"Where in Sätra?"

The female call handler's voice sounded tense, serious. Hamza couldn't remember the names of any streets in Sätra.

"Near the metro station, in the centre. Hurry up! They're dying!"

He clicked to end the call and felt sweat break out at the base of his spine. He leaned a little closer to the wing mirror to see what was going on behind the car. The police officer and Farid had moved slightly, but were still talking.

The policeman moved towards the boot of the car. Hamza could see his face clearly now, he was a huge man with a big beard. There was a purposeful look about him as he spoke to Farid, who looked like a frightened schoolboy.

Hamza had done what he could. If it didn't work, the only option would be to open fire. He reached for the gun, cradling the barrel. If the policeman moved any closer to the boot, he would shoot him through the rear window. Then throw the door open and shoot the other one so Farid could get back in the car.

The police officer held his hand up to Farid, who stopped talking and just stood there with his arms by his sides. Hamza saw the policeman's lips move; he was talking into his shoulder, where the microphone of his radio was attached. The driver's door of the police car opened and his colleague called something, waving anxiously.

The next moment the lights on the roof began to flash again, and the siren wailed. The policeman set off back to the police car at a run.

He leapt into the passenger seat and the car accelerated out onto the E4 and quickly disappeared from sight.

Farid stood there, leaning against the boot. Hamza got out. A truck driving past made the whole car shake. Hamza took Farid under his arm and led him to the passenger door, pushed him inside the car and slammed the door.

10

The bent, white-haired old man turned towards Vanessa and his face was lit up by the flickering, greenish light of the television. He gave her a long, disinterested look before turning back to the screen. There was an overflowing ashtray on the arm of his chair.

Vanessa straightened her back, which was aching after their drive up from Jönköping.

"Abbas Mansour," she said. "My name is Vanessa Frank, I'm from the police. This is my colleague, Samer Bakir."

The man in the armchair grunted something inaudible. The woman who had shown them in, Abbas's wife, pushed past Vanessa to get to her husband. She said something in Arabic and Vanessa caught the name Hamza.

"What do you want with me?" he said, reaching for the packet of cigarettes on the other armrest, taking one out and lighting it.

"To talk about your son."

The woman left the living room.

"Ahmed?"

"Hamza."

"I have only one son. Ahmed. The other is dead. Just as well. Should never have been born."

He had a very strong accent. Vanessa found the remote control and switched the television off. Abbas stared at her angrily. They glared at each other for a while until he looked away, took a drag on his cigarette and blew the smoke out between his lips.

"I've already said what I've got to say to the Security Service. A man called us from Syria a year or so ago, told us he was dead. My wife insisted we call the police. I didn't see why, because he was dead. But we called anyway."

"You don't seem particularly upset? You're not even saying his name."

"He was a loser. Weak, wanted to be liked. Accepted by people like you. I knew he'd come to a bad end by the time he was seven years old."

Vanessa sat down on the battered leather sofa, and sank deep into it. Samer remained standing with his arms folded, leaning against the door-post.

"Did you ever get any evidence to prove that he was really dead?" Vanessa asked.

"What do you mean?"

"A picture of his body?"

Abbas snorted.

"No."

Samer cleared his throat and took a couple of steps towards Abbas, who looked at him calmly. A thin, white tendril of smoke snaked up towards the ceiling from the cigarette in his hand.

"So he could be alive?"

Abbas gestured irritably with his hand, and there was a new intensity in his eyes.

"What do I know? Don't you hear what I'm saying? I don't care. He was dead the moment he set off to Syria. No one misses him except his mother."

"He hasn't contacted you?"

"No."

"Have you got anything that might have Hamza's DNA on it?" Vanessa asked.

"Why would I? I threw everything away," Abbas said, rubbing the palms of his hands against each other with a look of disgust on his face, as if he were rubbing something unpleasant off them.

They left the room and heard the television being turned back on. The small woman was standing in the hall, and gestured eagerly for them to go with her into the kitchen. There was a pleasant smell of food and spices. The dishwasher was whirring.

"Do you think Hamza is alive?" she asked hopefully.

"What's your name?" Vanessa asked.

"Shadia."

Vanessa and Samer exchanged a quick glance.

"We don't know, Shadia. That's one possibility we're investigating," Vanessa said gently.

The woman grabbed hold of the edge of the table and slowly lowered her body onto a chair and took a deep breath. Her small hand clutched the edge of the table until her knuckles turned white, and her arm was shaking. Vanessa realised that there was no need to ask if her son had contacted her, her reaction said it all.

They waited a few moments, letting her compose herself. Without any warning, and without looking up, she started to speak.

Her Swedish was much better than Abbas's.

"He changed. He started to go to that mosque. He started to get angry with anything and everything. Talked about God. About the wrath of God. About infidels. About Swedes. They were all going to die. He came home and lectured me and Nadira, his sister. Told us to obey him, not to argue. Nadira finally had enough when he hit her for refusing to take his plate away. She moved out. My friends told me he was walking around in Skärholmen telling women to dress decently. Called them whores. Harlots. He's always been lost, Hamza. But he changed. Became a bad person. A wicked, angry person."

She fell silent. She looked up at them in surprise, as she had forgotten they were there.

"But I still love my son. I wish I could hate him, forget about him the way my husband has done. But I can't. They say he has done terrible things over there. I can't believe that. For me, he's just my little boy. My sweet, frightened boy. I can't help it, but I dream that one day he might just show up here and I can hug him again, the way I did when he was a child."

She burst into tears. They ran down her face and dripped onto the table. She quickly wiped them away with the palm of her hand.

"I didn't even have a chance to say goodbye," she sobbed. "One day he was just gone."

"Do you know who Stig Boström is?" Vanessa asked.

Shadia sniffed.

"The teacher in Skärholmen?"

"Yes."

"He's a nice man. He tried to help Hamza. Asked him back to his flat, gave him books to read. Abbas didn't like him."

"Why not?" Vanessa asked in surprise.

"He doesn't like Sweden. I had to keep the fact that I was going to language classes secret." She gestured despairingly with her hands. "To start with he said that Stig wanted to turn Hamza into a Swede. Turn him into an Uncle Tom, happy to bow down to the Swedes. Get rid of everything Arabic. Then he started to say that

Stig was a pervert. That he asked the boys to his flat to... well, you understand."

"So Hamza and Stig got on well?"

"Hamza worshipped Stig."

"Stig's dead. He was found murdered."

Shadia's eyes opened wide before she shook her head hard.

"Hamza would never hurt Stig."

The dishwasher bleeped. Samer took a step closer and crouched down in front of Shadia.

"Do you have any mementos of Hamza? Anything you've kept?"

She nodded.

"A lock of hair from the first time he had his hair cut. My husband doesn't know about it, but I've still got it, in a box under the bed."

"Can you go and get it?"

"What for?"

"So we can find out if he's still alive."

11

Axel hardly ever drank alcohol, and couldn't remember the last time he had been drunk. But now he caught sight of a can of Carlsberg in the fridge. He wiped the condensation from the green metal against his trouser-leg and opened the can.

Rebecca and Thorsten's apartment was quiet and dimly lit.

Thorsten had moved out and was living in their summer house while he waited to get a flat of his own. Rebecca had gone out to meet a girlfriend. Simon, who had been allowed to leave hospital the day before, was sleeping.

Axel took the beer back to the sofa. Sometimes he listened to Lars Winnerbäck while he worked, but he didn't dare do that now in case Simon woke up and needed help going to the toilet.

It had taken longer than Axel had expected to track down the money that Johan Karlström had helped to launder through Gambler. There were a lot of false trails, and they had been skilfully laid out. Axel had been bounced between different accounts all around the world, but had stubbornly persisted with his quest. His investigation fell in a grey zone between what was legal and illegal, not least because he was using his security login from his work for Danske Bank to hide his digital footprint.

Now he thought he was getting close to finding the money's final destination.

Axel sank back down on the sofa, took a sip of the beer and rested his laptop on his knees. Before getting back to work, he listened to reassure himself that Simon was still asleep, but apart one of the neighbours apparently taking a late shower, the building was quiet.

He immersed himself in his work, carrying on with the search, and a hour later he finally got there. He leaned towards the screen and squinted. Was he reading this right? This can't be possible, he thought.

The money had been withdrawn, to all intents and purposes legally and cleanly, just a couple of kilometres away.

12

After quickly stopping off at Trude's flat to drop off the lock of hair they had been given by Shadia Mansour, Vanessa drove home.

Celine was waiting in the hall. Vanessa gave her a hug, then leaned over to unlace her boots.

"Shall we go and get some dough?" Celine asked hopefully.

Vanessa yawned.

"It's already half past nine."

"Time's relative. At least that's what our physics teacher says, and you've told me to pay attention in class."

Vanessa couldn't help laughing.

"Get your clothes on then, Einstein."

While Vanessa watched as Celine put on her coat and shoes, she couldn't help thinking that the world was a very odd place that she really didn't understand. Not that far away were a couple of parents whose son had joined one of the most murderous sects the world had ever seen. According to his dad, he had always been a loser, and according to his mum, a sweet little boy. It was too full of contradictions to make sense. It was impossible to fit the pieces of the puzzle together into a coherent image. Maybe that was why she had finally been able to let go of Natasha. How could the warm, intelligent, cautious girl she loved so much have been a member of ISIS?

It was impossible to make any sense of it. Yet, anyway.

They left the flat and walked past the Indian restaurant on Roslagsgatan.

"It's the first Sunday of Advent this weekend, what do you think of that?"

"What would you like me to think about it?"

"Do you like Christmas?"

They turned into Odengatan.

"To be honest, I hate it. What about you?"

"I love Christmas," Celine exclaimed. "It's the best time of the whole year!"

"Did you and your dad used to celebrate Christmas?" Vanessa held the door of 7-Eleven open for Celine. The girl ran over to the counter and nodded in recognition to the young man who had already taken two uncooked Lucia buns out of the fridge behind him. He put them on a napkin and Celine paid.

"Thanks, Steve," Celine said with a big smile, taking the napkin over to a free table. "No, Dad used to go on a bender at Christmas."

Vanessa reached for one lump of dough.

"A bender?"

"Several days of solid drinking. He used to disappear on 23 December and reappear on Boxing Day. Not that it mattered, I used to save twenty kronor each week all year long so I could buy Christmas food and a tree. I used to decorate the whole flat with Mum's old decorations."

"On your own?"

Celine nodded happily. She undid her coat, then bit off some of the dough.

"When Dad came home he said it was like climbing into a spaceship. He usually prepared to be scared, and ask if he'd been kidnapped by aliens, then he'd lie down on the sofa and moan, and I'd feed him leftovers."

Vanessa smiled. She imagined Celine sitting on her own in the gloomy, shabby little flat in Bredäng surrounded by twinkling lights while she waited for her dad to stop drinking. It was a tragic but beautiful image. It unsettled her, and made her think about the papers she had received, which were lying in her wardrobe. She put the yellow dough down on the napkin and wiped her fingers.

"Celine, would you… How would you feel about…"

The girl looked at her intently.

"About what?"

Vanessa felt her throat tighten.

"Buying more dough to take home with us?"

13

It was Sunday evening and Molly looked at her carefully made-up face in the rear-view mirror from her position behind the Uber Black chauffeur.

They turned right by the Kebab House on Kungsgatan and carried on towards Norra Bantorget. She had never been to the Clarion Hotel Sign before. They drove through the park, past the statue of Hjalmar Branting, and stopped in front of the entrance to the hotel. Flagpoles flying the flags of dozens of different countries rose up from the ground. The driver opened her door and helped her out. Molly thanked him with a quick smile, then adjusted her light-coloured trenchcoat before going up the flight of steps. Her heels clicked on the slabs, and she ignored the stares of a couple of men who were watching her. The glass door ahead of her was held open without her seeing who was doing it, and she headed into the lobby without slowing down.

She took the keycard she had been sent by courier that morning out of her handbag and held it in her hand as she walked towards the lifts. She tried to see if Thomas was there – he had said that members of the Security Service would be present – but she couldn't see him, or anyone who looked like they could be a colleague of his. Her palms felt sweaty and she wiped them discreetly on her trenchcoat before pressing the button for a lift.

When she got to the right floor she got out and made her way to the room. She held the keycard up to the door and stepped inside. She looked around the suite. Two west-facing rooms, and a large bathroom. The view out across the water of Klara sjö, the rooftops and the multiple railway lines heading into the Central Station was dizzying. She shrugged off her trenchcoat and looked at the black lace underwear she was wearing.

I look like a doll, she thought.

Molly opened the bar, took out two miniature bottles of whisky and unscrewed them. She sat down on the bed, leaned her head back and downed one of them, then grimaced.

"One last time," she said out loud to herself. "Then you're free."

She raised the second bottle.

"Free as a bird, cowboy," she sang in a Southern States accent, and drank down the contents.

There was a knock on the door and she got to her feet, dropped the bottles on the floor and kicked them under the bed.

The man in front of Molly took his glasses off, folded them up and slipped them into the breast pocket of his jacket. He was in his mid-forties, but looked younger. She knew he had been married for about ten years, she had seen them when they appeared on a chat-show on TV4, talking about how in love they were, their canoeing excursions out into the archipelago, the equality of their home.

Now his ice-blue eyes were studying her intently.

"It's been a long time, Molly."

She forced herself to smile in that girlish way she knew made him feel special. That was the trick. To make them feel specially chosen. They knew she could have any man she wanted, and her job was to make them believe they had something special, something that made her forget the others. She bit her lip, walked up to him and helped him take his suit off. She slowly undid the buttons of his shirt, one by one. She saw his penis swell up beneath the fabric of his trousers.

"Wait," he suddenly said. Molly stopped. He took out a blister pack of pills and held it up in front of her.

"What are those?" she asked

"Just Atarax, a mild tranquiliser. But if we take two or three of these and wash them down with spirits, it's like fucking on a cloud surrounded by angels."

Molly smiled and nodded.

"Do you dare? In your position?"

She knew he'd like it if she pretended to care, if she pretended to be impressed by his status.

"I'm no junkie," he said with a smile. "I get these on prescription."

Molly hesitated. Maybe the pills would help, stop her feeling so nervous? She went over to the bar, took out eight small bottles of spirits and lined them up on the bed. The man pressed out four pills, swallowed two, and handed the other two to Molly.

The lift stopped on the ninth floor. Hamza adjusted his black cap, and nodded to Sabina, who was wearing one just like it. On an armchair at the start of the corridor sat a large, blond man with an almost white beard. He lowered his newspaper and looked at them. He had an earpiece in one ear, the cord coiled down beneath his collar. Hamza recognised him as one of Khenziir's bodyguards at the ice hockey game.

Hamza and Sabina had already checked into the hotel on Saturday evening, and had left the automatic weapons in the room. They had hung the "do not disturb" sign on the door, to stop the cleaner going in. They had spent Sunday acting like a couple, wandering about in the hotel hand in hand to learn where the various entrances and exits were.

They walked into their suite and Hamza lifted the bag under the bed onto the bedspread. He unzipped it, took out one of the automatic guns and passed it to Sabina, who checked it with a practiced hand.

"Five minutes. I'll take care of the bodyguard. You wait here."

Sabina nodded. Hamza was stuck once again by how beautiful she was, with her full lips, dark eyebrows and jet-black hair that fell over her eyes when she wore it loose. Soon she might well be dead. But he was going to do his best to make sure they both survived and got out of there.

Hamza handed his automatic rifle to Sabina and pulled out his pistol. He released the safety catch and screwed the silencer onto it. He hung the now empty bag over his shoulder, and put both the pistol and balaclava inside it.

"You come out when he's dead."

Sabina pulled her own balaclava over her head. Hamza looked into her dark eyes for a few moments before turning away, pulling his cap down over his forehead and opening the door. He walked with firm steps towards the bodyguard, who looked up languidly. Hamza met his gaze calmly. Absentmindedly, as if he were looking for something, he put his hand into the bag.

But something about the movement or the look on his face must have given him away.

The man leapt up, reaching for his pistol. But it was too late. Hamza already had his finger on the trigger.

One bullet in the head, one in the chest.

The man was thrown backwards before he fell sideways and slid out of the armchair. Hamza pulled his balaclava on as Sabina came rushing out from their room.

Molly was sitting astride the man, moving rhythmically back and forth. The world was billowing and spinning around her. All sound seemed muffled, as if she were in an aquarium. It was nice to feel numb. No need to think. Just act, and pretend to be enjoying herself.

His mouth was half open, and he was groaning softly with each movement. One hand was cupped around her breasts, and he was squeezing one of her buttocks with the other. Somewhere outside she heard a dull thud. She jerked and stopped moving, turning her head towards the door to the room.

"Keep going, you little whore, keep going," he said, pulling her down onto him harder, pushing deeper inside.

It hurt. She resumed her movements, but was starting to feel unwell, and braced herself with her knees to save herself from losing her balance. She opened her eyes and focused on a point on the painting in front of her to stop her having to look at his sweaty, red face.

"Wait a moment," she gasped. The nausea was getting worse, she couldn't stop it. She stepped off him and tumbled off the bed, then got to her feet. He was shouting after her angrily.

She almost fell over, but managed to keep her balance, yanked open the door to the bathroom, hit the dimmer switch and the lights came on. She quickly locked the door behind her, fell to her knees in front of the toilet and threw up.

Pale brown liquid ran over the porcelain, clouding the water. She clung to the toilet seat as her head spun.

They moved towards the room where Khenziir and the whore were. Soon he would be dead, the man who hated Muslims, who had built his career on insulting Islam.

"Stand back," Hamza said, and aimed the barrel of the Kalashnikov at the door. Just as he was about to pull the trigger they heard screaming. He turned and looked towards the dead bodyguard. Two older women had just emerged from the lift and were screaming blue murder. Sabina quickly raised her gun and pointed it towards them.

"No," Hamza yelled.

She lowered the gun again. Hamza stood to one side of the door to stop himself getting hit by any ricochets, then quickly shot out the lock and kicked the door open. They rushed into the room with their guns raised. Khenziir was standing naked at the foot of the bed, staring at them with a confused look on his face. He raised his hands, and almost lost his balance as he did so. His eyes, which at first had been uncomprehending and angry, filled with terror. Sabina and Hamza stood side by side, raised their weapons and opened fire on his body.

Khenziir fell backwards across the unmade bed whose white sheets turned red with blood. Sabina pulled her balaclava off to uncover her mouth, then spat on his shattered chest.

The screaming in the corridor was growing louder as people rushed towards the stairs.

14

Max Lewenhaupt was on his way out of the *Kvällspressen* offices. His Taxi Stockholm car was waiting for him down in Gjörwellsgatan. He had spent a couple of hours in the newsroom sorting out his expense receipts, and trying to come up with an interesting article for the following week. After his scoop with Vanessa Frank he felt drained of ideas, and that could be lethal for a journalist. You were never better than your last headline, as the news editor, Bengt the Bun, always said. But Max had failed to come up with anything. He had stared at his screen without a single idea for an article popping up. Maybe that would get better if he went home and ran a hot bath. When he opened the door of the taxi his mobile phone rang. He said hello politely to the driver, gave his address, then took the call.

"Can you get to the Clarion?" Bengt asked at once. Max glanced up at the building he had just left, realising from the Bun's voice that he was wound up.

"What's happened?"

"A freelance photographer who was in the area says shots have been fired. He heard it on police radio."

"Gang-related?" Max asked.

"How the hell should I know? Can you get over there and check it out?"

Molly was holding her hands over her ears. She felt dizzy, and her head was ringing from the loud banging. What had happened? She heard voices, and looked up at the locked door. She had to get away from it. She crept towards the bathtub, crawled over the side and curled up inside it. Something had gone wrong. Why were they shooting? Thomas. Where was Thomas? He had to help her. Soon the agents he had said would be there would come to her rescue.

Molly thought about her father.

And about the fact that she didn't want to die.

A police car overtook the taxi at speed on Fleminggatan. Its siren was wailing, and the rotating blue light on top of the car was turning the facades of the buildings on both sides of the street blue. Shortly afterwards a second car raced past. This was something big. Max could feel it in his whole body. His mobile lit up. A newsflash from *Kvällspressen. Reports of gunfire at hotel in central Stockholm.* Before he had time to open it, another one appeared, this time from *Aftonposten. Newsflash: at least one dead in gunfight at luxury hotel.*

Max swore. *Aftonposten* already had people there. Their offices were within walking distance of Norra Bantorget.

He leaned forward between the seats.

"Can you put your foot down a bit?"

Panicking guests were rushing along the corridor. They were screaming, crying or simply howling in fear of the two masked gunmen as they hurried towards the stairs and lifts to get away.

Sabina walked over to the bathroom door and turned towards Hamza. She gestured towards the door with the barrel of her Kalashnikov. She seemed untroubled by what was going on around them. She raised her gun to fire just as the fire alarm went off. She lowered it again and looked at Hamza. He checked his Casio watch. One minute and forty-five seconds had passed since the first shot.

"We need to get out of here," Hamza said.

Killing the whore was of secondary importance. The idea was that they would drag her out into the corridor, make it look like she had just rushed out from a different room and got caught in the line of fire. But it would soon be too late, the first police officers could already have arrived at the scene. Every second they delayed reduced their chance of escape. The important thing was that Khenziir was dead.

Sabina pulled the trigger. The bullets shredded the bathroom door. Hamza looked out into the hotel corridor. He waved to Sabina. The tumult had died down. The corridor was empty.

"Come on."

They rushed towards the fire escape and shoved the door open. They could hear the sound of agitated voices from below. They pulled off their balaclavas, dropped their weapons and pulled off their outer layer of clothing. Sabina adjusted her long, thick hair while Hamza made sure that they hadn't forgotten any details that could give them away.

Molly took hold of the edge of the bath and heaved herself up. The tiled floor was covered with splinters of wood and fragments of glass. Dazed, she looked out into the suite through one of the bullet-holes in the door. The chaos, screaming and gunfire had been replaced by deafening silence. It didn't occur to her that she was still naked as she passed the bathroom mirror. The suite was empty. She let out a scream when she saw the body on the bed.

Blood was still pouring out of his stomach and chest, seeping down onto the floor.

Molly clamped her hand over her mouth. What if they were still there? If they were after her too? Where was Thomas? Had they killed him too?

She had to get out of there before they came back. Her underwear was in a heap by the minibar. She quickly pulled it on, not caring that the black silk underpants ended up inside out. She found her trenchcoat and handbag on a chair by the window. Police cars were pulling up outside on Norra Bantorget. Molly slipped her high-heeled shoes in her bag and peered out into the corridor. She ran towards the lifts and pressed the button desperately.

"Fuck, fuck, fuck," she muttered.

She turned round, looked up at the ceiling, and caught sight of the green sign pointing to the emergency exit. She made her way down the flights of steps, two steps at a time. When she reached the ground floor she stopped and tied her hair up, then wiped her cheeks with the palm of her hand. She took a deep breath, then pushed the door open and stepped out into the lobby.

After paying the driver, Max leapt out of the taxi on Vasagatan and started to run towards the hotel. He saw the rotating blue lights of the ambulances and police cars. The area in front of the hotel was complete chaos and a large crowd had gathered. The police were yelling orders at the confused mass of people, many of whom appeared to be foreign tourists who didn't understand what was going on or what there were being told to do.

One woman was sobbing that it was a terrorist attack.

"Move back!" one policeman was shouting, holding his arms out and shepherding them back, away from the hotel entrance.

Max pushed his way through the crowd and reached a different police officer. He held up his press ID and asked what had happened.

The officer snorted and turned away.

"Swedish press," Max called out in English, turning round and holding his press ID above his head. "Did anyone see what happened?"

He repeated the question in Swedish, but no one took any notice of him.

People were still pouring out from the exits of the hotel, some of them in nothing but their underwear or white dressing-gowns.

Two SUVs were approaching from Vasagatan. They pulled up, tyres shrieking, and heavily built police officers emerged, armed with automatic weapons and wearing face masks. Max felt his heartbeat thud harder.

The National Rapid Response Unit.

Maybe this really was a terrorist attack?

Molly kept her eyes fixed on the ground as she made her way away from the hotel. She walked quickly towards the Central Station to look for a taxi. At the Scandic Grand Central people had gathered to peer out of the big panoramic windows.

Emergency vehicles were still arriving, blue lights flashing.

She took out her phone and called the number Thomas had given her. His phone was switched off. According to the female voice, the number was no longer valid.

There were a couple of taxis waiting outside the Casino Cosmopol. She yanked open the door of the first one, not caring which company they were from.

She had to see Thomas. Now.

"Where are you going?" the driver asked.

"The Security Service."

"The Security Service?"

He turned round and looked at her in surprise. He probably thought she was drunk.

"Yes."

"Where's that, then?"

"I don't know. Hold on."

Molly took her phone out and googled it.

"They're out in Solna."

Hamza was moving calmly through the sea of people. He felt calm and focused. There was no sign of Sabina. They had different escape routes, and she had shown that she could take care of herself. He turned off into Torsgatan and quickened his pace. In his bomber jacket, hooded top, cap and jeans, he looked like someone out for an evening walk. It would take days to identify him among all the other guests. If they ever managed it. He and Sabina had made sure there were no security cameras where they changed their clothes.

Hamza stopped outside a 7-Eleven shop, crossed the street, found a bench in front of a flight of steps and sat down. He buried his face in his hands as he felt exhaustion get the better of him now that the adrenaline was no longer pumping round his body.

He had another hour before he was due to meet up with Sabina again, then they would set out to Lappkärrsberget together.

Khenziir was dead. Hamza had taken the first step towards avenging the women, children and fellow soldiers killed in the war. Centuries of humiliation. He had enjoyed seeing Khenziir's body riddled with bullets, each one of them resulting in an explosion of red on his body.

But his murder was only the beginning.

Before Christmas arrived, the headlines about the real attack would echo all around the world. He still didn't know how or where it was going to take place, but Farid had led him to believe that it was going to be large-scale. After that, no one would be able to say that the Islamic State was failing.

15

Molly walked over to the large reception desk, where two security guards with Kevlar vests bulging beneath their jackets looked at her warily. More cars were pulling up in the car park outside. People with serious, terse faces were streaming into the building, hurrying past reception towards lifts and stairs. She realised this had to be linked to what had happened at the Clarion.

"Yes?" one of the guards said impatiently. He was large, bald, and had reddish stubble. Molly saw that he had a pistol in a holster on his left hip.

"I'm looking for Thomas."

The man raised his eyebrows.

"Thomas. Surname?"

"I don't know, but he's from MI6. He's working with the Swedish Security Service."

The man exchanged an irritable glance with his colleague.

"We've got too much going on to be able to help you. If you haven't got a surname for this Thomas, we can't call him to say that you're here. Do you understand?"

Molly took her phone out of her bag and pulled up the picture of Thomas she had taken surreptitiously in the pub. She held it up towards the guard, who leaned across the counter.

"Never seen him before. And even if I had, I wouldn't be able to tell you if he works here or not. This is the Security Service, not the lost property desk in IKEA."

Molly felt panic rising inside her. The phone on the desk started to ring and the guard put his hand on it.

"I have to talk to someone," she whispered.

He sighed.

"Who, then?"

Molly sobbed.

"I don't know. Someone. I need to get hold of Thomas, he's working with you. I know he is," she said desperately.

The phone rang again. The guard picked it up.

Thomas had to be here somewhere. Molly turned round, looking at the people hurrying past and hoping that Thomas might be among them.

Molly walked up to one woman, grabbed her arm and held out her phone.

"Thomas. Do you know him? I need to talk to him."

The woman looked at Molly in surprise, shook her head and carried on into the building. Molly stopped a man in a suit and glasses. Repeated the same question. He held his hands up towards her and hurried past.

"Sorry."

"Thomas!" she cried. "Does anyone here know Thomas?"

16

Another police car raced past at high speed, siren blaring. That was the fourth in the past two minutes. They were all heading down Sturegatan towards the centre of the city. The footpaths of Humlegården were dark and slippery. Advent candles and Christmas stars shone out from the windows of the beautiful fin-de-siècle buildings that lined the park.

Nicolas had taken the metro to Stureplan from Södermalm. Since he had been dismissed by the Karlström family and AOS Risk Group he had been staying at the Hotel Rival on Mariatorget. He was back where he had been when he was forced to leave the SOG. He didn't know what he was going to do with his life, and was surprised when Axel Grystad called earlier that evening, suggesting that they meet. They arranged to see each other by the playground in the park. Nicolas was checking his surroundings out of habit, moving in a semicircle around the frozen grass, but he couldn't see anything unusual or worthy of note. Axel was alone, walking up and down across the frozen grass.

Nicolas stepped out of the shadows and raised his hand in a brief wave.

"C-c-can we walk?" Axel suggested.

"What's this about?" Nicolas asked as they strolled through the avenue of trees towards the Scandic hotel. The path was covered by patches of ice.

"I know where some of the money Johan Karlström has been laundering has gone. I thought you might like to know."

"Okay, tell me."

Another police car rushed past, and Axel waited until it had gone.

"I've managed to track almost two million kronor from the poker player to Babylon Exchange, an currency exchange office in Rinkeby. It took me a while, they're trying really hard not to leave any sort of a trail. They keep transferring sums smaller than ten thousand kronor so as not to trigger the warning system. That's professional."

"Why have you been doing this?"

Axel looked down at his hands.

"The maximum penalty for money laundering is six years. And for hit-and-run it's six months. Simple maths. I want to see Johan Karlström sent to prison. For a long time, so he doesn't have the opportunity to hurt more people. D-do you understand?"

Nicolas smiled.

"I understand. How is your son? Simon, that's his name, isn't it?"

"He's home with his mum at the moment. He'll probably never be able to walk again."

They walked on in silence, side by side. A jogger ran past in hi-vis running gear.

"I don't know how I'm going to tell him he's never going to be able to play football again, never be able to run around the way he used to," Axel said. "It's almost ironic. In the days before... the accident, I was wondering how on earth I was going to cope when he grew older and more independent. I was worrying about the day when he left the nest, didn't need me anymore. And now... Now he's probably going to need me for the rest of his life, every day, every second."

Nicolas didn't know what to say.

He felt sorry for Axel, guessing that he hadn't had an easy life. Nicolas, if anyone, knew how the slightest difference could be exploited by bullies in classrooms and changing rooms. He had seen how vulnerable his sister Maria had been from close up.

"Do you have children?" Axel asked.

"No, I..."

Nicolas was interrupted by his mobile phone buzzing. He apologised and looked at the number, which he didn't recognise, before answering. He recognised the voice at once.

"I'll come and get you," Nicolas said. "Stay where you are."

He turned to Axel.

"I know it's a lot to ask, but could I borrow your car? I'll get it back to you in a few hours."

Axel nodded and pointed towards Valhallavägen.

"We'll have to go back to mine to pick up the keys first."

17

Max Lewenhaupt was standing in the crowd outside the Clarion Hotel Sign. Twenty minutes had passed since the Rapid Response Unit had made their way inside the building, weapons drawn, and so far no shots had been heard. The atmosphere was tense. Max stamped his feet, he was freezing and feeling annoyed with himself for not wearing warmer clothes that morning.

It was going to be a long night. There was a group of photographers close to the cordon around the hotel. The flashes from their cameras lit up the darkness, as the pictures were sent directly to the websites of their newspapers.

"Excuse me. You're a reporter, right?"

Max turned his head. A blonde woman in her fifties was looking up at him.

"*Kvällspressen*. Max Lewenhaupt," he said, holding out his hand. The woman shook it.

"I know. I recognised you," she said, then lowered her voice. "I've got something I think you might be interested in."

"Okay?"

"I was up on the ninth floor when it all happened. I've… erm… I've got pictures of the man who was murdered."

Max led the woman aside so that no one could overhear them. "Can I see?"

She held up her iPhone, tapped in the code and opened the pictures. An image of a hotel corridor appeared, a man lying in an unnatural position in front of an armchair, with blood running from his forehead and chest. Max took the phone, covering it with his hand so no one else could see. He scrolled to the next picture. The same man.

"There's something I've been thinking," the woman said tentatively.

"Oh?"

"Here," she said, zooming in.

Max didn't realise what he was supposed to be looking at.

"Do you see?"

"That white thing? The cord?" Max wondered, feeling confused. She nodded eagerly.

"Isn't that an ear-piece? The sort bodyguards use, you know?"

Max's mouth fell open.

She was right. He moved across to the blue badge attached to the man's top. There was no doubt about it: it was the emblem of the Security Service. He studied the shot man's face, then his well-trained body. The man was a Security Service bodyguard.

He dug his fingernail into his palm so he wouldn't show how excited he was.

"And you heard shots after you took these pictures?" he said, as calmly as he could.

"Yes. Loads of shots."

Max was almost bursting with excitement, but managed to contain himself. The Security Service guarded politicians and the royal family. Sweden had lost two government ministers in the past thirty-five years. Prime Minister Olof Palme in 1986, and Foreign Minister Anna Lindh in 2003. Swedish history would be written tonight.

"Ten thousand kronor," he said, as relaxed as he could manage. "You don't show these pictures to anyone, or even mention them to anyone else.

The woman looked surprised and happy.

"Seriously?"

He nodded. He selected the pictures, then tapped in his own phone number and sent them to his phone.

"When will I get the money?"

"Tomorrow. Call me and we'll sort it all out. But remember – not a word to anyone else."

Max pushed his way through to the cordon, took out his phone and checked that the pictures had arrived before calling Bengt's number. While he waited for him to answer, he caught a glimpse of Vanessa Frank bending down under the blue and white tape and hurrying into the main entrance of the hotel.

"At last," Bengt said grouchily.

Max cupped his hand round his phone so no one else could hear him.

"Listen. I want you to dig out every picture we've got of government ministers, members of the opposition and the royal family from the past three days. You need to identify one of their bodyguards."

"What for?" Bengt said sharply.

"One of the victims, if there are more than one, I mean, is a Security Service bodyguard. I'm sending pictures to you now. If we can figure out who he's been guarding in the past few hours or days, that might tell us who's been shot."

"Are you serious?"

"Yes."

"Bloody hell. What do our competitors know?"

"Nothing, as far as I know."

Bengt started barking orders to the reporters around him before he ended the call without saying goodbye. Max slipped his phone back into his pocket and looked out across the cordon.

He was no longer freezing.

18

The police sirens were still echoing through the late Sunday evening. Nicolas was becoming increasingly convinced that what had happened at the Clarion wasn't some ordinary gangland shoot-out, but something altogether less common.

He drove past the Northern Cemetery and carried on towards Solnavägen and the OKQ8 petrol station where he had told Molly to wait. He pulled up at one of the pumps and got out. There were a few rental cars lined up by Solnavägen, but otherwise it was deserted.

Molly emerged from behind a container. She was so cold she was shivering. Nicolas quickly pulled his jacket off and put it round her shoulders. Her legs were bare, and her make-up had run beneath her eyes.

Nicolas led her towards the car, opened the passenger seat and gently pushed her inside. He got in the driver's seat, started the engine and turned the heating on full.

Molly was sitting hunched in her seat.

"What are you doing here?" he asked softly, taking her frozen hands in his and resting them on the dashboard, where hot air was streaming out.

She started blankly out through the windscreen into the darkness.

"Can we drive away from here?"

Nicolas put the car in gear, pulled out onto the roundabout and turned left towards Frösundaleden. Molly was sobbing silently beside him. He cast an anxious glance at her, but decided to wait. She would tell him once she had calmed down. They headed off towards Skytteholm, Nicolas pulled in at the Max restaurant and parked behind the football pitch. He left the engine running, leaned back in his seat and waited.

"Tell me, and we'll try to figure this out together."

She ran her hands over her cheeks.

"Thomas, the man who was in my apartment, the man you asked me about… I think he tricked me."

"In what way?"

"He said he was from MI6, that he was working with the Security Service." Molly swallowed and shook her head. "I believed him. I checked that that was how they worked. It all seemed to fit. He blackmailed me, threatened to show pictures of me to my dad, send them to the papers. God, I've been such a fucking idiot. Then at the hotel… they shot him."

"Thomas?"

"No."

"Who did they shoot?"

"Magnus Moheden."

Nicolas stared at her.

"The Minister of Justice?" Mikael nodded slowly. "He was the man who got shot at the hotel?"

"Yes."

"And you were there?"

"In the bathroom."

"You…" Nicolas tried to find the right words. "You'd arranged to meet?"

"Yes. Thomas arranged it on Wickr, an encrypted app. I gave him my login details. He said he just wanted to check if Magnus Moheden still did that sort of thing since he became Minister of Justice. It was a matter of national security, because he could get blackmailed. He told me this was the last thing I'd have to do, and that they'd leave me alone after this. Let me go. But they killed him."

"What were you doing?"

"I was in the bathroom being sick. They shot at the door, but I was hiding in the bath."

"Then what?"

"All I could think about was getting out of there. Finding Thomas. So I managed to get outside, got a taxi at the casino and went out to headquarters of the Security Service."

Nicolas was looking at her sympathetically.

"And they didn't know anything about a Thomas?"

Molly shook her head and burst into tears.

"It's my fault he's dead."

Nicolas leaned back against the headrest and looked out at the snow-covered football pitch. He wondered what he should do. Molly would have to hand herself in to the police, explain that she was being exploited and hope for the best. But her life from now on would be ruined. This was a global news story that was about to break. The international media would wallow in the details of her life. The tabloids would never leave her alone. And she would forever be a target. Thomas and the others, whoever they were, would want to finish their work. To prevent her talking, giving them away, whoever they were.

"I'm thinking of phoning a police officer I know. I trust her. She'll be able to help you. She'll listen to you."

"No, please."

She put her hand on his arm and looked at him beseechingly.

"You haven't got a choice. They could suspect that you were involved in the murder."

"Do you think?" she whispered.

"Yes."

"But no one knows I was there."

"They'll find out. And then it would look suspicious if you hadn't come forward to explain earlier."

"But…"

"Sweden's Minister of Justice has been shot. You have to help the police. You have a duty."

Nicolas called Vanessa's number. The call went through, but she didn't answer. He put his phone on his lap. Molly looked relieved.

He turned up the volume of the radio. A newsreader was announcing in a serious voice that gunfire at the Clarion Hotel Sign had led to two fatalities. But not a word about who the victims were.

Nicolas put his hand on Molly's shoulder. He felt sorry for her. She had been exploited, and the consequences had been terrible, for both Magnus Moheden and for her.

"It's going to be okay," he said, trying to sound reassuring.

But he couldn't help thinking that his voice sounded hollow, that he hardly believed what he was saying himself.

19

Trude pulled her white plastic hood back at the same time as she moved her mask down onto her chin. Her big brown eyes looked worried. Mats had been laid out in the hotel corridor behind her for people to walk on. Vanessa could see at least ten forensics officers working behind Trude's back. Samer glanced at the dead Security Service officer whose body was in the process of being photographed.

"So that's Minister of Justice, Magnus Moheden, lying in there?" Vanessa asked.

"Yes," Trude replied.

Many of the doors were open after people had rushed in panic for the stairs and lifts when the shooting began. A gym shoe lay upside down by one of the lifts. It looked like someone had tried to take their case with them, then dropped it as they fled. Vanessa couldn't help thinking that it was going to be a tough job for the forensics team. She felt oddly disconnected. The whole thing was too surreal. A member of the government, the Minister of Justice himself, had been executed in a Stockholm hotel room.

Her phone rang in her coat pocket, and she clicked to reject it without looking at the screen.

"When can we go in?" Vanessa asked, nodding towards the room.

"In a couple of hours."

"What can you tell us in the meantime?"

"He's lying naked on the bed. The perpetrator or perpetrators shot their way in through the door, walked in and hit him with automatic fire. His body's been ripped to shreds. Eighteen bullet cases so far."

"Does anyone know what he was doing here?" Vanessa asked.

Trude looked round, took a step forward and lowered her voice.

"I'm pretty sure he wasn't alone in there. The minibar has been emptied, I've found lip-gloss on two of the bottles. There's a pack of Atarax on the bedside table. And someone threw up in the toilet. The bathroom door was shot to pieces as well."

"Moheden had a family, didn't he?" Vanessa asked.

"Wife and two teenage children," Trude replied. "I read a cosy 'At home with' article about them in *Dagens Nyheter*'s Sunday magazine as recently as last week. Okay, I need to go back in."

She pulled her hood up and replaced her mask before turning away.

20

Nicolas found a free parking space close to the Södra Latin School and manoeuvred the car in between two dark SUVs. Seeing as Vanessa wasn't answering her phone and it was getting close to midnight, he had decided to take Molly to the Hotel Rival with him. Axel had told him it wasn't a problem if he got the car back to him the following day.

"Hold on," Nicolas said as Molly was about to get out of the car. "I want you to put my top on and pull the hood up. There are likely to be security cameras at the hotel, and I don't want you to get picked up on them."

Nicolas pulled off his top and adjusted the white T-shirt he was wearing underneath. He got out and stood with his back against the door while Molly changed and pulled the hood up. They walked in silence along the frozen streets of Södermalm towards the Rival. A mixture of snow and rain was falling. There weren't many people out on the streets; most of the bars had closed for the night.

Nicolas's single room on the third floor looked out onto Mariatorget. The furnishings consisted of a bed, an armchair and a desk. Nicolas put the safety chain on, then rifled through his suitcase and found a tracksuit that he handed to Molly. Then he went into the bathroom and removed the bin bag from the bucket under the basin.

"Change into these and put your old clothes in the bag."

"Is it okay if I take a shower? I'm still freezing."

"If you like. Are you hungry? I can go and get something from 7-Eleven."

"I'm fine, thanks," she said, giving him a quick smile before heading into the bathroom. Nicolas sat down on the armchair. He heard the shower go on. What he was doing was probably illegal, he thought gloomily. But at the same time he felt sorry for Molly. She had been deceived, and blackmailed. Her life had been wrecked, and tomorrow police and reporters alike would turn what was left of it upside down. Every juicy little detail would become a headline to be discussed and pored over. This night would define her forever.

But he could see no other option except to hand her over to Vanessa. It was at least something of a comfort to know that she wouldn't judge, and would be on Molly's side. And would at least listen to what she had to say. But that was the limit of what he could do for Molly. The alternative was helping her flee the country. Besides the fact that it was morally wrong, she wouldn't manage to stay hidden for more than a few days before she was found.

Inside the bathroom the tap was turned off and he heard her footsteps. It sounded like she was talking to someone. Worried that she had phoned someone, he went over to the door to hear better. But it seemed like she was just talking to herself, even if he couldn't make out what she was saying.

Slightly bemused, Nicolas went back to the armchair and put his feet up on the radiator. The bathroom door opened and Molly came over to stand next to him. The tracksuit was far too big and hung limply from her.

"I thought you could have the bed and I'll take the armchair."

"You take the bed. This is your room. Besides, I'm going to have trouble getting any sleep." She pulled up the sleeves of the top.

Nicolas stood up and closed the curtains. The bedside lamp was the only source of light.

"You probably need the bed more than me. You've had a rough day."

"Thanks," Molly said quietly.

Nicolas looked at her thoughtfully.

"I heard noises from the bathroom, it sounded like you were talking to someone?" He tried to sound unconcerned.

Molly seemed embarrassed.

"I talk to myself sometimes. I always have done. I grew up in Kiruna, outside Kiruna actually, and I didn't have many other people to talk to. Do you think I'm strange?"

Nicolas shook his head.

"I've met stranger people."

Molly went over to the bed, lifted the covers and got in. She reached her hand out and turned the light out. The room went dark. She shuffled awkwardly and Nicolas closed his eyes.

"By the way, I forgot to thank you," she said.

"Don't mention it."

"I should have listened to you from the start. But I've always managed on my own, I don't trust anyone. But I trust you. You're kind. If you think I should talk to your police friend, then that's what I'll do. I'll tell them everything."

"Good."

Nicolas saw his mobile light up in the pocket of his jeans. He quickly pulled it out, hoping it was Vanessa, but it was just a newsflash.

Kvällspressen exclusive: Justice Minister Magnus Moheden one of the victims of hotel shooting, it said.

21

When Max Lewenhaupt had gone to work early that morning, the city had been eerily quiet, like one of those disaster movies he had been so fond of as a teenager. He was too young to have even been born when Prime Minister Olof Palme was shot, and he only had very vague memories of the murder of Foreign Minister Anna Lindh. But as the taxi made its way across a dark Kungsholmen, he knew he would remember the previous day for the rest of his life.

What had happened would go down in history, and he was one of the people tasked with recording it.

The newsroom had been in a state of organised chaos all morning. Bengt was red-eyed, he had slept at work, and every so often leapt up from his chair to bark orders to his reporters before muttering and sitting back down again. The government had been meeting all night, and at nine o'clock a press release had been issued, announcing that the Prime Minister would be making a statement at one o'clock.

Max wasn't particularly disappointed not to be included among the reporters sent to the government offices at Rosenbad to cover the speech. He had been told to write about Magnus Moheden's life, from his upbringing in Gävle, his time in the Social Democratic Youth Movement, his legal studies at Uppsala University, his first years as a lawyer, then his appointment as a hard-line and controversial Minister of Justice. Max worked hard until lunchtime, calling Moheden's former colleagues at university and in the youth movement, teachers and childhood friends, the coaches of sports teams he was in. His political opponents and friends were competing to see who could heap the most praise over the deceased. Magnus Moheden had been a popular politician; only weeks before his death he had topped a list of most liked ministers in the red-green government. His tough stance against criminals had been appreciated even by the opposition.

By the time there were just five minutes to go before the Prime Minister's speech, Max had written enough to cover three tabloid pages. He was feeling happy. When combined with a generous helping of illustrations, what he had written would cover three double-page spreads.

Feeling satisfied with both himself and the article, Max wandered over to the coffee machine next to the editor-in-chief's room. Reporters and editors had started to gather round the newsdesk to watch the speech together, but Max felt a sudden need to be alone. Just as he was about to go back to his desk, he heard someone knock to get his attention. He spun round and saw the editor-in-chief, Tuva Algotsson, waving him into her office with her mobile clamped to her ear. Surprised, Max stepped into the glass box that made up her office.

"Speak later," she said to the person she was talking to, then put her phone down.

She looked at Max with satisfaction as she adjusted her trouser suit and put her feet up on her desk.

"Good work yesterday, Max. Really good work. The Bun, I mean Bengt, told me it was your idea to compare recent pictures of members of the government to see whose bodyguard had been shot. Excellent journalism."

"Thanks."

Max was beaming with pride, even if he was trying not to show it. Tuva Algotsson wasn't known for idle praise. From her laptop came the sound of *Kvällspressen*'s CNN-inspired jungle, then one of the reporters announced that the Prime Minister was about to speak.

"Grab a chair and sit yourself down here," Tuva said, pointing next to her. Max squeezed in beside the editor-in-chief. He couldn't help raising his head and looking past the screen and out across the newsroom where the rest of the paper's staff were gathered in a semicircle around a television. The Prime Minister, evidently moved by the seriousness of the occasion, cleared his throat. He was dressed in a black suit, white shirt and black tie. His neck was red, and he adjusted the collar of his shirt before looking directly into the camera.

"Magnus Moheden – father, husband, and Sweden's Minister

of Justice – was shot and killed yesterday in central Stockholm. A terrible blow to his family, to our country. To our democracy."

Max turned to Tuva, and they nodded to each other. Max thought that the Prime Minister, who wasn't renowned as a good public speaker, was doing well.

"Early this morning I was informed by the head of the Security Service, Gustav Sheen, that the terrorist organisation ISIS – the so-called Islamic State – has claimed responsibility for his death."

Max almost choked on his coffee. Tuva's mouth was hanging open. Outside in the newsroom there was a sudden buzz of activity. Bengt got up from his chair and started shouting and gesticulating.

"Once again, the hideous face of terrorism has shown itself in Sweden, but we will not stand idly by and let this happen. We will catch the culprits. We will punish them. I promise you that."

22

Hamza's ears were still ringing from the gunfire in the hotel room the previous day. He opened the pantry, which was full of tins, packets of pasta, rice and coffee. They had enough food for three weeks in case they had a long wait. But at least he wasn't alone anymore. There were three of them in the flat. Apart from him and Sabina, who always wore a niqab now, another person had moved in during the day. Hamza didn't know what his real name was, but he had told them to call him Thomas.

In marked contrast to his reaction to Farid, Hamza immediately felt a connection with him. It was obvious that he had been in battle. Had experienced the dangers, the struggle, the dust, the blood, the screams of the wounded.

They were sitting in the dim light on either side of the kitchen table with the blinds down, drinking sweet tea. Thomas was talkative, and had told him he grew up in west London – Pakistani father, British mother – and had interrupted his chemistry degree at King's College London to go to Syria with two friends in 2015. The two others had become martyrs.

There was something calming, almost touching, in meeting someone who knew what Hamza had been through. Who had been there, in Syria, and had fought for the Caliphate, for God.

"So he died like a dog?" Thomas asked, baring his white teeth. Hamza nodded.

"He begged for his life. Naked."

Hamza imitated Magnus Moheden. He felt relaxed, happy. It was like his first few months in Iraq, when they captured town after town. When nothing had been able to stop their advance. When the enemy's soldiers fled for their lives the moment they saw ISIS's warriors approaching. But this was even better. The events at the

Clarion Hotel Sign were just the first stage in an attack that would go down in history and be mentioned with the same respect at the attack on the World Trade Center on 11 September 2001. Hamza and the other martyrs' names would be sung by Muslims all across the world.

"But the woman escaped?" Thomas asked, and his smile quickly faded.

"She was in the bathroom, we couldn't take the risk of waiting, then dragging her out into the corridor to shoot her there. There wasn't time. But it looks like she fled. They haven't said anything on television about Khenziir not being alone."

Thomas snorted.

"They've been bought off, the whole lot of them. The media, the politicians, the police. They aren't going to admit that their minister's final act was fucking a whore. Hypocrites. Depraved hypocrites. And they accused us of having sex slaves. The only difference is that they pay theirs."

Thomas pretended to spit in the air.

"Who is she?" Hamza asked.

"Just some stupid little whore. I don't even know if she's realised that I wasn't working for MI6 yet."

"That's what she thought?"

Thomas grinned. He told her how they had taken the intimate pictures of Molly on board the *Lucinda*, and how he later contacted her in Stockholm.

"I spent weeks working on her."

"How?"

"She's the sort of woman all men dream of. She's beautiful, one of the most beautiful women I've ever seen. Girlish. Feminine. I ignored her advances. That made her feel uncertain, and I broke her down piece by piece. And she couldn't handle it."

"How did you learn that?"

"I've always found it easy to get women. Especially Western women. You know what they're like, you grew up in Europe. They're easy. They have egos the size of mountains. They talk about feminism, liberation, but deep down they want to be treated like whores in a brothel. It isn't really their fault, it's their parents'. That's how they're raised. They lack honour. Part of me just wanted to hold her down and fuck her, the way we did with our Yazidi guests during the war."

Hamza smiled. Even if he hadn't admitted it before, he had been having doubts, and had wondered if Western propaganda had made him weak.

Made him doubt what was right.

But with Thomas he started to feel like himself again – like one of the chosen warriors in God's own army.

"How did you get on?" he asked.

Thomas stood up and gestured to Hamza to follow him out into the hall, where the printer was. They had agreed not to send any information between them digitally. It could be catastrophic if their messages were intercepted and gave the entire operation away.

Thomas sat down at the pale-wood IKEA desk, connected his phone to the printer, and printed out a series of photographs. "It's all ready. The building is easy to get into, the office too. We're going to succeed, brother."

"Inshallah," Hamza muttered, leaning forward to study the pictures with a furrowed brow.

23

Nicolas was standing in the lobby of the Hotel Rival, watching Vanessa get out of the taxi. Small flakes of snow were drifting down from the dark sky, only to melt instantly on the pavements and streets. There was a sombre atmosphere over the whole city, a terse calm that Nicolas couldn't help but find rather moving.

Vanessa leaned into the car and said something that made the taxi driver laugh before she closed the door and the car drove away towards Hornsgatan. She stepped in through the glass doors and walked up to Nicolas. As always, he was struck by how beautiful she was. But there was something more. A feeling of camaraderie, of shared history, which he had never experienced with anyone except her and his sister, Maria. Vanessa seemed more friendly that the last time they had met, in Thelin's on Odengatan. He was still hurt by her chilly behaviour on that occasion, but had decided not to mention it.

They exchanged an awkward hug.

"Thanks for coming," he said.

"Let's go and sit in the bar, I need a glass of wine after the last twenty-four hours."

Nicolas felt very self-conscious about his movements as they walked across the lobby and up the stairs. He tried to interpret her body language, to figure out if she was happy to see him or saw the meeting more as a friendly favour.

The bar, which was on second floor, was almost empty. A bored bartender in a black waistcoat and white tie poured Nicolas a beer and a glass of white wine for Vanessa. They sat down facing each other.

"Before I hear what you've got to say, I'd like to apologise for the last time we met, at Thelin's. That was unfair of me. We've been through too much together for me to treat you like that. When you told me about Erica Karlström I guess I was... I don't know."

"What were you?" he asked, surprised.

She fingered her glass and looked down at the table.

"I don't know. I just didn't like it, and I know I had no right to react in that way. It's your life. Besides, I was the one who... put a stop to whatever we had, or whatever was on the point of happening, whatever it was."

"That other thing, with Erica, is over. And I've been sacked."

"Are you living here at the hotel?"

He nodded.

Vanessa couldn't hide a slight smile.

"You got found out?"

They looked each other hard. He waited for her to say something else, but she wasn't in any hurry. Nicolas gave up and cleared his throat.

"Well, that wasn't why I asked you to come. I appreciate that you've got your hands full with other things." He straightened his back. "There was a woman in the room where the Minister of Justice was murdered. I know who she is."

Vanessa put her wine-glass down on the table. She leaned forward.

"Where have you read that?" she asked.

"Nowhere. She called me afterwards."

"Why?"

"It's Molly Berg. The woman I asked you to check out."

"Where is she now?"

"In my room. She's in pieces, her life has been turned upside down. A British man calling himself Thomas was blackmailing her. He threatened to show compromising pictures of her to her father, and send them to the papers."

Nicolas moved his chair to sit next to Vanessa. He could feel the warmth of her arm, and smell her perfume.

"This Thomas, who I'm about to show you a photograph of, told her he was working for MI6 and was working with the Security Service. He's the same man who attacked me a couple of weeks ago. He set up the meeting between Moheden and Molly."

He played the recording he had been sent by Axel Grystad, the one showing Molly handing Johan Karlström's mobile phone over to the man who attacked him.

"Do you recognise him?"

Vanessa shook her head, and Nicolas moved his chair so they were facing each other again.

"Can you send me that video? Why did he want Johan Karlström's phone?"

Nicolas pressed *send*, and a moment later Vanessa's phone buzzed.

"I think it's to do with money-laundering through online poker games on Gambler, the company Johan is managing director of. But the money-laundering stopped back in the spring. The British authorities were starting to investigate Johan, and he thought it best to move back to Sweden for a while. I suspect that Thomas wanted to know how much Johan had actually told the Brits. What he'd confessed to."

Vanessa was looking expressionlessly at Nicolas.

"How long have you known Johan was involved in money-laundering?"

"A few days. A total of around two million kronor from Gambler has been moved around the world before ending up back here. In Stockholm, in an exchange bureau in Rinkeby called Babylon Exchange. I thought that might be of interest to you, not least in light of what happened yesterday."

"ISIS have claimed responsibility. The whole investigation is being handled by the Security Service, who are turning every basement mosque in Sweden upside down right now."

She stood up.

"I need to talk to this Molly."

24

Molly Berg wasn't wearing any makeup, her dark hair was tied in a scruffy knot, and she was wearing Nicolas's tracksuit. Even so, just as in the pictures Nicolas had shown her earlier, she was one of the most beautiful women Vanessa had ever seen. The features of her face were perfect, and there was something exotic and fragile about her whole appearance.

"Molly. This is Vanessa. Vanessa, Molly," Nicolas said.

A wave of jealousy ran through Vanessa's body when she realised that Molly had spent the night with Nicolas in the hotel room. She swatted the thoughts aside irritably, and gestured to Molly to sit down on the bed.

Nicolas cleared his throat.

"Molly, can you repeat what you told me?"

He sank down on the armchair while Vanessa sat down next to Molly and waited.

"I don't know where to start."

"Start with how you know Magnus Moheden," Vanessa said.

"I've been working as, well, an escort, I suppose, for the past few years. I used to live in Barcelona. He used to travel there a few times each year. I met him for the first time at a party in a villa three years ago, before he became a government minister."

Molly explained the rest. How she had been contacted by the man who said his name was Thomas, and who initially pretended to be a businessman. Then how he had told her he was working for the British secret service on an operation in Sweden, in collaboration with the Swedish Security Service. How she helped him steal Johan Karlström's phone, and how she had thought it was all over then, only for him to come and find her in Kiruna and blackmail her once more. The more Molly said, the more sympathy Vanessa felt for her.

She realised that she liked her.

When Molly had reached the final moments in Magnus Moheden's life in the hotel room, Vanessa was sitting in total silence. There was doubt that Molly had been deceived, and that Thomas – whoever he was – had exploited her to get at Sweden's Minister of Justice.

"You never saw the people who fired the guns?"

"No."

Molly fell silent, and was looking at Vanessa anxiously.

Vanessa crossed her legs and glanced quickly at Nicolas. She took her phone out of her bag, pulled up the picture of Hamza Mansour and showed it to Molly.

"Have you ever seen this man?"

Molly leaned forward and studied the picture before quickly shaking her head. Vanessa was about to put her iPhone away when she stopped herself. She pulled up the video from the ICA supermarket in Bergshamra, the one of Natasha and the unknown man. She pressed *play*.

"Do you recognise this woman?"

"No, I've never seen her."

"How about the man, do you recognise him?"

Molly leaned forward and squinted. She shook her head.

"Can you pause it?"

Vanessa did as she asked.

"What is it?"

"I do recognise him. Or the back of his neck, to be more precise."

Nicolas, who had been sitting there in silence, quickly got up out of the armchair and went over to stand by the bed.

"What do you mean?" Vanessa asked.

Molly pointed to the mark on his neck, just below his hairline.

"Last summer I was on a yacht in Puerto Portals in Mallorca," she said, unable to tear her eyes from the screen. "The *Lucinda*. That man was on board too. I recognise that mark. I saw it from my cabin when he left the boat."

PART VIII

1

It was half past five on Wednesday evening when Vanessa walked into McDonalds on Sveavägen. The restaurant was full, but she had no problem identifying the man she had arranged to meet.

Erik Giertz was wearing his police uniform and was sitting at one of the tables facing Observatorielunden. When Vanessa pushed her way through to his table he looked her up and down quickly before standing up and holding out a huge fist. She thought he could easily be an extra in some documentary about Vikings. He was almost two metres tall, and had a thick blond beard and blue eyes.

"Thanks for taking the time to see me," she said, looking at the three empty Big Mac cartons on the table.

"Just finished a shift. This has become something of a tradition. I actually used to work here, behind the counter, before I joined the police."

Vanessa sank down at the table. He had a piece of lettuce stuck in his beard.

She had handed over all the information she had got from Molly Berg to the Security Service via Mikael Kask, but what they were doing now, she had no idea. She hadn't heard a thing.

She had looked into Babylon Exchange – the bureau de change to which Axel had traced a lot of the money Johan Karlström had been laundering – and had found that it was owned by a fifty-two-year-old man named Farid Alami, who migrated to Sweden from Morocco in 1997. The business's turnover last year had been just over 4.3 million kronor, and among its assets was a silver-coloured Renault.

When Vanessa ran the vehicle's registration number through the police system, Storm, she discovered to her surprise that the vehicle had been stopped on the E4 close to Sätra, by Erik Giertz and a colleague as recently as last week.

"You pulled over a silver-grey Renault with the registration number NRM 127 on Friday?"

"That's right."

"Why did you stop it?"

"It was driving erratically," Erik Giertz said defensively.

Vanessa knew that many officers gave that reason when they wanted to check a vehicle without having any more tangible suspicions. She had to get him to tell her everything. The slightest detail could be vital.

"Really?"

Erik Giertz shrugged his shoulders.

"Two men had been found shot in a car, and witnesses mentioned two, well, what do we say...? Non-ethnic Swedes who they had seen leaving the scene in a similar car. So we took a chance."

"I'm going to show you a recording from a security camera, and I'd like you to tell me if this could be the man you stopped."

"Understood."

Erik Giertz picked up a French fry, drenched it in ketchup and popped it in his mouth. Vanessa played the clip of Vanessa and the unknown man talking outside the ICA supermarket in Bergshamra.

"Hard to say. You can only see the back of his head, after all. But it could be him, the body language seems familiar."

Vanessa leaned back in her chair and pulled up the picture of the man calling himself Thomas, then turned the screen towards Erik Giertz.

He shook his head.

"This guy was older. Around fifty, maybe."

Vanessa nodded. She took out the copy of Farid Alami's driving licence that she had printed out and pushed that over to Erik Giertz.

"Was it him?"

Erik Giertz nodded.

"And the other man?"

"I only got a quick glimpse of him. I'd say he was in his thirties. Short black hair."

Vanessa showed him the picture of Hamza Mansour, but Erik Giertz shook his head.

"I never really saw him properly."

She cleared her throat.

"You ran a check on the registration, but never checked the passenger's identity or searched the car?"

"That's right. I didn't have time. We got an alert about shots fired in Sätra and had to break off."

Vanessa sighed. She had been thinking she was onto something, and had been hoping she could link Farid Alami with the man in the security-camera footage from the supermarket and on the yacht. Possibly even to Hamza Mansour. But now her hopes were fading. She would have to investigate Farid and the money-laundering more closely, see if that came up with anything. After asking a few more questions, without much enthusiasm, she realised that Erik Giertz didn't have anything else to contribute, and said her goodbyes.

2

Johan Karlström leaned forward, covered one nostril and used a shortened straw to snort the cocaine from his desk. He closed his eyes, leaned his head back and rubbed his nose with his thumb and forefinger to ease the tickling. He really only took cocaine at weekends, but this Thursday was an exception. He was in a tricky situation, and needed to relax and clear his head.

He banged his fist on the desktop. The remains of the line of cocaine bounced. He repeated the gesture, fascinated by the movement of the tiny white granules.

"Cuntland. I hate this fucking socialist country."

He licked the tip of one finger and rubbed the remnants on his gums.

It was only a matter of time before the transactions were traced by the Security Service, and then he would be fired from Gambler. His foreign accounts would be found. He wouldn't be penniless, but he would be considerably poorer. And he might end up in prison.

He needed a lawyer. A hard-boiled, unscrupulous steamroller.

He was hoping that the Anders I Bladh he had emailed that morning might be his man. From the pictures he had seen on Google, at least he wore smart suits, had neatly combed hair and a wide smile. He looked like he enjoyed the finer things in life and liked earning money. Avarice was good. It made people fight harder. Freud was right, sexuality and aggression were the main driving forces for human beings. Men who didn't feel ashamed of wanting cunt were men who made a success of life. The rest were mediocrities. Jealous little robots.

Employing a lawyer like Bladh was the only way to avoid prison. Johan had suspected that something wasn't right back in January about the man who came to see him and wanted help laundering money. But the commission had been better than usual, a higher percentage. If he hadn't been so fucking stupid, he wouldn't be in this mess.

Sure, Johan had dealt with dodgy types before, he wasn't particularly fussy about who he did business with. Everyone was entitled to earn money the best way they knew how, and was responsible for their own conscience.

But Islamic terrorism?

Towelhead Nazis?

No, that was a step too far. When one of his less scrupulous contacts mentioned the rumours that ISIS was laundering money through gambling websites, he had put two and two together. When he received the call from the Financial Intelligence Unit of the National Crime Agency in London, he had realised he had a problem. The question now was, would the Swedish Security Service or police believe him if he contacted them himself and told them everything he knew about the man? Maybe then they wouldn't bother examining his accounts? And would help keep the journalists at bay?

He cut a fresh line. Inhaled it just as his computer let out a little chime. Anders Bladh wanted to meet, and suggested lunch at Operakällaren in an hour. That was a good start. A man after Johan's own taste.

Anders Bladh was impeccably dressed in a blue pin-striped suit, and was wearing a gold Rolex on his left wrist. His hair was slicked back and looked oily. The lawyer greeted the staff familiarly and was shown to one of the window tables with a view of the water and the Royal Palace. Johan was full of questions, but Anders stopped him and reached down under the table and opened his briefcase.

"Hold on a moment."

He handed over a gold pen and a document that he asked Johan to sign.

"This makes our conversation confidential. Lawyer-client privilege, as the Americans put it."

Johan signed without reading the document. He had taken a liking to Anders Bladh, even if the lawyer looked rather younger than he did in the professional portraits on his company's website. He leaned over the table and started to tell him about the man who had approached him a year ago and interrogated him in English about how they could help each other. He didn't say anything about his suspicions about Islamic terrorism. That was unnecessary, and anyway, he didn't really know. They could talk about that later. Anders listened in silence, with a neutral expression. He absorbed the information, and every so often jotted something down in his notebook. When their main courses arrived – meatballs with mashed potato and cream sauce – he pushed his notebook aside, tucked his napkin into his collar and began to speak.

"The first thing we need to do is get you and your family to a safe location," he said, helping himself to a gherkin from a side-dish.

Johan looked at him in surprise. Was that all he had to say after what he had told him?

"What do you mean?"

"You don't want to go to prison. Or have I misunderstood?" Anders raised his fork to his mouth. "Mmm, this is good. Okay, look. I have clients who have been in roughly the same situation as you. And I have a friend with a large house in Turkey. Do you like Turkey, Johan?"

Johan held his arms out. He felt confused by Anders Bladh's tone. He wanted another line of cocaine, he didn't want to sit here playing games with a fancy lawyer he was going to shower with money. Just because the guy had a degree from some university didn't mean he had to play the big guy.

"What should I be thinking?" he asked, slightly irritably.

"Turkey's a great country, that's what you should be thinking. Primarily because they don't have an extradition treaty with Sweden. That's why I think you and your family should take a little trip down there. My friend's house has every comfort you can imagine. It costs fifty thousand kronor a week, but that's hardly a problem for a hard-working man like you? Then we contact the police. If you're the one who takes the initiative and tells them how regretful you are, they'll be far better disposed towards you."

"Hold on a minute, now. I haven't even employed you yet?"

"You did that the moment you signed that sheet of paper."

First Johan felt angry, then his scowling face cracked slowly into a smile. He pointed at the lawyer, who was chewing calmly as he watched him with amusement.

"I like you," he said, wagging his finger. "Damn, I like you. Okay, Turkey it is. If you'll excuse me, I just have to go to the bathroom."

The sun was already going down outside the window.

"Bloody socialist country, here we are, having lunch, and the sun is already setting," Johan muttered on his way to the bathroom, but he still felt much brighter than he had done earlier.

3

The premises of Babylon Exchange were rundown. The paint was peeling, the furniture was shabby, the carpet stained.

Computer screens showed information about various exchange rates and currency regulations in Arabic, Spanish and English.

Behind a glass screen sat a guy in his mid-twenties with a pedantically neat beard. He looked at Vanessa and Samer with surprise as they walked in. Samer walked over to him as Vanessa peered into the space behind the counter. Another door led to what she assumed was an office.

She heard Samer conduct a quiet conversation in Arabic before he turned to her and shook his head.

"Farid Alami isn't here."

"When is he expected back?" Vanessa asked.

"He doesn't know."

Samer was gesticulating as he spoke. The man shook his head. Samer took out his police ID, held it up and the guy stood up reluctantly, opened the back door and let him through. Vanessa watched as Samer peered into the office, then shut the door.

They left the premises and stood in front of the plate-glass window.

"Farid Alami is registered at an address in Degerbygränd," Vanessa said. "If we hurry, maybe we can get there before hotshot there can phone and warn him."

The man behind the counter was watching them. Vanessa couldn't see what he was doing with his hands, but she was certain he was busy contacting his boss to let him know about the two visitors.

"Come on," she said, and jogged off towards the car.

They parked in a cul-de-sac outside Halal Wholesale, got out of the car and hurried up the steps to the five-storey blocks of flats. Samer led the way with Vanessa right behind him. As she glanced to their left, she caught sight of a silver-coloured Renault parked a short way along the street.

"You head up there. I'll stay here so he can't take the car if he makes a run for it," she called to Samer, who was already halfway up the steps. Vanessa checked the registration number before walking quickly back to her BMW, getting in and moving it so it wasn't quite so visible. She found a parking space four cars behind Farid's Renault, where she could keep an eye on it.

A few minutes later Samer came back down the steps. He looked around in confusion, and Vanessa flashed the headlights. Samer shook his head in disappointment.

Three hours passed without anything happening. Vanessa was feeling hungry and irritable. Samer was drumming the fingers of his left hand in the gear-stick as he checked his phone.

"Magnus Moheden is getting a state funeral," he said, holding his phone up towards Vanessa.

"What does that mean?"

"Good question."

Samer read more of the article.

"It means the state pays for it. And he'll be carried in a funeral cortege through the city. The ceremony is going to be in Storkyrkan, in Gamla stan."

"Like when Olof Palme was murdered?"

Samer shook his head.

"Apparently that one wasn't a state funeral in the formal sense seeing as it was organised by the Social Democratic Party."

"Do you know what my dad was doing when Palme was buried?" Vanessa said, staring out into the darkness.

"No?"

"He drank champagne the whole way through the broadcast. Then he took the family out for a meal. I've never seen him in a better mood."

"He didn't like Palme?"

"You could say that. He was a company director."

"You seem quite different?"

"I inherited his love of German cars," Vanessa said, running her hand over the blue and white logo on the steering-wheel. "When's the funeral?"

"Sunday, 15 December."

Vanessa was about to suggest that they take a walk to the square to get something to eat when her phone rang. It was Trude.

"The National Forensics Centre have been in touch. They've conducted mitochondrial analysis of the hair you got from Shadia Mansour. It matches the DNA found in Stig Boström's flat. There's no doubt that Hamza Mansour was there."

Vanessa turned to Samer.

"Listen," she said, then put the call on speaker and asked Trude to repeat what she'd just said. Samer, who had been half-lying in his seat, sat up with fresh intensity in his eyes.

"How are you getting on at the Clarion Hotel Sign?" Vanessa asked.

Trude was one of a number of forensics experts looking into events at the hotel who had been kept on by the Security Service when they took over the investigation. The amount of forensic evidence was huge, they needed all the help they could get.

"We're pretty much done. But a hotel is probably the worst possible place to have to conduct crime-scene analysis on. There have been literally hundreds of guests in every room. Every corner is contaminated. The NFC are working round the clock to deal with the results."

"Have the security cameras come up with anything?"

"Not as far as I know. There are only cameras in the lobby and on the doors."

A short silence followed.

"If you need me later, give me a call. I'm going to try to get away," Trude said.

"Thanks, we may need you," Vanessa said, and ended the call.

Samer was looking at her thoughtfully.

"Why would we need Trude?"

Vanessa pointed at Farid Alami's car.

She was starting to like Samer more and more. The time they had spent together had led her to trust him. But she didn't know how she was going to explain her suspicions without him thinking she was mad.

"We know that Babylon Exchange has paid out at least two million kronor from Johan Karlström's money-laundering. But we don't know on whose behalf. Or where the money has gone. But we have a possible connection between Farid Alami and Natasha.

I've spoken to a colleague who pulled Farid's car over last week, and who didn't think it was impossible that Farid is the person seen talking to Natasha in the recording from the supermarket. Natasha was a member of ISIS, we know that. And she was being threatened by the man in the recording. I think the money-laundering and Farid might be connected to ISIS murdering Magnus Moheden."

She left out the fact that Molly Berg had identified the man in the recording as one of the men on the luxury yacht. It would have been too complicated to explain how she had found out about that.

Samer sighed.

"You still don't want to say how you found out that Babylon Exchange is laundering money?"

"Not beyond the fact that I have a source."

"A source you trust?"

"More than any."

Samer scratched his stubble. To their right two women with pushchairs were walking past the car.

"Somewhere in Stockholm there is an active and highly capable terrorist cell," Vanessa said. "I've shared all I know with the Security Service, but I have no idea what they're doing with my information. The collaboration and openness that we shared before Moheden's murder is all in the past now. We have no idea what the Security Service are doing, except what Trude can tell us. And they could be on the wrong track, it's happened before."

4

Johan sighed loudly as he watched his son crying. James was sitting on Erica's lap on the sofa. She was stroking his hair, hugging him tight.

He was so weak, so pathetically fragile.

"Stop crying, for God's sake," Johan snapped. "It's only for a few weeks."

"But I don't want to go. I don't want to move again. Please, Daddy!"

Johan felt anger rising as he grabbed James hard by his arm and pulled him off Erica's lap and shoved him towards his room.

"Pack your damn things!"

Erica tried to calm him, and James slouched away.

"You make too much fuss of him," Johan said. "He's too spoiled, too weak. I don't know what's going to become of him. Fuck – I don't want a son I despise."

Erica hushed him.

"Please," she said. "Be quiet. He can hear you."

"Maybe that's just as well?"

They stared at each other until Erica looked away and got to her feet. She went over to the fridge, took out a bottle of wine and poured a glass. She drank a deep gulp.

"Who are those men upstairs?" she asked.

"IT specialists."

"What are they doing?"

"Checking that no one's infiltrated our mobiles and computers. It was the lawyer's idea." Johan's eyes narrowed. He walked over to Erica, towering above her. "Have you been fucking someone else again? Is that what you're worried they're going to find? That you've been flashing your fucking cunt to some personal trainer?"

Johan heard someone coming downstairs and turned away, and watched as Anders Bladh's shiny leather shoes appeared on the stairs.

"Can you come upstairs for a moment?"

"What is it?"

"We've found something."

The IT team, which consisted of three pale men in the mid-twenties, were sitting in front of Johan's laptop. Johan and Anders Bladh went over and stood by the desk.

"Arash, tell Johan here what you've found."

One of the men, who was wearing a red Star Wars T-shirt, adjusted his glasses and nodded.

"There's a third party that has access to your email account. Someone has…"

Johan clenched his fist and took a step closer.

"I don't give a shit how it happened. I want to know who they are."

The young man in the T-shirt looked at him in surprise.

"Out," Johan told him and the other IT guys. When they had left the room, he closed the door and sat down behind his desk. Anders Bladh remained standing with his hands behind his back.

"Then they know that I've contacted you. Shit. They know I'm going to talk."

"Have you got any way of contacting them?"

"You don't get it, these aren't the sort of people you can frighten. If you call and try to reason with them, they'll just get angry."

Anders Bladh sank onto one of the chair and crossed his legs.

"Tell me more about the man who contacted you."

Johan sighed.

"I've already told you what I know. He was British. Well, maybe not British. He spoke English, but he looked like an Arab. Well-dressed, well-spoken. He contacted me when I was living in London, told me what he wanted and what he was prepared to pay. I only met him that once. We did the rest via an encrypted app. But I've deleted my account, so I can't get hold of him that way. That was why he started emailing me."

Anders Bladh ran his thumb over his cufflink.

"I suggest you give me his email address. I'll formulate a message in which I explain the legal consequences for him. Believe me, I can be very persuasive."

Johan hesitated. He bit the end of the nail on his index finger, then spat it out on the floor.

"They already know that you've contacted a lawyer, so it isn't exactly hard to figure out that you're putting yourself at the police's disposal. You've leaving tomorrow. And neither they nor the police have any idea where you're going."

"Okay, do it," Johan said, getting to his feet. "Do whatever you have to do."

5

Sabina, Thomas and Hamza were sitting round the kitchen table. The blinds were down, and two tea lights on the windowsill were the only source of light.

Thomas was holding the laptop on his knees.

"Can I read the email from the lawyer again?"

Thomas passed the laptop to Hamza, who read the email from lawyer Anders Bladh.

"It all suggests that he's going to talk," Thomas said.

No one said anything for a while.

"There's no other option," Hamza eventually said. "We need to attack earlier than planned."

"But our orders are to stay here and wait," Sabina said carefully. She turned to Thomas, which irritated Hamza. They had no chain of command, but she evidently considered Thomas better suited to taking decisions.

Thomas cupped his hands over his mouth and closed his eyes.

"If Johan Karlström is going to talk to the police, then they'll be able to track the money to Farid. And he could lead them to us. That's a risk we can't take," Hamza said.

"Farid won't talk," Sabina said.

Hamza glared at her.

"You don't know what he might do. He's weak. He's a keyboard warrior. An organiser. If they put him under the slightest pressure, he'll crack. I was there when the police stopped us when we went to get the weapons."

"But Farid was the one who…"

Sabina stopped talking when Thomas stood up so abruptly that his chair toppled over behind him.

He was looking down at the table in front of him with his head bowed. Then he grabbed hold of her arm, pulled her off her chair and dragged her across the kitchen floor, dislodging her niqab.

"You need to learn to keep quiet when men are talking. Fucking bitch. What's wrong with you? Have you been in Sweden too long?"

He leaned over and slapped her across the face. Before he shut the kitchen door on her, he gave her a kick.

Thomas returned to the table.

"You're right. We need to get rid of Johan Karlström before he talks. I've got his address. We'll go there first thing tomorrow morning."

Hamza had just opened his mouth to reply when the doorbell rang.

They looked at each other, then Hamza snatched up the Kalashnikov that was leaning against the wall behind him. Thomas stood up, grabbed his own automatic weapon and hurried to the kitchen door. In the living room Sabina was pulling on her suicide vest. They stood in silence next to her, looking at the explosive device attached to the door.

If anyone forced the door open, the device would detonate. Killing everyone within a radius of three or four metres. The load-bearing wall that separated the living room from the kitchen would protect them.

Sabina closed her eyes, her head was bowed. Hamza realised she was praying, preparing for death.

He followed her example and mumbled a prayer for God's blessing. He hoped that God would receive him as a martyr.

6

Nicolas was sitting in his hotel room with his feet resting on the windowsill, watching people swerve the puddles of water in Mariatorget.

Once again he found himself at a crossroads in his life, without any plans for the future. He didn't know where he wanted to live or what he wanted to spend the rest of his time on Earth doing. Where would he have been if he was still part of the Special Operations Group? Perhaps he would have been dead, or perhaps he would have been even more lost. Time had an ability to give a particular gloss to your memories. One thing was certain: life had been simpler as a soldier. An officer had told him where to go, what his mission was. He hadn't needed to think. Just do what he was ordered, secure in the knowledge that it was right because he was acting on behalf of Sweden and was defending democracy and Swedish lives with a gun in his hand.

But now?

Someone knocked on the wall three times. That was the signal that meant Molly was hungry. He smiled and got to his feet. He knocked back twice, which according to their very simple code meant that the message was understood and that food was on its way.

After Molly told them what she had been through on board the yacht *Lucinda*, Vanessa had gone down to reception and booked a room in her own name. In all likelihood, it was illegal to conceal a witness in that way, but Vanessa had told them that she wasn't going to let the Security Service ruin Molly's life. At the same time she wanted her within reach in case she was needed in the investigation, but she had promised Molly that she could go anywhere she wanted as soon as this was over.

Nicolas pulled on his outdoor clothes and left the room.

Half an hour later he was in Molly's identical room. He handed over a plastic container from a nearby Thai restaurant. The television was on, tuned to CNN.

"Are you okay?" he asked.

"Can't you stay and eat here?"

Molly turned the television off and they sat down on the floor by the window. Nicolas with his back against the bed, Molly with her legs crossed.

"So where are you actually from?" Nicolas asked, putting a piece of chicken in his mouth with the chopsticks.

"Guess."

He looked at her. She gave him a big smile, and kept turning her head this way and that so he could get a good look.

"South America, somewhere?"

Molly laughed and shook her head.

"Mum was from Thailand. Dad's Swedish."

"Plenty of people have preconceptions about relationships like that," Nicolas said tentatively, reaching for his can of drink.

"You too, I'm sure."

He nodded.

"In their case, every single one was true," Molly said, unconcerned. "Dad found Mum in a bar in Bangkok. Offered her a new life. She had to choose between spreading her legs for drunk, drug-addled tourists, or moving to Kiruna. But sure, it wasn't exactly fun seeing the way people whispered and pointed behind our backs when we were in town. Or when the guys in school asked how many baht Mum wanted to suck their cocks or get gangbanged."

Her tone was cold, untroubled, even if Nicolas guessed there was a deep sorrow behind her words.

He tried to find something to say, but failed and sat there in silence. Molly tilted her head and looked at him with amusement.

"You don't have to look so bloody sad. Mum was a whore. I became a whore. Even if I earned an awful lot more than she ever did. It isn't the biggest thing in the world. But a psychoanalyst could probably find a few interesting things hidden away inside me."

She laughed.

"Here we sit, two tiny punctuation marks in the entirety of life on Earth, eating Thai food on a spinning globe somewhere in the universe," she exclaimed, gesturing with her chopsticks. "One hundred years from now we'll both be dead. No one will remember this moment. There won't be any pictures of it. So did it really happen, when there's no one left to remember it? Do you have any idea how many moments world history is full of? Moments no one remembers. People no one remembers."

She tilted her head again, and the look in her eyes turned serious for a moment.

"That's what I think about when I'm with men who have paid hundreds of thousands of kronor to stuff their genitals inside me. No one remembers this. You aren't that fucking important, Molly. It's only your body here in this bed. The rest of you, the bit that's really you, can't be bought by anyone."

Nicolas scraped up the last remnants of food from the plastic container.

"How come you haven't tried?"

He looked up and shot her a quizzical glance.

"To sleep with you?"

She nodded.

"Does it bother you?" he asked.

"Maybe a little, weirdly enough. Besides, I owe you a pretty big debt of gratitude."

"I don't think it would be appropriate."

Molly laughed, and repeated what he had said in a deep, serious voice, before putting her container down on the fitted carpet and looking at him.

"You're a good person, Nicolas. I like you."

7

The hinges of the letterbox creaked. Hamza and Thomas aimed their guns at the front door. Hamza was prepared for it to be forced open at any moment, triggering the explosives.

The voice that reached into the flat via the letterbox was familiar. Hamza and Thomas looked at each other questioningly as they slowly lowered their weapons.

"Open up," Farid said. "Quick."

Hamza handed his Kalashnikov to Sabina, who was looking pale beneath her veil. He wiped his hands on his jeans so he could deal with the explosive device.

"Wait here," he said tersely.

"Hurry up," Thomas hissed.

Hamza began to disarm it. He took a deep breath, then wiped his hands again, they seemed determined to get damp while he was working, then lifted the explosive aside and carefully put it down on the floor.

He unlocked the door.

"What are you doing here?" he asked. He checked there was no one else outside, then pulled Farid inside the flat and locked the door. Thomas pushed Farid up against the wall.

"They, they've found me."

Farid was terrified. Hamza could see beads of sweat on his brow. "Who?"

"The police. Or the Security Service. They've been to my home. And to Babylon. By God, they came close to catching me."

Hamza, who was busy arming the door again, spun round.

"And of all the fucking places you could go, you came here? We ought to cut your throat."

Thomas's grip tightened. He grabbed Farid by the throat and squeezed until he was struggling for air.

"They could have followed you here. You could have led them here."

The muscles in Thomas's arm tightened, rippling beneath his skin.

Farid shook his head desperately. He was choking. Thomas's grip eased slightly and Farid fell to the floor, gasping as he felt his throat.

"No one followed me. I spent hours travelling round."

"Your mobile?"

"I got rid of it."

Hamza and Thomas breathed out. Hamza helped Farid to his feet and guided him into the living room. Sabina was looking down at the floor.

"What happened?" Thomas said.

"Two police officers showed up at the bureau de change. I was at home, but I got a warning. When I looked out into the street before going out to the car, it was already too late. I snuck down into the basement and hid there for a while, then I got out the back way."

"You're certain you weren't followed?" Hamza asked.

Farid nodded hard, casting a frightened look at Thomas.

"Absolutely certain. I changed bus and metro ten or eleven times. No one's following me."

"Where did you get rid of your mobile?"

"I stamped on it till it broke. Then I threw it in a bin at the Central Station, and got rid of the SIM-card on the train. I wanted to call you first, but it was safest to get rid of it. There's nothing in my flat or in the office that could lead them here. I swear."

Hamza pulled Thomas into his bedroom and closed the door.

"What do you think?"

"I think we can use him," Thomas replied.

Hamza raised his eyebrows curiously.

"He's of no value at all. What for?"

"Tomorrow. You and I are needed for the next phase. Sure, if only one of us is alive we can still succeed, but it's better if we can both do it. If we get arrested or killed by the pigs now, there won't be anyone who can finish this. And then everything will have been in vain."

Thomas was right.

"We need two cars." Hamza sank onto his bed. "And we need

to get hold of them from two separate places, a long way from here in case anything goes wrong."

"You sort that out," Thomas said. "Set off now. I'll take Farid with me tomorrow and kill Johan."

"And his family?"

"We can't leave any witnesses. Not at this stage."

Hamza nodded.

"One more thing." He lowered his voice. "If anything looks like it's going wrong, Farid mustn't end up in the hands of the crusaders. We don't need him later, for the finale. His usefulness is at an end. After tomorrow he's just an unnecessary risk."

8

Trude Hovland and another forensics expert arrived at Degerbygränd around ten o'clock that evening. Vanessa had phoned and persuaded Mikael Kask to conduct a forensic examination of Farid Alami's Renault. The two forensics officers were tired and red-eyed, but they quickly set about the task. From the windows in the flats curious neighbours looked down on the scene. Because members of the emergency services often got attacked in the area, they were accompanied by a patrol car and two uniformed officers.

Vanessa and Samer headed home.

"Tomorrow I'll check the road cameras from 8 November to see if I can find Farid's car," Samer said. "It could have been in Östermalm when Natasha and Rikard Olsson were killed."

"Good idea."

"Do you think about her much?" Samer turned his head and looked at Vanessa.

"Natasha?"

"Yes."

"Not like I used to. I'm trying to see her as a terrorist, but... I don't know. I swing between hating her for deceiving me, for getting me to let her into my life, and more than anything wanting to catch the person who murdered her so I can find out what really happened."

"Would it make any difference if you knew for certain that she had defected, that that was why they got rid of her?"

"Maybe."

Samer nodded slowly.

"I think that's what happened," he said. "I think you made her believe in life again, and that's why they killed her."

Vanessa met Samer's gaze and they smiled at each other.

"Thanks," she said.

A different sort of silence spread through the car.

"You're special, Vanessa."

She waited for him to go on.

"You're so rich you don't have to look at the shit, don't have to be confronted with misery. Isn't that why people want to be rich? So they can live in a bubble, read about violence in the paper and think 'that doesn't affect me'. But not you. You seek it out, and I hope I'm going to get to know you well enough to understand why."

Vanessa didn't know what to say in reply. They drove a few hundred metres in silence until they were stopped by a red light.

"I'm sorry I ever suspected you, Samer, that wasn't fair of me."

"Yes, it was," he said, looking out at the dark streets.

9

Friday morning was ice-cold and dark, and there wasn't much traffic on the roads heading out of Stockholm. Heading into the city, in contrast, both carriageways were full of cars. An older driver from the security company whose name Johan hadn't bothered to remember was at the wheel. Johan was sitting in the front seat of the Range Rover, with Erica and James in the back. His son was lying with his head on his mother's lap, his eyes closed as she ran her hands soothingly through his blond hair.

Johan assumed he was crying, but didn't want to turn round to look. He didn't want to be confronted with his son's failings. Not now. Not this morning. Anders Bladh had sent him a text telling him that all the preparations in Turkey were ready. They would be flying to Istanbul with Turkish Airlines, then onward by an internal flight to Antalya. There they would be picked up by a Turkish security company recommended by Anders Bladh's friend, for the final, west-bound stretch of their journey.

The house was on the Marmaris coast, on a hill overlooking the Mediterranean. Most of the nearby villas were owned by international dollar-millionaires. It would be good to get away from the cold and darkness. From the tall-poppy syndrome that poisoned the air and conditions of life. Sweden was the only country in the world – along with North Korea and possibly Cuba – where it was forbidden to earn money.

The driver glanced in the rear-view mirror. Johan looked to his right, trying to see what he was looking at. Behind them was a silver Saab, an older model. Hadn't he seen the same car earlier, when they left Djursholm?

He checked the speedometer. A little under one hundred kilometres an hour.

"Maintain this speed. Stay in the right-hand lane," he said.

"Sure."

Ordinarily he would have told the driver to drive faster, but at this point it would be a disaster if they were stopped by the police. It was too much of an unnecessary risk. Johan was a gambler, and often played for high stakes, it made life more interesting, but only when the potential winnings were worth it. In this case they only stood to gain a few extra minutes in the VIP lounge at Arlanda. Their flight wasn't due to take off for another two hours.

Johan's phone vibrated. He answered.

"Just wanted to check that you're on your way," Anders Bladh said.

"We are. We're just passing Upplands Väsby."

"Splendid."

"As soon as the plane takes off, I'll contact the police and tell them that you're available."

"Good."

"Bon voyage. I'll fly down later in the week, once you've had a chance to settle in. That's when the real work begins."

Johan ended the call and turned round. Erica met his gaze.

She was wearing a white fur coat, with a low-cut dress beneath it. Her long legs were bare and she was wearing heels. Good. He didn't want them to look like they were a family going on a charter holiday. He liked showing her off, he enjoyed other men getting turned on by her. Erica was his. Everything she was wearing was his. And even if Johan knew that he could sometimes be difficult to live with, she had him to thank for everything. Without him she would have been a washed-up reality TV star, or – more likely by now – an overweight, miserable cashier in a suburban supermarket. He had given her a life she could never have dreamed of. That was why it was no more than right that she show a bit of gratitude.

"For fuck's sake, you could make the effort to smile from time to time," he muttered.

Behind her he saw the Saab indicate to overtake. Erica's lips moved, but he wasn't listening.

Instead he was watching the Saab.

It pulled up alongside.

Johan stared at the immigrant behind the wheel. What the hell was his problem? The driver turned his head as well to see what was going on, and muttered something. The back window of the Saab wound down.

Johan recognised the man in the back seat, but couldn't immediately place him.

10

Nicolas had bought a cup of coffee from the 7-Eleven on Hornsgatan and was now walking towards Gamla stan.

Out of the pit that would one day be the new Slussen traffic interchange, two large cranes reached into the sky, and several digging machines were making a terrible noise as men in orange overalls and hard hats wandered about inside the enclosed area. A white-haired woman was walking around sheepishly, checking the rubbish bins on the little square to see if she could find anything of value.

On the other side of the water the rides and attractions of Gröna Lund amusement park stood silent and abandoned, waiting for the heat of summer to return. He was seized by melancholy as he thought about the future. Where would he be the next time that rollercoaster was performing its gyrations, full of screaming passengers? When the cranes had been dismantled and Slussen was finished?

His mobile phone vibrated. He quickly took it out, hoping it was Vanessa, But it was a newsflash from *Kvällspressen*, with news of a car accident just north of Upplands Väsby. Three confirmed dead. A fourth person – a woman – was fighting for her life, according to the short text.

The cause of the accident has not yet been confirmed. But witnesses Kvällspressen has spoken to say that the driver lost control while overtaking.

Nicolas looked through the images, zooming in. A black Range Rover lay on its side in a muddy field. The body of the vehicle was completely mangled. The number-plate had been pixelated.

It couldn't be the Karlström family. After all, how many black Range Rovers were there in Sweden?

Even so, the thought wouldn't leave him alone.

After hesitating for a few moments, he called Erica's number. The call went through, but there was no answer. He tried again. Same result. Nicolas glanced anxiously at the organised chaos at Slussen.

He began to walk back towards Mariatorget as he called Vanessa.

"The car accident in Upplands Väsby. Can you find out the registration number?"

The line was silent for a few seconds.

"What do you want that for?"

11

The silver Saab had turned off the E4 and was now driving towards Fjällnora nature reserve, where Thomas and Farid had left the other getaway car at around five o'clock that morning.

The smell of gunpowder stuck in their noses and the Kalashnikov was still warm. Thomas leaned forward between the front seats and patted Farid on the shoulder.

"You remember the way?" he asked in English.

"Sure, no problem," Farid replied in Arabic.

None of the other people on the road seemed to have realised what had happened when they opened fire. The closest car had been about a hundred metres behind them, and it must have looked like the driver of the Range Rover lost control of his vehicle. The crash had been violent. The SUV had rolled over several times in the field. No one could have survived that.

Thomas turned round. The road behind them was empty, no one had followed them.

"The child died as well," Farid said, as if to himself, and wiped his sweating forehead on his sleeve. "Didn't he? He must have died too."

"What do you mean?"

"It's a shame he was in the car. He was young. Just a little boy."

Thomas leaned back in his seat and rubbed his sore eyes. They had got up at four o'clock to move the cars, and were outside the house in Djursholm by six o'clock in the morning. They had seen the driver packing the cases in the back of the Range Rover and realised that Johan Karlström was planning to escape.

Farid indicated right and they turned onto a muddy track that led into the forest, and drove another kilometre or so. The Toyota they had left in a clearing was still there.

Thomas waited until Farid had switched the engine off. He looked at the big, dark birthmark on the back of his neck before sticking the knife all the way to the hilt in his neck. Farid flailed with his arms, but not a sound came out of his mouth.

"You haven't got it in you. You're too weak. An infidel is an infidel. Child, woman or man. Boy or girl."

Thomas moved the knife around, cutting through tissue and blood vessels. Warm blood sprayed the inside of the car. The lower half of Farid's body was bucking, kicking and scrabbling.

"You were never in Raqqa. You never saw how their drones and bombs rained down on our children, tearing them to pieces, leaving them dead on the hot tarmac. You never smelled the stench of blood, of rotting flesh and crushed dreams."

Thomas pulled the knife out, pushed the passenger door open and gathered Farid's belongings in a plastic bag that he tied a knot in. He unlocked the boot of the Toyota, took out the petrol can that Hamza had left for them as arranged, so they could burn the car, then tossed the plastic bag and the Kalashnikov in the boot.

He went back to the Saab, put the petrol can on the ground, checked that he hadn't forgotten anything that could lead the police to them. He gather together all the empty shells he could find inside the car and put them in his pocket before pouring the petrol. He opened the driver's door, stuck his hand in the pocket of Farid's jeans and pulled out his lighter.

He found an old till receipt, lit it and let the flames take hold before tossing it onto the body, which immediately caught light. Thomas backed away a few paces, watching as the flames flared out from the open car doors.

12

Vanessa was sitting at her desk in the headquarters of the National Homicide Unit. The door to the corridor was closed. She got up and looked out of the window, down onto Polhemsgatan. A police car left the building, siren blaring.

If the Karlström family really had been in that Range Rover, then it was highly unlikely to have been an accident. She was expecting a phone call from one of the officers on the scene. Her mobile phone rang and Vanessa held it to her ear.

"Hello?"

"My name's Fredrik Karlsson, I'm a trainee, and I'm at the scene of the accident at Upplands Väsby. Erm, my boss wanted me to call you."

"What's the car's registration number?"

"JKL 172."

Vanessa didn't need to check the yellow Post-it note she had written the number on while she was talking to Nicolas.

It was the Karlström family's car.

"The witnesses have said it was an accident. What do you think?"

Vanessa heard the sound of wind blowing across the microphone and understood that he was still in the field where the car had ended up. They had probably cordoned the area off and left him to make sure people kept their distance.

"I don't get told much, but they've found something that suggests it wasn't an accident."

"And the victims?"

"Two men and a young boy were already dead. One woman was badly injured. I don't think she's likely to survive, it was a miracle she was still breathing. She's been taken to Danderyd Hospital."

Vanessa picked Nicolas up at Mariatorget in her BMW, then drove to Danderyd Hospital, where she parked outside the emergency room. An ambulance drove in as they crossed the car park and walked into the building. Vanessa showed her police ID to the receptionist and asked to speak to the duty doctor while Nicolas paced up and down impatiently. A nurse came to get them and led them in silence down a long corridor. She stopped at one of the doors, gestured to a sofa and asked them to have a seat before opening the door and disappearing.

"Are you okay?" Vanessa asked, taking Nicolas's hand. He shook his head as he stared blankly into the white wall.

"He was ten years old."

"Who?"

"James. Their son. Ten years old, Vanessa."

There were tears in his eyes, and Vanessa was struck by the fact that this was the first time she had seen him cry. She felt confused, unsure of what he wanted her to do. She moistened her lips, trying to think of something consoling to say, but stayed silent.

Vanessa let go of Nicolas's hand when the door opened and a green-clad doctor came out and walked over to them.

"Is she alive?" Nicolas asked at once, getting to his feet.

The doctor shook his head apologetically.

"Erica Karlström died on the operating table. I'm sorry. There was nothing we could do. It was something of a miracle that she survived as long as this."

Nicolas sank back down on the sofa again and buried his face in his hands. Vanessa and the doctor exchanged a long glance.

"What injuries did she have?" Vanessa asked quietly.

"Where should I start?" the doctor said with a sigh. "Let's see. Two gunshot wounds to the chest, compression injuries to the skull and torso, fractures to both legs and probably also back injuries. Like I said. Nothing we could have done would have kept her alive."

"Gunshot wounds?" Vanessa exclaimed. "Where are the bullets?"

"We removed them and are waiting for one of you to collect them."

"Can I see them?"

He shot her a quizzical look.

"Sure," he said, and held the door open.

Vanessa turned to Nicolas who was still sitting on the sofa.

"I'll be right back."

She followed the doctor, through the operating room, where two cleaners were hard at work, and into a small office. On the desk lay a bloody, resealable plastic bag. It contained two flattened bullets. She picked up the bag and inspected it in the light of the ceiling lamp. There was no doubt that they were from an automatic weapon. Just as she had suspected, they were the same sort of ammunition that had been found at the Clarion Hotel Sign after Magnus Moheden's murder. She was sure they came from the same gun, but that was something the ballistics experts would have to confirm.

Vanessa put the bag down, said goodbye to the doctor and left the room.

Nicolas was still sitting hunched over where she had left him. She sat down next to him and leaned her head on his shoulder. She had never felt more tender towards him, but didn't know what to say to comfort him.

"Is there anything I can do?" she whispered.

"No."

Two nurses approaching along the corridor lowered their voices, and passed by with sombre expressions on their faces.

Nicolas was breathing hard.

"Don't you have to go?" he asked.

She met his gaze, gave him a quick smile, then shook her head.

"No."

She moved aside, then gently laid his head down on her lap and stoked his hair. Nicolas's legs were too long to fit on the sofa and he bent them, so his knees jutted out over the edge of the sofa.

Vanessa saw Erica Karlström in her mind's eye. If she had survived, her only son would have been dead. And she knew that if she had been confronted with the same choice in Cuba, when Adeline stopped breathing, there was no doubt in her mind that she would have chosen to die there and then.

But now, in hindsight?

For several years she had just wanted to die. She never said so out loud to anyone but herself. But she had looked at life going on around her through a filter, like a performance on a screen that she had to watch all the way to the end before death took her and the pain of her daughter's death finally ended.

PART IX

1

It was half past six in the evening and Vanessa was knocking firmly on the bathroom door. Celine had discovered the bathtub, and was now spending at least an hour in it every day.

"I'm just coming!"

Vanessa went back to the living room, got out plates, cutlery and a bottle of cola and put them on the dining table where the pizza boxes were already waiting.

The bathroom opened and steam billowed out. Celine appeared in the doorway wrapped in a white towel. Her skin was bright red from the hot bathwater.

"You haven't considered lowering the temperature of the water a bit? You're steaming like a chicken that's just come out of the oven."

Celine grinned.

"I'll just put some clothes on," she said, and hurried into her room.

Vanessa pulled out her chair, wrapped her dark cardigan around her and sat down.

It was Friday, and with two days left before Magnus Moheden's funeral in Storkyrkan in Gamla stan, the hunt for his killers was still going on with undiminished intensity. The murder of the Karlström family was now also being investigated by the Security Service.

In a series of nocturnal searches and dawn raids, heavily armed police officers had turned neighbourhood mosques and flats in the Stockholm suburbs upside down.

But the terrorist cell always seemed to be one step ahead of them.

Not least the execution of Farid Alami, the Moroccan who had been found stabbed to death in the burned-out getaway vehicle north of Arlanda, which demonstrated that the members of the cell were systematically eliminating weak leaks to minimise the risk of being caught. Vanessa took the murder of Farid Alami, who appeared to have had some sort of organisational role, to mean that his usefulness was at an end, and that he had therefore become more of a risk than an asset.

Everything suggested that another attack was imminent. It would soon be Christmas, and the shops were already crowded in advance of the holiday, even though the national terror level had been raised from three to four. It was as if no one quite believed that what had happened at the Clarion Hotel Sign, and previously on Drottninggatan, could happen again, with even worse consequences.

Analysis of traffic cameras around Stockholm showed that Farid Alami's Renault had been in Östermalm at the time of the murders of Natasha and Rikard Olsson. Vanessa was convinced that Farid had been a participant, or was at least involved in events there. Rikard Olsson and Natasha were murdered by ISIS. But why they were murdered remained to be seen.

Two of the terrorists had been identified. DNA evidence from both Hamza Mansour and Sabina had been found in the Clarion Hotel Sign, in one of the suites on the same floor where the Minister of Justice had been murdered. The man calling himself Thomas, whose recruitment of Molly had been described in detail in a report Vanessa had sent to the Security Service, hadn't yet been identified.

It was frustrating not to be able to carry on working with the investigation. She wished she could be more involved.

Vanessa thrust her thoughts aside when Celine sat down at the dining-table with tinsel in her hair, and realised that it was St Lucia's Day.

They opened the boxes and sliced the pizza. Celine told her about the Lucia procession at school, but the conversation was stilted. Vanessa was distracted and was having trouble paying attention.

When they were halfway through the pizzas, Celine put down the slice she had been about to pop in her mouth and looked at Vanessa thoughtfully.

"Are you angry with me?" she asked. "Have I done something stupid?"

When Vanessa looked up she saw Celine looking at her with big, anxious eyes.

"No, not at all," she said quickly. "There's just something I need to talk to you about."

She pulled out the documents that she had tucked away in her back pocket, flattened them out and put them on the table in front of Celine. The girl's eyes darted between the documents and Vanessa.

"What's this?"

Vanessa cleared her throat.

"I wanted to ask if you'd like..."

Celine reached for the papers. Vanessa watched her face intently, trying to interpret the slightest movement as she read.

"You want me to live here?" she whispered. "Forever?"

Vanessa felt a lump in her throat.

"If you'd like that? There's no guarantee that the application would be approved, they take a long time, but..."

Celine stood up so abruptly that her chair toppled over. Vanessa barely had time to stand up before the girl buried her head in her chest, her still-wet hair soaking the thin white fabric of her T-shirt.

"I thought you'd changed your mind," Celine whispered.

"Changed my mind?"

"I found these papers in your wardrobe last week. But seeing as you didn't say anything, I thought you didn't want to go through with it. I promise to be good. I won't be difficult anymore. And I'll eat my vegetables. Spinach. And broccoli. I promise, I'm going to be crazy about broccoli."

Vanessa laughed.

"I want you just the way you are, Celine." She smiled and ran her hand through the girl's wet hair.

While Celine was taking the empty pizza boxes down to the recycling bin out in the courtyard, Vanessa's mobile rang.

"I've got something for you," Trude said.

She sounded tired, which was understandable. The forensics officers had been working long shifts pretty much every day since Magnus Moheden's murder, and as well as helping the Security Service, they also had to cover their usual duties.

"You were right. Hamza Mansour has also been in Farid Alami's Renault. His DNA is on the passenger seat. It matches what we found in Stig Boström's flat, and at the Clarion Hotel Sign."

This didn't come as much of a surprise, but Vanessa still had a feeling she was missing something.

"So he could have been there the night Natasha was murdered."

"We can't rule that out."

Vanessa thanked her for calling, then sat down thoughtfully at the table again. The dishwasher was rumbling. She drummed her fingers on the table. Hamza Mansour had been in Farid Alami's car. So maybe it had been him in there when Erik Giertz and his colleague pulled the car over on the E4. But they had been called away to a shooting before they had time to search the car. She could remember her conversation with the big policeman in McDonalds.

Vanessa reached for her phone and googled *29 November + shooting + Sätra*.

No results. There were no reports in the media about a shooting in Sätra that day. Which was strange. Every shooting or disturbance was usual given extensive coverage.

Vanessa called Erik Giertz's number.

He answered almost immediately and explained that he was out on a call, but that he had a few minutes to talk.

"That shooting you were called away to. What happened with that?"

A short silence followed.

"Nothing. It turned out to be a false alarm."

2

Mikael Kask ended his call with Vanessa and put his phone down on the white sheet. He gazed up at the cracks in the ceiling, then down at the terracotta-coloured wall. The window onto Markvardsgatan was open, and the wind was tugging at the curtains as it blew into the room.

Trude Hovland came in with a glass of red wine in each hand. He looked admiringly at her naked body before reaching for a glass. Trude lay down at the end of the bed with her head close to the open window, and balanced the wine glass on her stomach. He didn't know anyone who was so relaxed about being naked as her. He reached for the covers and pulled them over his hips.

"What did Vanessa have to say?" she asked.

"She asked me to track down an emergency call, and find out the number it was made from," Mikael said, sitting up in the bed.

Earlier that evening he had been getting changed in Harry's Bootcamp when Trude texted to ask if he wanted to meet up. He had immediately stuffed his gym gear back in his bag, walked to Stureplan and caught the number 2 bus towards Vasastan.

"And?"

"And what?"

Down in the street two dogs were barking angrily at each other.

"Are you going to help her with that?"

"Of course."

A short silence followed.

Mikael sipped the wine. He wondered if Trude wanted him to go, but if she did surely she wouldn't have poured them more wine?

He adjusted the pillow behind his back. You need to stop thinking so fucking much, he thought. Trude had a strange effect on him. He was completely natural when he was with her, in a way that he hadn't been with anyone for several years. At the same time, he was nervous about disappointing her and being asked to go home.

"You like her, don't you?" Trude asked.

Mikael searched hopefully for any trace of jealousy in her voice, but there wasn't any. Trude rolled onto her side, leaned her head on her elbow and looked at him with her big dark eyes.

"A lot," he replied. "Vanessa's special. The best detective I've ever worked with. But I can't make her out as a person."

Trude smiled.

"You don't have to be a therapist to see that she's been through a lot in her life. There's something there. But I haven't asked. She wouldn't like that. And that's fine, we don't need to know everything about everyone."

"Do you see each other socially?" Mikael asked in surprise.

"Sometimes. She lives nearby, on Roslagsgatan. We have a glass of wine together sometimes. Okay, you check out that emergency call and I'll grab a shower. Then what about going out for dinner? It is Lucia, after all."

Mikael looked at Trude in surprise.

"Sure."

She got up from the bed, put the empty wine glass on the bedside table, rested her hand on his hairy chest and kissed him on the lips before going into the bathroom.

Two hours later Trude and Mikael were sitting side by side in Nombre, the tapas bar. The big plate glass window was the only thing separating them from Odengatan, it felt almost like they were sitting on the pavement eating. At first Mikael had been worried someone would walk past and see them together, but the more red wine he drank, the more relaxed he felt. Maybe it would be a good thing if someone saw them together, that would be a natural way of prompting a conversation about where their relationship was actually going.

His mobile phone buzzed. An email from emergency call centre. Trude pulled a pair of earphones out of her jacket pocket, handed one to Mikael, then giggled as she inserted the other one in her own ear. He clicked to play the recording.

"*112. What's the nature of the emergency?*"

"There's been a shooting in Sätra. Automatic gunfire. Four men have been shot. They're bleeding, dying, please, get here quickly," a male voice said.

"Where in Sätra?"

A short silence followed.

"Near the metro station, in the centre. Hurry up! They're dying!"

The call ended abruptly.

Trude and Mikael looked at each other questioningly. The email also contained the number of the phone used to make the call.

"I'd better send this to Vanessa straight away," Mikael said.

3

Soft flakes of snow were falling from the dark sky above Stockholm. The white lawns of Humlegården were crisscrossed by the tracks of sledges and snowracers. Axel and Nicolas were walking slowly through the park before sitting down on a bench by the statue outside the Royal Library.

It was almost midnight and Axel had called Nicolas just an hour earlier. At first he had thought that Axel had changed his mind about the car, which he had asked to borrow on Sunday so he could drive Molly to the airport. But Axel had told him he had made an important discovery and needed to see him urgently.

Nicolas felt concerned at once, and quickly dressed and caught the metro to Östermalmstorg.

"I-I think it was my fault that the Karlström family were killed," Axel said.

Nicolas looked at him in surprise.

"D-d-did you know that Johan Karlström had contacted a lawyer?" Axel went on. "He wanted to talk about the money laundering, confess what he had done. Someone discovered the intrusion into his computer and assumed it was the people blackmailing him. His lawyer contacted them. He sent a threatening message from his own email address, using Johan's computer. But it wasn't the blackmailers who had accessed his computer. It was me. It's my fault they're dead."

Nicolas was staring vacantly ahead of him.

"I-i-it's my fault Simon will probably never be able to walk again, and it's my fault an entire family were shot and killed. I don't know how I'm going to be able to live with myself."

Axel paused. His breath formed white clouds that quickly dispersed in the darkness.

"My whole life, I've always been able to say that I've never harmed anyone. But now. I don't know… I can't sleep. I've just been sitting at the computer, finding out more about Farid Alami."

The tone of Axel's voice had changed.

"Have you found something?"

"I'm not sure. Farid Alami seems to have had access to another account, I don't know if the police or the Security Service have found that one yet. I found it just before I called you, it requires expert knowledge to understand how to look for it. Maybe they can use it to find something out?"

Axel took off one of his gloves, unzipped his jacket, took out four folded sheets of paper and handed them over. Nicolas leafed through them quickly.

"What's this?"

"Transactions."

"How…?" Nicolas began, but changed his mind. "It doesn't matter."

Axel leaned closer and pointed.

"It isn't much, but you see these three transfers? They're the only regular transactions that have been made, to one and the same account. The person who owns that account is a Jovana Babic, and she's a customer of Danske Bank where I work as an IT specialist. I've written the address the bank has for her on the back."

He looked up at Nicolas.

"Can you give this to your friend in the police?"

"I'll make sure she gets it."

Nicolas got ready to go, but sank back onto the bench when Axel showed no sign of moving.

"What are you doing?" Axel asked after a while.

"Keeping you company," Nicolas said.

Axel turned his head and looked at him.

"What for?"

Nicolas smiled.

"You look like you need it."

4

Vanessa tucked a lock of hair behind her ear as she looked in the rear-view mirror. Her body felt heavy and she sat there behind the wheel for a while. Just for once, she had found a parking space on Roslagsgatan, and because she had to get up early the next day she had decided to leave the car there. Her mouth tasted of coffee, and her eyes were red and stinging. Since three o'clock she had been sitting in meetings about the preparations for Magnus Moheden's funeral. She had been allocated a position inside the cordon that was going to be set up around Storkyrkan. During the ceremony itself she would be inside the church itself, because she was the only police officer who had actually seen Sabina Haddad in real life. After the meetings she had sat in her room, looking through the entire investigation once more in the hope of finding something they had missed. The terrorist cell was out there somewhere in Stockholm. Ready to strike against soft targets. Murder Swedish citizens. Vanessa had no doubt that they, if they got the chance, would try to take as many people as possible with them when they died. That was how Islamic terrorist groups operated.

Shadia Mansour had confirmed that the voice that had made the emergency call about the shooting in Sätra belonged to her son, Hamza. Thanks to that call, they had been able to identify a mobile number that had been used by one of the terrorists. Samer Bakir was currently working to get a list of calls linked to that number from the service provider. In spite of pressure from the authorities, the provider was taking a while to provide the list.

There weren't many hours to go now until the funeral, and the media were reporting that it would be the largest, most expensive security operation in the history of the Swedish police. After the ceremony in Storkyrkan, the coffin would be taken in procession to Adolf Fredrik Church on Sveavägen, where Moheden was going to be buried. The editorials of the newspapers were full of the importance of standing up to the threat of Islamic terrorism and not backing down.

Vanessa stared vacantly in front of her. The arrangements were a nightmare. A crowd of at least ten thousand people was expected around Storkyrkan alone. She, like most members of the Stockholm police, was of the opinion that the funeral ought to be postponed, or at least scaled back in view of the terrorism threat. But the decision to hold the ceremony as planned was political, and not something they could influence.

Her mobile vibrated in her hand, and it took a few seconds for her brain to realise that it was actually an incoming call.

"Were you awake?" Nicolas asked.

He sounded disconcertingly lively, as if he were out for a walk.

"For a while longer. The funeral's tomorrow, as you know. I'm going to be at the church, so I've got a fair bit to sort out."

"Have you got time to meet? I've got something for you."

"What?"

"A list of Farid Alami's account transactions. I don't think your lot have found this account."

She didn't reply at once. The final meeting about the security arrangements for Magnus Moheden's funeral was due to take place at seven o'clock, in about six hours time. She really ought to get some sleep.

"I can photograph the list and send that instead," Nicolas said quickly.

"Where are you?"

"In Karlavägen."

"I'm on my way."

Vanessa started the car and pulled out. As she stopped at a red light at the junction with Odengatan she saw a car take the space she had just left.

Nicolas was walking along Karlavägen close to Ellen Key's Park. He raised his arm in a wave and Vanessa pulled up gently alongside him. Nicolas opened the door, got in the passenger seat and held his hands out to the heating vents.

"I know you've got loads to do, but I met up with Axel. The guy who..."

"I know," Vanessa said.

Nicolas pulled a sheaf of papers out from the inside pocket of his coat and handed them to her.

"This is a list of payments made by Farid Alami in the past six months."

Vanessa unfolded the pages on the steering wheel.

"Look at this," he said. Vanessa followed Nicolas's finger as it moved down a couple of lines. "And this. And this."

"I don't understand?"

"In the past three months, Farid has paid a total of sixty thousand kronor to an account at Danske Bank, in three instalments. The account belongs to a Jovana Babic."

"Do you know anything else about her?"

Nicolas gently moved Vanessa's hand aside and turned the page over. On the back was an address in Vällingby, written by hand in blue ink.

"This is the address the bank has for Babic."

"Thanks," Vanessa said.

She was suddenly wide awake. Every cell in her body was telling her that this was important. Maybe it could lead them a step closer to the terrorist cell. She ought to hand the information over to Mikael Kask as soon as she could.

"Thanks," she repeated, and put the papers away. She looked more closely at Nicolas, who had dark rings under his eyes.

"How are you doing?"

"I'm okay."

"And Molly?"

"Good. I'm driving her to Arlanda tomorrow. Her flight leaves an hour or so after the funeral. She's going to stay with her dad in Kiruna for a couple of months."

Vanessa nodded.

"How about you? What are you going to do?"

Nicolas shrugged his shoulders.

"I don't know. I thought maybe... well, I thought I'd found something. But that didn't work out."

They looked into each other's eyes. Vanessa reached out her hand and stroked his cheek then his arm before quickly pulling it back again.

"I..."

"It's okay, Vanessa. You don't have to say anything."

Her smile turned into a laugh.

"Do you know, you have the most beautiful laugh I know?" Nicolas said.

She was pleased.

"Really?"

He nodded, then said with sudden serious in his voice:

"I think it's because you laugh so rarely. It means more then. Every laugh becomes so... intense, so important."

He felt for the door handle. She put her hand on his arm, holding him back.

"One day, Nicolas. Just not now. Now doesn't work."

She swallowed.

"I know." He got out onto the pavement, then turned and put his head back inside the car again.

"Take care, Vanessa."

She watched as he disappeared down the steps and into the shadows of Ellen Key's Park.

5

It was almost quarter to two by the time Vanessa and Samer, who she had picked up on the way, pulled up in a quiet residential street in Vällingby. At first Mikael Kask hadn't wanted to let them go, but Vanessa had insisted; Jovana Babic was the best lead they had, and besides, the Security Service had their hands full. They might not even think it was worth checking out, seeing as the amounts transferred had been so small. Nor was there anything in Jovana Babic's background to suggest that she had anything to do with Islamists. But Vanessa knew better than to believe what official records said these days.

The blinds of the address Jovana Babic was registered as living at were closed. There was a small white Ford parked in the drive. A child's bicycle was leaning up by the front door, next to some pots containing dead plants. They got out and approached the house warily. Vanessa stopped and took her Sig Sauer from its holster, and checked there was a bullet in the chamber before she tucked the pistol in the waistband of her jeans.

Samer rang the doorbell. They heard a loud ring. Vanessa peered in through the round window in the front door. All she could see was a dark hallway.

"Try again. There's obviously someone here," she said, gesturing towards the car.

A light went on and Vanessa saw a woman in her sixties coming down the stairs dressed in a pale-blue nightdress. Her movements looked sleepy, and her grey hair was sticking out in all directions. She peered at them anxiously through the glass. Samer held his police ID up to the glass, and after a short hesitation she opened the door.

"Are you Jovana Babic?" Samer asked.

The woman quickly shook her head and shivered.

"No, that's my daughter."

"Do you know where she is?"

She pointed to the ceiling.

"Upstairs. It's the middle of the night. What do you actually want?"

"We need to talk to her now, right away." Vanessa gently nudged the woman aside, quickly wiped her shoes on the doormat and walked in.

At that moment she heard the sound of children's voices. A woman in her thirties, with long, chestnut-brown hair appeared at the top of the stairs with two little girls by her sides. One of the girls started to cry.

"Jovana Babic?" Bakir asked.

"Yes. What's going on?" She looked frightened, and the girl's crying got louder. Jovana picked her up and stroked her hair.

"We're from the police, we need to talk to you," Vanessa said, a little louder so she could be heard over the crying.

Jovana shook her head firmly.

"Now isn't a good time. Can't it wait till tomorrow? What do you think I can do with the children?"

Her initial shock seemed to have been replaced by obstinate anger.

The other girl joined in with her sister's crying. Vanessa was reluctant to force Jovana to go with them in front of her daughters.

"Just come with us to the car, then," she said. "As I said, we just want to talk to you. It's important."

Jovana appeared to consider her options. In the end she nodded and put the crying girl down.

"I'm just going to put some clothes on."

Hamza stepped out of the lift in the block of flats in Lappkärrsberget. In his hands he was holding plastic bags containing his, Sabina's and Thomas's personal belongings. Mostly clothes, shoes and various forged documents. It was really rather unnecessary to get rid of everything, seeing as all three of them would be dead by the time the police found the flat.

The bags were too big to squeeze into the garbage chute, and he couldn't burn them without drawing attention to himself. But a hundred metres or so away was a green builders' skip that would do nicely.

Hamza slung the bags over his shoulders and pushed the door open. It was freezing outside.

He stopped in the yard, breathing in the chill night air and looking up at the glowing half moon. He knew it would be the last time he saw it. Soon he would be in Firdaws, the highest level of Jannah, paradise, where the martyrs, prophets and the most devout believers lived.

Sweden hadn't wanted to have anything to do with him, but after tomorrow he would be feted and remembered right across the Muslim world. For Swedes, the name Hamza Mansour would be synonymous with fear, but Muslims around the world would remember him with love, forever.

He would live in eternity.

Hated by his enemies, loved by his own.

Hamza carried on walking down the sloping path, past the football pitch and climbing frame. Music was streaming out of a flat on the second floor, he could see dancing silhouettes in the window. Young people dancing, smoking, jumping about in ecstasy. Did they understand what an empty, meaningless life they were living?

He walked between two blocks to where the skip was. He put the bags down on the frozen ground and looked around before throwing them in the skip.

When he was younger, he and the other kids in Skärholmen used to raid skips for anything useful that they could drag out into the forest. They once tried to build a space rocket, and another time a raft that would carry them right round the world.

Hamza smiled at the memory. He saw his father, Abbas's face in front of him, and suddenly felt great tenderness, to his own immense surprise. He wished he could have met his father, to explain that over the years he had realised that he had been right in his view of Sweden and the Swedes. They exploited Muslims. Humiliated them. Forced them to live like caged animals in the concrete ghettoes of the suburbs.

Perhaps they could have been reconciled, could have forgiven each other, if Hamza had admitted he had been wrong? And if his father had only found Islam, the true path, he would have been happier.

But it was too late for reconciliation now. As far as his father knew, Hamza had been dead for several years. And soon he would be dead for real.

Vanessa asked Samer to wait outside the car and to stay alert. She wanted to talk to Jovana on her own. She held the door open and the woman sank into the passenger seat. When Vanessa got in beside her she saw that the woman was wearing a gold cross on a chain round her neck. Jovana threw her hands out.

"So what's all this about, then?"

Vanessa took out the documents Nicolas had given her. She passed them to Jovana, whose hair was tied back in a knot, and tapped the list with her finger.

"You've received money from this account three times, a total of sixty thousand kronor. Twenty thousand kronor each time."

Jovana stared at the numbers. She shook her head hard.

"No."

"The account number is yours, we've checked," Vanessa said calmly. "And I want to know why."

Jovana cleared her throat.

"There must be some mistake. I didn't even know about this."

"Sixty thousand kronor appear in your account and you don't even notice?" Vanessa said. "What's your job?"

"I'm studying to be a civil economist."

Vanessa smiled.

"Maybe you should think about changing course? Economics doesn't really seem to be your thing."

The self-confidence Jovana had shown a little while ago seemed to have vanished. She looked down at her hands, refusing to look at Vanessa. It was obvious she was hiding something. Was she aware that she was involved with terrorists? Was she protecting them, or had she just received the money for something without knowing who the sender was?

"Is anyone threatening you?"

Jovana cast a surprised glance at Vanessa.

"No, definitely not."

Vanessa took the documents back and rolled them into a tube.

"You've got two daughters," she said. "I understand that you think you're protecting them by lying, but you aren't. You have to help me. I'll do my best to make sure you don't get into trouble, but this is serious. The man who transferred this money is a jihadist."

Jovana looked at her defiantly. Vanessa stared back.

Her mobile lit up. A text from Samer.

How's it going?

Vanessa looked at the time before slipping the phone into her pocket. 02.32. She leaned forward in front of Jovana, opened the glove compartment and pulled out a pair of handcuffs. She put one around Jovana's wrist, and attached the other to the inside of the door.

"What are you doing?" Jovana was looking at her in horror.

"The man behind these bank transfers is a jihadist, like I just said. He's involved with ISIS terrorists. Now he's dead. The Security Service and the entire Swedish police force are looking for his accomplices. Think about whether it was worth the money."

"Are you even allowed to do this?" Jovana shook her hand-cuffed wrist.

Vanessa shrugged.

"I'm as bad at law as you seem to be at economics."

She got out of the car and found Samer waiting for her.

"What's happening?"

"She doesn't want to talk. God, it's cold."

Samer shot Jovana a quick glance through the side window.

"I'm contacting the Security Service if she doesn't talk in the next five minutes," Vanessa said.

He nodded. Vanessa's mobile rang.

"Where are you?" Celine asked anxiously when she answered. "You haven't come home."

Vanessa a sudden warmth in her chest. She cleared her throat.

"Sorry, sweetheart, I've had to work late."

"Is everything okay?"

"Yes, fine. Don't worry about me."

"Okay, good."

They ended the call and Vanessa looked out at the yellow terraced houses that lined the street. She didn't want to let Samer see, but she was starting to get desperate. She felt they were close to something, something important. Jovana was helping the terrorist cell somehow, even if she might not have been aware of it herself.

She glanced as Samer before getting back in the driver's seat. She turned towards Jovana.

"The girl who just called me is thirteen years old. If the people you're trying to protect had their way, she'd be dressed in a niqab and be married to an old man stinking of piss. He'd be free to rape and abuse her. I don't know about you, but that isn't the sort of world I want to live in."

Jovana stared straight ahead of her as if she couldn't hear what Vanessa was saying.

"You know what these people are capable of. You've seen the footage from the slaughterhouse they called the Caliphate. The pictures of their victims in Paris, Barcelona, Brussels. From Drottninggatan, right here in Stockholm. One of the girls who was mown down there wasn't much older than your daughters. It's your duty as a fellow human being, as a mother, and a woman, damn it, Jovana, as a Swede to help me prevent something like that happening again. I'm giving you the chance to do the right thing."

For a moment Jovana's eyes seemed to waver and she opened her mouth, then closed it again.

"Okay." Vanessa got out of the car. She shook her head at Samer.

"What do we do now?" he asked.

Vanessa stamped her feet to warm them up.

"We call the Security Service in."

6

The sun's first rays were just appearing as Nicolas emerged from the metro station at the Stadium. The sky was clear blue and free of cloud. He had arranged to meet Axel in the avenue close to the Valhalla Grill to get the keys to the car.

It was Sunday morning and the streets were almost empty, with hardly any traffic on the roads. The thin layer of snow that had fallen during the night made him think of James, and his stomach lurched. It felt like a lifetime ago that they had played hockey together. Now the boy was lying in a mortuary waiting to be buried. Nicolas wondered who would visit his grave now that Erica and Johan Karlström were dead too. He decided to find out when the funeral was, and to attend in honour of James's memory.

He passed the black gates of Stockholm Stadium, and glanced in at the arena through the tall arch in the brick walls. As arranged, Axel was standing in the avenue that ran down the middle of Valhallavägen next to the white Passat, his hand raised in greeting. He had a black bag over his shoulder and was wearing a brown padded jacket.

"I'm going to stay with Rebecca and Simon," he said, gesturing towards the bag as Nicolas walked towards him. "W-what did your police contact say about those bank transfers?"

"We haven't spoken yet."

"I hope they were some use." The disappointment in Axel's voice was evident.

Nicolas's fingers felt his phone in his pocket. Vanessa was probably busy, but he understood that Axel wanted to know what had happened. Particularly given the risks he had taken when he was investigating Farid Alami's accounts.

"I'll give her a call and find out."

He moved away from Axel so he wouldn't hear the conversation. When Vanessa answered he realised at once that it had been a mistake to call her.

"Yes?"

She sounded tired, irritated in that way that only she could be, as if she were at war with the whole world.

"I was just wondering if you managed to get anything last night?"

"Hold on." He heard her close a door. "We got hold of Jovana Babic, but she's refusing to talk. The Security Service have got her now. I don't want to sound rude, but I haven't slept in over twenty-four hours. An hour or so from now I have to be in Storkyrkan, so things are crazy here. I need to get ready. We can talk later."

"I understand."

They ended the call. Nicolas turned towards Axel and held his arms out. A jogger ran past them at speed.

"Sorry. They got hold of her, but she's not talking."

Axel dug in his pocket and pulled out the car keys. But when Nicolas reached out his hand to take them, he lowered his arm.

"The money was always transferred into Jovana Babic's account on the twenty-fifth of each month, for three months. Almost as if it was her wages. Or…"

Axel leaned forward quickly and pulled a silver-coloured laptop out of his bag. He opened it and looked around for somewhere to sit, then unlocked the car and sat in the passenger seat instead, with his feet still on the ground outside.

"What are you doing?"

Axel raised his palm in a gesture of irritation. Nicolas smiled. Axel really did change when he was anywhere close to a computer. An empty bus drove past them towards the headquarters of Swedish Television. Nicolas watched it go, and by the time it had disappeared from view Axel had finished typing.

"The address Jovana Babic gets her mail sent to in Vällingby is a care of address."

"So?"

"Rent. Don't you see?"

Nicolas was looking at him quizzically.

"Look." Axel held the laptop up towards Nicolas. "Jovana Babic registered herself and her two children at a temporary address in September. The money Farid Alami was paying her must be rent for a flat or house. She's been renting out her own home to him unofficially."

"Which would explain why she didn't want to talk to the police. Do you know where she was living before?"

Axel tapped the screen with his index finger.

"Professorsslingan 37. In Lappkärrsberget."

Nicolas took his phone out again and called the last number. The call went through but Vanessa didn't pick up. He reached for the car keys where Axel had left them on the dashboard, hurried round the car and got in behind the wheel.

"Jump in," he said.

Axel tucked his legs in and closed the door.

7

Nicolas parked the Passat on a hill. To their right was a building site, to their left a small, fenced garden, and beyond that the red-brick complex of student residences rose up.

"That pistol," Nicolas said. "You wouldn't still happen to have it in the car?"

Axel shook his head.

"I threw it off the Lidingö Bridge. What are you going to do?" he asked anxiously.

"Have you got any way of finding out which floor Jovana Babic's flat is on?"

"Already done. Fifth floor."

"Thanks. Stay here."

Nicolas got out of the car and adjusted his coat. He went up some steps that led to a large open area containing a playground and a football pitch. He walked along the building until he found number 37. He stopped and looked up at the six-storey building before going over and trying the door. Locked. While he was thinking about how to get inside he tried calling Vanessa again, but she still wasn't answering.

Nicolas studied his reflection in the glass door. If the terrorists were up there they would be armed. If he smashed the glass to get in and they weren't there, they would realise that something was wrong when they returned. Change hiding place, disappear for good. Or even worse: panic and do something. He took a couple of steps to one side and peered in through the window of the flat on the ground floor.

He caught a glimpse of movement and tapped on the window. A young woman turned round and walked over to the window.

She had cropped hair and was wearing a long, white T-shirt over bare legs. She opened the window and leaned her head out.

"Yes?"

"I'm supposed to be meeting a friend, but she's not answering when I call. Would you mind letting me in?"

She looked at him for a few seconds. Nicolas could smell marijuana inside the flat.

"Sure."

A short while later she opened the door, now wearing a pair of jogging bottoms. Nicolas thanked her and started to go up the stairs.

He realised he hadn't thought the situation through properly. What was he going to do when he was standing outside the flat? He could hardly ring the doorbell to find out if the terrorists lived there. And if the flat was empty and he broke in, it wasn't impossible that they had set up some sort of alarm system, or, even worse, an explosive device that would be detonated if the door was forced open.

Nicolas stopped and took his mobile out again. Vanessa hadn't got back to him.

If Axel's theory was correct, this was the building where the people who had killed the Karlström family were holed up. James was only a young boy. A friend. And they had used Molly, leaving her life in ruins. And had murdered the Minister of Justice.

Nicolas felt in his coat pocket, found the white ear buds for his phone, and decided they would have to do.

He crept slowly up the remaining few steps to the fifth floor. On the door to the right of the lift a sign said *J. Babic*. He gently put his ear to the dark wood and closed his eyes. Silence. Not a sound. He crouched down and carefully opened the letterbox. A current of air laden with unfamiliar smells hit him.

There was no sound inside the flat. It must be empty.

He pulled out the ear buds and plugged them into his phone.

He pressed to start the video recorder before gently lowering his phone through the letterbox with the help of the wire from the ear buds, with the camera facing into the flat. In order to find out if the door was booby-trapped, he had to lower it all the way down so that the screen was facing the floor and it was filming upwards.

He managed to lower the phone so it was resting on its side on the doormat, and waited a few seconds. He rested his forehead against the door before peering down again and releasing a little more of the wire. His mobile twisted round, then landed with the screen facing up, meaning that it was filming the doormat.

"Damn."

Nicolas pulled the wire back ten centimetres and tried again. This time it worked. He let the phone lie there for a few seconds to make sure it had recorded the whole of the inside of the door before he began to pull it back up.

Just as it was about to reach the letterbox it caught on the metal edge. Nicolas heard his mobile come loose and fall with the dull thud onto the doormat.

Vanessa was sitting in one of the minibuses that was transporting police officers to Magnus Moheden's funeral service at Storkyrkan in Gamla stan. When they stopped at a red light by Strömbron she caught a glimpse of the statue of Karl XII in front of the Café Opera nightclub among the trees in Kungsträdgården. People in thick winter coats were heading towards the church and Royal Palace. Just like after the terrorist attack in Drottninggatan, Stockholmers had come out to demonstrate their support for an open, democratic society, and to show that they weren't going to be frightened of terrorism. Vanessa felt a degree of pride over their determination, but she couldn't help feeling worried. The terrorist cell was still out there somewhere.

Her body felt sluggish from lack of sleep, her eyes bloodshot and dry. She smelled of sweat and her white shirt was crumpled.

She leaned her forehead against the cold window to wake her up.

If only she had managed to get Jovana Babic to talk, to say why she had received that money. She smiled bleakly to herself. She had to put all that behind her now. The only thing that mattered was protecting the tens of thousands of people who would soon be gathered around Storkyrkan and on the streets of Stockholm.

Nicolas gave his lost phone one last look through the letterbox before standing up.

If the terrorists came back and saw it, they would realise they had been found. But this wasn't just about his phone. He needed to know what was behind that door.

He thought back to the outside of the building when he had looked up at it a short while earlier. If he wasn't remembering wrong, the balconies were lined up above each other. It ought to be relatively straightforward to get into the flat that way.

Nicolas went up to the sixth floor and rang the doorbell of the flat directly above Jovana Babic's. The name on the door was *Tandon*.

He heard footsteps approach the door, then a click as it was unlocked. A man around the same age as Nicolas, with a thick black moustache and side parting stuck his head out.

"Yes?" the man said in English.

Nicolas assumed the man was an exchange student.

"I need to use your balcony. One of my children is locked inside the flat and I need to get in," Nicolas said in English.

The man looked at him suspiciously.

"I haven't seen Jovana for several months."

Nicolas gave him a broad smile.

"She's back. We've been living in my flat. Listen, she's going to be furious if she finds out about this. Can you let me in?"

The man laughed and stepped aside.

"So you're her new boyfriend? You're really thinking of climbing down?"

"I haven't got a choice."

The man's suspicion seemed to turn into curiosity and he waved Nicolas into the living room, where the door to the balcony was.

The man opened it and gestured to Nicolas to go out first. Just as Nicolas had thought, the balcony was made of grey concrete, with a wide plank along the top for extra protection. At the bottom was a small gap between the floor and the railing. Nicolas leaned out and looked down. Much of his training in the Special Operations Group had involved practice in breaking into different types of building. They needed to be able to get themselves down from rooftops or helicopters as quickly as possible to secure a building. He ought to be able handle a jump like this without any trouble.

Besides, it was the only way to get into the flat and retrieve his phone. If he was lucky, the balcony door would be unlocked, but he could always break the glass. That would be very visible, of course, but at least he would have a theoretical possibility of warning Vanessa so she could send out her colleagues. It was a far smaller risk than him breaking in through the door of the flat and triggering some sort of alarm or explosive device.

Nicolas climbed up onto the railing and swung his right leg out, so he was lying on his stomach along the wooden plank. Holding on tight, he slipped his right foot into the gap between the floor and railing. Then he did the same with his left foot.

The man was watching him intently.

"You're not scared of heights?" he said.

"Not at all."

Now for the hard part. In order to grab the floor with his hand he would have to crouch down quickly, without being able to hang on anywhere.

"Are you okay?"

His voice sounded tense. Nicolas nodded quickly. He visualised his next movements, filled his lungs with air, and let go.

A moment later he was hanging down, his legs dangling above the tarmac below.

He glanced down quickly to estimate the distance to the balcony below before letting go of the floor of the balcony and dropping.

8

The man's face was masculine, with strong features, a heavy jaw and large nose. His skin was tanned, which Hamza assumed meant that he used a solarium. His salt-and-pepper hair, which had been combed back neatly, was now sticking up in all directions.

He held up his hands beseechingly and backed away as he begged for his life. But he wasn't going to get away. He was going to die here, in his office. That realisation was clearly visible in his eyes, even if he was still hoping for mercy. Tears were running down his cheeks.

"I've done everything you asked me to do. Please, let me go. I promise, I won't say anything. Never."

Hamza moved forward slowly but determinedly. He felt empty, numb. The man's attempt to escape ended abruptly when his back hit the edge of his desk. Hamza grabbed him by his collar and kicked him in the legs, forcing him onto his knees.

"No, please."

His upper body was bucking this way and that, trying to pull free, but Hamza was too strong.

He raised the knife he had been keeping hidden behind his back, and at that moment Thomas appeared in the doorway.

Thomas stopped, folded his arms and leaned back against the doorpost. He looked at the terrified man and smiled.

Nicolas hauled himself over the balcony railing and landed on the concrete floor.

"Are you okay?" the man on the sixth floor called.

Nicolas leaned out and looked up.

"I'm fine. Thanks for your help."

The balcony door was locked. He peered in and concluded that, just as he had thought, the flat was empty. But he had nothing he could use to break the glass. He quickly pulled his coat off and wrapped it around his elbow and upper arm. After another look at the glass he took his woolly hat off as well and wrapped that over his coat as an extra layer. He moved closer to the balcony door. He put his left fist in his right palm to maximise the force in the movement, then twisted his body and drove his elbow into the glass. There was surprisingly little noise as the glass broke. He took a step back and judged that the hole was big enough to stick his hand through to reach the door-handle. He checked he hadn't cut himself, then pulled his gloves on, carefully stuck his hand through and unlocked the door.

Nicolas went out into the hall, past an IKEA wardrobe and a desk with a printer on it. He quickly snatched up his phone from the doormat and saw that he had one missed call from Vanessa.

He called her back, but there was no answer.

"Shit, Vanessa."

It wouldn't hurt to take a quick look at the flat, at least until he managed to get hold of her. There might be something there that could help them trace the terrorists. Most of the police officers in the entire region were presumably busy with Moheden's funeral. By the time Vanessa managed to get officers to the flat, it could be too late. Not least if they were planning an imminent attack. If there was anything he could do to stop them, it was his duty to do it.

He tapped in Axel's number as he unlocked the door from inside.

"Put on a pair of gloves and come up here," he said. "I'm inside the flat, and I need help to look through it quickly."

"How did you get in?"

Nicolas ended the call.

Vanessa blinked in the bright sunlight, then rubbed her cheeks with her palms to help her wake up. In front of her the yellow-ochre walls of Storkyrkan, the site of coronations and royal weddings since the 1300s, rose up to its green copper roof. Just to the left of the church doors, in front of one of the large windows, was a metal detector that all the guests would have to pass through. There were already at least a thousand people crowded outside the barriers that had been set up beyond the thirty-metre-high obelisk in front of the church. Around fifty uniformed officers had been posted inside the barrier as an extra layer of protection.

Snipers had been stationed on the roof of the Royal Palace nearby. Another two lines of barriers formed a passageway down Slottsbacken towards Skeppsbron, so that the funeral cortege could get through the crowd. Inside a fenced-off area to the right of the church Vanessa could see black-clad reporters talking seriously into microphones. Their cameras were trained on the entrance to the church.

A police boat was bobbing on the waters of the harbour. On the other side of the water she could see the Grand Hôtel and National Museum.

Vanessa had never seen a security operation on this scale before. Storkyrkan had been under guard all week, and as recently as an hour ago had been searched by police dog teams. It would be impossible for the terrorists to get at the guests inside the church, utterly impossible. The most likely outcome, if the terrorist cell was going to attack again, was that they would target the crowd.

Her phone vibrated in her pocket, and she quickly pulled it out and answered. It was Nicolas again.

"The payments were rent for a flat," he said.

Vanessa didn't immediately understand what he was talking about. She turned, took a few paces towards the church door and put one finger in her ear to block the noise.

"Sorry, can you repeat that?"

"Jovana Babic was renting her flat to Farid Alami."

Vanessa's heart skipped a beat.

"How do you know that?"

"I'm there now. Professorsslingan 37 in Lappkärrsberget. The student residences near the university."

Vanessa glanced quickly at the time – there was only half an hour to go before the first of the nine hundred guests would start to arrive. Every minute, every second counted, if they had a lead on the terrorists. She had to call the Security Service and ask them to send forensics officers, say she'd received a tip-off from an anonymous source.

"Can you see any technical equipment? Computers, iPads, mobiles? Plans of buildings, maps?" The words were flying out of her.

"Nothing like that. We've looked. Looks like they've emptied the flat and cleared out."

Hamza and Thomas lifted the dead man under his shoulders and dragged him round the desk so the body couldn't be seen from the corridor. That wasn't really necessary; no one would be in the building for several hours, possibly not until the next day.

All they could do now was wait. Hamza sat down on one of the visitors' chairs while Thomas walked up and down with a tense expression on his face. Soddenly he stopped and started intently at Hamza.

"I'm going for a walk," he said abruptly.

Was that fear he glimpsed in Thomas's face? Was he going to run, leaving Hamza to carry out the last part of the attack himself?

He was about to protest, but realised that it didn't make any difference. They had nothing to go on until Sabina had played her part, and there was nothing they could do to help her now. If Thomas needed to be alone for a while to summon up his strength, that was up to him. If he didn't come back, Hamza would just have to do his bit of the job as well.

Thomas leaned his Kalashnikov against the wall and quickly left the room without saying anything else.

Hamza went over to the bookcase and ran his finger along the spines. He closed his eyes and conjured up Mazhar and Amina's faces. Their laughter. He felt it making him weaker, and opened his eyes. He wished he still had his mobile, then he could have kept an eye on the news bulletins. At least then he would have had something to do. Maybe he could have sent a text to his family, his mother?

Soon he, Thomas and Sabina would die. Probably in front of a live television audience, which meant that his family would see the final moments of his life. That felt strange. Even so, it pleased him. He wondered about the man – probably a police officer – who would eventually shoot him. Who was he? What was he doing at the moment? Maybe he was eating breakfast, blissfully ignorant of what was going to happen.

Axel watched as Nicolas disappointedly closed the door of the flat and pulled off the gloves he had been wearing. All that was left in the flat was furniture that presumably belonged to Jovana Babic.

"What do we do now?" Axel asked.

"I need to get back to Mariatorget to pick Molly up if we're going to get to the airport in time," Nicolas said as they made their way down the stairs.

Axel decided to walk to Rebecca's. He needed some time to himself, to wind down. It had been a hectic morning, and now it felt as if all the air had gone out of him. He really had believed that his discovery, the fact that Farid Alami's bank transfers had been payments of rent, would lead to something. After what had happened to the Karlström family, he had hoped he would be able to help stop the terrorists before anyone else got hurt.

But they hadn't found anything in the flat, and now all he felt was emptiness.

When they reached football pitch he told Nicolas he felt like walking to Rebecca's.

"Are you sure?"

"Yes. It's not a problem at all. I feel like having a walk."

Nicolas looked at him intently.

"It isn't your fault. None of this is. You do see that, don't you?"

Axel looked away and nodded quickly.

"See you soon, I'll drop the car keys back once I've been to Arlanda."

Nicolas carried on down the steps towards the car while Axel walked on. Two children in overalls were each pulling a sledge along the path. Axel stopped and watched them gloomily. Three hundred metres further on he stopped abruptly.

There was something they had overlooked in the flat. He really should have thought of it before.

Axel ran back, with the bag containing his laptop bouncing against his hip.

9

Vanessa was stamping her feet restlessly as she stood by the door of Storkyrkan, occasionally glancing at the mourners. Forensics officers were on their way to the terrorist cell's flat in Lappkärrsberget, but if it had been stripped like Nicolas had told her, there was little chance of getting any useful information until the lab results were processed in a couple of days. And by then it could be too late.

Back in Police Headquarters on Kungsholmen, Mikael Kask and Samer Bakir were working through the list of calls made from Hamza Mansour's burner phone, the one they had found out about thanks to the emergency call he made. If they succeeded, they might be able to identify more of the terrorists' phones. According to Samer's latest report, things were at least moving in the right direction.

Vanessa looked warily around at the crowd gathered behind the barriers in the hope of glimpsing some of the famous guests who had begun to arrive.

When her phone rang she moved a little closer to the church door before answering.

"Can you hear me?" Samer asked.

Vanessa pressed the phone closer to her ear and covered the other one with her hand so she could hear him above the noise of the crowd.

"We've identified two numbers that Hamza Mansour has been in contact with. They…"

Samer went on talking but all she hear was crackling. Presumably the mobile network was overloaded seeing as there were so many people in the same place. Vanessa walked quickly inside the church.

"…Vanessa? Can you hear me?"

"Yes, I can now."

"The two phones Hamza Mansour was in contact with were both

switched off at nine o'clock this morning. One on Kungsholmen, close to Hantverkargatan, and the other in Kungsträdgården."

Axel was staring at the sheets of paper the Canon printer was churning out. He ought to have realised sooner that the terrorist cell could have used it. Not least as a way to avoid sending information between them and risk leaving a digital footprint. The printer probably belonged to Jovana Babic, which was why it was still there. They probably had no idea that what they had printed on it was still saved in the memory cache.

Axel looked quickly through the printouts. The paper was still warm. The two last pictures were of a man in his fifties with slicked back hair. The man was getting into a car, a black Lexus, somewhere in the city centre. *Dino's Shoes*, a sign above the plate glass window behind him said. Next to the shoe shop was another shop, but only two letters of the name were visible in the picture.

Ce...

He took out his mobile and googled. Dino's Shoes was located at Hantverkargatan 21.

Nicolas lifted Molly's two cases into the boot. Mariatorget was practically deserted. There was hardly any traffic over on Hornsgatan, so the drive to Arlanda wouldn't take long. They were still early, in spite of the excursion to Lappkärrsberget; Nicolas had wanted to get going while there wasn't much traffic heading to the airport. Molly was already sitting in the passenger seat, dressed in jeans, a black woolly hat and black padded jacket. Her glossy dark hair was hanging loose over her shoulders. He liked Molly, he enjoyed talking to her and laughed a lot in her company, but at the same time he would feel more relaxed once he had got her away from the city.

He had been worried the terrorists would try to find her to finish the job they had started at the Clarion Hotel Sign. Or that some journalist would set their sights on her and show up at the Hotel Rival asking awkward questions. But none of that had happened, thank goodness.

Nicolas's phone buzzed and he took it out and saw that he had received a picture from Axel. He hardly had time to look at it before Axel called.

"I-I-I'm back in the flat again. The p-p-printer."

Nicolas told him to take some deep breaths and calm down. Axel cleared his throat and started again.

"There was a printer in the flat."

"Yes, I saw it."

"I forgot the memory cache. The picture I just sent you was printed thirteen days ago, probably by a member of the terrorist cell."

"Hang on," Nicolas said. He clicked to bring up the picture again. "Do you know who the man is?"

"No, but look at the name on the sign behind him. Dino's Shoes is located at Hantverkargatan 21."

"Good. I'll send the picture to my police contact. But get out of the flat at once. The police are on their way there."

Nicolas ended the call and forwarded the picture to Vanessa, with a brief summary of what Axel had told him. The break-in at the flat hadn't been entirely in vain. Perhaps the photograph could help Vanessa and her colleagues to locate the terrorist cell. The date checked out, the terrorists had definitely been renting the flat at the time. It must have been them who printed the picture.

He felt a little brighter as he got in the driver's seat and put his mobile down between the two front seats.

"Ready?" he asked Molly.

"It'll be good to get home."

Nicolas started the car and indicated to pull out. He checked the wing mirror, then drove off.

"I was actually planning to say this when we said goodbye at Arlanda, but I don't want to risk it going unsaid. Thank you. For everything. You saved my life, and you've been very kind to me."

Nicolas smiled and looked at Molly.

"You're welcome. I hope I can come up and visit you sometime. See how you're getting on."

"Of course."

At Hornsgatan they turned left to avoid any holdups in the traffic around Gamla stan and Slussen. Nicolas's phone rang.

"Who is it?" he asked without taking his eyes off the road.

Molly picked the phone up.

"Vanessa."

She passed the phone to Nicolas, who answered it.

"Are you on your way to the airport?"

"Yes."

"Can you go via Hantverkargatan?"

"What for?"

"A mobile phone that we believe belongs to the terrorists was switched off in the vicinity, and now there's this man in the photograph you sent. I just want to know what's there. But I don't want to divert any officers there, not right now. The funeral is using up all our resources."

Nicolas glanced at his watch, then at Molly.

"I should have time."

"Good. I think it could be important. Call me when you get there," Vanessa said, and hung up.

10

Vanessa was standing inside Storkyrkan which was starting to fill with the first mourners. An elderly man, who must have mistaken her for one of the guests, handed her an order of service. She took it absentmindedly as she looked around the church.

Heavy red-brick pillars were holding up the vaulted white ceiling. Up at the altar stood Magnus Moheden's coffin in the middle of a sea of floral wreaths. Vanessa hadn't seen the hearse arrive, so either the coffin must have been brought in before she got there, or they had used a side door.

Sunlight was filtering through the multicoloured rose window above the altar, casting prisms of light on the stone floor. She opened the order of service, the cover of which was adorned with a black and white photograph of a young, smiling Magnus Moheden, and looked through what was going to happen. After the address by the priest, the Prime Minister was going to speak, followed by a few others before the ceremony ended and it was time for the coffin to be taken to Adolf Fredrik Church.

Four police officers in dark jackets were posted inside the church doors, looking out, straight-backed, over the rows of seats. Vanessa recognised several of the black-clad guests from news broadcasts and television programmes. Now they were walking quietly and solemnly down the aisle to take their places. She decided to go outside to get some air, put the order of service down on a side table by one of the pillars and found a dark wooden door to the left of the pillar. She took a few steps towards it, apologising when she bumped one of the guests, and pushed the door open.

Inside the small room, which evidently served as a kind of

pantry, sat two suited men in their fifties at a rickety table, each with a cup of coffee in front of him. They didn't look like security guards or members of the Security Service, and Vanessa concluded that they were probably the drivers of the hearse, waiting to take the coffin to the interment after the service.

She closed the door and carried on towards the main doors, gently pushing past the guests who were making their way into the church.

A murmur ran through the crowd when the Prime Minister and his wife arrived. By their side was a blonde woman in black mourning dress, and two teenage children. Vanessa recognised them as Magnus Moheden's family. A wave of flashes followed them as the crowd filmed and photographed their every move.

There was still quarter of an hour before the service was due to begin.

The rows of seating inside the church were almost full now.

Someone let out a cry and Vanessa looked anxiously out at the sea of people. One senior police officer was talking into his radio and pointing out towards Slottsbacken. Two uniformed officers quickly made their way over the barrier.

A car pulled up inside the cordon and the Crown Princess and her husband got out and nodded sombrely to the crowd before hurrying inside the church, their Security Service escort following close behind them. Soon a black, top-end Volvo with tinted windows crept slowly up Slottsbacken. The doors opened and Vanessa saw that it was the King and Queen. They were helped from the car and four stern-looking Security Service officers surrounded them at once and led them through the metal detector and into the church. After the royal couple had disappeared from sight, Vanessa cast one last look at the obelisk and the sparkling water beyond before going back inside the church.

Nicolas and Molly turned off into St Eriksgatan at Fridhemsplan, then into Hantverkargatan. They drove past the fire station and Kungsholmen High School. Nicolas accelerated but didn't manage to get through the traffic lights. Two pedestrians walked slowly across the street.

"Can't you ever say no to her?" Molly asked with a mischievous smile.

Nicolas turned to look at her.

"No. I can't."

"Why not? What makes Vanessa so special?"

"We've been through a lot together."

"That's all?"

"That's all, Molly."

The lights turned green. Nicolas passed a stationary bus that was letting a white-haired woman off by Pontonjärsgatan.

"Are you in love with her?"

"That's none of your business."

His relationship with Vanessa was too private, too intimate for Nicolas to feel comfortable talking about it with anyone else.

Hantverkargatan grew narrower. They drove past small shops, tapas bars, pubs and legal firms.

Nicolas was keeping an eye on the house numbers... 17. 19. 21. He looked around, but couldn't see a free parking space. He double-parked, blocking a black Mercedes SUV, and turned the hazard lights on. He opened the car door, reached for his phone and called Vanessa's number. She answered on the second ring.

"I'm here. What am I looking for?"

"Hold on a moment, I just need to move."

He heard footsteps and echoing voices in the background, and understood that she was inside Storkyrkan.

"That's better," she said. "Okay, what can you see?"

Nicolas turned round, looking at the street with his iPhone pressed to his ear.

"A sushi restaurant. A bank. A coffee shop. A shop selling underwear. The shoe shop in the photograph. And a..."

There was a load crackle on the line.

"Hello, can you hear me?" he asked.

He was staring at one of the signs. His heart began to beat harder when he realised he had found what Vanessa was looking for.

"Vanessa?"

Sabina followed the column of people across Strömbron. Her head felt fuzzy and numb, and, like plenty of other people, she was hiding her eyes behind a pair of sunglasses. That morning, after praying, she had taken two tranquilisers. She hadn't mentioned that to Hamza or Thomas. She felt ashamed. She really ought to be feeling happy, walking towards death with a straight back and her heart pounding with pride.

At the far side of the bridge two uniformed police officers were watching the crowd walking towards Gamla stan. Sabina forced herself to smile stiffly when one of them lingered on her. She thanked God that the city was still cold and her suicide vest was well hidden under her red winter coat. She passed the policemen and checked her watch. She was going to reach the agreed location in plenty of time. She put her hand in her jacket pocket and ran her thumb over the detonator.

Vanessa stared at the phone in her hand. The call had gone dead. She called him back and Nicolas answered at once.

"What were you saying?"

"There's a funeral director's here, Cederdahl's."

The church doors closed behind her. Her mind was spinning.

She walked quickly towards the small room where she had seen the two men she had assumed were the drivers who had brought the coffin to the church.

"Are you still there?"

Nicolas heard Vanessa's shoes echoing against the stone floor again. The church bells began to chime. Molly went to get out of the car as well but he held his palm up and she closed her door again. He looked over at the closed funeral parlour, then crossed the street to take a closer look.

Sabina stopped on Skeppsbron and turned towards Storkyrkan and the Royal Palace. She felt the chill wind from the Baltic Sea on the back of her neck. The church bells were ringing loudly. She checked her watch one last time, then switched to counting the seconds. Were her lips moving? She pressed them together and closed her eyes behind her sunglasses. She tried to hold her shaking hands still in her pockets.

She was going to give her life for the greatest thing a person could die for. For God. She would not hesitate, she would fulfil her duty even though she was terrified.

It was time. She removed the transparent plastic covering from the button with her thumb. She opened her mouth to yell that God is most great, but no sound came out of her throat.

The two men looked up in surprise when Vanessa burst into the room just as the sound of the church bells began to fade away.

"Did you drive the coffin here?" she asked, holding up her police ID.

They stared at each other, then at Vanessa, and nodded simultaneously.

"Where did you pick it up from?"

"From Kungsholmen."

"Which funeral parlour?"

"Cederdahl's," they said at the same time.

"Who signed it over to you?"

"Jacob Cederdahl. The funeral director."

"Call him."

"Now?"

One of the men took out his mobile. He pulled up the number, then held the phone to his ear. The priest started to speak. The voice reaching into the small room was monotonous, hypnotic.

"Jacob isn't answering."

Vanessa quickly left the drivers and went out into the nave of the church.

"Get inside the funeral parlour, find Jacob Cederdahl!" she hissed to Nicolas over her phone. She could hear sobbing from the mourners. Vanessa looked at the rows of people sitting shoulder to shoulder, then at the priest who was gesturing beside the coffin.

A moment later came the muffled sound of a explosion.

11

Nicolas pressed his face to the plate-glass window. He could see a desk, some chairs, a green sofa. Above the sofa hung a small oil painting of the King and Queen. He jerked when he heard the rumbling sound on the phone.

"Vanessa? What's happening?"

"I don't know. Something just exploded outside the church. It sounded like it came from the quayside below the palace."

The priest fell silent. He stood there, straight-backed, looking out at the assembled guests. His lips were quivering and he seemed to be searching for words. People were looking round, shuffling in their seats, glancing anxiously in the direction from which the explosion had been heard. One woman started screaming. The suited police officers and the Security Service personnel held their hands to their ears to hear the instructions in their earpieces. Through the door, from the sea of people outside, came the sound of sporadic shouting. Vanessa rushed towards one of the windows facing Slottsbacken. Outside was a scene of total chaos.

From the quayside, a pillar of black smoke was rising into the clear blue sky.

"Secure the church. Seal the doors," one of the police officers shouted.

More officers came running over to take up positions by the church doors. Some drew their weapons, others made do with pushing their jackets back and putting their hands on their shoulder-holsters. Vanessa gazed out at the confused mourners. She tried calling Samer, but he didn't answer. She dialled Mikael Kask's number instead and gave a breathless summary of what had happened.

"Send Samer to Hantverkargatan."

"Not possible."

"Why the hell not?"

"I don't know where he is right now. Everything's in a state of complete fucking chaos."

Vanessa tried to shut out the noise and panic that was getting louder around her. Storkyrkan ought to be the safest place in the whole of Stockholm if a full-scale terrorist attack really was underway. All the guests had been handpicked, and had been made to walk through the metal detector and have their bags searched before they were let in. They were members of Sweden's political elite, and every single person inside the church had been thoroughly checked.

All except one, Vanessa suddenly realised.

Nicolas slowly pushed open the door of the funeral parlour. He took a couple of steps inside, then listened. He couldn't hear a sound from any of the adjoining rooms. Outside the window cars were driving past. Dark wooden panelling lined the foyer. The walls were full of landscape paintings, and the heavy furniture was all in muted colours. A framed newspaper article enlightened readers that Cederdahl's had arranged Princess Lilian's funeral.

Nicolas moved deeper into the premises.

Something was wrong.

He could feel in instinctively in his whole body.

He found himself in a narrow corridor, and opened a door. It led to a small office dominated by a huge mahogany desk. The walls were lined with bookcases full of old, leather-bound volumes. In the window, which faced an inner courtyard, was a collection of well-kept green pot plants.

He was just about to go back out into the corridor when he froze.

Two feet were sticking out from behind the desk. He walked closer, and found the body of a man in his fifties. Her eyes were open wide, staring blankly at the ceiling. Blood was running from his cut throat, soaking into the thick fitted carpet.

Vanessa stared at the Minister of Justice's expensive white coffin, then rushed towards it down the central aisle of the church.

People were getting to their feet now, looking around anxiously as the noise and shouting outside got louder. One woman was crying hysterically and clutching her children, while a man pushed his way out from one of the rows and ran for the exit to get out. One of the police officers caught him and led him away while another officer yelled that everyone should remain seated. Several of the guests threw themselves down on the stone floor, shaking as they clung to each other. Someone shouted that he needed a doctor for his wife, who had fainted. It was only a matter of time because a full-scale riot broke out.

Vanessa tried to block out all sound and focus on the coffin up by the altar. It was perched on a wooden platform, and was surrounded by floral wreaths and condolence cards. The people in the rows closest to her looked on aghast and she leaned over and began to feel beneath the platform and coffin.

She examined the lid of the coffin, running her hand over the polished surface until she felt a metal clasp with the tip of her finger. She slid it open.

"What are you doing?"

One of the bodyguards from the Security Service appeared beside her. Vanessa ignored him, which seemed to unsettle him. He stood there with his arms by his sides, staring at her warily.

She tried to open the lid of the coffin, but it was still stuck. The platform moved disconcertingly as she tried to open it.

She leaned forward, searching for the next clasp.

"Come on, now!"

She took a step back, looked at the coffin for a few moments, then took a deep breath. A murmur ran through the first few rows as she lifted the lid of the coffin. Two men leapt to their feet, shouting that someone should stop her, but Vanessa blocked out their voices.

Magnus Moheden's corpse was waxy and pale, eyes closed. He was wearing dark suit, a white shirt and a red tie. His hands were folded over his chest, with a red rose sticking out from them. Behind Vanessa the agitated complaints were growing louder. She clenched her jaw, reached her hand in and felt around the body, along the padded interior of the coffin. She leaned over the body and felt underneath the corpse.

"What the hell are you doing?"

She turned round. Another officer from the Security Service had appeared.

"Just wait!"

Her tone of voice made them stop abruptly. Vanessa turned back to the body again. She had managed to dislodge his tie when she leaned over, and there was a brown mark, the size of a fingernail, next to one of the shirt-buttons. She leaned closer. It could be blood. Oxidised blood. She unbuttoned two buttons of the shirt before tearing it open with a hard tug. The stitches across the chest from the post mortem had almost split.

One of the Security Service officers put a firm hand on her shoulder.

Vanessa quickly pushed her jacket back, shoved him aside, drew her pistol and aimed it at the man, who backed away. The cries from the mourners fell silent for a few seconds before a woman started to howl with fear.

Vanessa knew she wasn't going to get another chance. Putting her Sig Sauer within reach on the edge of the coffin, she ran her hand over Moheden's stomach and chest before pushing it into the post-mortem incision. She pushed into the cold innards until she touched something hard.

The Security Service officer beside her was staring in shock as she felt around.

"A bomb," Vanessa whispered. "The bastards have placed a bomb in his stomach. Give the order to open the doors. Get everyone out. Now!"

12

Vanessa pushed her other hand inside the body and folded the skin back, opening up the stomach.

"Get back!" the Security Service officer beside her was saying. He turned towards several of the mourners who were anxiously approaching the coffin, then repeated the order as he gesticulated above his head with his hands. "Get to the doors. Get out! Everybody needs to get out!"

The terrified guests got to their feet, screaming and pulling at each other to get as far away from the altar as possible. Complete panic had descended, and the police tried in vain to maintain some sort of order.

Vanessa examined the timer attached to the bomb. It looked like a relatively simple construction. The explosives were contained in three thermos flasks. Two cables were connected to a Casio watch with a black strap. She leaned forward and wiped the screen with her sleeve to see better. It said 12.11.

"What are you going to do?" the Security Service officer whispered. He was the only person who had stayed with her.

"I don't know."

"When do you think it's… timed to detonate?"

"I don't know for certain, but I'm guessing quarter past, because that was when the Prime Minister was due to speak, according to the order of service."

At that moment the numbers changed to 12.12. Vanessa looked up at the man, his face was pale.

"We haven't got time to get everyone out," he hissed, glancing behind him. "It's impossible. There are over nine hundred people."

"And there isn't time to get the bomb squad here?"

He shook his head quickly.

"No. They can't get through the crush."

Behind them the guests were still streaming towards the doors in panic. One woman fell, and howled in pain as other people trampled on her.

Vanessa licked her lips. She forced herself to focus.

"Can you remove the battery from the watch?" the Security Service officer asked.

"I don't think that's a good idea. Then the electronic signal would fail and the device would be triggered."

Molly recognised Thomas at once when he turned into Hantver-kargatan from the direction of Norr Mälarstrand, walking towards the door of the funeral parlour. She took out her phone and tried to find Nicolas's number.

"Fuck. Fuck. Fuck."

His phone began to ring just as Thomas disappeared inside the building.

His mobile was buzzing in his pocket. Nicolas saw that it was Molly, clicked to reject the call, and hoped she was waiting in the car like he had told her to.

The dead man in the office had to have something to do with Magnus Moheden's funeral and the explosion on Skeppsbron. But what? He hoped Vanessa was okay.

He went back out into the corridor. He heard a noise further inside the building. Was the person who had cut the funeral director's throat still there?

Footsteps were approaching from the foyer.

"Hamza? Time to go."

A toilet flushed and a door opened at the other end of the corridor. The man called Hamza was on his way towards the front door, and would spot him any moment.

"I'll wait outside," the other man called.

Vanessa turned the wristwatch over. The Security Service officer who had been standing next to her rushed away. She wondered desperately about trying to remove the battery as he had suggested, but it needed a small screwdriver to open the battery slot.

She swore. Wiped her hands on her thighs.

Twenty seconds until it was quarter past.

Nineteen.

She glanced over her shoulder again. There was complete chaos as nine hundred people tried to push their way to safety through the doors out onto Slottsbacken. The church itself was starting to empty a little, but there were still several hundred people left. Two men were fighting near the pulpit. Several bodies lay immobile in the aisle. Terrified screams echoed off the walls. From Slottsbacken came the sound of more screaming, as well as police sirens.

Seventeen seconds left.

Vanessa stifled the urge to just drop the watch and run for the exit. She would never make it anyway. The bomb was too powerful. The roof would collapse and she would be buried beneath the falling masonry along with everyone else who hadn't got out in time.

She licked her lips again.

Time is relative, she thought. What if I change the time? If I move the time on the watch back, would that fool the bomb?

Molly crouched down when she saw Thomas come back out and stand outside the door of the funeral parlour. He must be waiting for someone, she thought. Still crouching, she slid over into the driver's seat. The keys were still in the ignition. Molly kept her head down so Thomas wouldn't see her. At the same time she saw people on the pavement stop and stare at their mobile phones.

Vanessa wasn't even sure it was going to work, but it was her only chance, the only thing she could think of.

There were two silver-coloured buttons on the left side of the watch, and one on the right. Her hopes were fading with each passing second. She would never have time to figure out how to change the time on the watch. And if she changed it in the wrong direction, the bomb would explode.

Vanessa pressed one of the buttons and the digital numbers began to flash. Sweat was running down her neck, her shirt was soaked.

Five.

Vanessa was hyperventilating. She was going to be blown into microscopic particles. They would have to scrape her remains off the walls to find her DNA. She thought about Nicolas. She hoped he would look after Celine. She hoped they would have a good life.

Four.

Vanessa bit her lip so hard she could taste blood. She closed her eyes and pressed all three buttons at the same time. She screwed her eyes shut so tightly that dancing patterns appeared on the inside of her eyelids. She leaned her head against one shoulder and hunched up in anticipation.

She didn't want to die. Not now. A few years ago she wouldn't have minded, but not today. Not now that she had Celine in her life, something to fight for. Something good. Something beautiful. Celine trusted her, she needed her.

Three.

She felt tears well up. Her lips were trembling, the sinews of her neck stood out as she straightened her back, forcing herself to stand tall. She wasn't going to die cowering. She wasn't going to give the terrorists that. No one would ever know how she spent her last moments, but she would know. She told herself that that actually meant something.

Two.

"Fucking murdering bastards," she whispered.

She drew air into her lungs and realised that it could be her last ever breath.

One.

13

Nicolas just had time to throw himself through the doorway into the office before Hamza came out into the corridor. As soon as he walked past Nicolas stepped forward. The heavily built terrorist was holding a Kalashnikov in each hand, and Nicolas realised that he and the other man were on their way to finish the attack that had started at Storkyrkan. They would mow down adults, children, anyone they could find in the chaos that ensued. He had to stop them, otherwise hundreds of people would die.

Nicolas threw himself at Hamza, locking his neck and dragging him backwards, into the office. Hamza was kicking to get free, and a shot blasted into the ceiling. But it was only a matter of time until he was forced to drop the weapons and try to free himself from Nicolas's grasp, before he passed out through lack of oxygen. The man was gurgling, trying desperately to pull loose. His finger pulled the trigger again, and the automatic rifle hit the books in the bookcase and several portraits on the wall, which crashed to the floor.

Nothing happened.

Vanessa carried on pressing in all three buttons of the Casio watch. She opened her eyes, and almost let go of the watch in her surprise. The light pouring in through the large church-windows was blinding her. She blinked several times. Then looked down at the watch in her hand. All the digits were black: 88.88.88. She gasped. It was in some sort of indeterminate state, while it was evidently still sending electronic signals to the detonator. She looked down at the three metal thermos flasks in Magnus Moheden's stomach.

"Get the bomb squad here now!" she yelled, turning her head as she continued to hold the three buttons in.

No response.

"The bomb squad," she cried. "Get them here!"

Vanessa felt her desperation rising.

No one could hear her. There was no one there to help her.

Sweat was dripping from every pore. Running from her scalp, down into her eyes, itching. She blinked again. Her hands felt damp. Sticky. But she couldn't move. She couldn't let go of the Casio watch and the three buttons.

"Help!" she cried. "I need help over here!"

He rested her arms on the edge of the coffin in an attempt to find a more confortable position. Her hands were shaking, her joints felt stiff.

She leaned her head against her shoulder, wiping away the sweat that was running down her face and dripping onto Magnus Moheden's corpse.

Outside she could hear sirens and people screaming. She heard footsteps behind her, turned round hopefully and saw that it was Samer, running towards her up the aisle.

What was he doing there?

Molly stuck her head up above the dashboard in the car and looked over at the funeral parlour when she heard the shot go off. She watched as Thomas put his hand in his pocket, pulled out a pistol and disappeared inside the building.

"No," she whispered.

She dialled 112. There was no answer.

The edge of the desk was pressing against the small of his back. Nicolas squeezed his arm tighter round the terrorist's neck, aware that time was starting to run out. The other man must have heard the shots. He could appear in the doorway with a gun at any moment.

"Hamza," Nicolas heard someone call from the entrance. "Where are you?"

It was as if his comrade's voice gave Hamza fresh energy. He put up renewed resistance, tugging and jerking at Nicolas's arm. He wasn't going to have time to wait until Hamza lost consciousness.

Nicolas glimpsed a mug containing pens on the desk. Something was glinting among the pens. Instinctively he loosened his grip on one of Hamza's arms with his left hand and reached for the letter knife.

He raised it above the struggling man, and felt him stiffen when he realised what was happening, then plunged the blade of the knife into the terrorist's neck.

The body quickly became powerless, slumping in Nicolas's grasp. He pulled the knife out and dropped it on the floor. The footsteps in the corridor were getting closer. Nicolas heaved Hamza's body out of the way and threw himself at the two automatic rifles that had fallen to the floor during the struggle.

But it was too late.

He caught a glimpse of movement in the doorway, heard the sound of the gun firing. Pain exploded in his body where the bullets hit him.

"Vanessa?"

Samer's voice echoed in the now deserted church. His eyes were darting between Magnus Moheden's splayed-open corpse and her hands clutching the Casio watch.

"Where have you been?" she asked tersely. She stared at him. He seemed surprised by her reaction. "I spoke to Mikael. Where the hell did you get to?"

She glanced at her Sig Sauer, which was still lying on the edge of the coffin, but she couldn't reach for it without letting go of the watch.

"I went to Kungsträdgården, seeing as one of the mobiles Hamza Mansour was in contact with was switched off there this morning. I couldn't handle sitting there in Police Headquarters doing nothing. I wanted to see if I could find something, anything at all. Then I heard the explosion on Skeppsbron and made my way over here. What did you think?"

It sounded logical. Samer was on her side.

"I don't know what to think anymore," she whispered.

Samer gave her a long look and pulled his mobile from his back pocket. He called a number.

"We need a bomb squad in Storkyrkan. Immediately. Everything else can wait."

"We need to sent people to Cederdahl's funeral parlour on Hantverkargatan too," Vanessa said when he ended the call.

"What for?"

"That's where they did this," she said, nodding towards the thermos flasks sticking out of Moheden's stomach.

Samer made another call, then turned back towards Vanessa.

"Can I do anything? Anything at all to help you?"

She shook her head.

"Actually, can you wipe my forehead? The sweat's running into my eyes."

Samer looked round for something to use. Then he shrugged off his jacket, walked carefully towards her and wiped her brow with the sleeve.

"Better?"

"Yes. Thanks."

Vanessa forced herself to smile. Samer looked down at the watch in her hands.

"Bloody hell," he said, and sat down on the stone floor, cautiously leaning back against the platform holding the coffin and looking out at the empty rows of seats. He let out a deep sigh.

"Samer?"

"Yes?"

"You don't have to stay here. If anything happens, it's better if only one of us…"

"That's kind of you."

"Simple maths."

"What would you have done if I was the one standing where you are?"

Vanessa didn't answer.

"You'd have stayed and waited with me. Wouldn't you?"

The door to the funeral parlour opened. Molly hoped it would be Nicolas who came out, but instead it was Thomas who emerged, looking around warily. In his hands he was holding two automatic rifles. She felt her stomach clench.

Thomas unlocked a red car some fifty metres further down the street with the remote key. Molly started the engine of Axel's car and pulled away from the pavement. She watched as Thomas walked round the bonnet of the red car to the driver's side.

Thirty metres.

Molly lowered the sunshade to hide her face and increased her speed, but stayed on the right side of the road so as not to rouse his suspicion.

Twenty metres.

Thomas opened the driver's door, leaned over and tossed the weapons on the passenger seat.

Molly accelerated. The car reached sixty kilometres an hour before Molly wrenched the steering-wheel and swerved onto the other side of the street. Thomas turned round and shouted something. His eyes were wide open with terror as she rammed into him.

His body was trapped between the bonnet and the red car. He was lying doubled over in front of her windscreen. His arms were moving weakly. She put the handbrake on, leapt out of the car and began to run towards the funeral parlour.

"What do they say?"

Vanessa was looking on hopefully as Samer held his phone to his ear.

"Three dead. One seriously injured. Two of the dead have been identified. One is Hamza Mansour, the other is the funeral director, Jacob Cederdahl."

Vanessa took a deep breath. Her fingers were struggling to keep the buttons of the watch pressed in.

Nicolas could still be among the victims at the funeral parlour. But the only way to find out was to stay alive.

She heard footsteps and shouting from the door of the church. Samer craned his neck.

"They're here now," he said.

Vanessa turned her head as far as she could. Three men in dark clothing were slowly approaching along the aisle.

They stopped next to her, leaned forward and studied the explosive device.

"Are you okay?"

Vanessa grimaced. Then nodded with her lips tightly pursed.

"How long is it going to take?" she asked tersely. "Samer, can you wipe my head again, please?"

Samer moved closer.

"It's impossible to say," one of the men said. "But hopefully no more than a few minutes." Behind him the other men opened the two cases they had been carrying.

One of them took out a torch and shone it along the two wires connecting the thermos flasks and the Casio watch.

They conferred with each other in a whisper. Every so often they would approach the coffin, point and murmur something. After a minute or so, they seemed to have made a decision. They leaned over their cases once more and took out a selection of tools.

Samer smiled encouragingly at Vanessa.

"It's going to be fine," he said, then stepped back to give the bomb experts more room. He stood behind Vanessa and put one hand on her back.

Two of the men stood on either side of Vanessa. She looked from one to the other. Her mouth was dry. She ran her tongue around the inside of her cheeks to get her saliva flowing again.

They leaned over Magnus Moheden's body. One of them separated the wires from each other while the other took out a small pair of pliers. Beads of sweat were glinting on their furrowed brows. Their faces were taut with concentration.

"Ready?"

"Hold on a moment," Vanessa croaked.

She closed her eyes and took a deep breath.

"Okay, now."

She heard a click and opened her eyes.

They were all staring warily at the explosive device.

"You can pass the watch to me now," the man with the pliers said, holding out his hand and smiling at her in relief.

Vanessa breathed out. Her fingers felt stiff and numb as she passed him the watch. She leaned her head back and looked up at the ceiling of the church. She let out a loud laugh and gave the surprised and sweaty bomb expert a hug.

14

The lights were off in the hospital room. The machines keeping Nicolas alive were bleeping and hissing. His eyes were closed, but his heart was pumping, drawing digital lines on a black screen.

Vanessa leaned forward and smelled his warm skin.

Over the past couple of days she had only got a few hours sleep in the armchair by Nicolas's side. She got to her feet and looked out across the deserted car park.

What time was it? Gone dinnertime, she guessed. But surely it wasn't night, not already? There was a knock on the door and Mikael Kask's head appeared. He looked at the empty chair first before seeing Vanessa by the window.

They went out into the corridor. He gestured towards a sofa and armchairs a short distance away, where a television was on at low volume. They sank down next to each other on the sofa.

"How's he doing?" Mikael asked anxiously.

Vanessa mechanically repeated what the doctors had said, with her eyes glued to the news bulletin showing coverage of the terrorist attack. She watched as if hypnotised as covered bodies were removed from the quayside below Storkyrkan.

"Do they know if he's going to make it?"

"No."

Mikael picked up an old newspaper from the coffee table, presumably trying to find the remote control for the television. He gave up. Instead he put his hand in his jacket pocket and held up the black Casio watch.

"For you, from the bomb squad. They wanted you to have it."

Vanessa couldn't help giving him a wry smile. She weighed the watch in her hand, it was surprisingly light.

"I'd better make sure I know how it works."

A doctor walked past, nodding to them. Vanessa tucked the watch in the pocket of her jeans and stood up to go back to Nicolas.

"There's one more thing. Natasha. We've managed to reconstruct what happened on the night she was killed with the help of the terrorists' burner phones."

Vanessa sank back down on the sofa again.

"The ones who were there were Farid and Sabina. Sabina had arranged a meeting with Natasha at Gärdet – according to their messages, she had promised to help her move. Natasha wanted to get out. Sabina stabbed and killed her. Rikard Olsson, who was on his way home from going for a run, saw what happened and ran after Sabina as she fled the scene. He was shot from behind in Taptogatan, probably when he had almost caught up with her."

"By Farid Alami?"

"Yes."

When Vanessa got back to the room after going down to the cafeteria to get some coffee, a blond figure was sitting in the chair by Nicolas's side. It took Vanessa a few seconds to realise who it was.

"Axel?"

"I-I-I j-just wanted to see him. I'll get out of your way."

"No rush."

Vanessa pulled the other visitor's chair over next to Axel's.

"He likes you," she said, sitting down heavily. "It's quite hard for people to make an impression on Nicolas, but he likes you. I could tell by the way he spoke about you."

Even though Axel kept his eyes fixed on the floor, she couldn't fail to notice that he was touched.

Vanessa leaned forward and adjusted the blanket so that Nicolas wouldn't get cold.

"I want to thank you. Without you, we could never have stopped that bomb going off in Storkyrkan. You're very brave. If you ever decide to change your job, we could use someone like you in the police."

Vanessa could tell from Axel's reaction that he wasn't used to being called brave. His lips moved and he tried to say something, but nothing came out. Instead he gave a quick nod and wiped a tear from the corner of his eye. Vanessa solved his predicament by holding out her hand. Axel took it.

They sat in silence for a while, side by side, until he slowly stood up, waved and walked out.

Vanessa leaned over Nicolas again. She stroked his cheek, then ran her fingers over his cropped hair.

"I'm going to be alright. I have to be, because now it isn't just about me. Celine is waiting at home. And I love that girl, I want to see her grow up, graduate from high school, head off out into the world. This world needs people like her. And you. I want you to live so much, Nicolas. Do you hear that? You have to live. Otherwise I'll always be missing another piece of myself," she whispered.

Epilogue

In the weeks following the attack, Sweden mourned the people who had lost their lives, as more details about the terrorist cell's plans leaked out of the Security Service and were turned into headlines in the newspapers.

It soon became clear that an even greater disaster had been averted at the last minute.

The suicide bomber who blew herself up on the quayside below the Royal Palace so that the mourners inside Storkyrkan would be shut in and killed by the bomb in Minister of Justice Magnus Moheden's coffin was Sabina, or Fadila Khalili, as she was really called.

Five people lost their lives and another nineteen were injured.

Inside the red Nissan Note on Hantverkargatan, the vehicle used by terrorists Hamza Mansour and Thomas, whose real name was Wasim Sayyad, the Security Service found two automatic rifles, explosives, and a well-thumbed tourist map of Gamla stan.

The investigators came to the conclusion that they had been planning to use the chaos following the detonation of the bomb to mow down as many people as possible.

The family of funeral director Jacob Cederdahl were found bound and gagged, but otherwise unharmed, in his villa in Enskede. Wasim Sayyad, Fadila Khalili and Hamza Mansour had broken in at five o'clock in the morning and taken his wife and three children hostage. Then the two men had taken Jacob Cederdahl to the funeral parlour on Hantverkargatan and forced him to place the bomb inside the stomach of the deceased Minister of Justice before the coffin was collected and driven to Storkyrkan.

The identities of the police officers and civilians who worked together to prevent an even worse massacre were kept secret from the general public.

Author's Thanks

First and foremost, my beloved Linnea, who puts up with me and my erratic life. Your ideas and your support are invaluable. I love you.

I also want to say a special thank you to my little sister, Manuela, whose creativity and problem-solving abilities have – as usual – saved me from a lot of difficult narrative dilemmas.

Thank you to my family for their unfailing support. And thank you to Grandma and Grandpa Bengt for all that you have done for me throughout my life.

Thanks to Clas Ericson, Ebba Barrett Bandh and everyone else at Bookmark förlag who work so hard in various ways to make my books as good as they can be. And to Petra König-Kämpe for all the red notes and wise suggestions of how this story could be improved. Thanks to Joakim Hansson and everyone at Nordin Agency for your tireless work. Thanks to Simon Strand – one of the wisest people I know – who has had an interesting if somewhat calming influence on my working life. Thanks to X, who was the model for Molly Berg, and who generously shared her life, her story and her thoughts about the world in which she works. I would also like to extend a big thank you to terrorism expert Magnus Ranstorp for taking the time to sit down and talk to me about Islamic terrorism. I also want to thank police officers Therese, Ewa-Marie and Hasse Norlén who conscientiously worked their way through the manuscript and tried to hold me back when I was straying too far into fiction from the reality of police work.

Thanks also to: Seán Canning, Camilla Läckberg, Alice Stenberg, Johannes Selåker, Helena Jensen, Fredrik Feldt, Fredrik Moberg, Matilda Brinkeborn and Karin Sydholm for reading and offering opinions, criticism, praise and love. And thank you to Leonid Androsov, for so patiently sharing your knowledge of how to break into computers, Wi-Fi networks and printers. Mathias Emanuel, thank you for sharing your insights into life as a bodyguard. And thank you too to Martina Nilsson, strategic forensic coordinator for the Stockholm police region.

I would also like to thank Ann-Marie Skarp, who was the person who made me an author.

Finally I would like to thank all you readers, who get in touch daily to tell me how much you love Vanessa Frank. From the bottom of my heart: thank you.